THE BONNE CHANCE BAKERY

THE BONNE CHANCE BAKERY

A NOVEL

CHARLOTTE RAINS DIXON

WILD RUBY INK

Sign up for Charlotte's newsletter to be the first to find out about her new books, giveaways, and updates! charlotterainsd.substack.com

To learn more about Charlotte, visit her website at charlotterains dixonauthor.com.

Copyediting by Valerie Williamson

Cover design by Ebooklaunch.com

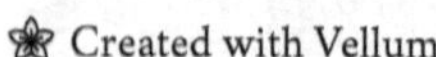 Created with Vellum

* * *

To Henry, Olivia, Owen, George and Tucker. You five own
my heart.

* * *

CHAPTER 1

Let me be the first to admit that sugar is bad for you. It makes you fat, messes with your blood sugar, and sends small children on crazy highs. But allow me also to submit that sugar is the basis of some of the most luscious confections in the world, none of which are more delicious than the macaron. Not the kind you're probably thinking about, the American macaroon, a lumpy cookie so full of processed coconut it makes your teeth hurt. No, I bake *macarons*, with one *o* only, please, and I make them in the Parisian style—two pastel-colored, almond-flavored meringue shells of delicate crispness with a rich, creamy filling of ganache sandwiched between. And, luckily for me, once Americans discovered *le macaron*, they had a ravenous appetite for them, if my fledgling bakery was any indication.

And that was where I stood the afternoon my new life began (although, like so many beginnings I didn't realize what was happening at the time)—outside my business, the Bonne Chance Bakery. I held a platter of macaron samples neatly arranged on a white paper doily in one hand and a stack of menus listing that day's flavors in the other. It was October and an early fall storm had blown in, forcing the line of people outside the shop to stand beneath umbrellas or don hoods in a steady Portland rain. I'd taken pity on them and donned my pink rain poncho to hand out samples.

"Thanks for waiting. I'm sorry our small space means you have to stand in the rain! Here's a free taste," I said over and over again.

"Num, I'll have the lavender."

"Oh, thank you, maybe I'll try the rose-colored one. Is it strawberry?"

"May I try the oatmeal raisin? I think I'm addicted to your macarons."

A gust of wind blasted down the hilly street on which the Bonne Chance was located, careening an umbrella out of the clutch of the next woman in line. I reached out with the hand holding the menus and whisked it back, handing it to her with a flourish.

"Thank you." She smiled. "Impressive save. You didn't lose a single macaron."

"Saving things is my superpower," I chirped.

I really hated it when I chirped. And more to the point would be I *wished* saving things were my superpower. There were so many things I'd not managed to save. But I wouldn't think about that now. I had customers to coddle.

So, I continued to smile and nod and chat until the samples were gone, and then I pulled my hood down and shook the rain off it before heading back inside my little bakery. And when I say little, I mean *little*. As in tiny, petite, wee, miniature. The Bonne Chance Bakery occupied a single storefront on a hill next to a coffee shop and a collection of food carts. Painted in broad stripes of pale blue and pink, with tasteful black outlines of Parisian landmarks decorating the walls, the interior looked like a French patisserie, or at least my Americanized version of one. And there was no other word for the smell of it but heavenly—that faint whiff of sugar, like cotton candy at the fair, or an ice cream cone on a hot summer day, the aroma that called to mind the best day of your childhood, or maybe your whole life.

The sales area was dominated by the display counter, which ran along the left side of the room, and was big enough for only three customers at a time. Patrons tended to linger, ogling the neat rainbow lines of macarons arrayed like pastel gemstones while they tried to make up their minds. My sole employee, Caroline, stood behind the counter, open tissue-lined box in one gloved hand, waiting for a knot of lanky teen girls to choose their macarons. It took a delicate touch to transfer the easily squished macarons from display to box and I watched for a moment as Caroline carefully selected them.

"All done handing out samples, Madeleine?" she asked as the teens dithered.

"I ran out. But that's enough for today. I'll be in back if you need me," I said as I breezed past. But in truth, despite the line, there really wasn't much I could do to speed things up, as there was only enough room for her behind the counter. I walked through the showroom into a short hall that led to the office next door, a room crammed with an old wood file cabinet and a pitted table that served as an all-purpose workstation. I pulled off my poncho and hung it on a rickety coat tree beside the door, then crossed to where my business partner stood.

"Hard to believe people will stand in the pouring rain to indulge their sweet tooth," Jack said.

He was peeking through the old-fashioned venetian blinds to view the line of rain-soaked customers. My hand brushed the soft flannel of his red plaid shirt as I reached to move a slat, so I could see through the window, too.

"We need to buy an awning," I said.

"It would be a good investment for the happiness of our customers." Jack glanced toward me. He had dark, intense eyes beneath bushy brown eyebrows, and cheekbones sculpted craggily. He wasn't movie star handsome by any stretch of the imagination, but there was something arresting about him. He was my manager, my assistant, my de facto accountant, and the one who had, along with my ex-husband, come up with the business plan for the bakery. Jack thought everything through before he talked, which sometimes caused him to speak slowly and pedantically. That day, I could tell by the way he carefully intoned his words what the answer would be.

"It sure would. But we can't afford it, right?"

"You are correct, Madame. I'm having a hard enough time covering our accounts payable. Not to mention—"

He stopped himself.

"What?"

Jack shook his head."I feel certain that with crowds such as these, that will change soon." He nodded his head toward the line out front. He looked at me and grinned. His face completely changed when he smiled, from serious to open and engaging. "Because, as you know, this bakery is charmed. Just like your life."

"Oh, my life is charmed all right," I said.

Jack winced, and his face returned to its stern demeanor. I realized immediately my words had come out harsher than I'd intended.

Because if charmed meant a successful business, he was correct. And for that I was grateful. Opening a bakery devoted to French macarons on a shoestring budget was perhaps not the brightest of ideas, so I was glad for the way

Portlanders had flocked to my doors. Even though their flocking didn't equate to making money. We weren't in the black yet, and I couldn't exactly figure out why. Jack mumbled that I spent too much on special touches like pink tissue paper in the macaron boxes when I asked him and then would say to let him worry about it. But still, because of the mere fact of its existence, the bakery felt charmed.

But my personal life didn't seem so charmed. You might actually call it cursed. Because the one thing I couldn't ever forget as I looked at the lines of people out the door to the Bonne Chance, or stared at the adorable window displays of our signature striped boxes topped with plates of macarons arranged in artful pyramids, was that the bakery had started as a joint venture with my husband, Will.

I'd started talking about opening a bakery years ago, encouraged by my mother, who taught me everything I knew about baking, but life had gotten in the way. Until finally, Will lost his job, and convinced me—and Jack—that the time was right.

Will had been certain the Bonne Chance would be a smashing success. (After all, with a name that meant good luck, what could possibly go wrong?) And Jack had gone along enthusiastically. Having recently sold a coffee shop in Washington State, he had some money to invest. Besides Jack, Will had pulled together the financing from an odd consortium of people—old friends, my father, and others he referred to vaguely and I never asked about. I let him and Jack focus on the numbers, so I could do what I did best —bake.

I'd wanted a macaron shop ever since we'd discovered the sweet confections on our honeymoon trip to Paris. One bite of my first macaron—it was a plump, snowy-white coconut number—and I'd been hooked. The moment was seared in my memory, helped, perhaps, by the fact that Will had nibbled on the other half of the macaron until our lips met and he'd kissed me full on in the middle of the patisserie. It sounds so sappy (not to mention gross) now I can barely stand to think about it. But love does strange things to people.

I'd been perfecting the recipe I'd found in my mother's papers, and the technique—because making macarons is all about technique—ever since, teaching classes, handing out macarons to friends, and finally garnering some wholesale accounts. The bakery was a natural next step.

And then Will had flown the coop shortly after the Bonne Chance opened.

Despite its immediate popularity.

Despite the accolades heaped upon his head for master-minding the business side of the bakery. (Never mind that Jack had been an equal partner in developing the business plan.)

Despite the fact that up until then, I'd thought our marriage strong, impervious to destruction.

And worst of all, *despite* the fact that I'd just told him that I was pregnant.

"I can't handle the pressure, Mad," Will had told me. Right before he and Hilary, the woman I'd hired to be the store's manager, had fled to Santa Fe.

Pressure, ha! Because, you see, scumbag-asshat-worm-jerk-insert-whatever-name-you'd-like Will started his own macaron shop with Hilary as soon as they settled in New Mexico. A shop that was doing quite well, helped along by Hilary's exotic looks and flair for publicity, not to mention, it turned out, money. The shop had already established a thriving online business selling all kinds of outlandish flavors, and been featured in *Elle* magazine, whose editors had loved the idea of a French-inspired pastry shop thriving in quirky, southwestern Santa Fe.

And never mind that they used my recipe and the skills I taught them. I shook my head, the movement making me notice my watery reflection in the window. My blonde hair was swept into a loose bun with a painted clip I'd found at a Paris flea market, and while it didn't look anywhere near as chic as the effortless way the French women did it, the style kept my hair off my face while I baked. Brown eyes beneath a fringe of bangs stared back at me in the glass. Once Will had compared them to the big eyes of the children in those creepy paintings popular in the seventies, which I'd never been sure if he meant as a compliment or not. My look was gamine, maybe even cute in the right light, but I didn't have the exotic beauty of someone like Hilary. Not to mention her tall model's body. Nope, not me—I was cursed with the petite gene from my mother's side, long legs and a short waist that guaranteed a muffin top—especially when I ate too many macarons. Which was nearly every day.

And now, staring out the bakery window at the rain, I pondered. My marriage was one of the things I hadn't been able to save. But at least Jack had stayed behind with me. For that, I *was* eternally grateful, because he was steady, loyal, funny and sweet. I relied on him to do the books, advise me on business decisions, and sometimes lend a hand with the baking. He was my best friend, and I couldn't imagine life without him.

"Now, if we were only making money, my life truly would be charmed, wouldn't it?" I said brightly. Jack had enough problems of his own without me adding to them with my attitude. Long story, but he had a bullet lodged in his back in a place much too delicate to extract, and it caused him constant pain in his right hip and leg. He did his best to hide it, but I knew that when one corner of his mouth turned down or that brief shadow crossed his eyes, he was dealing with another spasm. Sometimes—often—the pain caused him to limp as well, and it had cruelly curtailed his love of outdoor activities like hiking and rock climbing.

"Knock it off, girl, don't try your charming act on me."

"Sorry." I touched his arm. "I was trying to make up for sounding so harsh."

"You didn't sound harsh."

"It's true, though. Sometimes I think I'd give up my first-born child to make the bakery a success."

"Well, it's a good thing you don't have one then," Jack said. It took a second, but his eyes widened, and he clapped his hand over his mouth.

Because that was another thing I'd lost. I'd miscarried the baby I thought I was too old to have at age 38 shortly after Will left.

"Oh God, I'm sorry, Len. So sorry. I know you're still hurting over losing the baby and Will leaving."

Jack was the only one who called me Len, or sometimes Lenie. Everyone else usually just said Mad. And he knew about breakups himself, having lived apart from his so-called wife, Carla, , for years. She refused to divorce him, and uber-nice and overly-responsible guy that Jack was, he went along with it.

"By my calculations, you have three months to go to get over Will," a female voice piped up.

Startled, I turned to see Daisie, Jack's twelve-year-old daughter, who apparently had just come in the back door. She threw a backpack on a chair, shrugged off a shiny green raincoat, and took a seat at the old wooden table her father used as a desk. She was another reason he had his hands full —single parenting was not easy for anyone, but especially not for the father of an extremely precocious girl.

"Hello to you, too, Daisie," I said. "And on what, pray tell, do you base your calculations?"

"You figure out how long you were together and add in

the cause of the breakup and then you can get a good estimate," Daisie said.

"How do you even know that?" I asked.

Daisie shrugged. "I Googled it. Since you and Will were married for four years, and you broke up because he cheated, I figure it will take you a year to recover." She pulled a binder and a stack of books from her backpack and arranged them on the table. "And, he's been gone nine months. Thus, you've got about three to go."

Oh lord, I hoped she was right. Because I was damned sick and tired of the simmering anger that erupted at odd moments, and the nights I awoke at two in the morning and started sobbing when I realized I was alone in the queen size bed we'd wedged into our tiny bedroom.

But, enough of all that. Enough of thinking about Will. I needed to get better at focusing on the positive, not dwelling on the negative, as my father would no doubt advise me.

"What are you working on, Dais?" I asked her. She had dark hair, like Jack, which was held back in a messy ponytail, and she wore glasses that magnified her dark eyes. The private school she attended required uniforms, and that day her white blouse was askew beneath a navy-blue cardigan.

"It's homework for my social studies class. I'm doing a paper on migration patterns of indigenous people in America. The other kids each just chose a state to report on, but that sounded boring to me, so Mrs. Eckman let me do this instead."

"Oh, of course," I said.

Jack caught my eye and we both smiled.

"I saw that," Daisie said. She pushed her glasses back up her nose and bent her head to her work, pen gripped in her hand like a five-year-old. I felt sure she would one day either be president or the CEO of a large and powerful corporation. One way or another, Daisie would rule the world. And we'd all be better for it.

A splatter of rain blew against the window. I glanced outside. The line had shortened some, but at least ten people still waited to get in the front door. Out there, it was rainy and unseasonably cold, but inside our little room it was cozy and warm. I looked from Daisie to Jack, glanced at the file cabinets and bookshelves that lined the small office, and then gazed into the adjoining baking area, which often looked like an Easter egg factory with its trays of colorful macarons.

And I realized that in some ways I *did* lead a charmed life. I had wanted this for so long—my own macaron shop, the pleasure of doing something I loved for a living, the wonder of almost making the bakery a financial success. I adored my bakery and everything to do with it, even getting up before daylight to bake the macarons. It had given me the sense of purpose I'd sought for so long and I wouldn't trade that for anything. And I was determined to make it a success. It was for damned sure that I would do anything—anything—to save the bakery.

"But, Lenie, we do need to talk. "Our balloon pay—"

The phone rang. Jack and I both reached for it but Daisie lunged and got there first. Later, I would wish I'd paid more attention to what Jack started to say, that I'd asked Jack to keep talking instead of listening to Daisie on the phone.

"La Bonne Chance Bakery, this is Daisie speaking."

Daisie always insisted on using the French definite article *la* instead of the English *the*. It drove her crazy we'd named it the way we had, but Will had insisted Americans liked French things as long as they weren't *too* French.

Her cute little eyebrows furrowed, and her glasses slid down her nose as she listened to the person on the other end of the phone and made noises like "hmm" and "umm" until she finally said, "if you could be so kind as to hold for one second, I will check with Madeleine on that."

Daisie covered the phone with her hand and looked up. "It's this woman, an assistant from Richard Bishop. He would like to visit the store, but he needs you to close it for him so that he doesn't have to deal with the crowds."

Richard Bishop? *The* Richard Bishop? The business mogul slash movie actor slash author? Here in Portland?

Jack and I looked at each other.

"Maybe it's a joke?" I asked.

He shrugged. "He has been in town, Len. I was reading about the movie he's making last night."

And then I vaguely remembered hearing that he was here to shoot a film, Portland with its quirky ways and gorgeous scenery being a current darling of the industry. "But he wants me to close the shop? Can you say arrogant?"

Jack put his finger to his lips and rubbed it up and down, which was the thing he always did when he was thinking. "Maybe so. But his patronage could be good for the shop. It might get us some free publicity."

Daisie was madly nodding her head up and down. "Yes, say yes. I want to meet him." She snuggled the phone between her ear and shoulder and put her hands together before her in the sign for prayer. "Please, please, please, Mad."

I clutched the edge of the table for a moment, the old wood soft beneath the palm of my hand. My world felt like it was tilting on its axis. Richard Bishop wanted to visit my little bakery. How cool would that be? Because: *Richard Bishop.* One of the best-known men in the world. And a favorite of mine since forever. Another burst of rain hit the window and I glanced toward it. A few people still huddled as close to the building as they could get, waiting for their macarons. That gave me pause. Was it fair to them to close the shop just so a famous business tycoon or movie star or whatever in the hell he was these days could shop by himself?

I made my decision. "No, tell them no. It's not right, and it's not fair to the other customers. If he wants to buy my macarons, he can come wait in line like everyone else."

A rush of adrenaline surprised me as Daisie talked to the assistant and hung up the phone. It felt good to stick to my guns, even as disappointment covered me like a shroud. As soon as she set the phone back in its cradle my shoulders slumped. Had I done the right thing? Had I just lost my best chance at boosting the Bonne Chance into the black? Oh, God, I probably had. But then I looked at the customers out front and calmed myself down. *They* were the ones who mattered, not one arrogant famous person who felt he was too good for everyone else.

"Damn it," Daisie said.

"Don't swear," Jack said.

"But I wanted to ask him how he got started!"

Daisie was a budding entrepreneur, selling clever crocheted bracelets that could also be worn as necklaces on Etsy and at local craft fairs when she could convince Jack or me to help her with her booth. She had a business plan—handwritten on several pages of college-ruled notebook paper—and made enough money to buy her family and friends Christmas and birthday presents.

"You did the right thing," Jack said to me.

"You think?"

He nodded. "If you don't maintain your integrity in business, you're doomed."

I nodded my head, too, and blew out a long stream of air, wishing I felt better about maintaining my integrity versus losing future sales. By the scowl that Jack tried to hide, I could tell he was thinking along the same lines.

"Oh, God," Daisie said.

"Language," her father warned.

Daisie held her iPad in front of her and was scrolling through it. "Richard Bishop started his first business when he was ten." She looked up. "Sort of like me, only I was eleven." She looked at the tablet again. "He made and sold fishing flies. Ick. He started his first store—outdoor stuff—at age twenty-one, acted in his first film at twenty-three. That was *Car Thief*, and it was huge." Daisie looked up. "Can we watch that one tonight, Dad?"

I listened with half an ear to Daisie go on about Richard Bishop's accomplishments—the chain of outdoor stores, the line of sporting apparel, a whole collection of travel agencies, and his recent forays into transportation—and thought about him as an actor. Or more to the point, I thought about his alter ego, Ford Dooley, the character Richard Bishop had played in three movies—the character that had made him famous.

He also happened to be the character I'd been in love with since I was a teenager, so much so that my sister Natalie and I to this day traded Ford Dooley quotes. She and I had watched all three Ford Dooley movies together a million times. He was our go-to choice for an uplifting film, because despite suffering greatly for his family lost through his own wrongdoing, Ford did the right thing through many terrible trials and eventually won them back. But, mostly, he—or more to the point, Richard Bishop—was just so adorably cute in the movies, with his ready grin (despite all that suffering), his lively blue eyes, and his thick, glossy dark hair. I slumped my shoulders. It would have been fun to meet him.

I tried to recall what I'd read about Richard Bishop lately. Not a lot. Mainly because I didn't have time for surfing the Internet or reading the Hollywood gossip blogs, where he was a staple of breathless reporting and photos. I knew that he preferred the nickname Rich (maybe because he was, hahaha) but many people called him Dick behind his back—and not in a positive way. In a life that included as many successes as his you made some enemies. He was leading-man handsome, yes, and he also had a reputation for womanizing, with one female or another on his arm at seemingly every moment. Actresses, businesswomen, authors, models—he wasn't picky, though often of late, his dates of choice had come from the entrepreneurial ranks.

I pulled myself out of my own head when I saw Jack shaking his. "What?"

He grinned. "I told you—you lead a charmed life. Richard Bishop. Geez, Lenie."

"Yeah, well, like I said, it's not so charmed, now is it, seeing as how I told him to take a hike."

"Or a ride in his limo," Daisie said. I noted out of the side of my eye that she had set down the iPad and picked up her crocheting. I couldn't concentrate fully on her, though, because I was still looking at Jack, trying to discern the expression on his face. We worked so closely together; I thought I knew all his nuances. But this one was different, something shaded and cloudy in his eyes.

"All that is gold does not glitter," Jack said.

"Not all those who wander are lost," Daisie piped up. "The old that is strong does not wither, deep roots are not reached by the frost."

The awkward moment was gone. I grinned. "You're reading *Lord of the Rings*."

"You bet we are," Jack said, and a smile lit his face at last.

The world tilted back to its proper rotation and everything felt right again.

But then there was a sudden commotion out front, a burst of noise and energy. The crowd started squawking like a murder of crows and Daisie threw her crocheting down and ran to the windows. She turned around with a triumphant smile on her face.

"It's him! It's Richard Bishop after all!"

"Oh, come on, of course it isn't. I told him no," I said.

Jack joined Daisie at the window, and then talked to me over his shoulder. "There's a limo pulling up in front, Len. And the door is opening…get your butt into the showroom, right now. Daisie is right; Richard Bishop is here."

CHAPTER 2

I watched Richard Bishop alight from his long black limo and thought three things nearly simultaneously: first, that I'd forgotten to remove my apron, which was dotted with specks of pink macaron batter, bits of pale blue butter cream, and a huge dab of yellow ganache. Second, that it was amazing how quickly and efficiently crowds parted for someone famous. Third, that Richard Bishop was the most freakishly attractive human being I'd ever laid eyes on.

He was handsome in a the-Gods-bestowed-every-blessing-known-to-man-and-heaven kind of way. In a superhuman way. Apparently, also in a movie star way, though I'd never actually seen a movie star in person. But I was awed by his appearance, nearly knocked over by the sight of him. Especially because he seemed to me like my fictional idol Ford Dooley come to life, walking into the Bonne Chance.

Jack and I stood in the doorway from the back hall to the showroom, watching as Richard made his way through the crowd outside, smiling, nodding, shaking hands, and pointing at people. His assistant held the bakery door open for him, while customers who had been in line gawked and craned their necks to watch him enter, then rushed to get a glimpse from the doorway behind him. Those who couldn't see from the door peered in through the glass door and storefront windows.

And now Richard Bishop stood just inside the front door, grinning like a dog who knows he's about to go for a walk. He had the same eagerness as a dog, too, and a sense of being *present* unlike anybody I'd ever met. He wore a black turtleneck and trousers that fell in a perfectly cut line from waist to ankle. With his dark hair and dark clothes, he stood out among the pale blue and pink decor of the showroom and the muted jewel tones of the macarons, like a raven amid a flock of hummingbirds. He looked like he carried his own permanent illumination source, as if the sun shot beams of light upon him wherever he wandered. The man radiated charisma, and he wielded it effortlessly, smiling at each person in the crowd peering in the door one at a time and finally beaming his sunny grin at me.

I was not only awed by him, I was speechless, too. Because what do you say to a legend when he appears in your tiny little shop on a rainy September afternoon? Especially after you refused to close said shop for his benefit?

If you're me, you say, "So you came anyway," and then wince because it sounded so snotty.

But Richard just grinned—that blinding smile—and walked toward me with his hand extended. "Madeleine Miller? I'm Richard Bishop. Pleased to make your acquaintance." His voice was deep and low, his hand warm and soft, and then, unexpectedly he said, "Can I hug you? I'm a hugger."

Do you say no to a hug from a movie star slash business mogul? Do you say no to a hug from Richard Bishop slash Ford Dooley? Even when it strikes you as the tiniest bit creepy? Um, no. And so, I let him enfold me in his arms. His turtleneck pressing against my cheek was as soft as cat's fur, and smelled vaguely of cinnamon, like the apple pie macaron I'd been trying to perfect. I tore myself from him before he pulled away from me, grimaced briefly at the crumbs my hug had deposited on him, then smiled in what I hoped was a bright, perky manner.

"What can we do for you, Richard Bishop?" And then I realized how dumb that sounded. Seeing as how the only thing we sold were macarons, clearly, he was here to buy some. I took a deep breath to calm myself and tried to think of something more intelligent to say. But I got lost once more in the glare of his presence. Dimly I noticed movement, and then Daisie was scooting around me and placing herself next to Richard.

She pulled herself up as tall as she could and squared her shoulders. She had straightened her blouse and gotten it tucked neatly into her plaid skirt and she'd taken her hair out of the messy ponytail and combed it. There was no sign of her glasses. She took a deep breath. "Hello, sir. I'm Daisie Rogers, and welcome to our shop. We offer a wide variety of flavors of macarons with some new specials each morning. May I interest you in our flavor of the day, the cinnamon roll?"

"Daisie, let him choose his own macarons." Jack's voice came from behind me, rife with a warning tone to his daughter, and he walked around me and tried to pull her back, but she held her ground.

Richard smiled at her, seemingly unconcerned with her interruption. "That flavor sounds delightful, I must say. I will certainly try it. But before I make my selections, I'd like to talk to your mother for a minute."

"Oh, she's not my mother," Daisie said. "Her husband left before she could have babies. Well, actually, she was preg—"

"Daisie," Jack warned.

I felt my cheeks color and realized they were probably the same rosy hue as the pink peppermint macarons that sat behind the counter, between the chocolate hazelnut and vanilla cashew.

"Some people believe there are more important things in life than making babies," Richard said.

Jack grabbed Daisie by the collar of her blouse and pulled her back a step.

Richard turned his focus on me.

"I'm delighted to make your acquaintance, Madeleine, babies or not. " Richard smiled again and his eyes swept around the room as if to ascertain that everyone in it was still focused on him. They were. People held their phones up, snapping photos. "We drove by here recently and I noticed the long lines. When I asked my driver what the crowds were for, he told me about your bakery. I sent my assistant to buy a box of your macarons—she chose the egg cream and watermelon—and I swooned. Your macarons, my dear, are better than Ladurée or Pierre Hermé, I must say."

Richard Bishop had just named the two most famous and prestigious macaron bakers in Paris. I stammered a thank you.

"I'm always impressed by successful businesses and so I decided to visit in person. Would you be so kind as to help me make my selections?"

And so even though being within a foot of him made me nervous as all hell, we walked together along the counter and Caroline picked up each type of macaron he ordered, until she had filled five of our largest boxes for him. By the time she was finished, I was no longer nervous around him, but giddy instead. Was it from being in his presence or because he was about to drop several hundred dollars on macarons, an amount that would sail our weekly take into the black before we even got to the weekend?

Daisie trailed along behind us, her eyebrows getting more and more knitted together, watching every move of Richard's as he pointed to macarons. "And I'll take a dozen of the pink, and give me two dozen of the yellow—what flavor were those again?"

"Banana split," Caroline said, smiling up at him from behind the glass. *Everyone* smiled at Richard as if he had just told them he was giving them a million dollars.

Finally, Daisie spoke. By this time her eyebrows were totally entwined. "But that's a lot of macarons!"

Um, thanks, Dais.

Richard turned to her and, of course, smiled. "Yes, indeed, it is. Should I not be buying so many?"

"It's just that you don't want them to get stale," she said. "They taste best when eaten within a day of being baked and if you can't do that, you need to get them into a refrigerator."

Richard looked at her and the bemused expression on his face instantly changed to an I'm-taking-you-seriously one. "Thank you for your concern. But I'd planned to pass them out on the movie set for our wrap party, and there's a lot of people involved in making a film."

"Oh," Daisie said. "I get it. That's okay, then." She reached an arm to the counter, grabbed a piece of paper and handed it to him. "Here's an instruction sheet that will tell you how to store them. Mad insists we put one in every box, even though my Dad says it costs extra money. But Mad says teaching people about macarons is the most important thing."

"I would say that Madeleine is a very wise woman." Richard caught my eye and smiled. I smiled back, of course.

"Can I ask you something?" Daisie said.

I marveled at her ability not to be intimidated by him.

"Ask away," he said.

"Do you have any advice for a woman in business?"

I glanced at Jack, who still stood in the doorway to the back room and we smiled at each other—the first smile I'd seen on his face since Richard's arrival. Luckily, Daisie was so focused on Richard she didn't notice. She hated when she thought we were patronizing her.

"And would that woman be you, perchance, Daisie?"

Oh, lord, he even remembered her name.

Daisie nodded.

"Do whatever you do with passion and don't do it unless you love it."

Daisie's mouth hung open as she looked up at him. She had a big forehead—full of brains, we always said about it—and I could practically see the synapses firing as she gazed at Richard.

I wrinkled my brow and tried to pull a distant thought into my brain. Then I realized that what Richard had just said sounded a lot like a Ford Dooley quote.

"And now," Richard said, "I must return to the set."

His assistant materialized from the background and paid his macaron tab.

Richard turned to me and bowed slightly. "Madeleine, it has been a pleasure." He nodded to Daisie and Jack and Caroline and all the people watching him. And then he was gone.

The room came to life all at once, and only then did I realize we'd been suspended in amber while watching Richard. My customers managed to re-form themselves into a rough line as they chattered with excitement. Many of them typed into smart phones, hopefully Tweeting and Instagramming and posting on Facebook about the Richard Bishop sighting at the Bonne Chance Bakery, emphasis on the bakery.

I joined Jack and Daisie in the back hall. "Is it just me, or does he take all the air out of a room?"

I expected Jack to be grinning like a man who'd just met Jesus—after all, Richard had bought two hundred dollars' worth of macarons, our biggest sale ever, and moreover, he clearly was impressed with the business. And I'd gotten to have my macaron and eat it, too—I had stuck to my guns about not closing the shop and Richard had come and bought goodies anyway.

But Jack's face was sober as a criminal facing his sentencing.

"He's something, all right," Jack said.

I poked him in the side above the waist of his Levis. "C'mon, you have to admit it's exciting. Richard Bishop likes our macarons!"

"Yeah, it's great, Mad."

Jack never called me Mad.

"What is up with you?" I asked, following him into the office.

"It's nothing." He shook his head.

"It is too. It's something. I can tell. You never act like this."

Jack's shoulders slumped. "It's just...I don't trust him. He's such a pretty boy and he's so aware of the impression he's making at every moment."

"Pfft. Like we're ever going to see him again anyway."

Just then, my cell phone, tucked in my front apron pocket, rang, and I answered it even though I didn't recognize the number.

"Madeleine? It's Richard Bishop."

Oh, God. Something in me told me to turn away from Jack, perhaps realizing that he would read the expression on my face—no doubt a look of shock, and maybe, yes, pleasure —as easily as I read his.

"How'd you get this number?" Lame, I know, but it was

the first thing I thought of. He—or his assistant—had called the bakery line earlier, so why was he now calling my mobile? I tucked my head down and ducked into the back room, away from Jack, where I leaned against a counter laden with bowls and mixers.

Richard's laugh was melodious, like the tolling of a bell. "Oh, I have my ways, my dear. I'm sorry to bother you so soon—I know you have a line of customers awaiting your attention, but something slipped my mind while I was there, and I needed to ask you."

What on earth would he want to ask me? "Fire away," I said, wondering why every word I uttered around him was so ridiculously stupid.

"Would you be so kind as to have dinner with me this evening?"

I dropped the beater I'd been idly flipping about, and it clattered to the floor. Jack peeked his head through the door and gave me an "Is everything okay?" look. I waved him away and tried to concentrate. My thoughts came fast and furious, all in a jumble.

Why did Richard Bishop want to have dinner with *me*?

Could I handle sitting across the table in the glare of his attention?

What would I *say* to him over the course of a meal?

Then:

What would Jack think?

And finally:

Daisie would kill me if I didn't say yes.

And so, I did.

I headed for home earlier than usual that day, because dinner with Richard Bishop was an event that would require scrambling through my closet for attire. Not to mention ample time to fuss over hair and makeup. I lived just a few blocks away from the bakery, and luckily, that afternoon the rain had finally let up. I punched the button at the crosswalk that would make the light turn red so that I could cross busy Sandy Boulevard, the street the bakery sat on, but I really didn't need to. Cars slammed to a halt and motioned me forward, Portland being the politest city on the planet. Navigating a four-way stop could be hellish in this town, with every driver motioning for the other one first. "You go." "No, you go." "No, you." And changing lanes on the freeway? Not a problem. There's always a nice Oregonian wiling to wave you in.

Waving a thanks to all the people who had stopped for me, I pulled out my cell and punched the number for my sister, Natalie, thinking that she would be able to advise me on my clothing choices. Nat lived in L.A. and followed movie news avidly. But all I got was her plodding voice mail, as she slowly told callers to leave a message. She taught religion and anthropology at UCLA, and as a soon-to-be tenured professor, she felt the need to impress people with a grave greeting. Never mind that she dressed like a rock star and had spent years working in the film industry before she got her Ph.D. I left her a message saying I needed help with clothing for a hot date—that would get her to call me back promptly—and walked on through the residential streets of my neighborhood.

Called Rose City Park, the name fit, as it was an area of near-century-old homes, gardens, and lots of trees. The wind came up and blew my bangs away from my face, and I knew it was a signal that the rain would soon return. I quickened my pace. Another block south brought me to Jack and Daisie's house, a big old bungalow that perched majestically on the corner. Three houses down and across the street sat my little home. I felt the first drops of rain on my face as I headed up the stairs to my front door and unlocked it.

I loved my little house, even though it echoed with the absence of Will. Something else ricocheted through it, too, and that was a whiff of fear. Because if the bakery didn't start making money soon, I'd have to sell my house and move. Housing prices in Portland were high, and I wasn't quite sure where I'd go. Too often now I dipped into my savings to pay my mortgage. Said savings were growing thinner than the parchment paper I used to bake my macarons on.

Inside, I threw my keys in a bowl that sat beside the door on a small table. My heart twisted as I remembered the day Will and I had bought the bowl—it was yellow, red, and turquoise, and embellished with images from antique wood stamps—at a flea market in Paris. I ordered Will out of my brain and cast my gaze into the living room. It was all velvet, silk and tapestry textiles, in colors similar to the bowl, with a healthy dash of pink thrown in. Think elegant (or so I hoped) French boudoir and you'll get the picture.

Sometimes I worried that Will left me because of the way I decorated the house. I know, that sounds silly—but my house was well, um, *girlie*, and I wondered if I didn't leave him enough room for his masculinity. You know, guilty of being an emasculating woman and all that. After Will and Hilary flew the coop, I couldn't help but compare myself to her in every way. With her black pageboy hair always perfectly combed, and her makeup, complete with pale foundation and kohl eyeliner, expertly applied, Hilary was polished.

"She's sleek, Mad," Will had said when we hired her. "And she'll add a cachet that we don't have to the bakery." Hilary carried that sleekness through in her clothing, which leaned toward silk tunics that rustled enticingly as she wafted about, and formfitting pants that emphasized the endless swaths of her long legs. I favored more of a boho look, similar to my home décor. And, neither the way I dressed nor the way I furnished my house would ever be called *sleek.*

I'd visited Hilary's place once to pick her up when her car was in the shop. She lived in a newish loft condo down in the Pearl, one of the trendiest and most expensive parts of the city. Located on the other side of the river, it's an area of lofts, art galleries, pricy shops, and high-end restaurants. I got a good glance at her apartment when I stood at the door, as far as I made it because she sure didn't invite me in. (I wondered later if Will was hiding in a closet.) What I saw was modern furniture—white with black accents—and gleaming stainless steel, of course, in the kitchen. I figured the monochrome color scheme was designed to show off her exotic presence.

Of course, it didn't occur to me at the time to wonder why a woman who lived in such an expensive apartment wanted a menial job at a bakery. Later, I understood it all too well. She wanted to learn everything there was to know about macarons at my elbow and then go off and start her own bakery with her family money, taking my husband along with her.

I shook myself to clear the memories and headed to the kitchen. Very unlike Hilary's. The cupboards were creamy white, some glass-fronted, and I'd arranged my thrift store finds—colorful vintage glassware and cute salt and pepper shakers—along the windowsills. As I entered the room, I pulled an apron off a hook by the door and tied it around my waist. This was my sacred ritual, a habit so long-standing it was as ingrained as drinking coffee first thing in the morning or brushing my teeth after dinner.

Because it wasn't just *any* apron. It was my mother's apron, a special white chef's apron that she had sewn herself and then embroidered on—images of a rolling pin, a chef's hat, a spoon, a whisk, and an oversized bowl. I'd worn the apron so much the fabric was thin and softened with use in places and some of the embroidery stitches were broken. But it was my good luck charm and my touchstone, my emblem and shield and precious memory of my mother. One of my goals for the bakery was to be able to reproduce the apron for use there. Jack, of course, had no intention of approving such an expenditure, so in the meantime we made do with plain white aprons.

My phone rang as I boiled water for tea. I'd considered a glass of wine to calm my nerves for the upcoming dinner, but we'd have wine with dinner, no doubt—wait, had I ever read anywhere that Richard was an abstainer? No, I didn't think so. Anyway, I didn't want to drink too much—I did have to get up at 4:00 a.m. and bake the next morning. I saw it was Nat returning my call and answered as I pulled a tea bag out of the canister on the counter.

"Baby sis!" Nat screamed into the phone. My sister was nothing if not dramatic. It was why her students loved her—she had a knack for making religion interesting. Proof of her theatrical flair came when I told her about my date with Richard Bishop, in the form of screams so loud I had to put down the phone.

"Oh, for the love of flipping Jesus, tell me how this happened."

I explained about Richard's grand visit to the bakery and how he'd called me a few minutes after he left to ask me to dinner.

"Amazing. My sister, dining with Richard Bishop. The one and only, inimitable Ford Dooley."

"I know. Remember how in love we were with Ford?"

"Oh, lord, do I. Remember when the angels told him, 'you're only given as much as you can handle—'"

"—and he said, 'I've been given so much good, I will learn to handle the rest.' Oh God, I repeated that to myself over and over again after Mom died. And then again after Will left and I lost the baby."

"I know, sweetie," Natalie clucked. "On a cheerier note, what, pray tell, are you going to wear?"

"That's exactly why I called. All I've got is a bureau full of jeans and T-shirts and a closet full of dresses and skirts from Target."

"I know. Your love of clothing from that store is one of your tragic flaws."

Natalie wore only brand-name clothing, and when I say brand name, I mean expensive brand name, names I don't even recognize, though they fell from her lips as easily as waves gliding up onto the beach. I poured a dollop of honey into my tea mug—a cute one that said Paris on it and featured an image of the Eiffel Tower—and took it to the table by the window.

"Accessories," she said. "You may have a closet full of crappy-ass clothes, but you are wonderful when it comes to accessories."

I preened under my sister's compliment. Like most younger siblings I was very susceptible to praise from my elder sis and I realized she was right.I had scarves and boots and jewelry aplenty. I could jazz up one of my plain outfits and it would be just fine for Richard. After all, what did it matter? It was only one dinner, and it wasn't even exactly a date.

"Honey," Natalie said, "promise me one thing: that you'll be very careful with Richard Bishop. He's got a reputation as a lady charmer."

I sipped my tea. "Let me remind you I'm a nobody baker from Portland, Oregon. There will be no lady charming going on here, at least on his end."

"Yeah, well, he's also got a rep for going after ordinary women."

"Thanks."

"Oh baby, you're anything but ordinary. What I meant was that he likes women from ordinary walks of life, not those involved in the film industry necessarily, though he's had plenty of those, too. He especially has a rep for dating entrepreneurs."

"Well, he's not going to *have* me, or be interested in me beyond tonight, Nat. "

There was a moment of silence and the sound of clicking keys.

"Hello? Did I lose you?"

"Hmm." Nat made a murmuring sound as the key clicking continued. "Sorry, sweetie, I was just Googling Richard Bishop."

"No need. Daisie read me everything she could find on him."

"I suppose we all know the broad outlines of his life by heart now, but I was just checking..." Click, click, click. "No, I can't find it. I'd heard a rumor that he *is* married. Wait, here it is. Yes, his first wife died in a tragic car accident—"

"Just like Ford Dooley," I said.

"Right. And he remarried soon thereafter. Hang on..."

I heard more clicking.

"Hmm, hard to tell what happened to the second wife. One site says they divorced a couple years after they married and another one says they are legally separated. Oh God, this blog says she died, just like the first one. Anyway, I guess something happened to her. Because woo-ee he has had a lot of women. And now you, sweetie pie."

I made a dismissive sound. The thought of living up to all of Richard Bishop's other women made me feel glum, because I truly was an ordinary baker. "Stop, Nat. Anyway, things haven't been going so great for me lately. Which seems to be the story of my life."

"You have got to quit saying things like that, sis. Truly. You get back what you put out."

"Spare me your woo-woo," I said. "You sound just like Dad."

"Honey, every religious tradition in the world says something like what I just told you. Can fifty gazillion people over time be wrong?"

I watched a tiny little brown bird flit around the bush outside my window. If Will were here, he'd know the name of the bird and the bush. One of many things I loved about my ex-husband was his eclecticism. A mathematician and engineer, he also got outside as often as possible and had an amazing memory for the flora and fauna he found there.

"Okay, okay, I'll try to be more positive," I said to my sister, though inwardly I was disagreeing with myself.

"And by the way," Nat said, "speaking of our father and

being positive, rumor has it, Earl is coming to town. Your town."

"Oh goodie, I love seeing Dad."

We ended the conversation with Natalie wishing me luck. No sooner had I hung up than my phone rang again, and I saw it was Daisie.

"Hey, Dais," I said, standing up and walking to the sink to dump the dregs of my tea.

"Italian Delight."

"What?" I asked.

"Dad's cooking Italian Delight for dinner tonight."

Oh my God, how could I have forgotten? It was Thursday, which meant I ate dinner with Jack and Daisie. The three of us ate together every Thursday, no matter what. But tonight, I'd agreed to meet Richard Bishop. And, I hadn't mentioned the small matter of the date with him to Daisie, or Jack. It just didn't feel right somehow.

"Oh dear, Daisie, something's come up. I can't make it tonight." Of course, lying didn't feel so good either. But I couldn't bring myself to tell her about Richard.

I was greeted with a frosty silence on the other end of the phone. I held out my phone to see if icicles were forming on it. Finally, she spoke.

"How can something come up? You always eat dinner with us on Thursdays. And Dad's making my most favorite dish ever, Aunt Betty's Italian Delight. And I was going to show you my new product line. And how I've rearranged my studio to accommodate it."

"I'll see it another time, honey. Maybe this weekend? I just can't tonight."

"Why?" Daisie demanded.

I said the first thing that popped into my head. "Because I have a stomachache." And I did, sort of, if feeling an adrenalin rush every time I thought of Richard Bishop counted.

"I'll have Dad bring you soup. Chicken noodle soup has been proven to help with stomach ailments."

"No!" I said, a little too fast and too adamantly. "I think it's best if I just take it easy tonight, sweetie. I do have to get up early and bake tomorrow, you know."

Mentioning work always soothed any objections Daisie might have. That seemed to do the trick and I said goodbye, not without an enormous load of guilt that I was missing our weekly dinner. And besides guilt, I felt a sudden wave of sadness at not being able to see them. Don't be silly, I told myself. You get to see them all the time—every day! But that wasn't the same as our weekly dinners, where we had a chance to really relax and talk about everything going on in our lives. But duty called. If Richard Bishop could be called duty.

CHAPTER 4

Standing in the bakery showroom with Richard was overwhelming but sitting across a table from him at the restaurant was positively surreal. He was like a super-human being, his glossy black hair flawlessly arranged, his blue eyes sparkling merrily, not a wrinkle on his face. I tried to remember how old Daisie had said he was—at least in his mid-forties. And yet he looked like a fresh-faced thirty-five-year-old.

The restaurant Richard chose surprised me. I'd have thought he'd opt for some fancy French place, or one of the trendy foodie spots my fair city is known for in the food world. Instead, he'd chosen an old Portland institution near the waterfront. I parked in a garage and walked across the street, nervously straightening my skirt—I'd opted for a floral number with a plain black wrap top that flattered my macaron-burgeoning stomach and accessorized with a white lace scarf and red and black cowboy boots, topping it all off with a jean jacket. An oversized crocheted rose pin decorated the lapel, another of my prized purchases from Paris. Natalie had said I was good at accessories, so accessories I would do.

I found an almost matching rose-decorated clip for my hair, too. I wore my hair down, using the clip to pull just a section of it back, and allowing the rest fall in loose waves, which was the best I could do with my curling iron.

And yes, I drove my own car—at my insistence. Richard had offered to have the limo pick me up, but I wanted to show my independence. And there was the small matter of Jack and Daisie living so close by. It wouldn't do for them to see a town car stopping at my house after I'd pled a stomachache. I thought of Jack's cheesy Italian Delight casserole and the Caesar salad he made from scratch—he was a fantastic cook—and my stomach growled. I felt a pang. Maybe I should have said no to Richard in favor of my weekly intimate dinner with Jack and Daisie. But it was too late now. I squared my shoulders and walked on.

When I arrived, I saw why Richard had chosen the restaurant. The unctuous host looked me up and down with what appeared to be disapproval when I told him who I was meeting, and then he ushered me through the front room of the restaurant and down a flight of stairs to a private space. The room was the wine cellar, with walls of wine bottles on three sides and an antique sideboard on the fourth. A large round table filled the space, and it had been set for two. Richard sat at one of the spots, sipping wine and looking at his phone. He raised his head when he heard us approach, stood and smiled.

That dazzling Richard Bishop smile. It couldn't help but make you smile back. Which I did. In fact, I was so busy smiling at him that I tripped on the last step. The maître d' held out his arm to catch me and his face once again held that faint whiff of disapproval—the sly raised eyebrow—or perhaps it was wonder that Richard was dining with the likes of *me*. Well, I was in wonder about it, too.

Richard stood, hugged me, and then kissed me on each

cheek—what the French call *le bisou*—and I returned the gesture, saying, "Hi, Richard."

"Sit, sit, Madeleine," he said. "I took the liberty of ordering wine. I hope you like Chateau Lafitte Rothschild."

"Well, duh, who doesn't?" I said, although of course I had no idea about the wine, other than it sounded expensive. Very expensive.

Richard laughed and nodded to the waiter, who poured me a glass, famous people apparently not capable of doing such things on their own. After my jean jacket, held by the host's fingertip, I kid you not, was hung on a peg in the corner and I was sitting with wine, I noticed that Richard had left his phone on the table, so I made a show of pulling mine out of my purse and setting it beside my place. Maybe it was immature, but I didn't want to let him establish that he was so busy and important he needed his phone, but I didn't.

Once I was settled, he dazzled me once again with that blinding smile. His lips looked as soft and velvety as a rose petal and his teeth were as white as fresh coconut. The rest of his face was all smooth planes, and the overall result was so appealing it made my breath catch.

He held up his glass. "To all things new."

It took me a minute to be able to speak. "To all things new," I agreed, touched his glass, and then took a bigger drink of the wine than usual.

"Will there be anything else for the moment, Mr. Bishop?" the waiter asked.

"Give us a few minutes to enjoy our wine and then we'll order," Richard said.

And then something funny happened. Once the waiter left, Richard Bishop relaxed into himself. Was relaxed the correct word? I wasn't sure. Maybe molted would be better. It was as if his protective shell—the dazzling smile, the intense focus, the glib words—disappeared and he became a real person. I swear, he even looked less intimidatingly handsome.

And finally, I could relax too, even though it felt like every cell in my body was straining toward him.

Richard focused on me and smiled one of his real smiles, and I admit, my heart did a little flip.

"So," I said, to distract myself from his charm, "How does one get to be Richard Bishop?"

He waved his hand in front of him and sipped wine. "Hard work, mostly, which is what most people fail to realize. And a lot of luck, too, I will admit. But my life is a boring story, told too many times. I want to hear about you. And that delightful bakery. How did you learn to bake macarons?"

"I taught myself." Talking about myself made me uncomfortable. What could possibly be interesting enough about me to capture his interest? I took a big gulp of wine. *Tell him about the macarons. You can do this.* "I fell in love with macarons on a trip to Paris and when I came home, my mother shared an old recipe for them. She was quite the Francophile."

"Was?" Richard asked.

I nodded. "She died a couple of years ago. She's the one who taught me everything I know about baking. And she was the one who gave me the idea for opening a bakery in the first place. She always thought it would be the perfect occupation for me. Once upon a time, she dreamed of opening one herself." I took another gulp of wine. "After she died, all I did was bake macarons and eat them for a month. I gained five pounds. That's when I knew it was time to sell the macarons—so I'd quit eating them."

"So we can thank your mother for the delightful Bonne Chance bakery," Richard said.

"Yeah, but don't tell that to my sister. She's got a sore spot when it comes to our mother." Why was I telling him all this?

Now that I'd started, I couldn't seem to stop talking. It was something in the way he looked at me so expectantly, as if I were the most fascinating woman in the world. "She insists that Mom liked me best, which is probably true. But Dad likes *her* best, so it all worked out."

"Your sister is Natalie, the religion professor?"

I nodded.

"And your father is Earl Miller, right?"

I nodded again. And then it hit me.

"Wait a minute. How'd you know all that about my family?"

He laughed. "I'm always curious about the people I'm interested in. And these days, it's easy to find such things out, Mad. Do you mind if I call you Mad?"

I shook my head and took another sip of wine. Richard could call me any old thing he wanted, as long as I could keep looking into those amazing blue eyes. And then I had a horrible thought. Maybe Richard was using me to get to Earl? But a man of Richard's stature could call up Dad—or his agent—and get an audience with him immediately.

"I'm a big fan of your father's work," Richard said. "His first books advanced the self-help industry by leaps and bounds, and he continues to write compelling material."

"Thank you. I'll tell him."

Richard touched my hand again and this time his finger stayed there longer. "But we keep getting sidetracked. I want to hear more about you."

And so, I told him about how we'd started the business. Luckily, the waiter came to take our orders about the time I got to the part about William and Hilary leaving, so I glossed over that. Richard ordered the salmon, and I chose the osso bucco. After Richard smiled his dazzling public smile—I was starting to think of it as the Public Option—the waiter left.

"What's the deal with the guy?" Richard asked.

"What guy?"

"The dark one who glowers."

"Oh, you mean Jack. Does he glower? I just think of him as intense."

"Is he your boyfriend?"

I sputtered out the wine I had been sipping. "Oh no, Jack's just a friend. And my right hand at the bakery. He does environmental consulting to pay the bills. He used to be big into the outdoors."

"Hmm."

"What?"

Richard shrugged. "I just caught something in the way he looked at you."

I shook my head. "Jack thinks of me like a sister."

Richard raised his eyebrows. "If that's the way a brother looks at his sister; I'd say we have scandal afoot."

I scowled at him. "No, he was probably just in pain. He has a bullet lodged in his back from when he interrupted a robbery at his coffee shop in Olympia."

"I see." Richard nodded.

"He saved the life of his wife by stepping in front of her and taking the bullet. Of course, some people might say it would have been better if he'd let the ditz get shot." I clapped my hand over my mouth. I shouldn't be saying such a thing, especially not to Richard Bishop.

But he just laughed and poked a finger at the hand covering my mouth. "Oh, Madeleine, your candor is so remarkably refreshing."

The waiter brought our food and we ate in silence for a few bites. Then Richard set his fork down and looked at me. "You're probably wondering why I wanted to have dinner with you."

"Because of my scintillating personality and good looks?" I asked, then laughed in what I hoped was a merry way to show that I was just kidding. Except I wasn't. Because deep down inside I *had* thought that. But as soon as I said it, even in a joking way, I realized how ridiculous it was. Jesus, this guy had access to the most gorgeous women in several worlds. And here I was, sitting across from him in the stupid skirt I'd bought at Target. I did get points for the jaunty scarf I'd purchased in Paris, but *still.*

Richard flashed his signature grin. Suddenly we were back to the Public Option. "That goes without saying. But I'm also interested in your fascinating business."

I nodded. I wasn't sure that getting up early and baking as many kinds of macarons I could manage before the bakery opened was fascinating, but I'd go with him on this anyway. And squelch the tiny bit of disappointment when I realized that he really wasn't much interested in me. So, I went on about macarons and how I baked them, how funnily enough the so-called French recipe I'd gotten from my mother turned out to be for Italian macarons.

And then, just as I was about to explain how I now bought my egg whites in cartons rather than separating them myself, he held up his hand. I sat back in my chair, embarrassed at how I'd run on yet again. I reached for my glass—we were on the second bottle, though Richard seemed to have drunk most of the first one, or so I told myself.

"I love hearing about all this," he said. "But before it gets too late and we run out of time, I must tell you—I see all kinds of possibilities with your bakery, Mad."

"Possibilities?"

"You could take it big. With your baking skills and sense of style—"

Richard Bishop thought I had a sense of style? Wait until I told Natalie.

"—I envision a chain of little Bonne Chances across the country."

"You mean, like a franchise or something?"

Richard nodded. "I'll tell you, Mad, acting is great, but it's such a superficial world. Business is my true love. Until I tasted your macarons, I haven't been this excited about a business opportunity in a long time."

I reached for my wine. I mean, really, what else could one do except drink in such a situation? Because Richard Bishop was interested in franchising my little bakery. I was so shocked I couldn't even sort out how I felt.

"Um, I don't know what to say," I said, because it was clearly the truth.

He leaned toward me. Oh God, those eyes. Knowing that Richard was interested only in my business was both a relief and a disappointment. "I understand that this must be surprising, Mad. But I want to invest in your business. I want to invest in *you*. You proved your business acumen to me when you refused to close the business for my sake."

"I did?"

"Yes. A businesswoman who puts her customers first is a good businesswoman. What do you think about my idea?"

"I'll have to think about it," I said weakly.

"Of course you will; I'd expect no less. But let me tell you this: it is one of my ongoing goals to help women in business." Richard cast his eyes downward for a minute and then gazed steadily back into mine. "I do it in honor of my wife."

"So, you are married," I blurted.

He shook his head and waved his hand in a way that I took to mean no. "I'm talking about my wife Grace." He cast his eyes down to the table and a long, mournful sigh escaped his mouth. "She died in a car accident when we'd been married only a short while." He looked up at me. "Oh, Madeleine, I loved her so."

I gazed steadily into his eyes. And all I could think was

how wonderful it would be to be the woman that Richard Bishop loved *so*. "I'm sorry."

He nodded. "She was the impetus for everything that I am. It was Grace who had the idea for the sporting goods store that was my first venture. And it was her business acumen that made it take off as fast as it did. When I met her, she was the proprietor of a very successful business selling table linens. If she were still here—"

Agog. There was no other word for it. I was agog. So agog that all I could do was nod my head up and down in encouragement for him to continue.

"If she were still here, that would be a business to rival Ikea." Richard heaved a heavy sigh. "I just didn't have her sense of style." He cast his eyes down and then back up at me. "You can see why I have a special interest in women-owned businesses. I have a good success rate at helping women succeed. I've had a few failures, and those pain me. But I so admire people—especially women—who dare to follow their dreams."

"Just like Ford Dooley," I breathed.

He leaned closer to me and I stared into his eyes, those blazing robin's egg blue eyes. "Like Ford Dooley, I strive always to do the right thing. Though I'm afraid I sometimes fall short."

"Oh, so did Ford Dooley, though! And he just kept taking action until he learned what he was supposed to learn!"

Richard placed his hand over mine, the one that moments earlier had been snaking toward my wine glass for a drink. "And that is exactly why I wanted to play Ford so badly. Even though he was only a fictional character, he was an incredible man."

Like you, I almost blurted out, but stopped myself just in time. Richard sat back in his chair and so did I.

"What I propose is this: you come to L.A. in the next week

or so. You can meet with my business advisors and see if we can come up with a plan to move forward on this. The trip will be all paid for, of course."

L.A.? I could see Natalie! And get some sunshine before the fall rains and winter cold set in. But would going make us beholden to Richard? Oh God, I wished Jack was here to guide me. Just then my cell rang.

"Oh, I'm so sorry, I forgot to put it on silent." I grabbed the phone and pushed the button to silence it, but not before I saw that it was Will calling. Will? What was he doing calling me? And that's when it hit me—if Richard Bishop invested in the Bonne Chance, I could outpace Will and Hill, with their fancy-schmancy online business and stupid Santa Fe style macarons. But, still. I wasn't sure I was ready to give up control of my business to someone else. Even someone as brilliant and focused as Richard Bishop.

"You're scowling," he said.

"I'm not, I'm just thinking. I'm confused."

"I know you are, and that's okay," he said. "Promise me you'll think about it."

"I will."

Richard and I finished our dinner and wine to the accompaniment of amusing stories of his rise to fame—the disastrous antics of his costar on his first movie; how his first business, the outdoor store, almost didn't open on day one because he and his manager were locked out; the time he accidentally stood up a *New York Times* reporter. I relaxed and forgot about Richard's plans for world domination through macarons. Talking to him like this felt intimate and satisfying and I could have stayed at the table hours longer.

"Alas, Mad, I have an early call on the set tomorrow. It's our last day. So I must bid you adieu."

He held my jacket for me as I put my arms into it and then we walked back through the restaurant, the Public

Option on full display, to the front sidewalk where his limo idled at the curb. To my surprise, a photographer also awaited, and he snapped a photo of us as we left the restaurant. I flinched at the unexpected intrusion, but Richard was smiling and waving. Damn, the man was always on.

"Where are you parked?" he asked me. "Silly girl, insisting on driving yourself."

I pointed to the parking garage across the street and shrugged. "I value my independence," I said.

"I'll walk you."

And he did, across the street and up the elevator to the third floor, where we walked a few feet to my car. He laughed when he saw it. "Of course you have a Fiat 500."

I opened the door to my bright blue car, glad that it was clean for once. I turned around to say goodbye and thank Richard and whoa mama, he was right beside me.

He touched my scar. "Where did this come from, my sweet?"

His finger felt light on my face, and yet ponderous at the same time—as if it were the harbinger of something huge. I couldn't speak. Apparently, he took that as reluctance to tell him about the scar.

"It's okay, you don't have to talk about it if you don't want to." He looked down at me soulfully. "I'll be ready to listen whenever you want to tell me about it."

I nodded.

And then he took me in his arms and kissed me.

CHAPTER 5

I arrived at the bakery a little later than usual the next morning, closer to 5:00 a.m. than 4:30. It wasn't that I'd gotten home so late, but rather that I'd had a hard time sleeping. A kiss from Richard Bishop will do that to you. His lips had been soft and slightly moist, and when his tongue found its way into my mouth, it was as if fireworks went off overhead. Okay, we were in the parking garage, so not a good metaphor. But the kiss was amazing. Mega-amazing.

"Wow," I'd said when we finally broke apart.

Richard laughed and patted me on the shoulder. "Drive safe," he said, and then he leaned in and kissed me again.

Finally, I pulled myself away from him and got in my car, so he couldn't kiss me again. I *wanted* him to kiss me again. And that was the problem.

"I'll be in touch," he said, and I pulled out of the parking space faster than I probably should have. Getting out while the getting was good, so to speak, or before the kissing started again. When I looked in my rearview mirror, he stood there grinning in the middle of the parking garage, looking like the larger-than-life Richard Bishop whose most recent movie had been a blockbuster action flick in which he had performed feats of superhuman daring.

Oh, my freaking God.

I shook my head to clear the memory and unlocked the back door of the Bonne Chance. We always left one little light on in the showroom overnight and I used that to see by as I navigated into the baking room, where I took off my coat and stashed it and my bag in the corner. I tied on a clean apron—one of the plain white chef's jobs, because I kept my mom's special apron at my house—and set to work. I pulled egg whites from the fridge and set my big mixing bowls out and then stood with my hands resting on the big old wooden worktable, willing my mind not to keep going back to Richard Bishop and his kisses. I was so confused. Initially I'd thought he asked me out solely for the sake of investing in my business, but then he'd kissed me.

Richard Bishop was the first attraction I'd allowed myself to feel for a man since Will left me. It scared me. Passion is wild and wooly and wonderful, whether it's for a hobby or a business or a person, and I'm convinced that the wildness is what stops most people from following their heart's desire. It's frightening. And when the passion you suddenly feel is for a man of the stature of Richard Bishop, it's terrifying. Thoughts coursed through my mind: why had he kissed me? What did it mean? Did he want a relationship with me? And if so, *really*? Why? And how did it even work to have a relationship with a famous man like Richard Bishop? Did I even *want* a relationship with him? One kiss did not mean a relationship, I chided myself. I was getting way ahead of myself. But wouldn't it be nice to have a man interested in me, someone to ease the disappointments of Will?

I placed parchment paper on baking sheets and pulled out the scale and the almond flour. Soon I got into the rhythm of my work. Thoughts of Richard disappeared as I baked, with my mind roaming all over the place. My free-floating brain was one of the reasons I loved baking so much—it was my own form of meditation. And these early morning hours, when I was alone in the bakery with my macarons and my thoughts, were most often my favorite time of day.

I'd not told Richard the full story of how I fell in love with macarons, because I preferred to keep it to myself, and that was because I didn't want anyone else to sully it. Because there was more to it, much more. And that more was my mother.

I could still see my mom's face as we sat in the kitchen of the house I grew up in, located in an area of stately old homes. Ours was a three-story number with a kitchen nearly as large as the first floor of my current house. It was the day after I'd arrived home from my honeymoon, and she and I ate the macarons I'd picked up for her at a kiosk at Charles de Gaulle. Mom—the original Francophile—was always elegant and composed, with her hair perfectly arranged in a short shag and just the right touch of makeup gracing her face. Jet-lagged and bleary-eyed, I laughed to see her attacking the macarons, eating one after another as pastel-colored crumbs fell down the bodice of her white blouse, one even sticking to her mouth.

When she was finished, she sighed with pleasure. "Oh, Madeleine, what a treat." Mom, of course, never called me by anything other than my full name. Then she held up a finger and rose from her seat to rustle around in a cupboard. She came back to the table with her recipe notebook, licking a finger to turn the pages, a neatly arranged mélange of hand-written recipes and ones copied in other hands, some cut and pasted in.

"Ah, yes, here it is," Mom said. She pulled the rings of the binder apart and carefully removed the sheet of paper and handed it to me. On it I saw a recipe snipped from a magazine, and it was for macarons.

That's when it started. She and I made the first batch of macarons together later that week. Shortly after that, her cancer came back. But even as her lovely silver hair fell out and she refused most food, she still had an appetite for macarons. They were hard to find in Portland in those days, and so I kept baking them, thinking as long as she'd eat them, she'd stay alive.

One day, Mom said to me, after she'd polished off two blueberry macarons and one chocolate, "You know, darling, maybe this is your thing. Maybe you've found it at last." We'd call it a life purpose now, but back then the best expression Mom and I had for it was a *thing*.

"I would have been better off with a thing, like your father and sister both have," Mom had said.

I'd protested, pointing out how beautifully she arranged the house, what a great mom she'd been to Natalie and me, how she dressed people at the boutique where she'd worked part-time for years.

She'd raised a perfectly manicured hand which, even at her age, looked like that of a young woman. "All well and good, and I am beyond proud of all of it, but I always wanted something to be passionate about. I wanted a thing of my own."

She took another bite of macaron, closed her eyes and chewed and then spoke again. "You know I had ideas about selling my tarts for a while. But then—" Mom paused, pressing her lips together, then waved her hand. "Oh, never mind. That was another lifetime ago. Just remember, passionate people are happier people, darling. I want you to be one, too."

I knew exactly what she had glossed over—the death of my baby sister Cecily. I touched the scar on the side of my face. It happened in an accident when I was eight. Mom was driving when a car ran a red light and broadsided us. I sat in the back, next to Cecily's car seat and I'd just screamed with excitement when I saw an announcement for the latest My Little Doggie movie on a theater marquee. To this day, I blame myself for my sister's death. I was leaning as far toward the window as possible to see the movie poster and if I'd been closer to her, she wouldn't have taken the brunt of the collision as she did. The shattering glass would not have pierced her neck. And there was also the fact that my scream had distracted my mother. Had it not, she would have been able to maneuver around the oncoming car.

We didn't talk about any of that. But at least macarons, and my bakery, had made me into a passionate person. They'd given me a *thing*. And Mom was right—life was better that way. Which was why I'd do nearly anything to hang onto the Bonne Chance. Not to mention the fact that I'd not been able to keep my mom alive with all my macaron baking—but I could damn well keep her dream alive in the form of my bakery. And it was also why Will's desertion rankled more than just your garden variety divorce would have—in leaving, he'd struck at the very core of my being.

Oh God, speaking of Will, he had called last night. I set out the first trays of macarons to rest, took off my gloves, washed my hands, and looked at my phone to see if he'd left a message. There was one, and it was short and sweet and inscrutable, Will's voice saying, "Mad, I'm sorry. Just know that, okay? We'll talk soon." I held the phone out to look at it after his message ended. What was *that* about? Was he saying he was sorry about leaving me now, all this time later? And why did a mere whiff of his voice still make me clutch my heart to keep it from leaping out of my chest? I shook it off, literally, holding my hands over my head and shaking my entire body. And then I felt better. A little.

I put Will and even Richard out of my mind as my macaron baking did its magic. I worked steadily, putting several batches of macarons in the oven, and was startled when I heard the back door opening and people entering. But a glance at the clock showed me it was 8:30 already, and I'd been working for three hours.

"It's just us," Jack's voice called out.

"Good morning," I yelled back. I was in the middle of loading a pastry bag with macaron batter, so I waited until I'd piped it onto baking sheets. The macarons had to sit for at least a half an hour before cooking, so I used that chance to go see Jack.

And it turned out that Daisie was with him as well.

"It's a teacher planning day," Jack said when he saw my questioning look at Daisie. She was ensconced at the table, notebook paper and pens arranged in front of her, iPad to one side, basket of crocheting to the other. But what caught my attention was the thing she had on her head—it looked like a pillowcase draped over her crown and tied with some kind of headband around her forehead.

"Um, what's up with the headgear?"

"It's a wimple." Daisie gave me a look like I was the resident idiot. "Duh."

"Oh, of course, how could I be so stupid?"

"Richard Bishop grew up Catholic and attended Catholic schools all his life," Jack explained. He sat across the table from Daisie with his computer open and I could see from where I stood that he was looking at an Excel sheet.

"He says everything he knew, he learned from nuns," Daisie said. She smoothed the part of the pillowcase that lay on her shoulder and bent to her work.

"Well, that explains everything, of course," I said. Daisie ignored me.

"Hey, Len, could I talk to you a second?"

"Talk away, but follow me to the back. I've got to get the next batch of macarons piped."

"What flavor?" Daisie asked.

"Lemon-coconut, I think I finally got the recipe right."

Jack stood and winced and at first, I thought it was due to the mention of coconut, which he hated. But then he rubbed his back and I realized it was because of his injury. I started to say something, but he quickly recomposed his face into a pain-free demeanor, even though I suspected he was totally faking it. I closed my mouth. I knew better than to mention it because that just upset him more.

I slid four trays of macarons each into their ovens, set the timer, and then turned to Jack.

"You feeling okay?" he asked.

"Of course," I started to snap, me being one of those people who got irritated when someone asked how I was. But then I remembered the stomachache excuse I'd used to plead off dinner. I caught myself and said, "I'm doing fine, thanks."

"We missed you last night," he said.

I felt a twinge of guilt. "And I missed you—and your aunt Betty's famous Italian Delight." At least that was the truth. I stared into Jack's eyes, hating that I'd fibbed to him. Sometimes—and this was one such moment—I reveled in just being in Jack's presence, in feeling the Jack-ness of him. I wanted to fling myself into his arms and stay there forever, safe and warm.

"So, Mad." Jack looked at me with what I called his piercing glance, wherein he stared at me intently for a moment and then ducked his head. It was his signal that something was up—something big.

I set down the plastic scraper I'd been using to mix batter. "What?"

He looked at me. "We can't hire someone to help you yet."

My shoulders slumped. "But I thought you said I'd be able to start looking this month."

"I did. But I was wrong."

Something in the way he said the words made me look at him more closely. "Is everything okay?"

"Everything is fine," Jack said, albeit weakly. "It's just that the almond meal you buy is expensive and...."

"I know, I know, the tissue papers we put in every box cost a small fortune. As do printing the care instructions that go along with it."

Jack raised a hand and then took a deep breath. "That's not what I was going to say, Len. The landlord is raising the rent."

"He is?" I was filling a pastry bag with yellow-colored batter. "But I thought you talked to him and he said he'd keep it where it was for a while."

Jack shrugged. "Guess he sees the long lines and thinks we can afford it. This stretch of buildings is getting popular, with the food carts down the street and the coffee shop next door."

I coveted hiring help with all my might. I loved baking, but working to create so many different flavors and come up with new ones was exhausting me. And there were also tedious jobs like sorting through the baked macaron shells, checking for less than perfect specimens, that took forever. Often, I paid Daisie to do it, but despite her drive to earn money, even she tired of it.

"I just wish the house in Olympia would sell." Jack shook his head. "That would solve all our problems."

Jack owned a home up in Washington, where he'd lived with Carla before he and Daisie came to Portland and Carla moved back to L.A. The house had been on the market for a year without selling.

I shook my head at him. "Even if it sold tomorrow, I

wouldn't let you put the money from it into the bakery. You already put everything from the sale of the coffee shop in. And you've got Daisie to think about."

Jack stared at me beneath knotted brows. "It's a moot point for now. And, Len, there's more. We've got that big payment coming up."

"Big payment?" I had no idea what he was talking about. From the very beginning, we'd split duties at the bakery. I baked, Jack and Will dealt with the finances. Whenever I asked about money, they told me not to worry about it, to concentrate on what I did best—bake. Later, I'd realize that I should have paid at least a little attention. But I hadn't. Because, baking, not numbers, was what I did best.

Jack nodded. "A balloon payment coming due on the loan."

"Weren't we planning to go back to the bank to cover it?" I thought I'd heard something to that effect at some point.

"There's not a bank in the world that would loan us money at the moment. And the people we owe the balloon payment to are getting cranky. To put it mildly."

"Yeah, bankers are such assholes, aren't they?" I said.

"These aren't your average garden variety bankers, Len. They're a consortium Will put together from his contacts in Vegas. I didn't like the idea at the time, but—" Jack spread his hands.

A loud Daisie scream split the air. Jack and I exchanged a glance and then he ran out the door. I dropped my pastry bag on the counter and followed him.

I expected to see her fallen on the floor in agony by the sound of her scream, but instead she sat where we'd left her, holding her iPad in her hand. And the look on her face told me everything I needed to know.

"You," Daisie said, glaring at me. She opened her mouth, but no words came out. It took her a second to continue.

"You didn't have a stomachache. You had dinner with Richard Bishop last night." She turned the iPad toward me so I could see she'd landed on a photo someone had tweeted. And yep, that would be the one of Richard and me leaving the restaurant. My eyes were closed, and my mouth was open, and I looked like I was drunk.

The look of shock and betrayal on Daisie's face was bad enough, but Jack's expression was even worse. "I thought you had a stomachache," he said.

"Well, I did." And I tried to explain about the adrenalin and how it had made my gut hurt but then I stopped. Jack and Daisie deserved a real explanation. "I'm sorry, you guys, I really am. He called and asked me to dinner after he left. And for some reason it felt weird to tell you about it. I don't even know why." And that was the truth.

"What did you talk about? I can't believe you didn't tell me, I would have provided you with a list of questions," Daisie said.

"Well," I said, "he's actually interested in the business."

"He is?" Daisie jumped out of her chair and her wimple went askew.

I nodded and looked at Jack. "He wants to invest in it."

The expected look of horror crossed Jack's face, his eyes blazing beneath a scowl. He spoke slowly. "And what did you say to him?"

"Pretty much no."

"Richard Bishop wants to give you money and you said no?" Daisie yelled.

"I told him I'd think about it."

Jack did his finger rubbing up and down his mouth thing. Then he pressed his lips together and all his features rearranged, like puzzle pieces falling into place. "Actually, this might be a good thing."

I shot him the dirtiest look I could muster. "You said you

didn't like him. But now you think taking his money could be a good thing?"

"Of course, it's a good thing!" Daisie shouted.

Jack opened his hands in front of him in a questioning manner. "We do need the money." He paused a second. "Badly."

"But you said you didn't trust him!"

He raised his hands again. "I don't know. I really don't. But it might be the answer to all our problems." Jack shrugged. "Maybe it's a dream come true."

"Guys, it's not that simple. He wants to franchise. He sees a whole chain of little Bonne Chances across the country."

"And your problem with that is what?" Jack asked. "You've always said your goal is to make macarons as popular as chocolate chip cookies."

I drummed my fingers on the desk and bit my lip, thinking. "It feels like selling out. All I want in life is for my bakery to be successful. *This* bakery." I tapped my finger hard on the table.

"I really can't say I like the guy," Jack said. "But he may be our best hope."

I shook my head. "I don't know. It feels…weird to me."

"Are you sure you're not just scared, Len?"

"I'm not scared." I scowled, ignoring the voice inside my head that said, *yes you are.* "What would I be scared of?"

"Success."

I waved my hand in front of my face. "I'm not scared of success. It's all I've ever wanted. Anyway, he wants me to fly to L.A. to talk about it more."

"L.A.!" Daisie hollered. "I can go visit the La Brea tar pits."

For reasons known only to herself, Daisie had developed an obsession with the La Brea tar pits. Fossils were one of her many passions.

"And I could see Carla," Jack said. He looked over at Daisie. "*We* could see Carla."

Daisie wrinkled her nose. "Or I could shadow Richard Bishop while you see her."

In case you hadn't guessed, Daisie wasn't the hugest fan of her mother. I spoke before the two of them could spat any longer. "Actually, he only mentioned me coming."

Daisie sighed dramatically.

"You should go, Len, and at least see what he has to say."

The nuances of this discussion had caused a fog in my brain and I couldn't sort through it all. "I'll tell you where I'm going. I'm going to go clean."

"Richard Bishop only supports businesses he passionately believes in," Daisie called after me.

I waved a hand as I fled to the sanctuary of my kitchen.

CHAPTER 6

I was rinsing a sponge after spraying disinfectant and wiping down my worktable when Caroline stuck her head in the door.

"There's a man here to see you."

I clenched the sponge as my heart did a tricky gymnastics maneuver. Was it Richard? Who else would it be? Caroline would tell me if it was someone she knew. But then again, she would also tell me if it was Richard Bishop. I told myself to quit with the fantasies and go see who was here.

There was a crowd in the showroom, as usual, but this time the four customers who constituted a crowd in that tiny space were staring not at the gorgeous rainbow display of macarons, but at something in the corner. The man nearest me had his phone held out, taking a photo. Another woman raised her cell and snapped a shot. Again, my heart clenched. Were they gaping at Richard? I elbowed between the two people standing nearest me, my heart pounding.

But it wasn't Richard Bishop. It was my father, Earl Miller, standing in the corner of the showroom next to the front door.

Only he was upside down, head to ground, elbows slightly bent, feet in the air. As I watched, he lithely swung his feet to the ground and hopped back onto them with a flourish of his arms in the air. The crowd clapped and cheered.

"And this, my friends, is what seventy looks like when you do yoga every day," Earl said to more cheers. "And follow my simple spiritual principles. Which include not eating sugar, I might add." Earl swiped a sidelong glance at the macaron display.

"Knock it off, Dad; you're scaring my customers away!" I said, smiling, as I walked toward him.

"Forgive me, dear daughter." Earl turned to the group of customers who still watched him. He had the knack for enthralling groups gleaned from years of lecturing to large audiences. "If you must eat sugar, this is the place to do it."

"I'm working on a healthy version of macarons, made with honey, just for you, Dad. And you know they are gluten-free."

"That, at least is a wonderful thing," Earl said, and then, "Hi, baby," as he enfolded me in a hug.

Earl—these days I called him that more than I called him Dad—smelled like a fresh fall day outside in the high desert —a tang of leaves and a hint of sage, perhaps. Being in his arms reminded me of everything good in the world and a sense of relief settled over me. I shook off the nagging worry of my conversation with Jack, and the idea of Richard Bishop franchising my little bakery suddenly seemed far away.

I stepped back from his embrace and looked at my father with delight. He was elegantly bald, with intelligence blazing from his brown eyes, and naturally tanned skin. One of my father's many core beliefs was the benefit of spending time in the sun. He wore a Hawaiian shirt in shades of blue, green, and magenta, cargo pants, and thick-soled sandals, despite the fact our early fall rains continued. This, or slight variations thereof, was Earl's signature uniform in all seasons, even though the southern Oregon town of Ashland where he lived did get somewhat nippy in the winter.

I pulled Earl into the back hall, with him smiling and waving and calling out "My new book on following your soul releases in time for Christmas," to the bakery customers. Far from being offended at his blatant marketing, they seemed to be delighted.

Daisie and Jack were still in the office and Daisie screamed in joy when she saw Earl and ran to him for a hug. This caused her wimple to fall to the floor and necessitated a long explanation of the reason for it. Which Daisie gave with relish, including highlights of my conversation with Richard Bishop at dinner the night before.

When she finally stopped, Jack shook Earl's hand and said, "Good to see you." He turned to Daisie and told her it was time for them to go.

"But I want Earl to tell me how to write a best-selling book!" she said. "Richard Bishop's book went to the *New York Times* best-seller list, you know."

"We can have that discussion any time," Earl said to her. "As a matter of fact, I'm here in town for a few days. Might we arrange a lunch just for the two of us?" After much consulting of phone and computer calendars, the date was set and a contented-looking Daisie scampered off after Jack, who appeared the exact opposite of his daughter—he still wore that worried, distracted air.

"So, Richard Bishop, eh?" Dad said after they'd left. He sat on Jack's chair, with his legs crossed in lotus position. I'd thought about taking him next door to the coffee shop, but that would have necessitated sharing him with his adoring public and I wanted him to myself. I set a plate of macarons in front of him and plugged in the electric teakettle.

I nodded. "Yeah, it was wild. And an interesting evening, to say the least."

"Isn't he the actor who played that movie character you and Natalie liked so much?"

I nodded. "Ford Dooley."

"And remind me of Ford Dooley's story?"

I took a bite of a Mom's Apple Pie macaron. "Oh, Ford Dooley was so inspiring. He taught religion—"

At this Earl's eyebrows shot up and he interrupted me. "And this was a big, popular Hollywood movie?"

I smiled and nodded, then popped the rest of the macaron in my mouth. "I know, shocking, huh? Anyway, Ford taught religion at this small private college and he had a wife and three kids. Problem was that Ford was not making enough to support his family. He loved what he was doing—it was his true calling—but he just wasn't making enough money. So, he was about to go back into advertising, which he hated."

Earl's hand hovered above the plate holding macarons and finally landed on a lemon thyme one. "Sounds like someone I know."

"I didn't hate advertising. I just like macaron baking better." I stood and pulled two mugs from a small wall shelf, plopped tea bags in them, and then poured water. My career previous to baking had been writing ad copy for local businesses like muffler shops and insurance companies and I'd lied to my father. I had disliked it intensely.

"Oh God, these are good," Earl said, reaching for another macaron.

I smiled, handed him his mug, and sat back down.

Earl finished chewing. "These should be illegal. I've eaten more sugar today than I have all year. Carry on with the story."

"Well, so then Ford is carrying the weight of the world on his shoulders and because he's so distracted, he gets in a car accident when he's driving his kids to school. But he and his kids are rescued. Ford swears it was by an angel."

"Of course," Earl said. "Because they do like to be helpful, you know."

Dad had written a book about angels and was a huge proponent of, as he said, getting to know your guardian angel.

"So then, a few months later, after everyone is all happy, an angel comes to him and tells him it's time for him to start giving back. So, Ford Dooley goes around helping the angels and rescuing people."

Earl pursed his lips. "And this was a big blockbuster movie? I can't believe I missed it."

"It wasn't just one, it was three of them. Rent them sometime. But watch them in order because there's a big twist at the end of the last one."

"I will. Meanwhile, I am curious to know more about how your evening with the real Ford Dooley went."

I filled him in on the details that Daisie hadn't mentioned, though there were precious few of them because she didn't miss much. "He wants to franchise the Bonne Chance."

"And how do you feel about that?" Earl asked.

"Jack says we need the money, but on the other hand I don't want to sell out."

Earl sat in perfect stillness as he listened to me.

I hesitated. "And Jack says I'm just scared."

"Are you?"

"No. Yes. Probably. I don't know. This is all so confusing." And then I thought of something. If we could get an infusion of money, I could forget Richard Bishop's interest in the bakery. "Hey, Dad, would you consider—"

Earl raised his hand. "I'm sorry, baby. I'm totally tapped out with the new center; I can't afford to give you a cent. You know I would if I could."

Dad was building a retreat center where his followers could come study with him in Santa Fe. Yes, the one and only Santa Fe, that self-same place where Will and Hill had gone to open a macaron shop with my recipes. The hell part of it was that *I* was the one who introduced Will to Santa Fe, taking him there to visit Earl, who kept a home in town. Something in the tone of Dad's voice set off a vague bell of alarm ringing in the back of my mind, but unfortunately, I was so distracted with my own worries that I didn't pay much attention.

"How do you do that?"

"Do what?"

"Read my mind?"

"It's all in staying present, my dear daughter. Let me ask you something that might help. How do you feel when you envision a chain of your bakeries across this vast land?"

I shook my head. "I don't feel anything, because I can't envision it."

"Oh, Mad." Earl grabbed another macaron. "Rule one of everything. You must be able to envision your success to achieve it. Or the message to the devas will be muddy."

"Devas, Dad? Really?"

He nodded solemnly. "The subject of my next book. Amazing creatures. They will help you succeed, but only if you know what you want." Earl stood, brushing crumbs off his shirt. "And now, I must attend yet another meeting with the bankers."

"I love you, Dad," I called as he walked out the back door.

He raised a hand in a wave without turning around. "Remember, Mad, devas."

I shook my head. I wasn't even sure I knew what a deva was. And just then my phone buzzed. Of course, you know who it was. Richard Bishop. I picked up the phone and answered his call.

CHAPTER 7

Richard picked me up at the Burbank airport, zooming up to where I stood at the curb with the Public Option grin plastered on his face. He wore his signature black T-shirt and slacks and when I got in the car I smelled mint and lime—like a combination of aftershave and breath fresheners. When I look back now, I realize how silly my reaction was, but I was touched by this—as if Richard, *the* Richard Bishop, had gone to extra lengths to smell nice for me.

I would have been knocked out regardless. To be inside the enclosed space of a car interior was far more overwhelming than sitting across a table from him at dinner. His aura—charisma? —filled all the space inside and made it hard to breathe. I was in sensory overload.

He drove a Tesla, of course. It was a beautiful rich brown and Richard seemed to delight in telling me how much money he saved on gas. "And it's the right choice for the environment, too," he said as we zoomed along the freeway.

I had no clue where we were headed or what his agenda might be. On the phone he'd made vague noises about choosing locations for the bakery, but that was all I'd gotten out of him. It felt weird to place myself solely in his hands, so to speak, but I was determined to keep an open mind about his ideas for the business. Because it appeared Richard's ideas might be the only way to actually continue to *have* a business.

But still and all, I wanted to have some clue what I was getting myself into.

"So, um, where are we headed?" I asked.

He glanced at me with a smile. "Places."

"What kind of places?"

"My kind of places."

Oh God, this was like a child's game. But I was into it anyway. I tilted my head to one side in an effort to play coy. "Will I like your kind of places?"

"Is your neck bothering you? Did you fall asleep on it awkwardly on the plane?"

I straightened my head. So much for my efforts to be coy. "Um, no, I'm fine." I rubbed my neck for show. "Though those airplane seats are murder on the neck, right?"

Richard laughed heartily, and I got the impression he knew what a fake I was. But then he looked at me with a serious expression, no glitzy smile.

"I want to share a little bit of myself with you, Mad. I want you to get to know me. And I want to get to know you better, too."

I nearly gasped with the wonder of it all. Down, girl, I told myself. He's just a man who puts his pants on one leg at a time, like everyone else. He smiled at me again, then stepped on the gas, zooming around a slow car ahead and barreling down the fast lane. I decided that there was no cop on the planet who would dare to stop Richard Bishop. Or maybe his Tesla had its own force field around it.

Once we exited the freeway he spoke again. "I'm going to start by showing you one of my houses."

Houses? As in plural residences? Well, why not—he had the money for it. But who needed multiple homes in the same city? Richard Bishop, apparently. The ways of the rich and famous were opaque to me.

We turned down a winding road through golden hills that passed a school and some other buildings, and then the terrain opened, and I could see that we were at the base of a canyon—Malibu Canyon, as it turned out. A little further on, the buildings were replaced by huge mansions that sprawled over the burnished land. After a while, we turned again and then again, and soon we were in an area of modest (by Malibu standards) homes located on curvy streets beneath old oak trees. A burbling creek ran along the road with little pedestrian bridges crossing it periodically. One house featured a huge fenced area out front with a horse in residence. The shade from the oaks dappled the sunlight as we zoomed through the neighborhood. Finally, Richard pulled into a driveway and then ran around to open my door for me.

"This is your house?" I asked.

"Sure is."

Frankly, I was surprised. The house wasn't much. We walked past an outdoor area with a barbecue covered in a bright blue tarp and dry leaves skittering across the patio, and then inside through a glass slider, which led directly into the dining room. Don't get me wrong, it was a nice house, a California rambler, all one level, with a long hall beyond the (tiny) kitchen that led to bedrooms, or so I assumed. And the location couldn't be beat—if you liked living at the bottom of a canyon amid a hazardous fire area with no clear, fast way out.

Richard stood in the dining room and put his arms out to his sides and said, "What do you think?"

"Um, it's very nice," I said

"It was my first home here." Richard looked around the space. I followed his gaze. There was a huge framed map of the world on the wall, and beneath that a hutch on which rested a decorative vase and two candles. The one thing missing was any personal touch—I saw no photos of Richard, no mementos, no signs of actual living in the place.

"But you don't live here now?"

He shook his head. "My other home is over on the beach. But this, dear Madeleine, is the place you will stay when you come to run the flagship bakery."

"Oh, really." I felt my entire body stiffen and I took a step back from him. He was assuming a lot.

He nodded. "Do you like it?"

Suddenly, it was all too much for me. I got fed up with Richard Bishop and his presumptions. He'd presumed I would come to L.A. to do...I wasn't exactly sure. He'd assumed I'd want to go wherever he took me, do whatever he wanted. And now he was presuming that I would live in this house. We hadn't even talked details of opening a bakery down here. Yet he thought he could dazzle and charm me into acquiescing to his desires. Well, he had another think coming.

"I like it fine, thanks," I said, even though its décor looked like a bland designer had created it and it couldn't be further from my taste. "But you're presuming a lot, Richard."

"Oh, now I've riled you." Richard strode across the room and grabbed my shoulders. "I'm so sorry, Mad, dear. That's the last thing I want."

Even though my skin tingled where his fingers gripped me and standing so close to him was as intoxicating as the smell of the honeysuckle that grew along my back porch, I held my ground. "I don't like to be taken for granted. I don't like it when people assume I'm going to do things I haven't decided on yet."

"You are so very correct. I have been thoughtless in my assumptions, Madeleine." And then he did the most amazing thing. He got down on one knee and looked up at me. "I want to give you so much, Mad. I want to give you everything. That's my only intention. So please forgive me if I get overbearing."

I stared down at him, and I'm certain my mouth was open in my characteristic unattractive fashion. Because Richard's behavior was big, so grand, so larger than life, I almost couldn't handle it. I'd never known a man like him before. But then it occurred to me—maybe this was the way men of his stature behaved. Every cell in my body sang as I stared into his eyes, sang in a way that made me delirious. It was the way I wanted to feel, always, every minute, every second of my life, forever. Up until now, the only time I'd felt this way was while baking. But here was Richard Bishop, handing that feeling to me, showing me I could own it, luxuriate in it, *live* in it—that it was mine for the taking. For that, I could forgive him his assumptions and his overbearingness and a whole hell of a lot more. I could forgive him everything for *this*, for this moment.

"Life is like a fishing net, Mad, a vast web in which we're all connected." His eyes glittered up at me. "And some of us are more connected than others."

Oh, God, I really couldn't take it—he'd just uttered one of my favorite Ford Dooley quotes. And then I recalled the scene in *Take Back the Night* when Ford got down on his knee in exactly the same way for a woman he was trying to save. I looked down at him and my heart flipped over. I swear, I *felt* it flipping. I was helpless to resist his charms.

"Just tell me one thing," I said.

"Anything."

"Why me?"

"Oh God, Mad, you really don't get it, do you?" Richard

stood. "You're adorable. Fresh, unique, yet not over the top. Stylish and talented. A diamond in the rough. I want to polish your edges."

Then he took me in his arms and kissed me. And I quit worrying about the gulf between our stations in life, or how I should respond to him. I decided that grand gestures came with the territory of the rich and famous, that maybe they were even how one acquired wealth and fame, and I should just relax and enjoy. Because his kiss was as amazing as the first time, in the parking garage across from the restaurant in Portland. Only this time it was early afternoon, not late in the evening, and through the windows streamed soft golden light filtered by the oaks that surrounded the house.And when we broke apart, he gazed down at me. I looked into his eyes, expecting to see guile, or triumph, an air of patronizing. But all I saw was what no doubt shone in my own eyes —desire.

"I want to polish *all* your edges," he murmured.

And polish them he did. Then, he was kissing me again. He pushed my little lace cardigan off my shoulders and suddenly it had landed on the floor. His hands—they were big and strong, but soft, too—roamed over my neck and down lower and then the strap of my sundress got pulled aside and he'd connected with my breasts. He deposited little kisses down my neck, and chest and cleavage. Before I knew it, we were working our way down the hall, items of clothing —his shirt, my dress, his belt, my bra, his pants, my panties— falling away until we made it to the king-sized bed in the master bedroom, totally naked.

I didn't have time to stop myself to think about what I was doing. Okay, I didn't *take* time to stop myself. I didn't want to. Because Richard's hands on me were like the ulti- mate best massage you've had, *ever*, and his mouth on me made every cell in my body sing. Richard inside of me was flowers blooming and windows everywhere opening; it was birds singing and rainbows appearing in the sky.

And any worrisome thoughts I had about Richard Bishop were dispelled. Because, as you might have guessed, Richard was tres bon in bed. About as tres bon as you could get. And macarons were the furthest thing from my mind that October afternoon in L.A.

CHAPTER 8

I stayed in L.A. three days longer after that golden afternoon. When I look back at that time, it's a blur. A happy blur, but a blur nonetheless. After we left his original home, Richard ensconced me in a room on the top floor of the Peninsula Hotel, and only later, much later, did I wonder why he'd never taken me to his "real" home, the luxurious one in Malibu. But I was too entranced by staying at one of the finest hotels in the world, and by Richard, so I never thought to ask.

There was also the small matter that Richard never spent the night. He stayed at the hotel late, and arrived early—but he never, ever, spent the night. Why? Was it because he was afraid somebody would find out? But why would that matter? Or, more problematic, was it because staying the night would indicate a certain level of intimacy that he wanted to avoid? Probably the latter. But I didn't want to think that.

So I ignored those little niggling thoughts.

Because *Richard.*

I got used to being followed everywhere by photographers shouting his name and relaxed when I realized they weren't particularly interested in me. And some days they didn't follow Richard, either. I couldn't quite figure out the metrics of it. On the day we drove to Hollywood to see one of the potential locations of the L.A. Bonne Chance, there was not a paparazzo in sight.

"Where'd they all go?" I asked as a uniformed doorman held the front door of the hotel open for us.

"Anita Carole is taking her baby girl to lunch today. It's the child's first public appearance," Richard said.

"Oh," I said, with grave seriousness. "Of course."

Richard just laughed and chucked my chin. But I wondered: how did he know this? He didn't spend any time with his head buried in his phone, as most humans on the planet did these days. When we were together, he was present, not half with me, half paying attention to his phone. That was one of the things I liked best about him—his ability to make me think I was the only person in the world at that moment. Yet he always knew exactly what was happening in the world of entertainment, politics, and current events. And when I asked him how he did that, he just laughed again, and steered his car down busy Hollywood Boulevard toward the Bonne Chance location.

I was shocked when I saw it. Richard had said "his people" had found a fantastic location in an area called Noho. The way he talked about it, I'd envisioned an arty enclave magically set away from the L.A. bustle. But the empty storefront Richard showed me was smack in the middle of the tourist traffic on Hollywood Boulevard, near the gaudy TCL Chinese Theatre which I'd always heard called Grauman's, and next door to a tacky store that sold hats, mugs, and snow globes featuring Oscar statuettes or movie studios in them. The crowds of people who thronged the area walked with their heads down because the sidewalk was emblazoned with black stars containing the names of famous actors and actresses. Yup, the proposed location was right next to the Walk of Stars. Even I knew that this was as Hollywood ground zero as it got.

"This is it?" I said as I stood on the sidewalk before it. I turned to Richard, stunned. He'd gotten waylaid by a group of tourists with cameras slung over their necks and fanny packs around their waists. After he signed a few autographs, he unlocked the front door and beckoned me in.

The space was empty and echoing. And it was *huge*. I couldn't believe such a spacious store might be devoted to my macarons. I followed Richard through the rooms, stepping over boards and nails that had been left lying on the ground, to a back area where he pushed me in front of him and then stopped. "This will be your baking area." He spread his arms wide and grinned, then wrapped his arms around my waist from behind. "You can advise us on how to best outfit it."

I leaned my head back against his chest. Cloaked in his arms, I felt excited about all the possibilities in the world. But I remembered my doubts about the location and wriggled out of them. "This isn't really what we would call Noho, is it?"

Richard spread his arms and, of course, grinned. "It's Hollywood, baby! The land of dreams."

I swallowed. "It isn't exactly the kind of location I think of when I think about macarons."

Richard stepped closer to me. "I understand what you mean, Mad. But the first rule of retail is location, location, location. You saw the tourists out there. Your L.A. Bonne Chance will be swarming with macaron buyers."

I glanced around again, trying to envision it all decked out and ready for business, but I couldn't quite pull the vision into my head.

"Now come check out the space back here," Richard called.

I looked around the space. Someone had used it as a kitchen before and there were a couple of stainless-steel racks, a sink, and an oven. A good start. I glanced around further and noticed a glass door.

"Where does that lead?"

Richard shrugged. "I'm not sure."

I walked over, opened it, and stepped outside into an alley lined with back doorways from the neighboring businesses, each one with its own set of garbage cans. The alley was empty and a little creepy, the kind of place you probably wouldn't want to linger at night. Or even early in the morning, on the way to bake. I shuddered and started to close the door and then I saw movement, a flash of purple.

Someone had just come out the back door of the tacky tourist store next door. I craned my neck. A young woman dressed all in black and with short bright purple hair—not a color seen anywhere in nature—had emerged and her head was now bent, lighting a cigarette. She got it going, took a drag, and looked up. When she saw me, she nodded her head in that studied casual manner hipsters affected, a slight uplift of her chin.

"Hi." I nodded back.

She stared at me, appraisingly. Took another drag, blew out more smoke. Something about the girl—because she *was* a girl, probably in her late teens—mesmerized me and I couldn't help but gaze at her. She was tall and slender, and beneath her purple hair she had tanned skin and fierce dark eyes.

"Do you like working here?" Yeah, lame conversation starter, but I felt compelled to engage her.

She shrugged. "It's a job." The word *job* ended on a high note, and she drew it out, as if she were questioning why anyone would ask if she enjoyed it. She held my stare with a dark, intense gaze, keeping eye contact. This girl was ferociously tough and wanted to make sure I knew it. But then her expression changed and softened into childlike curiosity.

"Hey, you're that famous guy!"

I looked behind me and there stood Richard, peeking out the door. I'd been so focused on the young woman I'd momentarily forgotten about him. He nodded and flashed the Public Option.

"Wow." The girl stared at him, and then a slow smile spread across her face. "Am I, like, supposed to ask you for your autograph or something?"

I expected Richard to dissemble, to mumble some platitude or another and pull me inside the store. But he stepped out into the alley and grinned. And it was a real grin, not the Public Option, which astounded me. "How about a photograph?"

The girl's smile faded. "I don't have a phone."

"Well, I guess it will have to be an autograph, then." He pulled a pen from his pocket and advanced toward her. "Do you have a piece of paper?"

Instead she held her arm out. I felt a smile growing on my face as I watched Richard write out his name, then lean down and pat her on the shoulder.

"Thanks," she said, stubbing out her cigarette and springing up. "My boyfriend will be amazed."

"Give him my regards," Richard said, and he followed me back into the store. Inside, he clapped his hands together. "Now, where shall I take you for dinner? Would you like to drive down the coast? Or just return to the hotel room and get room service?"

I threw my arms around his neck and kissed his cheek.

"What was that for?"

"You being wonderful."

"You're the one that's wonderful, my Madeleine." He wrapped his arms around my waist and held me close for a minute. If I could have frozen that moment in amber to preserve it for all time, I would have.

Richard nuzzled my neck, kissed my cheek, and then disengaged from the hug. "Let's go eat dinner, my lovely."

And I followed him out the door.

LATER, after dinner at Nobubo, and once we were back in the hotel, I forgot all about the girl with the purple hair. Because once Richard and I climbed into bed together, I forgot about *everything*, except him. Sappy and schmaltzy as it sounds, we explored each other's bodies, and after making endless love, we explored each other's brains and stories. I hadn't felt such intense chemistry since Will and I reconnected while watching an Oregon Ducks football game at a sports bar. We'd never made it to the end of the game, instead watching the final play on a tiny TV from Will's bed, naked and wrapped in each other's arms.

But Will was the furthest thing from my mind those days in L.A. Even Jack and Daisie and the Bonne Chance bakery faded away. Over the next few days I forgot about every aspect of my life in Portland. After a while, I didn't think about opening a store in L.A. I didn't think about franchising the bakery. I didn't think at all about whether we were going to take Richard up on his offer, and Richard seemed content not to press me on it. I didn't even worry about Richard's continued breezy reluctance to spend the night with me. Instead, I just *was*. I was in the moment, in the present, in love with Richard and happy just to be in his presence. Finally, after all these years of listening to Dad, I got what he meant by telling people to "relax into the eternal now."

Maybe it was because of all the relaxing that a funny

thing happened. I got to the point where I could see myself letting it all go. I awoke in the hotel bed on the morning I was due to fly back home to Portland and I knew with a clarity I hadn't felt since Will left that I didn't want Richard messing with my bakery. Forget franchising. I didn't want a Hollywood version of the Bonne Chance loosed upon the world. I wanted my bakery to remain as it was—a sweet little single location shop in northeast Portland. Somehow, Jack and I would figure out a way to make it successful on its own terms. Somehow, I'd be able to save my house. Somehow, I'd have my macarons and eat them too.

And somehow, someway, one day far in the future, I'd be able to forget Richard Bishop and the time I had with him.

When I told Richard my decision, he laughed. "I figured you might feel that way."

"You did?"

We were at the table in the hotel room's sitting room (it was the first time I'd stayed in a hotel that *had* a sitting room), eating a breakfast that room service had brought up right as Richard arrived—croissants nearly as good as the ones I'd loved in Paris, bacon, sausage, scrambled eggs, yogurt, granola, orange juice, fruit.

"I did." He nodded as if to accentuate his words and smiled. I swear, nothing perturbed the man. He always smiled. He poured me more coffee. "All I ask is that you return to Portland and think about it. Keep an open mind, Maddie. Your business could be huge in my hands."

I sipped at my coffee and stared out the window at the city far below. This life that Richard had showed me the last couple of days was incredible, no doubt about it. But I wasn't cut out for it. Suddenly, all I wanted more than anything was to get back home, home to my bakery. Home to Daisie and Jack and my quirky little house. Home to waking up early to bake my macarons. Home to good old Portland rain.

But then Richard rose from his chair and came over to kneel beside mine. The man knew how to stage himself expertly. It looked like a tableau from the movies. He knelt before me, crazy, glorious Los Angeles spread out beyond him. "Maddie, listen to me."

I nodded, more than a little overcome by everything.

"No matter what you decide about the business, that doesn't affect us, okay?"

I stared down into his eyes.

"Answer me."

I nodded again. "Okay."

"Because these last few days have been magical for me. For you, too?"

"Yes, " I said.

"Then let's keep it going."

All I could do was nod once more and laugh as he stood and pulled me to my feet. He clapped his hands together like an eager little boy. "And now, what shall we do today before you have to leave?" He swept his hand toward the view outside the window and quoted a Ford Dooley line. "The whole, wide, wonderful, magical world awaits."

CHAPTER 9

Jack insisted on picking me up at the airport, despite my protestations I could call an Uber for the short distance to my house. My plane arrived around dinnertime, and I met Jack on the curb outside the baggage claim. A thick mist fell, the kind that hung in the air and collected on everything, leaving beads of moisture glistening in the dark. The damp always made it feel colder to me, and I rustled in my suitcase for a scarf and hopped from foot to foot to stay warm.

And then there was Jack, pulling carefully alongside the curb where I waited. He turned off the car engine and got out of the car to retrieve my luggage. Oh God, Jack in all his Jackness was the best sight ever. I lunged at him and threw my arms around him, pressing my nose against the soft, worn cotton of his shirt. He held me tight for a minute, then squeezed me, kissed my head, and let me go.

"You hungry?" he asked after he had stowed my luggage and we were both snug in our seats.

"Always," I said, which was true. I seemed to be ravenous

these days. Not just for food, but for life, and every experience I could wring out of it.

"Want to grab a bite at the Laurelwood? I could stand a beer. And, we need to talk."

Uh-oh. Jack only said that when it was something important. But I needed to talk to him, too, I realized—to tell him that I had declined Richard's offer of help for the bakery. I hoped Jack would be okay with that decision. I looked over at him, realizing all over again that he was incredibly handsome, as handsome in his own way as Richard was in his. All Jack lacked was Richard's calculated star power.

The Laurelwood was our favorite brewpub right down the hill from the Bonne Chance, and it was a short distance away from the airport. We drove through rain-slicked streets in the November early dark, the SUV windshield wipers straining to keep up with the downpour. Despite the weather, it felt good to be home, back to my familiar stomping grounds of northeast Portland—NEP to proud locals—which didn't appear to have changed much in my absence. We drove past the Bonne Chance and my heart leapt when I saw it. The bakery was closed by this time in the evening, but we always left a light on inside and it looked like a little glowing jewel, cozy and sweet and charming.

The pub was warm and brightly lit and hopping with customers, but we were still able to get a prime spot, a booth near the long bar where bartenders poured the pub's award-winning beers. Portland is a beer town beyond all others, with more brewpubs per capita than any other city in the U.S., so much so that it is often called Beervana. Just about anyone who ever drank a beer seemed to be brewing their own in the garage, and microbreweries dotted the city with as much regularity as coffee shops and wine bars. Despite all that, I hadn't been much of a beer drinker since my college days and ordered a glass of red when the waiter came.

"So," Jack said after we'd both gotten our drinks and taken sips, "how was the rest of your trip?"

It was such a normal question, and yet coming from Jack it seemed inane, because Jack was not one for small talk in any way. I cocked my head and looked at him, only now noticing how the worry lines around his mouth and eyes seemed to be more deeply etched.

"It was good," I said. And then, because it seemed like more was needed, "I finally got to eat at Brava Nueva and it certainly lives up to the hype."

"Great."

This would be why Jack and I did not normally engage in small talk—because we weren't good at it. But I plunged on. "How's Daisie?"

"Ha! She's lobbying to be home schooled, so that she doesn't have to put up with the 'stupid idiot teachers who know less than I do,' and that was a direct quote."

"And where is she, by the way?"

"At the neighbors. She was supposed to be playing with the kid who's in her class, but the father is a top exec at Nike. When I left, Daisie was quizzing him on the global supply chain."

I heard a bell chime and my heart leapt. Maybe it was Richard texting me. But when I pulled out my phone, no messages had come in. I looked up and realized Jack was reading something on his phone—must have been his cell that I heard. He grimaced, typed a few words, then set the phone down on the table and looked at me.

"Lenie, we have to talk."

"So you said earlier."

He took a deep breath. "I really don't know how to tell you this," he said and then sat silent for a few moments.

I realized my heart was pounding. Now that I was paying

attention, everything about Jack's demeanor screamed anxiety.

"What? Is it something with Daisie you're not telling me?"

Jack shook his head and rubbed two fingers between his eyebrows and up this forehead. "She's fine. And thank God for that."

"What then? Just tell me."

"We've run into some trouble with the bakery."

Now my heart quit pounding. Instead, I was sure it quit beating. Trouble with the bakery? What?

Jack laid a hand flat on the table and blew out a long stream of air. "It's about Will."

My stomach clenched like the hand of God had taken a fistful of my intestines. Hearing the words *Will* and *trouble* in the same discussion made my heart stop beating all over again. I put a hand to my chest. "Oh God, is he okay?"

Jack held a finger in the air and nodded. "It's more about something he did. Something bad."

"You mean worse than running off with the bimbo and leaving us in the lurch?"

"I'm afraid so."

My shoulders slumped. "What? Tell me!"

"It has to do with murky financing."

That didn't sound so bad to me. "How murky is murky?"

"Think sleazy loan shark and then quadruple the image. I'm not exactly sure, but there's evidence it could be worse."

"I don't get it."

"These guys are thugs, Lenie. Like Mob-type thugs. The kind who break body parts if you don't pay them."

Slowly it was dawning on me what he might mean. "And they invested in the Bonne Chance?"

Jack nodded. "Apparently so. Will arranged that part of the financing."

I sat back in my seat. And then I reached for my wine and belted down the rest of it. "And are they, by any chance pressuring us to pay them? That was the big payment you told me about?"

Jack nodded again.

"And we don't have any way to pay them, right?"

The waiter walked by and I hit him up for another round of drinks. I held my breath waiting for his answer, even though I knew what it would be.

"That is correct. They've been raising the rates every month. And couple that with the credit cards we maxed out to get started, not to mention the money from your father, and the regular bank loans…"

Suddenly I remembered a couple of weeks ago when I'd gotten that weird message from Will. What had he said? Something to the effect that no matter what happened, I should remember that he was sorry. I hadn't thought much of it at the time, but now, in retrospect, it seemed very ominous.

"There's more," Jack said.

My shoulders slumped.

"Will and Hill's bakery burned down a couple nights ago. It was arson—intentionally set to get the insurance money. Because he was into it for a lot from the same guys."

"Oh, Jesus." I could only begin to imagine how badly Will must be hurting. To lose his business, the thing he loved more than anything else in the world—or so I assumed, because that's how I felt about my bakery, and Will and I always saw eye to eye on such things—must be absolutely devastating. And I was devastated for him, surprised at how much my heart hurt at the thought of his downfall.

"You've talked to him?"

Jack nodded. "Earlier today."

"Is he okay?"

"Hanging in there, considering the circumstances."

I reached for my phone. "I've got to call him."

Jack held up a hand. "Hang on, Lenie. We need to discuss the implications this has on us."

I looked at Jack. "Is there a chance the same thing could happen to us?"

"I think anything is possible with these guys," Jack said. "We've got to get the loan paid back as soon as possible." A funny expression crossed his face, one I'd never seen before. "I'm hanging on by a thread, Len. I'm a month behind on my mortgage and I know you're sweating paying yours."

"Oh God, Jack, I had no idea." It was one thing for me to be struggling with my monthly bills, but quite another for Jack. He had Daisie to think of. He'd invested a substantial sum of money from the sale of his coffee shop—his nest egg. And now it was gone, apparently. Thanks to me. And my insistence that we could make the bakery a success. How blind could I be? I dropped my head into my hands and then looked up. "I am so, so sorry."

Jack shook his head. "It's not your fault, Len. I invested in the bakery willingly. It's just that I'm not getting the consulting jobs like I used to. This damn injury. And I can't leave for months at a time with Daisie, either. I called the real estate agent in Olympia to see if there's any hope of selling the house soon, but no such luck. That house is cursed, for some reason. Which is why it's a damn good thing that we've got Richard Bishop to back us. Much as I dislike the guy and his plans, he's our only option."

I rubbed my hand along the edge of my temple, where a headache knocked on the door. I felt it threaten to pound with every financial woe that Jack listed. "Um, about Richard." I looked into Jack's eyes. "I kind of told him no."

"Oh, Lenie, really? Why did you do that?"

"It just didn't feel right. And you yourself didn't appear to like the idea much. You told me to be careful."

Jack spread his hands in the air, as if to indicate helplessness. "I don't like it. But, according to what you texted me, he is offering us a golden deal. Clearing away all the debt, money to buy more equipment, and a generous operating fund. Plus, paying both our mortgages."

"Yeah, too bad we're selling our business lock, stock and barrel at the same time. That's why I told Richard I couldn't do it. I couldn't see us selling out that way."

"You're going to have to un-tell him, Len. I know how much the bakery means to you, and I just don't see any other way forward." Jack rubbed his hand to his forehead. "Because apparently Will sold us out long ago."

My heart twisted. Really, it felt like it did. I was so confused. On the one hand, I ached for Will, I really did—to see his dream go up in ashes at the hands of a bunch of thugs. On the other hand, anger had begun to rise inside me. How dare he jeopardize *my* dream this way? And why hadn't he told me who he'd gotten the money from? Will had grown up in Las Vegas and being the affable type he was, I wasn't surprised he knew the kind of lowlifes that Jack described. Suddenly, I realized that beyond everything else—my fears for my own business, the unreal time I'd just spend with Richard Bishop, Jack's scowl—lay one pure, undeniable fact: I still had strong feelings for Will. And my heart hurt for him.

"I've got to call him."

"While you do that, I'm going to use the restroom," Jack said. I pretended I didn't see the way he stumbled a little bit upon standing.

I plucked my phone from the tabletop and punched the button for Will's phone. His number was the same from back when he'd still lived here and though I'd told myself a million times to delete it, I hadn't been able to bring myself to do it.

The phone rang and rang and finally the voicemail clicked on. I listened to his deep, low voice on the same goofy message he'd had for years, "Dude—or maybe you're a dudette—you know what to do. Leave me a message, telling me what's up. Catch you later."

I didn't leave a message at first. Because Will and I had developed a thing where we didn't bother to leave messages with each other. He never listened to them anyway. "If I see you called, it's faster for me just to call you back than listen to your message," he always said, and I saw the logic in it. So that night I thought maybe he would call back right away. But I waited and that didn't happen. I called again. This time I told him to call me as soon as possible, ending with, "And Will? I'm really sorry for your loss."

I frowned as I hung up the phone. That sounded…well, I don't know how it sounded. I sat there, drumming my fingers on the table, my thoughts flying in so many directions I couldn't settle on any one to attend to. And then I heard those bells chiming again. I grabbed my phone; ever hopeful it might be Richard. Nope, it wasn't my phone, but Jack's. I noticed that he had left his phone on the tabletop. And I couldn't help but see the name on the text that had just come in.

Carla.

Carla, Jack's wife, who had previously been known to be unresponsive to texts for months on end was now apparently texting him nonstop.

I popped my head out of the booth and looked to see if there were any sign of Jack returning from the bathroom and when there wasn't, I used one finger to turn his phone around and read the text. I had to push the button to light up the screen again, but there it was: *I can't wait to see you again when you come to Texas.*

I gasped. Jack was going to see Carla in Texas? What was that about? And why was Carla being all lovey-dovey?

"Hand me the phone, Len."

I looked up. Jack stood there with his hand outstretched.

I winced. "I'm sorry, I was just curious. I couldn't help it, I heard the text come in and I, um, noticed who it was from."

Our eyes met, and I don't know what he saw in mine, but I know what I saw in his: hurt, anger, anxiety, all mixed in one desperate expression.

"Um, so, er, are you…." I couldn't quite find the words. "Are you guys back together?"

"We were never really apart, Len." He slid into the booth. "She'd live here in a second if there were any acting jobs."

Ri-ight. Because Carla seemed just like the kind of woman who'd love living in a place where it rained six months out of the year.

"She's got a part in a movie that's shooting in Texas so Daisie and I are going to fly there to join her for a few days next week. Carla really wants to develop a relationship with her daughter."

And Carla had Mom of the Year stamped all over herself.

"Really," I said. "It's only just now occurred to her, some ten-odd years later? And what does Daisie think of all this?"

The thought of Daisie being anywhere near her ass clown of a mother infuriated me. Carla wasn't mean, and she wasn't abusive. She was just not interested—in anybody but herself. How any woman could treat both Jack and Daisie so cavalierly was beyond me. To say she had left me unimpressed would be an understatement as vast as my love of macarons. And I knew that Jack sent her money every month, which was why, I suspected, that Carla continued to string him along.

"She has mixed feelings," Jack said, holding my gaze.

"Mixed feelings, my ass." The only time I'd heard Daisie

speak of her mother it was in the terms of utmost derision. Jack's expression didn't change, but I noticed a tic throbbing beneath his right eye.

"And what do you think of it, Jack? I mean, really? After all this time when she's kept you at arm's length, she's suddenly wants you and Daisie with her again?"

"I don't know how I feel, Len, I really don't. But I do know that I have to find out. This is something that both Daisie and I need to follow up on, no matter what the outcome. We need to put it to rest, one way or another."

I stared into his eyes. All the emotions I'd seen earlier still roiled there, but now I identified a new one. Love. Jack was still in love with Carla. Maybe not in a big way, but in that way when there's one last part of your heart that feels incomplete. And a chunk of you is missing in a way that you fear you can never get back. I knew this landscape of the heart intimately, because it was the way I still felt about Will. If Will called me back at that very moment and said, *Come to Santa Fe, I love you, I need you,* would I? Would I leave Jack and Daisie and my burgeoning relationship with Richard to go to him?

Well, no. Probably not. Mostly because of my fledgling relationship with Richard. But I would at least be tempted. Because that's what you do when your heart feels like it is missing a piece.

And that was no doubt how Jack felt as well. The changes that were sweeping over my life were nearly overwhelming: the thing with Richard, whatever in the hell it was, the bakery teetering on bankruptcy, the disastrous plans for expanding the Bonne Chance, Will and Hill's bakery burning down, and now this—Jack defecting to Carla. Not to mention all that had gone before: my mother's death, Will leaving, my miscarriage.

I reached for my phone.

"You calling Will again?" Jack asked.

I shook my head. "Nope. I'm calling Richard. To tell him I've changed my mind." Because now it wasn't just about saving the bakery, it was about saving Jack, too.

Jack nodded. And then I saw a new emotion in his eyes: devastation.

CHAPTER 10

In L.A. in January, most of the time it's warm enough to sit outside. Who knew? Well, I did, sort of. I just hadn't experienced it. But I'd been living there for a week now and so far, the sun had shone every day. Every damn day. I couldn't get over it. In Portland in January, it rained every day. Every damn day.

I luxuriated in the warmth as I sat outside at a restaurant in Santa Monica with Natalie and Daisie. We were at Cave, which was, according to Nat, the hottest new place in West L.A. It served keto food, which meant, of course, no carbs, so I had hidden the box of macarons I brought for my sister in my messenger bag. Yes, macarons are *gluten-free* but that doesn't mean they are *carb-free*. No sense riling the locals. But I would have eaten anything. I was so happy to be with Natalie and Daisie.

"So, Daisie, you've managed to trump me," Nat said, "I've never been on a private plane."

"It was a Cessna 525 CitationJet," Daisie said. "Not as luxurious as I might have imagined—"

"She was sorely disappointed, in truth," I said. Richard had sent one of his planes up to Portland to collect Jack and Daisie. I was a little envious, because I'd driven myself down in order to have the things I wanted, like my apron and baking sheets, and my own car. Richard had said he'd lease one for me, of course, but I wanted at least some vestige of familiarity. The waiter set a plate of food in front of me: a nice slab of grass-fed steak and a mound of fake mashed potatoes, made from cauliflower.

"—but a smooth ride nonetheless. And I have it on good authority that Richard Bishop owns a fleet of private jets, this one being one of the smallest, suitable for travel up and down the West Coast." This was Daisie of course. She finished her mini-lecture and looked somewhat askance at the food the waiter set before her. It was a hamburger with no bun and a huge pile of vegetables.

"You are really something," Nat said to Daisie. I was having a blast introducing Nat and Daisie, as they were two of a kind. They each had a certainty in the way they viewed the world and their place in it, and utter confidence that the world would open its arms to accommodate them in all their glory.

Today, Daisie wore her hair combed back neatly from her face and oversized black-rimmed glasses she'd begged Jack to buy for her. She wore the white blouse from her school uniform beneath a black blazer that she'd found at Goodwill. The crowning touch was the man's tie she wore. "I'm experimenting with what kind of sense of power it will give me," she had explained to me earlier, when she and Jack picked me up at Richard's house in Malibu Canyon, where I was indeed staying.

But she hadn't lingered over her explanation long, because instead she prowled every inch of the house and finally returned to where I waited in the living room.

"This isn't much of a house. I expected more from Richard Bishop," she'd said.

"It's just one of them. He owns a bunch, apparently."

"Oh!" I could see the synapses firing in her forehead. "I get it. He stuck you in the crappy one."

"Thanks, Dais."

"C'mon, let's get going. I'm sure Dad's about ready to split a turbine."

Daisie had informed me upon her arrival that Jack refused to come in because, "he can't bear to see your love nest."

I'd been about to ask her where *that* had come from, but she'd been already out the door to the car. The house wasn't exactly a love nest, though I did have to admit that Richard and I had made love in the bedroom several more times. But he was gone a lot, too, and that had made my first week in L.A. a little lonely. Anyway, I happened to know that Jack had plans to pick up Carla after dropping us at the restaurant.

"So, what's on the agenda for today?" Nat asked, taking a bite of her vegetable puree, "Seeing as how your meeting is not until tomorrow. Disneyland? Universal Studios?"

The meeting. The thought of it made my stomach thunk and my heart pound. Tomorrow was the big day—the meeting with Richard Bishop and his people, who were ready with plans and designs for the L.A. Bonne Chance. It made me nervous to think about what they'd cooked up, even though I'd shared my vision and was assured it would be followed.

"This is not a girl who goes to Disneyland," I said, as my phone buzzed.

"We're going to visit the Museum of Death," Daisie said.

I looked at my phone. There was a text from Richard: *Just got in from London, will see you soon, please?*

"And why, pray tell, does an eleven—"

"I'm twelve," Daisie said.

"Why does a twelve-year-old want to go to a death museum? Which I didn't even know existed, by the way, " Nat said.

Daisie looked at Natalie as if she had offered her a Barbie doll to play with. "Richard Bishop says you must face your own mortality to achieve success on this planet."

"Sounds like Dad," Natalie said.

"Richard's an admirer of Dad's," I said.

Natalie rolled her eyes. "Figures." For reasons I had not been able to ascertain, Nat was not a big fan of Richard. And though she loved our father as much as I did, she often poked fun at his philosophies, which I, in turn, thought hysterical, because she and Dad were both cut from the exact same cloth.

"Daisie's obsessed with all things Richard Bishop," I explained as I tried to unobtrusively answer Richard's text.

"Sounds like you know quite a lot about him, too," Nat said to me, one eyebrow raised. It killed me that she could do the eyebrow-raising thing, but I couldn't, no matter how hard I tried.

"Who, me?" I set my phone down and shook my head vigorously.

"Methinks you doth protest too much," Nat said.

"*Hamlet*," Daisie said. "I love Shakespeare. And in case you're interested, the actual quote is 'The lady doth protest too much, methinks.'"

"Methinks what?" Jack had appeared at our table. He looked spiffy wearing a blue pinstriped shirt and neatly pressed khakis, a departure from his usual flannels and jeans. In the southern California sun, he looked healthier, less sallow, and I could tell, too, that the warmth made his back hurt less, and his limp was thus less pronounced. But still, I thought, as I watched him hug Natalie, there was a faint tinge of worry in his eyes, a funny way his mouth twitched that I knew meant he was stressed. Maybe the meeting with Richard Bishop's people would cheer him up.

"Methinks your daughter is brilliant," Natalie said.

Jack nodded. "I have a hard time keeping up with her now. I can only imagine what it's going to be like in another year or two."

"I don't get all this methinks stuff," another voice spoke up.

Oh, God. That would be Carla, Jack's erstwhile wife. She appeared behind them, having apparently first stopped to chat with someone at a different table. Movie star gorgeous (no surprise, as that is what she aspired to be), even with no makeup on and her black hair pulled into a ponytail, she had cheekbones you could ski jump off and smoldering dark eyes. I watched a man at a neighboring table sneak glances at her.

Daisie gave Carla a withering look. "It's Shakespeare language. You're an actress. Don't you know this?"

"Daisie," Jack admonished.

"We've been studying the twentieth-century playwrights in my acting class. Torvald says they are the most relevant these days. Torvald says relevance is everything." Carla had an earnest affect that came across as, dare I say it, just short of simple. A few sandwiches short of a picnic. A few kernels shy of a full bowl of popcorn. I chastised myself and took a deep breath, striving to see her in a more positive light. The way Jack apparently saw her.

"Torvald says— "

"Who's Torvald?" Nat asked. "For that matter, who are you?"

Silently I blessed Natalie for interrupting the Torvald tirade. Jack made the introductions and I tried to be pleasant to Carla and tell her it was nice to see her.

"It is just so wonderful to see you, Marsha. You and Jack are doing such amazing things at the bakery."

How difficult was it to remember my name, especially seeing as how I was the business partner of her husband? And was it just me, or was Carla's enthusiasm a little forced, her speech a little stilted? Her eyes, vacant and dull, signaled that she could care less about our business. She and Torvald would need to work on her delivery. I looked at Jack, expecting to see a shrug or eye roll or something. But he seemed as entranced with Carla as every other man within a five-mile vicinity. I rallied the polite me. "Thanks. We're having a good time."

Finally, Jack turned to Daisie. "You ready, pumpkin?"

"I sure am." She jumped up and then stooped to retrieve her bag from beneath the table. It was a square boxy black leather briefcase she'd taken to carrying her schoolwork in. No pink princess or Disney character bags for her. Carla reached out to ruffle her hair and Daisie pulled away.

"You'll be able to get back to the house on your own?" Jack asked me.

"I'll figure it out. I can take a Lyft or something. Have fun at the Museum of Death."

"Oh, I'm sure it will be fascinating. I'm also sure you'll hear all about it."

I watched him walk away, pondering how Carla had shown way more enthusiasm for the legendary Torvald than she had for either her husband or her daughter. And shouldn't the look of worry in Jack's eyes have been replaced by excitement to be in the presence of his wife, who he didn't get to see all that often?

After they left, threading their way through the crowded tables, Nat turned to me. "She's not the brightest bulb, is she?"

I grimaced and shook my head. "I try so hard to like her. But..."

"And I can't figure what he's doing with her, when he's obsessed with you."

For a minute, I thought she meant Richard, seeing as how I was using the time Nat was focused on Jack and Daisie and Carla to text him. *I can't wait to spend time with you,* I'd written after some thought, because I wasn't sure what he'd meant by seeing me soon. A brief chat? Coffee? Dinner? But then it dawned on me what Nat meant, and I set my phone on the table.

"You mean Jack? You think he's obsessed with me?"

"I sure do."

"Oh God, Natalie, don't be crazy, we're very close but not in that way."

"I love you, sis, but you can be incredibly dense at times. Don't you see the way he looks at you?"

"You're crazy, Nat." I scowled, even as my insides squiggled at the thought. I shook my head to brush the feeling away. "Anyway, he's committed to Carla."

"And this is why men are an unsolvable puzzle." She shook her head. "I don't get it."

I ticked reasons off my fingers. "He feels responsible to her. She's the mother of his child. She's gorgeous."

"Vapid is not gorgeous, baby. Smart wins every time."

"Ri-ight." I wasn't at all sure I agreed with Natalie on that, given the standards of our youth-obsessed culture. "Anyway, enough about us. I want to hear about you. What's going on in your life?"

Nat took a deep breath. She looked like a carbon copy of me, if you added five inches to my height and gave me brunette hair. Make that black hair—Nat helped herself look more dramatic by coloring it darker. But we both shared the same big, dark brown eyes inherited from our mother, and button-ish nose from Dad. And then, of course, there were our clothing choices. Mine ran to boho-casual, while hers could only be called dramatic. That day she wore an outfit of royal blue from her head to her toes: blue leggings, blue boots (even in the southern California heat), blue blouse, and blue sweater. Her arms and neck were rimmed in silver and, you guessed it, turquoise jewelry. It was a striking look, I had to admit. It just wasn't *my* look.

"You really want to hear?" Natalie said.

"Of course."

"I'm having an affair."

I took a sip of my water, which was ice cold and flavored with a slice of lemon. The sun was creeping toward my seat and I was getting warm, even in my sundress. I shrugged the lace cardigan off. "Um, news flash Nat, you are no longer married. So technically you are not having an affair."

"The other party is married."

"The other party? What kind of talk is that? Just tell me who he is."

"She."

"She?"

"Oh God, Mad, I'm so in love. I've never felt this way about anyone before, ever. She is just so incredible."

I sat and stared at my sister, probably with my mouth open, as usual. I had absolutely no problem with her falling in love with a woman, I just never thought it would happen. Nat was famous for her string of men and her bawdy descriptions of their working parts. ("His Chunk O'Love wasn't working right," or "King Dingalong renounced his throne," or "That man really knew how to work his joystick.")

"I'm happy for you," I finally said.

"There's one little problem."

"What's that?"

"She's married to the head of my department."

"Oh lord, Natalie," I said.

She shook her head in agreement and her huge silver triangle earrings bobbed. "I know. But the heart knows what it wants, you know?"

"Now you sound like Dad."

"But it's true. When Sarah and I ran into each other at the faculty tea that day, wow, I'd never experienced anything like it."

I nodded my head in agreement. I got it; I really did. Witness my recent experience with Richard Bishop. But this was dicey territory my sister was entering. "Um, I hate to be a naysayer, but aren't you up for tenure this year?"

"Yes." Nat drummed a finger on the table. "Yes, I am."

I was about to tell her to be careful when there was a commotion on the edge of our outside seating area.

"Over here, Richard!"

"How's that new movie going?"

"Who's your new girlfriend?"

The shouts of the paparazzi were accompanied by camera flashes, weirdly visible even in the daylight. I saw the maître d' move to prevent the paps from coming onto the patio. And suddenly Richard Bishop loomed into view, the Public Option in full display as he beamed a munificent smile at each table he passed. I watched him approach, and half of me wondered who he was coming to meet, while the other half knew it was, of course, me. But Richard Bishop was so larger than life that he always engendered a kind of bewildered wonder within—had this amazing creature really chosen me?

When he got to our table, he stopped and beamed the Public Option at me. "They told me I'd find you here."

I smiled up at him. I swear to God, he carried his own light source with him—he appeared to be bathed in golden, shimmering light. "*Who* told you?" I asked, brilliantly. And then, "And I thought I wasn't going to see you until tomorrow?"

He waved his arm as if my questions were of no concern whatsoever, then pulled a chair from the table. "May I join you?"

I nodded.

Once seated, he turned to Natalie with his hand out. "I'm Richard Bishop."

"Duh," she said. "The entire world knows that." But even through Nat's bravado, I could see that she was as dazzled by him as everyone else. "Natalie Miller."

"The religious studies professor, right?" Richard said.

Now my sister was really impressed. The two of them chatted about her job and I wondered if I should be creeped out that Richard seemed to know exactly where to find me. But then I decided it was business as usual for someone like him. Wouldn't he have to be cognizant of everyone he was dealing with? I tuned back into the conversation just in time to hear Natalie.

"So, Richard, tell me something?"

"Of course." I couldn't help staring at him, he just had that effect on people. He wore a black T-shirt (as far as I could tell, he always wore black in some form or another) emblazoned with a white heart and the word, LOVE, in block letters and it fit tight over his muscular chest and arms, so tight there were no wrinkles in the shirt anywhere. Maybe his housekeeper ironed it. Did he have a housekeeper? We'd talked about many things in our late-night phone conversations before I'd moved down, but mostly since I'd been here, I'd seen him in dribs and drabs, long enough for a rousing romp but that was about all. So I was unclear on the mechanics of how a star like him lived his day to day life. He smiled at Natalie and she held his gaze.

"What are your intentions with my sister?"

"Natalie," I said. I mean, really?

But Richard didn't miss a beat. He reached for my hand, which was the tiniest bit awkward, as I was taking a drink of water at that moment, and stared into my eyes.

"I adore her," he said.

Water dribbled down my chin. "You do?"

He nodded.

This was when he would say something about the bakery and how as much as he adored *me,* it was really the business he was after. But he didn't. He just sat there and smiled at me as I sat speechless. And then he turned to Nat. "And this is why. She is so ingenuous, genuinely so. She has no idea how charming she is."

Nat shook her head and stood. "And I thought I had it bad. I am leaving you two lovebirds—"

"Nat," I said, in a warning tone. Because Richard and I were not lovebirds.

"—and continuing with my afternoon. Because I, unlike some people, have to work."

I jumped up to hug her goodbye and then sat back down after she left. Her sudden absence raised an awkward silence with Richard.

"Let's go back to the house where I can ravish you," he said, smiling at me. *Still* smiling. I wasn't sure how he did it. He must have trained his mouth muscles over the years, because mine would hurt if I smiled that much. "And afterwards, I'm going to take you back to Nobubu. For once, my sweet, I have time to spend with you, and I'm going to take advantage of every minute."

And of course, there was nothing to do but agree.

CHAPTER 11

The next day, a woman wearing a very short miniskirt and stiletto heels met us in the lobby of Richard's office building—because of course, not only did his company have its headquarters in the high-rise, he owned the whole thing. *Of course.* Everything with Richard seemed to be an *of course.* The woman introduced herself as Fiona, Richard's personal assistant, and spoke in a charming English accent. I recognized her from the visit to the bakery last fall —she was the one tasked with paying for Richard's macarons. And was it my imagination, or did she shoot me the stink eye every chance she got?

I told myself it was because my clothes were not up to L.A. standards. My signature look—floral skirt and cute top —apparently didn't much impress Fiona, even though I'd swapped out my usual boots for strappy sandals in deference to the relatively warmer January days in L.A. But fashion notwithstanding, my jealous little heart suspected that Fiona had a thing for Richard. But then, who didn't? Daisie was foaming at the mouth at the thought of getting to see him again. And I was doing my best to stay rooted in the present

—even though all I wanted to think about was the day before, when I'd spent the afternoon being "ravished" by Richard, and then enjoyed dinner at one of the swankiest restaurants in L.A..

As if reading my thoughts, Fiona smirked at me. She wore hot pink lipstick that she'd applied unevenly, causing it to bleed into the skin lines beneath her lower lip. This little detail made me feel better, that she wasn't quite as perfect as she seemed. "Richard regrets that he'll be unable to be with us today," she said in clipped British tones.

"Oh, I'm sure we can accomplish what we need to do without him," I said, even though my breath had caught in my throat at the thought of not seeing Richard. I said it as airily as I could possibly muster, which fooled nobody. I know this because Daisie stopped short on the marble floor of the lobby and glared at me.

"We will not be okay! I haven't gotten to see him this whole trip!"

Fiona, who seemed to be as taken with Daisie as she was unimpressed by me, patted her on the back. "Well, we'll just have to make sure you get time with him before you leave then, won't we?"

Jack and Daisie and I trailed after Fiona into the elevator. Fiona smiled and chatted with Daisie but ignored me as the elevator whisked us up forty-two floors to Richard's offices. When the elevator stopped, the doors opened, and we walked directly into his suite of offices. A woman who could be Fiona's twin sister, at least as far as youth and saucy style went, sat behind a low curved desk, which was situated in front of a wood wall emblazoned with a sign saying *Richard Bishop Enterprises*.

Daisie gasped. "This is exactly how I want my offices to be," she said.

I understood her enthusiasm. The offices weren't exactly

my style, but then working in a cubicle wasn't either. I'd worked in them for years—first at my Dad's advertising agency in downtown Portland, and then at the hottest ad shop in town, Weiden+Kennedy. Even though both places were hip and happening, as they say, and did their best to mitigate the whole office cubicle vibe, I still hated the grind of working at a desk. Give me a sore back from standing on my feet baking any day. But Richard's offices were beautifully appointed—the wood of the front desk backdrop was repeated throughout, the chairs were leather, and the floors were all marble, which made me feel like I was going to slip and fall at any moment.

Fiona waved at her twin and led us around the desk, down a hall past a warren of offices and one big room where a lot of people sat in cubicles, and into a room on the corner. Walking into it gave me an immediate sense of vertigo—the windows were floor to ceiling and the entire city of Los Angeles was spread out before us. I grabbed the doorjamb to steady myself.

"You okay?" Jack asked.

I nodded. He smiled at me. I smiled back. And suddenly I felt like everything was going to be all right. I'd been pitched into a new world so suddenly and so dramatically that I felt I was on ground as shaky as the San Andreas Fault. A big business opportunity, a relationship with Richard—Was it a relationship?—this move to L.A. Oh, and let us not forget that my sister was having an affair with her boss's wife. But Jack's smile steadied me. I was so lucky to have him in my corner. I took a deep breath and walked into the room.

A huge table sat in the middle, and with the view beyond, for a minute it looked like it was suspended in space. Just as Fiona looked a twin to the receptionist, so, too, did all of Richard's business underlings look alike, each of them in a dark suit with white shirt and dark tie, which puzzled me, since I'd never seen Richard in anything fancier than jeans. And they all had dark hair, cut neat and short and combed back from their foreheads just so. After Jack and Daisie and I took seats, the minions went around the table and introduced themselves, but it was like watching robots say their names and I couldn't remember any of them except for the first one, Ryan. I'm afraid I took to calling them all Ryan in my mind, and for the life of me, I couldn't see that it made a difference—they all seemed to be interchangeable.

We introduced ourselves and the Fiona twin came in and took our drink orders. I stuck with water—didn't need any more caffeine as I was already buzzy enough, what with all that was happening. Once we were settled, the real Ryan stood and pointed to an easel at the edge of the table, which was loaded with oversized display boards. I peered at them, eager to see what they'd dreamed up, but the top board had been turned backside out. "We're very excited to work on the La Bonne Chance bakery project launch," Ryan said. All the other Ryans around the table nodded their heads in unison. The real Ryan walked to the easel and turned the first board around.

"So, the macaron," he said, pointing to the board on the easel. It featured a giant image of a macaron—a pink one, perfectly baked to my eye. Even in the oversized photo, it looked light and airy. "Let's begin with some history."

Daisie's hand shot up just as Ryan took another breath and opened his mouth to say something. It looked to me like he was irritated with Daisie's interruption, but Fiona smiled and said, "Yes, Daisie?"

"I have a question," Daisie said. She had folded her hands in front of her on the table and sitting next to her I could see where her cuticles were dry and bleeding from her gnawing at them.

Fiona raised her eyebrows at Ryan and he grudgingly

said, "Go ahead." Clearly pontificating on the history of the macaron was of more interest than a young girl's ideas.

"Why do you use those unwieldy boards? Why don't you use a PowerPoint and a projector? Wouldn't that be more efficient?"

Ryan opened his mouth as if to say something and then closed it again. His Adam's apple bobbed. He took a deep breath and then spoke.

"Richard Bishop prefers the creativity and purity of hand-drawn boards."

One of the things I loved best about Daisie was that you could practically see the neurons firing in her brain. "Ohhhh," she said, nodding her head. I predicted an interest in drawing would soon be forthcoming, along with a request for art supplies.

"May I continue?" Ryan said. He looked to Fiona for veri-fication, but Daisie nodded her head and said, "Go on."

"So, the macaron," Ryan said, and pointed to the image. "The preferred cookie of the French, the de rigueur treat at Parisian tea salons, actually was invented in Italy in 1533 by the chef to Catherine de Medici." He pulled the board off the easel, showing the one beneath, which featured an image of a jeweled crown superimposed on a picture of multicolored macarons. "Soon thereafter, she married the Duc d'Orleans, who became the king of France in 1547 —Henry II."

I glanced over at Jack. He sighed loudly and waggled his head back and forth, a sign he was getting restless already. And with good reason—Ryan's presentation was snooze-worthy. He was managing to take the topic I loved more than any other and make it boring.

"An interesting side note," Ryan continued. "The word *macaroni* and the word *macaron* both have the same origin, which is the word meaning *fine dough*. And fine dough a macaron is, with its ingredients of sugar, almond flour, and egg whites." The next board was a photo of these ingredients.

This was excruciating. I tried to catch Jack's eye as Ryan droned on, thinking we might share a covert smile, but despite my best efforts, he remained fixated on Ryan's presentation. Ryan went through more history and delved into the macaron's current popularity in France and the burgeoning interest in them here in the States. My mind roamed, lulled by Ryan's droning voice. I couldn't help but think of my time with Richard the night before, the way his eyes had sparkled as he listened to me across the candlelit table, how he'd listened to my stories with such interest, and the luscious feel of his lips on mine as he left me at the house with one final kiss. I shivered with pleasure as my brain wandered even further back, to our time in bed. But then some slight variation in Ryan's voice captured my attention.

"Which brings us to our current situation. While the Portland La Bonne Chance…"

I tried not to wince at the way he mangled the pronunciation.

"…has achieved a modest level of success with its macarons, we feel that much more is possible. We take as one example an innovative macaron bakery out of Santa Fe, that is absolutely killing it online."

Ryan flipped a whiteboard to an image of Will's *Macaron Madness* logo, a macaron surrounded by confetti. I groaned, both at the corny logo and the fact that Ryan was calling up Will as an example. "This company combines an array of exotic macaron flavors with a deft knowledge of internet marketing to sell their goods."

I glanced at Jack, who sat next to me. He looked down at me and raised his eyebrows.

"And while we anticipate following suit and crushing it

with Internet sales soon, everything starts with the bakery itself, of course. We've taken our cues for image and branding from the existing bakery," Ryan said and pointed to several images on the next board, an enlarged photo of the exterior of the Portland Bonne Chance in all its glory, and one of the interiors as well. "Now this is all well and good." He nodded at me. "Madeleine, we have told you how much we appreciate your sense of style and the esthetic you have brought to La Bonne Chance and the style suggestions you shared with us. We don't want to lose that. We just want to tune it up a little."

He paused for a moment and then turned the next board. I gasped at the image on it. Jack and I met each other's eyes, both of us with scowls on our faces. Because their idea of "tuning up" my style was apparently making it look like a Las Vegas attraction. The picture showed a storefront like mine, but *more so.* Like a lot *more so.* The store was painted in a myriad of pastel colors, pink and blue and green and yellow —so many it looked like a basket of Easter eggs had exploded. It seemed every surface had some sort of curlicue or doodad hanging on it. The front windows were strung with multiple strands of lights. I don't have a problem with lighting things up, especially around Christmas, but this image featured enough lights to sap the energy from every power station for miles around.

"What do you think?" Ryan asked.

"I'm speechless," I said.

He beamed. "And here's an image of the inside." This board was, if possible, even worse. The gaudy colors and overuse of lights continued, and besides the macaron display case there was an area of tables and chairs. Which would have been fine except each one seemed to have a miniature Eiffel Tower on it. And a bunch of other supposedly French geegaws I couldn't quite identify.

"What's all that stuff everywhere?" Daisie asked, echoing my exact thoughts.

"You mean the bric-a-brac?" Ryan asked, and then without waiting for an answer, he pointed to the board. "This is one of our designer's key elements. The stores will be decorated with items found in antique and thrift stores—items that evoke the feel of Paris and romance. While each store's decor will carry this broad theme, because all the items will be handpicked, each will be unique to its location as well. And, let me just add, we've already settled on our first location, which will be..." and here he shrugged his hands out for effect, "....in Noho!"

I looked at Jack and Daisie, and each of them wore the same blank expression I assumed my face featured. In Ryan's faux-enthusiastic voice, NoHo sounded like something a pirate might say. *No ho ho and a bottle of rum.* No wait, that was *Yo ho ho.* And I knew, because I'd already seen the space they'd rented, that it was really just plain old Hollywood.

Daisie spoke up. "Excuse me, but could you please explain where Noho is?"

Ryan beamed. "It's one of the hippest spots in SoCal, with an art district and an edgy feel to it. We think it will be perfect for La Bonne Chance."

"The," I said.

Ryan furrowed his brow at me.

"It's, *The* Bonne Chance, not *La* Bonne Chance."

"Oh, right. *The* Bonne Chance," Ryan said. "So, what do you think?"

"I'm astounded," I said, truthfully. Because everything he had said sounded like the worst idea ever in the history of the world. The inside of the Bonne Chance in Portland was simple and elegant, and if I do say so myself, charming. And it was that way because it most specifically was not full of crap.

"We're so pleased you like it," he said, looking like an eager kindergartener who had just presented his mother with a goofy handmade present.

Clearly Ryan had not been taught to assess body language or tone of voice in his business training. Because I didn't like it, in any way, shape, or form. I *hated* it. I didn't want to see my simple concept for a macaron bakery bastardized into this Disneyland version. I looked to Jack and Daisie, both of whom sat staring at the images as well.

"It's a little on the, uh, overwhelming, side." I wished Richard were there. Because if Richard were there, I would feel as if I could protest, ask questions, respond. But with bland Ryan—and all the other Ryans, who sat nodding their heads with smug smiles on their faces—at the helm, the meeting was covered in a fog of corporate monotony that was difficult to pierce.

And then Jack punctured it.

He abruptly slammed his hands on the table and then stood. His face looked like the visage of an angry thunder god—his eyebrows scowling deeper than I would have thought possible, his eyes flashing with anger, and his mouth turned into a frown. But he didn't say a word, he just got up and left the room, his chair turning over behind him.

Ryan stared at his retreating back. Daisie and I looked at each other and both of us pushed back our chairs at the same time, ready to follow him. Fiona murmured something that sounded like "oh dear," then nodded at Ryan as if to carry on.

But just as he opened his mouth again, somebody else entered the room.

It was Richard. Of course.

"Was it something you said?" Richard directed this comment to Ryan and then threw back his head and laughed. Everyone in the room laughed along with him, and just like that the mood shifted and everything was okay again.

Richard strode across the room, kissed me on the head, and then took a seat beside me. Everyone looked at him expectantly, but he focused his attention on me.

"What do you think of the team's plans, Madeleine? Personally, I'm quite excited about them."

I took a deep breath. This was when I should smile and nod and tell him how wonderful everything looked. Because: money. As in, we needed it. And because: I'd uprooted my life for this expansion, moving to L.A., leaving everything I knew and loved to fall into the arms of Richard Bishop. So I should just be grateful for what they were showing us and be a good girl and go along with it all. I looked around the long table. The Ryans appeared bored. One of them flipped a pen over and over and another stared out the window at the city arrayed beneath us. Fiona was frowning at her phone. It seemed clear that they all expected me to toe the party line and tell them the plans were fabulous.

But I just couldn't do it. And now that Richard was here, I felt able to speak up.

"I don't think—" I paused, having just remembered that women too often prefaced comments with phrases like *I think* and *I feel,* when what we really needed to do was just flat out say what we meant. If I was going to operate in Richard's grand world, I'd need to be aware of such things. I took a deep breath and started again. "The design is too much. It's too over the top, not at all in keeping with the original Bonne Chance vision."

That was it. That was all I had in me to protest. I raised my shoulders, then lowered them. Heard Daisie sigh as if the stock market had just crashed, watched as the Ryans sprang to attention and Fiona looked up from her phone, her eyebrows arched in alarm. Inwardly, I winced. By the looks of things, I'd just committed the unpardonable sin—

disagreeing with Richard Bishop. As if they were watching a ball bounce toward him, every head turned to Richard.

His hands rested on the table in front of him, and his face was serious. So serious. Too serious. Oh crap, I'd totally blown it. He cocked his head to the right and stared at the design board, then tilted it the other way. Finally, he turned toward me.

"You have an excellent eye, Madeleine. I do believe you are right." Then he snapped his fingers at Ryan. "Tone it down and start over. ASAP. See what you can do that doesn't look quite so garish."

I felt a strange mixture of relief and giddiness. And when Richard covered my hand in his and smiled at me, I decided maybe I could play in his world, even though it still seemed as foreign as waking up on another planet.

CHAPTER 12

Daisie and I found Jack sitting in the lobby, scanning his phone and texting. He acted like nothing was wrong, but I knew he'd had time to compose himself and was faking it. I tried and tried to get him to talk about it as we loaded ourselves into my Fiat for the drive to the airport.

"That was over the top, wasn't it?" I said as I steered onto the freeway. "Can you believe the ideas they came up with? And how they used Will's bakery as an example?"

Jack grunted.

"I liked it." Daisie, sitting in the back seat with her head buried in her iPad, looked up. "Richard Bishop is the most successful businessman in the world and thus I think it is important to listen to his ideas carefully."

I tried to catch Jack's eye to share a smile at Daisie's insistent reverence of Richard, but he stared out the window. I turned my attention to a black Lexus that cut in front of me. There was no doubt about it—my relationship with Daisie and Jack was strained, not helped by me decamping to L.A. and spending time with Richard. Even though I was doing it with the best of intentions. I tried again to make conversation.

"I couldn't believe all that crap they wanted to put inside the shops—bric-a-brac my ass," I said.

Another grunt.

"I thought the design had a lot of potential," Daisie said from the back seat. "I can't believe you told him to change it, Mad." She was hopeless, a sycophant for whatever Richard did.

At least that broke Jack free from the prison he'd locked himself in. "You told Richard to change the design?"

"I did."

"I'm impressed, Lenie." Finally, he looked over at me. "Good for you."

"Good for her! Are you crazy?" Daisie yelled. "Richard Bishop is the most successful human being on the planet and Mad told him she didn't like what he'd done. She's insane."

Jack laughed, easing the tension in the car, then reached over and patted my leg. "I'm proud of you."

When we got to the airport, I pulled over to the drop-off curb and Jack and Daisie got out, Jack pulling luggage out of the trunk. I hopped out to hug them goodbye.

Daisie submitted to my hug for as short a time as she could and when she broke away, she handed me a piece of paper. "These are some questions I still have for Richard."

I laughed and glanced down at the paper, a sheet of yellow legal notepad with a torn edge at the top, with Daisie's neat printing filling the page. 1. WHAT IS YOUR FORMULA FOR PRICING? 2. TIPS ON TIME MANAGE-MENT. 3. WHEN SHOULD I START TAKING A SALARY? The list went on. I tucked it in the pocket of my long cotton cardigan.

"She's not going to have time to ask Richard your ques-tions," Jack said.

"I'll do my best," I protested.

"You can email me answers as you get them," Daisie said.

"Dais, go sit on that bench over there for a second, okay? I need a moment with Len."

Daisie slunk off to the bench, iPad in hand, but not before calling out, "Don't forget the questions."

I smiled up at Jack. "You have produced far and away the most unique girl ever born."

His face lit up briefly at my compliment. Then, he nodded, and his face turned dark. Once, when I was in the New Mexico desert with Will, a cloud scudded across an otherwise flawlessly blue sky, casting a moving shadow along the land. That's what Jack's face looked like that day at the airport.

"What, Jack?"

"Is this the direction you really want to go? Are you really ready to give up your original dream for…?" Jack swept his arm vaguely toward the city. "… for someone else's idea of what the Bonne Chance should be?"

"He said he'd change the design. And I believe him. He didn't hesitate at all when I said I didn't like it. And besides, we don't have much choice now, do we?"

Jack stared down at me, his eyes blazing like sparklers on the Fourth of July. And then his eyes softened and he grabbed my shoulders and leaned toward me. For a moment I thought he was going to kiss me. He opened his mouth, then stopped, dropped his hands, and took a step back.

"What?" I asked.

"Be careful, Len."

"About what?"

"You know."

"You mean with Richard?" I looked up at his face, searching for clarification about what his words meant in his demeanor, searching for some clue as to what he was thinking.

But he gave up nothing, just looked at me for a long moment and then turned away with a wave of his hand. "Just be careful."

"Have a good flight," I called, flummoxed as to what else to say. I watched him walk away from me, wondering what had just happened.

A few weeks later, I stood in Richard's house at the bottom of Malibu Canyon, surveying my handiwork. Baking sheets topped with parchment paper covered every countertop and surface in the kitchen, and more baking sheets crowded the dining room tables and chairs. That would be because the kitchen was tiny, a cramped space separated from the dining room by a countertop, and above that, a row of dark cabinets. It seemed almost like an afterthought, and it was hard to work in. But, while I waited for the bakery to pass its last inspections, I needed a macaron baking fix.

My life had become a whirlwind since I moved into the funny little canyon house in Malibu. Between checking on equipment installations at the bakery, doing publicity at Fiona's behest, and, well, spending as much time as possible with Richard, I didn't get much time to myself. That afternoon I was blessedly free, and so a macaron baking spree was in order. It had been too long since I'd gotten a baking fix in.

But why did it sound like someone was pulling into the

driveway? Not that many vehicles drove by the house, since it was in a secluded area. If my ears did not deceive me, I'd say it sounded like Richard's Jag. I'd gotten very good at discerning which car he arrived in, be it the Tesla, the Mercedes, or the Porsche. And sometimes he used the limo service as well.

And then the front door opened, and Richard appeared. He threw his keys into a wooden bowl on a table beside the door and then stopped in his tracks with the door open behind him.

"Let me guess." He pointed a finger at me. "You robbed a baking supply store." Then he opened his arms wide.

I laughed and ran to him, allowing myself to be enfolded in his hug. It was warm out, of course, so he wore one of his signature black T-shirts, the expensive knit fabric of which felt soft against my cheek. I closed my eyes and reveled in his presence, the sheer Richard-ness of him. He kissed me on the head and then pulled away from me. I looked at him, puzzled. Richard was usually one for long, involved hello kisses, especially when he hadn't seen me for a couple of days, which he hadn't, as he'd just returned home from London. But then I noticed that a set of keys dangled from the end of his finger, attached to a keychain that looked suspiciously like a miniature Eiffel tower.

"The keys to your kingdom, Madame."

I cocked my head.

"Don't look so confused." He grinned down at me. When I didn't respond, he shook the keys. "They're for the bakery, my sweet dunderhead. We pulled some strings with the permitting office and got the inspections moved up. La Bonne Chance Bakery, Los Angeles, officially opens next week."

I screamed and threw my arms around Richard again, hoisting my legs around his waist. He mock-staggered, laughed, and kissed me on the cheek as I put my legs back on the ground, and for good measure, jumped up and down a couple of times. The bakery! Last I'd seen it, five days ago, it still had that not-quite-finished air, with stray lumber and nails littering the floor. And there'd been an issue with the ovens not working. Plus, the contractor had glumly informed me that inspections were backed up and it might be weeks before we could get someone in to approve us. In the interim, Fiona had somehow managed to fill my time with PR appearances.

But I was itching to see the bakery ready to open. And I was so, so ready to bake—in a kitchen where there was space to do so, not the cramped galley setup at the canyon house. I missed the Bonne Chance something fierce. I missed rising early, *really* early, and arriving at the bakery. I missed baking macarons for hours, listening to a book on my iPhone, or letting my thoughts run down arcane and interesting alleys.

"Let's go see it," I said. "I haven't actually started the batter, so I can leave all this." I indicated the mess of baking sheets.

"Ah, Maddie, I do so love your enthusiasm. Now run change your clothes and we'll go celebrate. And you can tell me everything that's happened while I've been gone."

"But I'd like to go see the bakery." I shrugged. "I didn't realize you were coming home today."

"If you ever looked at your phone, you'd have known I was on my way. I texted you, dear girl."

He had a point. I'd gotten overwhelmed with Richard's people calling me about one thing or another about the bakery, so I'd kind of quit paying attention to my messages.

"Now go make yourself gorgeous." He grinned. "Not that you aren't always gorgeous, my sweet."

I could always rely on Richard to lay it on thick. Sometimes, to be honest, it irked me that he laid it on *too* thick. It came off as disingenuous, much like the Public Option.

"If you hurry, we'll have time to run by the bakery before dinner," he said.

That was the other thing about him. He invariably knew when I was thinking less than charitable thoughts about him and managed to pull himself back from the brink of pandering.

It *had* been four days since I'd spent time with Richard. It took me about two seconds to whip my apron off—it was my mom's special apron, of course, my lucky touchstone—and hang it on the hook by the entry to the kitchen. Then I set off toward the bedroom, down the hall past the kitchen, and chose a simple black dress, sleeveless with a round neck. It was one of the few nice things I owned, and I wore it with filigree silver earrings I'd bought in Paris and strappy sandals. Richard had urged me to go shopping for clothes, but I hadn't quite been able to bring myself to do it. I still felt it necessary to be cautious about money, even though everyone around me in this new life seemed to throw it around without any thought whatsoever.

I fastened a chain with an Eiffel Tower charm encrusted with diamonds around my neck. Richard had given it to me for Christmas, and it was the most expensive piece of jewelry I owned. I'd opened it in front of Jack and Daisie at Christmas, which had been a mistake.

"Wow," Daisie had breathed as I'd held it up for them to see.

"Nice, Len," Jack had said, noncommittally.

I'd dangled it in front of my face, somewhat taken aback, to be honest. Wasn't the Eiffel Tower motif a bit too on point? And didn't the diamonds look a bit too gaudy? But probably that was just me. I tried to remember to wear it as much as possible so that Richard would know I appreciated

it. And now he'd brought me a keychain with another bejeweled Eiffel Tower on it. Oh, well, so what if his taste ran to
the obvious?

I walked back to where he waited in the dining room.

"My darling, you look like a goddess," Richard said. He
took my hand, raised it to his mouth and kissed it, then
deposited kisses up my arm, finally landing one on my lips.
Then he took a step back and clapped his hands. "Chop chop.
If you want to see the bakery, we need to get going."

I believed him, of course. Why wouldn't I? I let him usher
me to his car and drive me off into the night.

BUT THERE WAS a slowdown on the freeway and even Richard
Bishop couldn't wave a hand and make L.A. traffic disappear.
There was also the slight matter that we headed in the opposite direction of the bakery, which I didn't realize until too
late, because I'd been absorbed in telling Richard about the
interviewing process for our macaron bakers. I'd never been
interested in managing people, but I found I enjoyed talking
to prospective employees and imagining myself baking
alongside them. There were several I had enthusiastically
recommended we hire.

But then Richard pulled the car to a stop and I realized
what had happened. We were at Tangent, one of his
favorite places to eat in Malibu. He smiled at me, then
turned off the engine and started to open his door. As a
valet came to open my door, I overcame my momentary
confusion.

"Wait," I said, as Richard was halfway out his door. He sat
back down and looked at me over his shoulder, his face a
glassy lake of composure.

"We're in Malibu."

Richard grinned. "We sure are, my sweet. Horst is

offering a special four-course meal this evening and I knew I had to return home in time to treat you to it."

I scowled in frustration. "But we were going to stop by the bakery first!"

He reached across the gear shift and took my hand, looking into my eyes. "I'm so sorry, Madeleine. But when I got the message that Horst had moved the dinner time up, it was imperative that we came here first." He paused and smiled. "One does not take issue with what Horst decrees."

As far as I was concerned, Horst could take his hissy fit decrees and throw them in the Pacific, which roared quietly behind the restaurant, this being Malibu, where God forbid the stars couldn't tolerate their oceans too loud. I was pissed. And feeling pissy. My mind scrolled through options. Book an Uber and go to the bakery myself? Get a Lyft back to the house and drive my car in from there?

"Richard, over here!" The shout came from near the restaurant's front door. The paparazzi had arrived.

"Let's go, my darling."

I sat firm in my seat, pondering what to do. Yes, I could get a ride to the bakery but to what end? I didn't want to rile Richard. Because, at that moment it felt like everything in my life depended on keeping him happy. What if he got angry and decided to defund the Portland bakery? What would Jack and Daisie do? I'd committed to doing whatever it took to save the bakery and I'd accomplished that. With an infusion of cash from Richard's bankers, Jack had paid off Will's thugs, which was all it took for the business to reach equilibrium. And besides, dinner at Tangent with one of the most famous men in the world was hardly torture.

I made my decision. At the last minute, I faced forward, gazed out the car window, and smiled as Richard grabbed my hand and raised it to his lips. Flash. I knew I'd see the shot on the gossip sites tomorrow.

"That's my girl." And with that, Richard exited the car and waved to the assembled photographers. By now I knew my role. I followed his lead, allowing the valet to help me out and lead me around the car, where Richard took my arm and turned us toward the paps for one last shot.

I smiled, leaning into Richard, then walked with him into the restaurant.

CHAPTER 14

After we'd eaten Horst's four-course meal, which wasn't that great, to be honest (I'm sorry but sea anemones in a blackberry reduction are not my idea of a tasty appetizer), and Richard had dropped me at home, I found I couldn't sleep. I couldn't get my brain to turn off. Number one, I worried about the bakery. We'd never made it there that evening, obviously, even though I'd tried again after dinner. But Richard mumbled something about a Zoom "with his people in Mumbai" and I gave up. Why was he so intent on keeping me away from the bakery? Did he think I was incompetent? But if so, why buy into the bakery in the first place? Or was he truly trying to please me, wining and dining me, not wanting me to fret about business? I didn't know the answer, and my pillow did not tell me, either. And when my brain grew tired of obsessing over Richard, I worried about Daisie and Jack.

Well, mostly Jack, because Daisie could be plopped down in the middle of the African savannah and figure out a way to rule the local tribes within five minutes. But, Jack. Earlier that day when I had Skyped with the two of them, he looked thinner and more anxious. I knew he still brooded about money, with consulting jobs in short supply, but it seemed like there was more going on, too. Like the strain of keeping up with the young, beautiful, and impossibly ditzy Carla.

It was at times like this when I couldn't sleep—and there were many of them recently, as my brain processed the elements of my new life—that I thought about the day I had said goodbye to Jack. And the thing that had happened.

It had been a cold morning in early January, and my little car was packed for my long drive to L.A. We'd gotten Daisie off to school, which had been a production, seeing as how she desperately wanted to come with me and "shadow Richard Bishop so I can learn everything he knows." It was only after I'd promised to write down anything of importance Richard might utter that Daisie had trudged off.

But my mind cycled back around to what had happened next. I'd planned to take a walk to get some exercise before the long drive, and Jack decided to come with me.

"You going your usual route?" he'd asked.

I hesitated. I *had* been planning to take my usual route, but with Jack along I wasn't sure. I most often walked along a trail that bordered a nearby golf course. I loved it, because it was like a little piece of country in the middle of the city, but with the greens on one side and a steep, brush- and tree-lined ridge on the other, once you got on the path there was no way to get off it. I fretted that Jack wouldn't be able to make it all the way.

"Don't worry about me, I can do it," Jack said.

"I'm going to miss the way you can always read my mind."

We walked the few blocks to the trail through the neighborhood I loved so much, with its Craftsmen style homes interspersed with miniature Tudors and large cottages. The lawns were green from the winter rains, and all the garden beds dormant, but in a month the crocuses would be peeking out, and soon after daffodils and tulips. And the daphne! I'd miss the sweet February smell of it. I did my best to ignore the way Jack walked with a limp and stopped myself from reaching out to him when he stumbled over a root at the beginning of the trail.

The dirt trail lay damp from rain the night before, and we skirted mud puddles and dodged piles of rain-slicked leaves. Jack's limp became more pronounced as we walked, and I eyed the path ahead, hoping to see the end soon.

"Do you mind if we stop for just a minute? I find the pain eases if I can just pause occasionally."

"No problem."

Jack stretched his arms over his head and then bent over at his waist. When he came back up, he inhaled deeply. "It feels good to be outside." Another deep breath and long exhale. "I miss the outdoors. Seems impossible to believe I used to climb mountains and raft rivers."

He shook his head and fixed his gaze across the golf course, to some distant point. I was about to say something—I was formulating words of sympathy—but he spoke again.

"I try not to, but times like these, I think about what I've lost, Lenie. Mountain climbing, my marriage—"

"You're still married," I said, shocked by his comment.

"Trying to be." He was still staring across the greens. "It is just looking less and less likely it will work out." Jack unfixed his far-off gaze and stretched his head back against his neck, and then turned to me. "And you. Now I'm losing you."

I opened my mouth to respond but no words came out.

"I've rested long enough now," Jack said and started off down the trail.

I ran after him and grabbed his elbow to stop him. "Maybe I shouldn't go. Maybe I'm not doing the right thing."

Jack gazed down at me. In his eyes I saw everything, all the emotions I'd ever felt. "You are. You're doing the right thing, Lenie. I don't see that's there's any other choice if we want to save the bakery. But all the same, I'm going to miss you something fierce."

"And I will miss you."

I stood on tiptoes and kissed his cheek. His arm circled my waist and suddenly his lips were on mine. I opened my mouth and welcomed him to me. It was a natural reaction, done without any thought, just instinct. And, oh God. He tasted like the best macaron I'd ever created, the most amazing delicacy in the world. All the sweetness and light in the whole world was in that kiss, all the good things I'd ever experienced in the past and the wonderful things that waited for me in the future. I pressed myself closer and opened my mouth wider.

And then I heard footsteps and the sound of leaves crunching. Jack broke away from me. A runner appeared on the path and tipped his ball cap at us as he ran by. I stood on the path, staring after him, because suddenly it was difficult to look at Jack. What had just happened? When I turned my attention back to Jack, he patted me on the shoulder and nodded his head in that way he had, as if to emphasize a point he'd just made. Boy, had he ever. I just wasn't sure what his point meant.

"I think I see the end of the path," I said.

"Good, I'm getting tired," Jack said

And we walked home in silence.

Back in Malibu, I flopped over in bed, burying my head under the pillow. But that didn't help. Finally, long about two in the morning, I realized three things: that I couldn't help Jack, that I'd probably never figure out Richard's inscrutable ways, and that I wasn't going to get back to sleep any time soon.

I climbed out of bed and finished the batch of macarons that I'd been making when Richard arrived. I was playing with a lavender/vanilla flavor and they came out amazing, despite my cramped working quarters. As I took a bite of the lovely pale-violet colored confection, I had an idea: what was to stop me from heading to the bakery now? Not a thing. Not one damn thing.

I ran to my room, threw on an old stretched-out T-shirt and jeans, and laced up my athletic shoes. I grabbed my purse and my phone, which I told myself I really should check for messages and headed out the door. Even though I'd had a couple of glasses of wine the night before and hadn't gotten any sleep, I felt only the slightest edge of tiredness. I stopped at a Starbucks drive-through for their largest Americano and a sausage, cheese, and egg breakfast sandwich, and drove on along the weirdly busy L.A. freeways.

It struck me for the umpteenth time how odd this was. Not that I was out and about after not sleeping all night, though that was unusual for me, too. My new life was what was strange. One minute I'd been happily ensconced at the Bonne Chance in Portland and the next I was transported to L.A., spending time with Richard in bed and out, and working with his team to plan the opening of the new location. I'd forsaken my old life in Portland and the bakery for the sake of saving it, which seemed like weird, twisted logic to me.

But the most important thing was that my little love child —the original Bonne Chance—was doing well. People still lined the sidewalk rain or shine to buy the macarons I'd painstakingly trained Caroline to make, but now we could afford equipment (including an awning) and cash flow was no longer an issue.

Yes, that was the important thing. Never mind that I was not that there to enjoy it, that I didn't get to observe Daisie's crazy obsessions or Jack's grumpy glares turn to smiles. Skype was wonderful, but it wasn't the same as spending hours every day alongside them. Never mind that I didn't get to revel in the bakery's success. It was a success precisely because I wasn't there anymore. I pulled up in front of the new Bonne Chance in Hollywood. As long as the Portland Bonne Chance was successful, that was all that mattered. Right?

I stared at the bakery. I'd done my best to have my voice be heard on the design, and Richard had backed me, but somewhere along the line my voice had gotten lost in translation.

The way the design had come out, it fit right in with the tacky Hollywood businesses around it. The window looked like a display stolen from Macy's at Christmas time, only without the Christmas. It was crammed with miniature steel Eiffel Towers, tiny tables and chairs, and mock-ups of ornate old buildings, all of which were supposed to evoke Paris. And let us not forget the macarons. They are, by their very nature, delightful to look at. Their gorgeous jewel-like colors, their puffy little shells, and their smooth fillings are inherently attractive. But someone had piled a huge number of them in the center of the so-called Paris geegaws. Correction. It looked like somebody had thrown them. The macarons were flung every which way into a mountain of macarons, or more like a mockery of them. I think the look Richard's designers were going for was casual hip, which I knew something about from living in Portland, which was the hipster capital of the country. The result was a terrible mishmash that just looked tacky.

I walked around back to the alley that ran along the back door of the bakery, glad to see that it was illuminated by lights on the buildings, and not as dark and creepy as I'd imagined. Even so, I startled when I realized there was a person standing there. I held my keys out in front of me, the way I'd learned in the self-defense class I'd taken in college, keys being an effective weapon in a pinch. But I relaxed when I realized it was the purple-haired girl I'd seen when Richard had first shown me the location.

She shrank toward the wall of the building when she saw me, but I called out to her anyway. "Hey, you surprised me. I didn't expect to see anyone else here at this time of the morning." I glanced at my watch. It was just a little bit before six.

The girl shrugged and blew smoke, which curled up to the sky, visible in the streetlight that shone at the end of the alley. What *was* she doing there so early, anyway? Surely a souvenir shop didn't open until midmorning.

"They must make you come in early to get the souvenirs organized, huh?"

Another drift of smoke. I could feel her anxiety waft into the air with it. "Not really. Sometimes I just get here early to, um, get away."

I took a step closer to her. She sported ripped jeans with a short black skirt appliquéd with huge pink flowers on it, and a gray hoodie that looked like it had seen better days. She wore the hood up, covering her purple hair, but I could see hanks of it sticking out over her forehead. Dark circles rimmed the space beneath her eyes, as if she'd not sleep well for quite a while. "Get away from someone in particular?"

She waved her hand, then tossed the cigarette and used her black-boot-encased foot to stomp it out. "I gotta go." And she headed toward the back door to the souvenir shop.

"Wait," I called.

To my surprise, she paused and looked over her shoulder.

I held out the Starbucks bag with the breakfast sandwich in it and my cup of coffee. "You hungry? Take these. I haven't touched them, I promise. They were too hot when I got them."

"Nah." She shook her head. "I don't need your food."

"I actually wasn't planning to eat them," I lied. "I won't have time now, because I need to get going on the baking."

She darted across the alley and grabbed the bag and cup from me. "Thanks," she said. And then she was gone.

I wondered what was going on in her life that she had fled to hang out at the souvenir shop hours before her shift began. Well, at least I'd gotten her some food and coffee. I used my key to unlock the back door to the bakery, which opened onto a dark hall. It was arranged not unlike the Portland location: on one side of the hall sat the retail area and on the other the actual bakery—though you could have put five Portland baking rooms in this kitchen. As I walked toward it, I saw light spilling out from the doorway and heard the clatter of pans and the hum of voices. That surprised me. I'd imagined having the place to myself, happily baking, as I used to do in Portland.

When I stepped into the doorway I stopped in my tracks, dumbfounded. I'd seen the bakery area before, of course. I'd helped choose most of the equipment. But I'd never seen it in full-on action, as it was that morning. In a corner in the rear of the room, a white-jacketed woman tended the macaron-making machine, a huge contraption with an arm that poured precise amounts of batter onto an endless line of baking sheets. In the other back corner, a bank of ovens appeared to be full of macarons. And at the vast table in the middle, two men piped filling into macaron shells, then carefully pasted them together.

And even though I'd been involved in the interviewing for the baking positions, I'd never seen any of these people before. Which meant that my hiring choices had been overridden. As Daisie would say, duh. Was Richard aware of this? Was this why he'd kept me away from the bakery?

The man closest to me started when he noticed me and dropped his macaron shell. He had very dark hair beneath his white chef's hat, and dark eyes and a few days stubble on his chin. He reminded me of Will and my heart did a little *kerthump*.

"How'd you get in here?"

I held up my key. "I'm Madeleine Miller. The, um, owner." It sounded odd to say that word, *owner*, because was I really? Clearly there was a lot I didn't know. Like the hiring of the bakers who stood before me.

The baker removed his gloves, and a cloud of suspicion crossed his eyes. "So, you do exist. We were just taking bets on whether you were real or not."

The woman at the machine glanced over her shoulder at me. "Or if Richard was just using his latest squeeze as the face of the bakery."

I winced. Ouch. But their comments were well deserved. Despite what I thought were my best efforts to oversee every aspect of the bakery, I hadn't even known this crew had been hired. I nodded, as if accepting their summations. I could blather on about my intentions to be a hands-on owner, but that wouldn't convince them of anything, based on what had happened so far. "Where can I find an apron?"

"What for?" The dark-haired baker glanced at the other man across the table, who raised his eyebrows in a quick puzzled expression before he rearranged his face and went back to work. Hostile energy filled the room.

"Because I'm going to work, of course."

He stared at me for a long moment, and then a resigned look crossed his face, and he nodded his head toward the corner, where an iron rack held white chef's jackets and aprons. I grabbed one, wishing I had my special apron with me to help dispel my chilly welcome, tied it on, then joined the two men at the table.

"Pastry bag?" I asked.

He pointed to a shelf beneath the table. I reached for one,

then looked around for plastic wrap to line it with. I found it on a shelf against the wall. He watched me as I inserted the plastic wrap and then spooned huge dollops of filling into the bag.

"Makes the pastry bag a lot easier to clean," I explained to his puzzled look. And then I pulled on plastic gloves and set to work. I couldn't really blame them for their suspicions about me.

After a few minutes, the dark-haired man spoke. "By the way, I'm Jacques-Pierre and this is Thomas and Ellie." I nodded hellos at all of them and went back to work.

As always, within minutes I was absorbed in my task and totally lost in thought. I can't say that the bad juju Jacques-Pierre and the others radiated went away. But as I got into the rhythm of my work, I tuned it out. I filled macaron shells to the sound of the piping machine and felt my body ease and my mind relax. This was what I loved in life. This was what I wanted to do.

"Aiyee!"

I dropped my pastry bag on the table and looked toward the source of the screech. Fiona, Richard's erstwhile assistant, stood in the door to the room, her eyes ablaze with anger. "Richard told me to look for you here but I thought he was crazy. Madeleine, what on earth are you doing?"

"Filling macaron shells." I shrugged and picked up the pastry bag.

She wore a black pencil skirt with a short black jacket and royal blue blouse beneath it, and when she took a step toward me, I put my hand up.

"Don't come in here."

"Of course I'm coming in," Fiona snapped.

I shook my head and pointed to her feet. She wore patent leather open-toed, strappy high heels that looked like sandals on stilts.

"It's too dangerous with those things on." It was an iron-clad rule to always wear closed shoes in the bakery; there were just too many accidents that could happen.

I heard a noise beside me and glanced at Jacques-Pierre just in time to see a smile traverse his face and then disappear.

Fiona exhaled a huge sigh. "Well you come out here, then. It's time to get your clothes on and get going."

I filled another shell. "I have no idea what you're talking about."

"Oh Jesus, please spare me. Really?" Fiona now had her hands on her hips. "You've got an appearance on *Good Morning Southland* this morning in," and she checked her watch, "two hours. You've still got to get dressed and to the studio and it's an hour away at this time of day."

"Nobody told me about an appearance."

Fiona let out another of her screams, her mouth open as wide as the Grand Canyon. "I left fifty gazillion messages on your phone! I emailed you! I texted!"

Oh God, I really did need to be better about checking my phone.

"So, let's get you changed, and we can get going," Fiona said.

"I don't have any clothes." I gestured to myself. "This is all I have with me." I braced for another scream, which came on cue.

"Oh my God, Richard does not pay me enough to deal with you. You cannot go on the air like that."

"This apron covers a lot." I looked down. It was also covered with green and pink macaron batter. And the thought of making a TV appearance made my heart pound.

"How about one of the chef jackets?" Jacques-Pierre said. He nodded toward the corner rack. Was it my imagination or was he trying not to laugh?

"Oh no, that's not the look we're going for at all." Fiona glanced down at herself and then back at me. "You'll have to wear my clothes; I think they'll fit. And I will—" she looked at my scruffy jeans and T-shirt and grimaced, "wear yours. Now come along. Chop chop. There's no time to waste."

I hung my apron on the rack and turned back to wave to Jacques-Pierre and the others. "Bye. See you bright and early tomorrow."

I earned a grunt in response from Jacques-Pierre, and a couple of "see yas" from Thomas and Ellie. That would do for a start.

CHAPTER 15

I tuned out Fiona's chatter as we drove across town in the back of a limo, she in my clothes, me in hers, which fit relatively well, even if the skirt hit mid-thigh instead of my knees, as it did on her. Truth is, I was terrified. I'd done several media interviews since I'd been in L.A., even one on the radio, but not one on TV. If I'd known about it, I never would have stayed up all night. I looked a fright, with huge bags and dark circles beneath my eyes. And the energy that propelled me to the bakery a few hours earlier had largely deserted me. I had only myself to blame. I needed to be better about checking my phone and email.

"Okay, good, good, thank you." Fiona spoke into her cell and then pressed the off button as if spanking a child. She turned to me. "It's a damn good thing that we hired someone to do the prep work on set, or we'd be shit out of luck. But it sounds like Mary has everything under control. You should have everything you need."

"And, um, what is it exactly that I'm doing?"

"Oh, good lord. Did you not read the précis I sent you? I

swear, Madeleine, I don't know how you expect to be a famous food star if you don't pay attention to such things."

I started to say that I had no desire to be a famous food star, but she ran on. I was to talk about the process of baking macarons while doing a TV version of making them.

"Damn it, this traffic is atrocious!" Fiona yelled. "Wouldn't you know that the 10 would be clogged on this, the one day I need to get somewhere fast." She scooted to the edge of the seat and leaned forward to talk to the driver. "Can't you drive up the shoulder or something?"

"I'm going as fast as I can, ma'am."

I couldn't imagine why she was complaining about the mass of cars we sat in, because as far as I could tell, there was always a mass of cars on L.A. roads. Fiona steamed and stewed and screamed as we progressed slowly along, then took to doing whatever it was she did with her cell again. The farther down the freeway we got, the more I felt like hyperventilating. I couldn't believe I was going to be on television in just a few minutes. Fiona's sound effects didn't help, as she oohed and aahed over something on her phone.

"Oh blimey, we so need to do this."

"What?" I asked.

"They have special macaron flavors of the month. This month is St. Paddy's day." Fiona turned her phone around, so I could see. Above a picture of a kelly-green macaron was Will's obnoxious Macaron Madness logo. His online business seemed to be thriving, despite the loan sharks and fire that had burned his brick-and-mortar location.

She flipped the screen around, so she could see it again and pushed more buttons. "Oh crap! This is freaking brilliant! They have celebrities designing flavors!"

"If you don't mind, I'd rather not hear about that right now."

Fiona scowled at me. "And why bloody not? Why don't

you want to hear about ideas that might improve La Bonne Chance?"

"Because I'm already a nervous wreck about going on TV," I snapped. "I don't need to hear about how freaking bloody great my ex-husband's macaron business is doing, okay?"

Fiona's eyes widened, and she waved her phone. "This is your ex-husband?"

I nodded.

"Well, he's a genius, is all I can say."

A few minutes later we got to the station. Fiona directed the town car to pull up in front of the main entrance and instructed the driver to wait for us. Then she looked at her watch, turned to me and said, "Run!"

I took one step in Fiona's strappy shoes and knew there would be no running in them. I reached down and pulled them off my feet, then pattered after her, down a hall, up an elevator, down another hall, and into a room that turned out to be the Green Room (even though it wasn't painted green), where you waited before going on camera. Though there wasn't any waiting involved. Because as soon as we reached it, Megan, the perky blonde host of the show saw us. "Thank God you are here; your segment is next."

Before I knew it, I was pushed onto the stage where a kitchen had been set up and bright lights blinded me. Megan and I stood behind the counter and a voice counted, "And we're on in 5...4...3...2...1."

Megan smiled at the camera, at least I thought that's what she was doing. Once I was standing on the stage, I realized I had no idea where to look or how to act. And the lights were not only bright, but also hot. A bead of sweat rolled down my back and the underarms of Fiona's silk shirt were wet. But at least none of that showed on camera. I just hoped my head didn't start sweating, because that would be painfully obvious.

"And we are back with our next guest, Madeleine Miller, the owner of the brand-new NoHo bakery, La Bonne Chance, which opens today. This bakery is unique in that it features only one item—French macarons. Can you tell us a little bit more about them, Madeleine?"

"Yes, thank you, Megan, I can." I looked around on the counter in front of me for a macaron to hold up as an example, as Fiona had told me that the prepper she'd hired would have them ready on the set. But there was no plate of macarons. Instead there was a plate with a sheet of paper on top of it. The sheet of paper had photos of colorful macarons and I realized in a flash of clarity that the prep person had that there as a place holder and had then forgotten to place the macarons.

"Um, yeah, so the macaron. The French have been enjoying them for years and anybody who goes to Paris falls in love with them."

"Can you explain what they are?" Megan seemed suddenly to realize the lack of macarons in front of us.

"A macaron is made with almond flour, so it's gluten-free, and it's a little sandwich made of two shells and a layer of frosting. A delicious treat." I felt a few beads of sweat blossom on my forehead and wondered if there was any way I could surreptitiously wipe them off. But instead, I held up the piece of paper with the macaron images on it.

"And you're going to show us how you make macarons, correct?"

"Yes, I am."

"They look difficult to bake," Megan said.

I was glancing around the set looking for the baking setup and didn't see anything. "Macarons have a reputation for being finicky, but once you learn a few simple tips, they really aren't."

"Well, great. Why don't you show us?"

At the very last minute I saw the mixing bowl set way off to the side of the counter and I grabbed it and proceeded to explain to Megan the fine points of mixing the simple syrup and then adding in the almond flour. As I added almond flour to the simple syrup, a huge splash of it landed on my shirt. Well, Fiona's shirt. I startled and then laughed self-consciously.

"So much for this blouse," I said, without really thinking. "Good thing it's not mine."

Megan cocked one eyebrow at me.

"I had to borrow it from my keeper. Apparently, the clothes I usually bake in weren't really camera ready." Shut up, Madeleine, I told myself. But I was in that weird fugue state you reach when you've not slept in a very long time and my mouth just kept going, seemingly separate from my brain. "I was actually up baking macarons all night."

"Were you now," Megan said.

I nodded. "Yup. Made some delicious lavender-vanilla ones. Too bad you can't taste them. They were divine." I felt something moving on me and looked down to see the splash of batter rolling down Fiona's blouse. I used my finger to gather up the batter and stuck it in my mouth. "Num. These are pretty good, too."

Megan twisted her mouth in a grimace and shuddered, then seemed to get control of herself and smiled. At least with her mouth. Her eyes shot daggers at me. "And now that you've made the batter and told us how to cook them, you're going to show us how to assemble them, right?" Megan nodded toward a pastry bag lying on the counter. The prepper had gotten that part right. Only problem was the lack of macarons—and macaron shells—to use in the demo.

"Yes, yes, I am," I said, stalling for time. "You know, since we don't seem to actually have a macaron shell here to show you, I'll just give you an idea how it works." I grabbed the sheet of paper with images of macarons on it and held it up. "See? Macarons." Then I laid the paper flat on the countertop and squeezed a dollop from the pastry bag.

"Well now, that doesn't look too appealing," Megan said.

The frosting that came out of the bag was black. A deep, horrible, profound black. It made a nice little dollop when I first squeezed it onto the paper and then it started oozing off the sides of it. I had no clue how the prep person had even gotten that color, let alone the consistency.

"Um, if I had actual macaron shells here, I'd put another one on top and it would be like a sandwich, okay?"

"Right." Megan nodded her head definitively. She knocked the paper into the sink. "Thanks for that demo, Madeleine, and now let me ask you something."

I rubbed my hands together. "Ask away." This appearance couldn't get any worse. It just couldn't.

"Richard Bishop is the money man behind the bakery, correct?"

I nodded. "He's a big fan of the macaron."

"And sources tell us he's a big fan of you, as well."

"Apparently so." I smiled. "Lucky me, huh?"

"Indeed," Megan said, and I could tell by the look on her face she was wondering what in the hell he saw in me. "Well, thank you, Madeleine, for sharing your baking, um, skills with us this morning. And the bakery opens when?"

"Today," I chirped brightly.

"Coming up next, attachment parenting—good or bad theory?" Megan said.

"And we're at break," the producer called.

I turned to Megan, but all I saw was her back as she strode off the set. Alrighty then. Apparently, she wasn't too happy with the way that segment had gone. I blew air up my face, cooling my sweaty brow. And then I walked offstage to face Fiona's wrath.

CHAPTER 16

took one last look at the copy I'd just written and decided it sounded perky and cute enough (Fiona's orders) for a first post. I pressed publish on the blog post and pushed myself away from the table, stretching my arms, then reached for my paper cup of coffee.

My days had developed a rhythm over the last week. I headed to the bakery every morning at five, where I joined Jacques-Pierre, Thomas, and Ellie in the back room, and we churned out reams of macarons. By sheer virtue of me showing up every day, I seemed to be slowly winning my baking crew over. Now Jacques-Pierre said good morning to me instead of grunting, and Ellie had flashed me a smile after I mastered the piping machine. I counted that as huge progress. And when I was done in the back, I went up front and fussed over the macaron arrangement and kept an eye on customer service. And then I came here, to the Coffee Bean and Tea Leaf, where I sat outside, glorying in the warm temperatures, and worked.

I decided to see how the post looked on the blog. I clicked over to the page and eyed it. Not bad. Of course, it helped that the blog, *Macarons and Magic*, had been professionally designed and created for me by one of Richard's web designers. Unlike the so-called designers who were responsible for the bakery, I liked the web guy's aesthetics—my blog was pink and black, Paris colors (or at least an American's idea of Paris colors) with subtle French design elements throughout.

I also had managed to snag myself a book contract. Well, I hadn't had a whole lot to do with it. One of Richard's minions had sat with me to talk concept, then written a proposal. Et voila, next thing I knew I was talking to my editor, Amelia, about how long I would need to put the manuscript together. It was to be a book all about macarons, their history, how to bake them, the usual suspects. But it was also going to be about more—sort of a Madeleine's guide to living life the way the French do. It floored me that both blog and book had been handed to me on a silver platter, but that was the way things happened in Richard's world. If there was one thing I'd learned over the last few months, it was that money could buy you anything. And I do mean *anything*.

I opened the file where I'd been saving notes for my book, and then couldn't think of a thing to write. Staring at the page didn't work, so I stared off into space. And noticed a gorgeous woman with black hair, doe eyes, and cheekbones as chiseled as the Alps walking by arm and arm with a good-looking man. Correction, she was draped over him, as close to another human as you could be and still walk. Why did she look so familiar?

I gasped when I realized. My God, that was Carla! Or was it? I squinted toward where she and her paramour—might he be the famous Torvald? —had stopped on the sidewalk to share a kiss. It was difficult to tell with her face buried in his, but I was sure it was her. Carla. Who was supposed to be in Texas, working on her movie set, while Jack and Daisie caught up on things in Portland.

And, wouldn't you know it, right then my phone dinged with a text from Jack.

Good morning sunshine, the text read. *Hope you have a great day.*

Oh, God. Would he be so cheery if he knew that his so-called wife was here in L.A., canoodling with someone who looked like a pastiche of every leading man ever born? No, he would not. And it was not my place to ruin that cheerfulness because I wasn't even sure the woman who had now wandered off down the street was Carla. After a few deep breaths, I convinced myself it wasn't her, then I texted him a simple reply. But my concentration was destroyed. I clicked over to read the latest news.

And there was a story about my father. Not that that was so unusual; he got written about all the time, most often fawning articles about his massive success and popular self-help theories. But this one was different, starting with the headline that blared: "Earl Miller's Financial Woes. New Age Self-Help Author Tangled in Money Mess." Uh-oh. I scanned the article, which mostly focused on the retreat center Dad was building in Santa Fe. No wonder he'd not been answering my calls and texts.

I reached for my phone to call Nat and find out more. But before I could call her, an alert that I'd gotten a tweet came through. When I looked closer at the tweet, though, I realized it had Daisie's name on it. Oh, God. The girl had discovered Twitter. I hoped the Twitterverse was ready for what was to come. I scrolled through her feed. She had tweeted about the bakery, along with a couple snide remarks about Dallas, glowing comments about Portland, information about several business sites, a link to a Richard Bishop biography, and a picture of the correct business attire for women.

"Excuse me? Are you Madeleine Miller?"

I looked up. A slender man with a head that was disproportionately large to his body and a haggard face stood before me. He carried a black laptop bag over his shoulder and held a small notebook and pen in his hand.

"I am."

He stuck out his hand. "Winston Herman, with the L.A. *Times*. I was wondering if you could answer a few questions?"

"About what?"

Winston's Adam's apple bobbed. "About Richard Bishop. And his pattern of wooing women and taking over their businesses."

I wrinkled my brows. What was he talking about? I waved my hand. "I don't know what you're saying. He takes over women's businesses?"

Winston nodded. "He's all into it because of his wife, the one who died. But then he can't help himself. He goes overboard and sucks the life out of them."

"I'm not interested in talking to you." The guy sounded like crazy cakes to me, and I wasn't even sure I believed he was with the L.A. *Times*.

"It's a story I've been following for a year or so now, and since you are Richard's latest conquest, I thought I could get your take on it."

Something rang a bell with what the man was saying. *Richard was into taking over businesses because of his dead wife.* He'd told me how everything he did was in honor of his wife at our first dinner—and several times since. But it was going overboard to say he took over the businesses he helped. I mean, the Bonne Chance was doing just fine. Great, even.

"Have you noticed any sign of him or his people edging you—"

We were interrupted by shouting. I looked up. A black limo had pulled to the curb in front of the coffee shop and a crowd of paparazzi clustered around the back door that was slowly opening.

"Richard, look this way."

"Hey, Bishop, over here."

"How was your trip to Brazil?"

Oh God, he was here. My heart did its usual Richard samba. And then I thought: Brazil? I thought he'd been in Barcelona.

Winston glanced in Richard's direction and then thrust a business card at me. "Here. Call me if you change your mind."

And then I lost track of Winston because suddenly Richard was in front of me, smiling the Public Option. I was dimly aware of everyone at the tables around me staring.

"How do you always know where I am?"

He laughed. "I have my ways. And you're nothing if not predictable. If you're not at home, you're at the bakery, and if you're not at the bakery, you're here."

I didn't ask him how he knew about my coffee shop habit, since it had only started in the last few days, in the time he'd been gone. Behind him, on the perimeter of the coffee shop property, the paps hung out. Richard seemed to thrive on their presence and know just how to pose without looking like he was posing, while I always ended up looking like a wild beast.

He held out his hand to me. "Would you like to come with me? I have a surprise for you."

"Hmm, let me think. Sit here and pretend I'm writing or go with you and find out what your surprise is." I stood, then sat back down again. "I think I'll just stay here."

Richard laughed, and I stood again and kissed him on the cheek. "Of course, I'll go with you." I gathered my things and stuffed everything into my bag and preceded Richard to the car.

"I hope we're not going anywhere fancy, because I'm not dressed nicely."

"You look wonderful."

"You're a terrible liar," I said. I was wearing my usual baking outfit—jeans and T-shirt. Once in a while, just to mix it up, I wore leggings and a T-shirt, but only when I was really feeling wacky. And of course, I had my sturdy athletic shoes on. I'd run a brush through my hair and pulled it into a ponytail at 5:00 that morning, but lord only knew what it looked like by then. Quickly, I redid my ponytail and bit my lips to make them look like I wore lipstick.

Richard handed me a bag after we'd settled in the back seat of the town car. "We *are* going someplace nice. But I bought you this, so you can change when we get there. Open it."

I pulled layers of pink tissue from the clear bag imprinted with the name of an expensive Beverly Hills store and uncovered a sky-blue dress. It was a simple A-line with no sleeves, but the fabric felt deliciously soft beneath my hand and I knew it would drape just so along my body.

"That color of blue looks so good on you," Richard said. He scooted closer to me and nuzzled my neck. And then his nuzzling turned into a kiss as he planted his lips on mine and probed my mouth with his tongue. I wanted to melt into him, to rip his clothes off and feel his skin on mine. But he broke away from me.

"There will be time for that later, darling," he said. "I always miss you so when I'm gone. Dig further in that bag—there's more."

I pulled a box from the depths of the tissue and when I opened it, I gasped—it was a lovely oval pendant in deep royal blue, a hue that would look stunning with the lighter blue of the dress.

I threw my arms around his neck. "It's gorgeous, Richard, thank you!"

And I have to admit, I thought, *so he does manage good taste once in a while.* I swatted the thought away.

"I can't wait to see it on you," he said.

"And I can't wait to find out where we're going."

Richard leaned toward me again but then his phone rang. Unlike me, he always answered his phone. His eyebrows knotted as he listened to the person on the other end, interjecting an occasional "uh-huh" and "really" and "okay." Then his face broke into a big smile. "I'll tell her," he said, and ended the call.

He turned the grin on me.

"What?" I asked.

"Fiona says you owe her a blouse."

"Oh, God." After my disastrous TV appearance, I'd handed Fiona back her blouse, and she'd eyed it with distaste. Not only did it have a huge stain of batter down the front, its underarms were, how shall I say it, completely pitted out, with huge wet crescents beneath each. She'd refused to put it back on and worn my T-shirt home.

I shook my head. "That was such a train wreck."

Richard's smile had not disappeared.

"What now?" I asked.

He raised his eyebrows.

"Tell me!"

"Do you promise to be very, very good?"

"I'm always good," I cried.

"You promise to do that thing you do to me that drives me wild tonight when we're in bed?"

I felt my cheeks redden. I had discovered Richard's secret pleasure spot and learned to use my fingers and my tongue on it liberally. "Not a problem."

"Okay. The Cook & Eat Network called. They're interested in doing a show with you."

I screamed a scream worthy of Fiona, a scream so loud our driver swerved for a brief second.

"They want me to do a show?"

Richard nodded.

"But my appearance was a disaster."

"Not everyone thought that, Mad. You came across as real and funny and natural instead of stiff and programmed. That's rare these days." He reached a finger out to touch the back of my hand. "It's what so attracts me to you."

His gentle touch sent shivers throughout my body and I reached for his finger and brought it to my lips, kissing the pad of it. Thanks to Richard, I was living the dream, and it was easy to forget my occasional qualms. I stared into his eyes as I took his finger into my mouth, and he leaned over and kissed me. His touch had set me to shivering, but the kiss caused every cell in my body to explode. He kissed me long and hard and deeply and just as his hands snuck up to my breasts, he unlocked his lips and pulled away.

"Oh, Jesus, Maddie, you tempt me so." He leaned back against the seat, panting and laughing. "But we really need to talk before we reach our destination."

I inhaled deeply, then exhaled, my tongue out. "Okay." Another deep breath. "Fire away."

Richard, of course, was now completely composed. He could go from passionate lover to logical businessman in seconds. "I hear we had a little trouble at the shop?"

I scowled and shook my head, not sure what he was talking about. Then it occurred to me. "Oh, you mean with the macaron machine? Yeah, it's a little balky. Ellie is having a hard time with it."

"No, no." Richard shook his head. "I meant with the shoplifter."

I looked at him, stunned. How did the man manage to know *everything* about all the businesses he was involved with?

There'd been a ruckus in the shop a few days earlier when one of the cashiers had found someone snitching a macaron from one of the window displays. When I'd gone out front to see what the fuss was about, I'd recognized the girl with the purple hair I'd given my breakfast to a few days earlier.

"The shoplifter was no big deal. Her name is Tansy. You met her out back of the store. And you don't have to worry about her anymore."

"The police handled it, then?"

I shook my head. "Of course not! She was just hungry. I took her down the street to McDonald's and bought her lunch. You have never seen a human being scarf food down so fast." I looked out the window and laughed, remembering. "She's really a sweet young woman. I gather she doesn't have much money and skips meals a lot."

"Shoplifters are not exactly the kind of people I like to think of you hanging out with."

What was this about? Richard usually spouted off such platitudes as, *the importance of helping those less fortunate than ourselves.*

"Richard, she was just hungry. She works at the shop next door and lives in some crappy apartment with her boyfriend." I leaned away from him, my back against the window. "You're the one always talking about giving back and doing nice things."

He gazed at me with what I was starting to recognize as his soulful look. Usually, it made my heart flip. But that day it felt like a performance. I glanced away. I didn't want to see that.

"And those actions are ever so important." Richard reached a hand to me. After a moment, I took it grudgingly. "I trust your judgment, Maddie, so I'll accede to your greater wisdom on this. But, in general, we've got to watch out for this sort of thing."

His phone buzzed, the signal he'd gotten a text. Richard smiled, held up a finger, and tended to his phone. I stared out the window and pondered what I hadn't told him about Tansy, that since the day I'd met her I'd taken her out to eat several times. I'd learned that she made quirky skirts with material bought cheap at Goodwill and that sewing was her passion and that more than anything she'd love to sell her creations someday. I'd found out that the boyfriend she lived with and professed to love—Brad—had a mean streak. Hence me finding her lurking about the alley early that morning.

I glanced over at Richard, both thumbs flying over the face of his phone. And I certainly didn't tell him what she'd said to me over cheeseburgers at McDonald's the day previous.

"Can I ask you something?" she'd asked, wiping a smear of ketchup from her face with her finger. After I nodded, she went on. "Why are you with Richard Bishop, anyway?"

I pulled my head back, surprised by her question. "Well, he invested in my bakery and saved my bacon, for starters."

"Yeah, but does that mean you have to, like, *be* with him?" She crammed a handful of french fries, dripping with ranch sauce, into her mouth.

"He is rather attractive," I said. "In case you hadn't noticed."

She wrinkled her nose. "But he's a jerk."

I remembered how nice he'd been to her the first time I met her and scowled in puzzlement.

"Do you know how many women I've seen him with over the time I've worked there?"

"Richard's love of women is well known."

She shook her head. "Yeah, but it's weird how fast he goes through them. And the businesses, too."

"The businesses?"

"There's always a new store going into that location."

I was sure that Tansy was mistaken, because when we'd had the initial meeting with the Ryans, they'd acted as if the location had been chosen just for the Bonne Chance. But it had caused a glimmer of unease inside me. And what was it that reporter had said?

I eyed Richard as he put his phone away.

I certainly was not going to confess that I'd invited Tansy to attend the grand opening of the bakery, which was coming up in a couple of days, now was I? No, I wasn't. Because I knew how well that would go over. But I had no intention of uninviting her, either. I liked Tansy a lot. She activated my mothering instinct big time, and I loved our forays to fast food places and coffee shops together, despite her dubious opinion of Richard.

"And that just emphasizes my other point," Richard said. He'd finished his texting and had resumed exactly where we'd left off. The man's powers of concentration and focus amazed me.

His tone unnerved me. "What's that?"

"You've got to stop spending your mornings at the bakery."

"But why? That's what I do."

"I know you love it, darling, but we're going to need you to be available for other things, especially as we get closer to the grand opening. Like publicity. And me." He leaned toward me and pressed his lips over mine.

He broke apart from me. "You're okay about the baking?"

"No, I'm actually not," I murmured, but he didn't seem to hear me, and I let him pull me back to him and kiss me even deeper. I figured I could handle the publicity plans he had for me *and* my early mornings at the bakery.

He simply wouldn't need to know about it.

CHAPTER 17

few minutes later, we pulled up in front of a gorgeous grand hotel in Pasadena. By now I was used to the fawning service Richard got from valets and I dashed into a restroom in the lobby while he dealt with them. As I donned it, the fabric of the dress felt soft and substantial at the same time, and I realized that was what expensive textiles were like—just *different* from what I was used to. Sort of like the life I suddenly was leading.

When I came out in the shimmering blue dress with the pendant at my neck, Richard stood waiting for me in the lobby. His face changed when he saw me—his eyebrows raised, and a slow smile spread across his face. He held out his arm. "My goddess."

I smiled and let him lead me into a windowed area that looked out over lush green lawns and potted flowers arrayed around flagstone patios. The room was decorated with tufted white chairs and couches and it was beautiful. But by then, everywhere Richard took me was either incredible or beautiful or over the top, so even I was jaded as we walked in.

Then I saw the woman ensconced at a prime table by the window, the very table Richard was leading me toward. I would have noticed her even if we hadn't clearly been heading to meet her, as she stood out in the room. She was elegant—slender, with short gray hair beautifully coiffed in soft waves around her head. She was also very tanned.

"And this, my lovely, is my mother. Edna Bishop, meet Madeleine Miller. Madeleine, Edna." Without standing, Edna extended her hand to me and I took it, and then Richard leaned down and gave her a hug.

Some advance notice that I was going to meet someone as important as his mother might have been nice, but I managed to not embarrass myself as we made our introductions. Once we got seated, Edna nodded toward me. Her every movement was gracious, and by the look of it, she had given Richard his piercing blue eyes. Hers gazed at me, taking my measure. "You are the macaron baker, correct? Tell me a little about yourself."

I usually hate it when people say something like that. Because, where do you begin? How did I distill the essence of my life into "a little?" But there was something so warm and open about Edna, even in the face of all that elegance, that I found myself relating the story of the Portland bakery, how Will left and Jack and Daisie and I rocked on, and how Richard had appeared there one day and changed my life.

We were interrupted by a white-jacketed waiter bearing champagne, a pot of tea, and a three-tiered tray of tea sand-wiches, scones, and tarts.

Edna smiled and nodded in all the right places and when I was done, she patted my hand, then smiled at Richard. "She's a good one, Richard. I like her."

And was it my imagination, or did she give him a *look*? Raised eyebrows, quick dip of her head, a firm set to her jaw?

Like a look a mother would give her son, as if to emphasize her words?

But Richard blithely ignored her, gracing her with what I decided was a Mom version of the Private Option and then turning it on me. I smiled back and popped a bite of scone in my mouth. "So, you live at the ranch that Richard grew up on?"

"Yes," Edna said. "I'm at heart a ranch girl, though more and more these days my life seems to be taking me away from it." I pictured her in jeans and a tee, inseminating cows, bossing ranch hands, and mucking out stalls. I could see it. Edna emanated a sturdy toughness beneath her graceful demeanor.

"So, darling," Edna said, turning to Richard, "how is Grady? It seems like it's been forever since he and I had any time together."

"Who is Grady?" I asked. And then, I couldn't help it—I snitched another bite of the scone. They were almond poppy seed and just so good, like the proverbial melt-in-your-mouth good, like the Bonne Chance macaron good.

"How's your champagne, Mom? It looks like you need some more." Richard bent to retrieve the bottle from the champagne bucket and once again my imagination activated as I caught him glaring at Edna.

The look on Edna's face as she stared at her son was like that of an angry empress displeased with her subjects. "You haven't told Madeleine about Grady, have you?"

Richard's shoulders slumped. He poured himself more champagne and then offered some to me. I accepted, intuitively sensing that I might need it.

Edna drew herself up into an even more intimidating presence. She smiled at me and delivered her bombshell. "Grady, my dear, is Richard's son."

The champagne I'd been sipping at the precise moment

she delivered that bit of information dribbled down my chin. I wiped it away and kept the napkin at my face to hide the fact that my mouth had dropped open in a most unappealing way. It took me a minute to say anything and slowly it registered that Edna and Richard had moved on and were now talking about Grady's progress in school and how much he liked art.

Grady. Richard's *son.* His *child.* A very important part of his life—at least, presumably so—that he'd failed to mention to me.

"Um, excuse me for a minute, but Richard, really? You have a son that you've never bothered to tell me about?" The champagne bubbles buoyed me and gave me the courage to confront him. Because, really? Did he think I was so easy to distract? Just give me a pretty dress and necklace to match and call it good?

"Oh dear," Edna said. "It seems I've put my foot in it again."

Richard poured himself a half glass of champagne, all that was left in the bottle, and signaled the waiter for more. Then he took my hand and smiled at me. This time it was more like the Public Option, which meant he was going to dissemble. "Forgive me, Mad. You know how much I like to compartmentalize. I just didn't think you would have any interest in hearing about a teenage boy. I decided I would wait to mention him when the time was right."

"He's a teenager?" I cried. "You have a freaking teenage son and you've never mentioned him to me? Where does he live? And please don't tell me that he lives with you and that's the reason I can't ever stay at your house."

"Mad, darling." Richard put his hand on my arm. "He lives on the ranch in Montana. And, please, let's discuss this later, okay? I only have a limited time with my mother and I'd like to enjoy it."

I took a deep breath and pushed his hand off my arm, then turned a bright smile at Edna. Two could play at this game. If he wanted to save the discussion of why he had never bothered to tell me about his teenage son, the flesh of his flesh, I could wait to talk about it. But oh boy, would we talk about it.

"I'm so sorry to have upset you, Mad," Edna said. And even though she delivered the words in her contained, elegant way, I believed her. "And since Richard won't tell you, I will. Grady is a lovely young man, a junior in high school, interested in art. He loves Montana, where he lives with his mother, and prefers not to come to L.A. often."

I glanced at Richard and couldn't believe what I saw. He sat slumped—Richard Bishop, slumped!—over his champagne glass and as I watched he belted what was left in his glass down. It was a good thing he wasn't driving, I thought. And then I realized what I was witnessing: the awful toll it took on him to contain his private self into his public persona.

If I had been a smart woman, instead of one blinded by desire to save the bakery at all costs, and, oh yeah, let's not forget awe at the glamorous life I was leading, I would have stopped it all right then. Smiled and nodded at Edna as we finished our tea and then let Richard and the town car drop me off at home and hightail it back to Portland.

But I didn't.

I thought about it, because I was royally pissed. For a moment the thought of being back in Portland with Jack and Daisie and forgetting this crazy L.A. life seemed like the best idea ever. But then I started thinking again about how that might affect the bakery. How it might jeopardize this business relationship. How Jack and Daisie were all tied up with Carla now anyway. How it would be one more damn thing that didn't work out for me just when it looked like every-thing was going great.

And I had another thought, as I stared at Richard.

I decided that I could rescue him. That it was up to *me* to save him from himself, and that it was I who would help him unite the two dueling halves of his personality. I'd lost Will, and I'd lost Jack and Daisie, too. So maybe Richard truly was my destiny. After all, he had plucked me from the obscurity of an ordinary life in Portland, and didn't that mean that at least part of him desired to be more in touch with his ordi-nary life? I could help him with that. Yes, I could. And by the by, save the bakery and Jack and Daisie, too.

I leaned toward him and kissed him on the cheek. "You can tell me more about Grady later, Richard." I waggled my finger at him. "But I'm not letting you off the hook on this one."

I turned to Edna. "How long are you in town?"

She stared at me, her eyes steely. "For the next few days. I'm here to meet with my ghostwriter. I'll leave the morning after your grand opening. I need to get back to the ranch."

I started to comment on the fact that she was writing a book when she leaned over and patted my hand. "You're something special, Mad. Most of his women never challenge him on anything. Including Sa— "

And then the waiter came with more champagne and topped off all our glasses, then glided away after leaving the bottle in the ice bucket beside our table.

Edna took a delicate sip. "Now, where were we? Oh yes. You're a pistol, Mad. Lots of spunk. Please don't let my son change that. Now tell me, who is running the Portland bakery while you're down here?"

And even though I should have listened more closely when she said, "most of his women," I didn't. Instead, I talked more about Jack and Daisie, and how wonderful and unique

Daisie's ideas were. The conversation flowed on and the planet got tilted back on its axis again. It turned out that Edna knew a lot about baking and had taken a baking course in Paris as a younger woman, "though I've never attempted macarons," she said, and so we had quite a lovely time chatting. And through it all I could forget that Richard had a son he'd never told me about. *Almost* forget.

After an hour or so, we said goodbye and I was left with the feeling that she genuinely liked me. I knew I genuinely liked her.

Ensconced in the back of the car for the drive home, I snuggled into Richard's arms and leaned my head against his shoulder. "So, do I get to meet Grady some day?"

"Of course, darling," Richard said. Then he nuzzled my neck and kissed my ear. "But for now, I want to experience the jewel of your being."

I exhaled with pleasure at his quoting another Ford Dooley line and ignored the unbidden thought that he seemed to rely on Ford Dooley lines an awful lot. Then I leaned into his caress for a moment, but all that filled my brain was his mother saying, *Don't let him change you.*

"Does he come to town very often?" I gently swatted his hand from my breast.

"Once in a while," Richard murmured, his lips on my cheek.

"Next time he comes, I want to meet him."

"You will." His lips connected with mine and I gave into the feel of them. But then I thought of something and pushed him away.

"What?" he said, sitting back in mock anger.

"I don't suppose you have a daughter hiding away somewhere, do you?"

Richard laughed, a true, honest, open laugh that

reminded me of water burbling on a hot day. "No, Mad, no daughters. I promise."

"Your mother is wonderful. It sounds like you had an amazing childhood."

Richard leaned back against the leather seats. "We did. I spent hours outdoors with Rhonda."

At least I knew about his sister Rhonda. She was a midwife in Montana with a gazillion kids of her own, content to live a quiet life away from the limelight of her brother. Richard funded her clinic and contributed to a public health nonprofit that she ran as well.

"To us, it seemed like the whole world was our playground."

I squinted my eyes, trying to picture Richard romping across the rangelands with his sister. Couldn't do it.

"What?" Richard asked. "Why are you shaking your head?"

"You just don't seem like the outdoorsy type to me."

He angled his chin up. "What you don't know about me might surprise you."

I giggled. "Such as?"

"Such as…." And here Richard stopped and thought for a minute. "Such as if I had to choose between being an actor or being a businessman, I'd choose—"

"Acting!" I yelled.

Richard shook his head and stared at me solemnly. "I wouldn't be able to choose. I'd have to retire from both."

"Give me another such as." I was happy in the backseat, playing this game with Richard.

He raised his eyebrows, then let them drop down. "Such as, the reason I was keen to play Ford Dooley was that I wanted to be him. I wanted to be as much of a man of character and integrity as he turns out to be."

My heart leapt. "That's beautiful, Richard."

"I've got one more," he said.

"Lay it on me."

"Such as, from the moment I first laid eyes on you, I've been entranced. And all I can ever think about when I'm with you is this."

And then he kissed me. And I let him. And off we sailed, in the back of the limo, on the freeway.

CHAPTER 18

"Madeleine."

Will stood above me on the sunny beach, laughing. He reached an arm out to pull me up and I stood, then ran after him to the waves. He grabbed my hand as we raced into the water. Laughing, I turned to look at him. But he was Richard, not Will. And then Richard was clutching my arm hard and saying my name.

"Madeleine!"

But why did Richard suddenly have such a female-sounding voice? And how come he was now grasping me and shaking me? I opened my eyes. And saw, not Richard, but Fiona. I closed my eyes again, hoping that she was the dream and the part about Richard and Will on the beach was the reality.

"Open your damn eyes! It's time to get up."

Oh crap. Fiona was for real, not Richard/Will. But what was she doing in my bedroom? And, oh God, what time was it anyway? I rolled over and glanced at my alarm clock. Well, it wasn't really mine, it was Richard's, like everything in the house. Its digital display read 8:00. The bakery! I should have been there hours ago.

"Come on, sleepyhead, get up."

Fiona.

"Why are you here?" I asked her.

"We've got a meeting at headquarters." She checked her watch, though clearly the clock was in her line of sight. "In one hour."

"And there's a reason you're in my house telling me this?"

"Because you never answer your damn phone. Come on, Madeleine, we've got a full day ahead of us."

Even in my sleepy haze I realized something was different with Fiona. I squinted up at her. "You're not wearing any makeup."

She threw the covers back on the bed—good thing I didn't sleep naked—and pulled at my shoulder. "That's because you and I are getting our hair and makeup done later. After our facials. But first we have a meeting at headquarters."

"And you couldn't have told me all this ahead of time?" I asked as I swung my feet unto the ground.

"It was in the monthly schedule I presented to you."

I groaned, both from the shock of standing upright and the mention of Fiona's schedule, which she regularly sent me as an attachment on my email and I regularly ignored. It was likely sitting, still unopened, in my inbox. As long as I was baking every morning, and seeing Richard, I was happy. I tended not to pay attention to the rest of it.

Thinking of Richard, I groaned again.

"What's wrong?" Fiona asked.

I waved my hand. "Nothing you can help me with." Richard was the reason I'd stayed awake all night and hence overslept. Once I had laid my head on my pillow, all I could think about was Richard—and his son Grady. Despite my brave words to myself, I still harbored deep doubts. Why had he kept such an important aspect of his life secret from me? And what did that say about our relationship?

Fiona clapped her hands together. "Chop chop. Throw some clothes on."

She looked different without makeup, *very* different—more approachable and less British-y efficient and intimidating, I decided as I rummaged in my closet for something to wear and she kept talking behind me.

"Since you've failed to read my schedule, I'll review it for you. Meeting at headquarters, shopping for something for you to wear tonight—"

I turned. "Tonight?"

"No." Fiona gave me the exasperated teenage girl look. "Tell me you didn't forget that tonight is the grand opening of the bakery."

"Oh, that's right. But wait a minute, the bakery—oh crap, I've got to make a phone call."

"You can make it in the car, Madeleine. Honestly, get a move on. After the meeting and shopping we've got hair and makeup. Everything is scheduled. We can't be late today, so move it."

"Can we at least stop for coffee?"

"I'll have Hans pull through a drive-in for you. And bring a coat, it's cold out."

Fiona's idea of cold was anything under seventy degrees, but I was glad I'd grabbed a sweater when I walked outside and found that it was raining. I tried to remember—was this the first time it had rained since I'd moved here full-time in January? I put the call through to Jacques-Pierre at the bakery as we rode along the freeway into L.A.

"Sorry I didn't make it in this morning; I overslept," I said when I got him on the phone.

"We were told not to expect you to come in anymore," he said.

"And who told you that? Never mind, it doesn't matter. How is everything?"

There was a slight hesitation. "Good. Fine." Another pause. "Actually, it's not. And maybe you can advise me, since it's your recipe."

"What's wrong?"

"The shells are cracking once they are out of the oven."

"That's a problem with the macaronage."

Fiona raised an eyebrow at me. I covered the phone. "It's a fancy term for how you mix the batter," I explained.

"We're mixing it the same as we've always been doing it," Jacques-Pierre said.

I looked outside as a few drops of rain hit the windows. "You might have to monkey with the amount of egg whites you put in. This rain could be making a difference."

"I didn't think about that," Jacques-Pierre said.

"Being in L.A. you probably wouldn't. I used to have to adjust regularly in Portland, depending on if we were having a dry spell or our usual rain."

"I'll work with that," Jacques-Pierre said. "And Madeleine? Thanks."

"Not a problem," I said as blithely as I could, though inside, I exulted. Jacques-Pierre *thanked* me.

"Can I ask you something?" Fiona asked after I'd ended the call. I was surprised but pleased. Fiona never had shown the least bit of interest in finding out anything about me, or my life before I came into her tending. "Sure."

"What's it like to be with Richard?"

Well, you could have knocked me over with a wire whisk, I was so surprised at Fiona's relationship question. I squinted over at her. Even without any makeup on, or perhaps because of it, she was beautiful. Fiona had the English complexion that the term "peaches and cream" had been invented for, and her blonde hair fell just so at her chin. I could tell by the uniform look of the ends that it had been recently cut. I'd always been so intimidated by her that I'd never taken the time to really look at her. At the moment, her face wore a soft, far off expression on it, one I'd not seen on her before—or maybe just hadn't noticed. Perhaps the thought of a restful afternoon at the spa was allowing her to relax.

And then it hit me—that expression didn't stem from her excitement about the spa. It stemmed from pondering Richard. Was she in love with him?

I answered her carefully. "In some ways—most ways—it's everything I've ever dreamed of and more."

Fiona nodded her head eagerly, and her face was open and alight.

I gestured around the car. "I mean; I didn't ride in limos or go to all the most exclusive restaurants before I met him. And when Richard is with you, he's fully with you."

"I love that about him," Fiona said.

I did too. Richard's ability to make you feel you were the only person on the planet was one of his best qualities.

"But he's gone a lot," I said. "And..." I let my voice trail off. I was probably already saying too much.

"What?" Fiona had leaned forward, as if to catch every word I said.

Oh, what the hell. "I'm learning that with him, I have to settle. I have to be content with what he's willing to give me and not want any more."

Fiona nodded. "That's how it is with Ryan, too. We've been dating for a few months now."

"Which Ryan?"

She looked at me strangely and I remembered there wasn't more than one Ryan except in my own mind. I still grouped all of Richard's yes men into one heading under the name Ryan because I couldn't tell them apart.

"You know, Ryan. Richard's right-hand man, of course."

"He seems nice." In truth, he seemed like an insufferable, self-important jerk to me, but I could hardly say that to her.

"He is. When he's not obsessed with work."

I thought about Richard, constantly flying off to some city or another. "Guess it comes with the territory when you play with the big boys."

"Sometimes I think it's easier with women." Fiona glanced out the window, then back toward me. "Of course, then I get into a relationship with one, and it is just as complicated."

I cocked my head to the side. "But didn't you just say you were dating Ryan?"

"Oh, I can go either way. Story of my life—terminally indecisive."

"Hey, can I ask *you* something?"

"Sure."

"What's up with Richard's son?"

"You mean Grady? He's a typical teenager. Wants to be a comic book artist when he grows up. Obsessed with games and gaming." Fiona shrugged. "I've only met him once. He tends to stay in Montana with his mother."

"And his mother is…."

She curled her lip, as if the woman was not even worth talking about. "I've never met her. She doesn't like L.A., apparently."

"But they're divorced, right?"

And then Fiona's phone rang. Unlike me, she never kept it on silent. And she never didn't answer it. Her face changed as she reached for it. I could almost see the Fiona business mask return. All evidence of the personal Fiona fell away as she talked.

"Uh-huh, uh-huh, I see. Good. That will be fine. Okay."

She pushed the button to end her phone and pointed at me. "Pressure's on. The Cook & Eat Network execs will be at the opening tonight. We have got our work cut out for us."

And, just like that, the sweet, earnest Fiona was gone, replaced by the one whose eyes narrowed into dark, hard slits as she surveyed the wreckage (me) that had to be salvaged. I looked for that sweet, earnest girl all day, but I didn't find her again. Not during the meeting at headquarters, where I was handed a script—a script! —to memorize so I could spout it at just the right moment during the opening (which would be when Ryan and Fiona deemed there was a critical mass of people in attendance). She didn't reappear during our shopping trip, where my idea that a simple black wraparound dress with a lace cardigan over it would be just the right look was overruled by Fiona's insistence on a sleek burgundy number. And I didn't see the thoughtful Fiona again at the spa, where we had massages and facials, and I preened with pleasure at the luxury that surrounded me.

I pondered Fiona and life in general as I lay on the table being pummeled by the masseuse. Fiona had seemed so wistful earlier, so full of longing, and so open and alive. And then she'd shut it all down. Was that the price you paid for success? Surely not. Surely you could do it on your own terms, without succumbing to the strictures of others. However. All I had to do was look at myself as example 1. I was allowing Richard's people—Fiona and the Ryans—to make me over, tell me what to say, and how to run my life. And it was about to get worse, I feared, remembering the Cook & Eat Network's interest, which most of the time freaked me out so bad I pushed it to the recesses of my mind. But I was doing it for a cause, I reminded myself. As a means to an end—to save the Portland bakery, which was now doing just fine, I reminded myself for the umpteenth time.

When everyone was done fussing with me, I looked in the

mirror and gasped. The makeup artist had rimmed my eyes in black pencil and smeared my lips with red, which in my modest opinion overwhelmed my blonde hair, that had, by the way, been curled and sprayed and teased within an inch of its life. I looked like a little girl who'd gotten into her mother's makeup and put on way too much of it.

But Fiona disagreed. "Perfect," she pronounced. And off we went into the back of the town car again, to be signed, sealed, and delivered to the opening.

CHAPTER 19

"You look like a prostitute," Daisie said.

She stood outside the door of the L.A. Bonne Chance, alongside a phalanx of paparazzi who ignored us with great focus. They were no doubt waiting for Richard and some of the other stars rumored to attend that night. I was so happy to see Daisie I wanted to gobble her up, the way she was gobbling a pink-hued macaron. She wore a black dress with a lace collar that made me wonder if she were still in her nun stage and when she finished the macaron she paused and thought for a minute and then said. "White chocolate with a hint of cherry. Not as good as ours in Portland."

"And it's wonderful to see you, too, Dais." She submitted to my hug for exactly one second before she pulled away and held up a soft blue object. "My latest creation. I'm hoping Richard Bishop will want to invest in it. I need an infusion of capital to bring it to market. And then he can buy me out like he does with all his other businesses."

Lord, I'd forgotten how incredible Daisie was. I gave her

167

another quick hug. "Oh, I'm sure he'll be quite interested in talking to you about it. Um, but what is it?"

Daisie looked at me as if I were wearing a dunce cap. "It's a scarf with a pocket that folds up to be an iPad cover. Duh. Where is Richard? Why aren't you with him?"

"He'll be here eventually," I said, not wanting to admit that I had no clue when Richard would show up until he did.

"She insisted on standing by the door, waiting for him," Jack said, coming up behind her.

I caught my breath when I saw him. When had Jack gotten so handsome and self-assured? He looked spectacular in neatly pressed brown slacks and a dark shirt, a far cry from the plaid flannel numbers he usually wore, and his face looked clear and open, unburdened with worry and woe. Seeing him this way made me realize how much of a weight the finances of the Bonne Chance had been to him last fall. I threw myself into his arms.

"I cannot believe how good it is to see you."

He smelled like chocolate and espresso, exactly like the latest macaron flavor I'd been experimenting with, and I pressed my cheek against his chest, feeling safe and content and happy. I burrowed in deeper, content to stay in his arms. But then I heard a shriek.

"Your hair! Your makeup. Oh God, Mad, I should have known you'd go and hug somebody and ruin it all." It was Fiona, of course, and she yanked me away from Jack and pulled at my hair and pressed a finger to my temple to deal with my makeup. I glanced at Jack to exchange looks with him. But he was smiling down at the woman who had come to stand beside him. Carla.

I stared at her, trying to ascertain if she was the same woman in the indelicate embrace I'd seen at the coffee shop a few mornings ago. Maybe she felt the weight of my gaze because she turned toward me.

"Oh." She looked me up and down as if I were a supplicant come to ask the queen a favor. "Hi, Melissa."

But before I could open my mouth to correct her, she went on. "You really need to come see me for a reading." She jutted her chin toward me. "Because you have so much going on in your aura. Wow. I don't see that very often."

"A reading," I said.

Carla nodded. She wore her black hair loose around her shoulders and it had the effect of softening her features, making her even more drop-dead beautiful than usual. "I'm a spiritual counselor when I'm not acting. And a psychic. I could tell you a lot about what's going on in your life. But you'll have to come soon." She looped her arm through Jack's elbow and smiled up at him. "Because I'll be heading back to the film set in Texas in a few days. Jack, too."

"And what about Daisie?" I asked.

"Oh, her too." Like she was a flea. Or an unavoidable, uninvited guest.

In a move that made me believe there was a god, another partygoer jostled me and by the time we'd made our apologies the press of the crowd, which was growing larger by the second, carried me away from Carla. I looked around. The shop had been festooned with streamers and confetti sprinkled delicately everywhere. There were even balloons, elegant (if a balloon could be elegant) metallic-y ones. I had to admit it looked good—fun and happy with an L.A. sheen to it. Macarons were everywhere, plates of them in piles, trees of them, pyramids of them, circles of them. The space was so much larger than the Portland location that there was no problem fitting in the hordes who seemed to be appearing out of nowhere.

Across the room, coming in the front door, I saw my father and my sister but because of the press of the crowd I couldn't quite get to them. I did what any self-respecting baker of macarons would do—I snitched a macaron from one of the displays. It was a soft red color and I expected it to be berry flavor. With a good macaron, there'd be a bit of flavor up front, and then a full burst of it once you quit chewing. But when I bit into it, the taste was more like plain sugar. I closed my eyes, waiting for the pop of strawberry that would recall sunny days in June, with the promise of many lazy summer afternoons to come. But nothing came. There was barely any other flavor to it, and furthermore, it was dry and felt mealy in my mouth.

Oh, this was not good. This was not good at all. I reached around a portly woman in yellow and grabbed a pale green macaron. Key lime pie, I assumed. One of my favorites. I always made them with an earthy undertone and a festive top note. This macaron tasted only faintly of lime. The flavor, like the berry macaron, was not strong. And it, too, was overly dry. I looked around and saw Jacques-Pierre standing with a couple of the other bakers by the door to the bakery, all of them dressed in baking whites and toques. I made my way over to them, grabbing a glass of wine from a waiter with a tray full as I went. Because if bad macarons didn't call for wine, I didn't know what did.

"Did you taste the macarons?" he asked, as soon as he noticed me.

I nodded.

He shook his head. "We've tried everything. And concluded it's the almond flour."

"Could be. You're grinding it?"

Jacques-Pierre nodded. "Multiple times. As fine as I can." He tilted his head toward where Fiona stood with Ryan. "The bean counters made us change to a cheaper supplier."

"That's what the problem is. It's making a huge difference."

"Same thing with the flavoring?"

Jacques-Pierre nodded. "That guy—I don't know his name —checked over all our ingredients and substituted less expensive ones after the first financial reports came in."

I groaned, then grabbed another macaron, a yellow one, pulled it apart, and poked my finger into the shell. There was a big air hole in it. But, might as well test the ganache. I stuck my tongue into the creamy yellow.

"Oh, here she is. My darling Madeleine, you look stunning this evening."

Richard. I was so startled to see him—I hadn't noticed the hoopla that usually surrounded his arrival anywhere—that a blob of yellow ganache fell from my tongue onto my dress. Another thing to talk to Jacques-Pierre about. Clearly the ganache was too runny. Richard wore the Public Option and his eyes glided right over Jacques-Pierre and the other bakers, as if he'd not seen them.

"Madeleine." He kissed me on both cheeks, in the manner of the French *bisous,* and simultaneously turned me away from Jacques-Pierre. "I'd like you to meet Ted Palmer, vice president at the Cook & Eat Network."

I wondered if there were any way I could surreptitiously remove the glop of yellow frosting from my dress. But Ted leaned in and extended his hand and there was nothing to do but take it. "Wonderful to meet you."

Ted was impeccably dressed in a dark three-piece suit— no globs of ganache for him—and with such shockingly pale skin and black hair and eyebrows that he looked like a Mexican Day of the Dead sugar skull. When he smiled, his skin stretched thin over his facial contours and he looked even more like a skeleton.

"We're very enchanted with your macarons, Madeleine."

"Thank you," I said. "I do love me my macarons." And then, I did a minor little act of rebellion. "And you should meet the other bakers here as well." I turned toward the line of them in white, and said, "This is Jacques-Pierre, and Thomas and Ellie."

Richard nodded at them cursorily, but Ted smiled and shook hands with them, making some little comment to each one. That made me like him right away. The ever-growing crush of the crowd bore Richard away from me. For once I wasn't sad about being separated from him. I seemed to be attached to Ted at the hip, however.

"We truly would love to talk to you about your own show, Madeleine," Ted said.

"I'm flattered." Somebody bumped me from behind and I struggled to maintain my balance. Suddenly, and uncharacteristically, I wished for Fiona. Because what was I supposed to say to this person who seemed to be offering me a television show? I was totally out of my depth.

"But, um, don't you think viewers will get a little bored watching me make macarons week after week?" Way to go, Mad, I told myself. Talk him out of giving you the show before its even offered. I tried to recover. "Though I'm sure I can make the process fascinating."

Ted threw back his head and laughed a deep, hearty, belly laugh. The contrast between his sepulchral features and the jollity was startling—but it was also infectious.

"No offense to you, Madeleine, I find you charming, but watching you bake macarons every week would make the ratings plummet quickly. No, we have a bigger picture in mind—something about French culture. We're still playing with ideas. Are you interested?"

"You bet I am! Sign me up," I said. Okay, that was about as unsophisticated a response you could give. I mentally slapped myself on the forehead. "I mean, I'm not the world's greatest expert on France or anything, but sure, yeah, that sounds great."

And I was only making things worse.

But Ted laughed again. "Your enthusiasm is so refreshing. And now that I've met you in person, I can see for sure it is real and not staged. We'll schedule a meeting soon, okay?"

I nodded.

And then he was gone, weaving through the crowd with a dexterity that astonished me. For a man who looked as if he had one foot in the grave, he was amazingly frisky. I liked him. I allowed myself to think that maybe I could do a cooking show. I mean, why not? I looked around. A year ago, when I was mired in misery over Will leaving, who would have ever thought I'd be celebrating the opening of the second Bonne Chance bakery? My eye fell on a macaron display. My enthusiasm for the moment fell also. Because if we didn't get the current problems with the macarons under control, there wouldn't be a bakery for long.

I sipped at the wine in my glass, looking around for Jack and Daisie. After my brief glimpse of them, I hungered for more. I stood on my tiptoes, looking toward the front of the bakery, where I'd last seen them, but the crush of bodies was too great.

"Hey."

I rocked back down onto my heels and turned toward the voice. It was Tansy, erstwhile shoplifter, worker at the souvenir shop next door. She wore purple lace tights and a very short red skirt that barely covered her bottom. The skirt was one of her original designs, I assumed, seeing as how it was decorated with yellow flowers made from netting and stems made from what looked like pipe cleaners. Atop it, she wore a hot pink top and a jean jacket. On her head was some sort of hat with a black veil that she had pulled down to cover half her face.

"Oh, hi, Tansy. Thanks for coming."

She shrugged and raised both hands. One held a glass of

wine and the other a fistful of macarons. "Free food and drink."

I grinned. "Figures that would get you here."

"So, like, do you know all these people?" she asked.

I shook my head. "Some of them. But most of them were invited by Richard's publicity department. And, like you, they found the prospect of free food and drink hard to pass up."

Tansy's eyes darted around the room. I knew from our conversations at McDonald's that she was inordinately impressed with the rich and famous. I watched her as she watched the room. She was so beautiful, even with—or maybe because of—her fierce façade. But as I gazed at her I realized something was off. She didn't show quite her usual amount of bravado. And was it just me, or was that a hint of something black around her eyes? I looked closer. Tansy was not a girl to leave smudged makeup on her face. She was far too concerned about her appearance for that. But there *was* something dark there.

"I like the veil," I said.

"Thanks."

"But it's a shame you hide your pretty face." I reached for the black netting and pulled it gently. She jerked away from me, but not before I saw the reason for her makeshift veil. Beneath it she sported a shiner as black and blue as my licorice and blueberry macarons.

"Oh honey, who did that to you?"

"Nobody. It's nothing." She bolted the glass of wine, ditched it on a display, and turned on her heel. Then she fled out the front door, but not before grabbing another handful of macarons.

"Tansy, wait," I called. A flash of purple and the door closed behind her. I set my glass of wine down and went after her, finding her right outside the door, bent over at the waist. She held her hat in her hands, and they were crossed around her middle, her body heaving as if she was trying to catch a breath. Or sobbing.

"Tansy."

She looked up, and when she saw me, scowled, then raised her shoulder and wiped her cheek on it. When she faced me again her expression was stern and set. "Don't tell me to leave him. I don't have anywhere else to go."

"Oh, sweetie." I reached out to give her a hug, but she flinched away from my touch. A group of partygoers surged around us and opened the door to the bakery. Festive noise rose in the night air and then fell when the door slammed shut behind them.

"How often does he do this to you?"

She looked away and shook her head.

"Tansy."

Reluctantly, she spoke. "Only when he's had too much to drink."

"Do you have any family nearby?"

"Pfft. I don't have any family, period. My Dad's been in prison since I was a baby, and I haven't seen my real mother since I was six. The last family—" and here she used her fingers to make air quotes—"I had was a foster home in Diamond Bar where the mom drank all day, and the dad came into my room every night."

"Oh honey, I'm so sorry."

"Yeah, me too." She shrugged.

My mind was racing. What to do, what to do? What could I do? Have her come live with me at Richard's house? Yeah, that would go over big with him. Not that I cared. What seemed more to the point was that it would be a difficult sell to Tansy herself. Another group of partygoers surged around us. And then I had an idea.

"Listen, take my phone number. And then you call me

anytime, you hear? I mean it, anytime of the day or night. I'll come get you."

Tansy shrugged in the nonchalant way she always affected. But I saw a glimmer of light in her eyes. A glimmer of hope. It gleamed for one brief second before she shut it down again.

"I don't have a cell phone."

"You could call me from the apartment."

"But he's always there."

I screwed up my face. "Doesn't he work?"

"Some. He's a stunt man." She made air quotes again when she said stunt man. "But he doesn't have enough experience to get hired very often."

Oh God, this was worse than I thought. "You could call from the souvenir shop," I pointed out.

She tipped her head to one side as if conceding the point.

"Take the number, okay?"

Tansy nodded. I reached for a piece of paper from my pocket and then realized the getup Fiona chose for me had none. And I'd left my purse inside. "Crap. Do you have paper?"

"Nope."

But the look on her face made me even more determined, because it was triumphant. As in triumphant that I was wrong, and she was right—her situation was hopeless. I couldn't allow that to stand.

I held up a finger to her and turned my head to a clump of people standing nearby. I couldn't tell if they were tourists looking at the Walk of Stars in the fading light, or on their way to the grand opening. "Excuse me, do you have a pen and paper I could borrow?" I asked a tall man dressed in a three-piece suit.

He smiled down at me. "I have a pen, but no paper, will that do?"

"I'll take it!" He reached in his pocket, pulled the pen out and offered it to me. And, gods be smiling on me, it was felt-tipped. "Thanks, hang on just a second and I'll get it back to you."

He waved me away and shook his head. "No need."

I returned to Tansy just to see her hind side. The back of her jean jacket featured a huge magenta dahlia embellished with all manner of embroidery. She was trying to flee yet again. The girl was as stubborn as, well, me. "Not so fast." I grabbed her shoulder. "Hold out your hand."

She sighed heavily and rolled her eyes, the picture of a Valley girl, but she did extend her arm. I uncapped the pen and wrote my number on the edge of her hand, right below her thumb. "Now write that down somewhere as soon as you can, before it fades."

Tansy nodded. I stared into her eyes, wondering what secrets they harbored. Then she broke the gaze abruptly and turned away. "I gotta go."

"Keep in touch, Tansy. I mean it."

But all I saw was a spray of black veil as she bobbed and wove her way through the crowds. I watched her go as people jostled around me. I made my way back to the entry and edged my way in through the crowd, which had grown exponentially in the time I'd been with Tansy.

I felt at sea for a moment, like I was a D-list bystander rather than the so-called star of the party. The macarons were terrible, and I didn't know any of these people. And then a firm hand grasped my elbow.

"Dad!" I cried happily.

"Hey, baby, congratulations," he said, and then enfolded me in a hug.

"Oh, God, I've missed you," I said to him. "How are things?"

But as he released me from his grip and I inspected him, I

got my answer. Earl looked tired. And bear in mind, he *never* looked tired. His health regimes might seem crazy to some (or had a few years ago), but all the meditation, standing on his head, and intermittent fasting had a positive effect on him. Usually he looked glowing with health, lit from within with an unquenchable fire. But not that day. To my eyes, he looked shrunken, and sunken.

Earl wagged his head back and forth in response to my question. "Things have been better."

"What's wrong? Is it the financial stuff I read about?"

Earl nodded. "The retreat center financing is a disaster." He waved his hand. "But I prefer not to think about it. We shall dwell on more positive things. Like this wonderful new bakery you've put together."

"It actually sucks," I blurted.

Earl cocked his head to one side in an inquiring manner.

"The macarons are terrible, and the place looks like a kid's toy store. Despite my best efforts, I've had very little input into anything here." I grabbed a glass of wine from a passing waiter's tray and took a drink. I followed that with another gulp of wine and looked around. The party swirled around me, all the guests having a riotous, festive time when I felt anything but festive. But there was nothing I could do about it now.

Earl looked deep into my eyes. He shared that quality of presence with Richard, the sense that, despite being surrounded by hordes of people, in Earl's eyes, I was the only person on the planet. In his parlance—I had learned *something* from him through the years—it felt like he held a space for me and my concerns. And instead of trying to put a positive spin on things as so many people would have, he just nodded.

"I see," he said. He looked around. "And what are you planning to do about the situation?"

That was Dad, too, not letting me wallow in the situation, instead asking me to figure out how I was going to move forward. But before I could think of an answer, a clipped voice spoke in my ear.

"There you are, Mad. We're just about to put you onstage, okay?"

"Sure," I said. I took another sip of wine. I was feeling okay with the world. Dad's ear and the wine had taken the edge off my angst. "Hey, Fiona, this is my dad. Fiona, Earl. Earl, Fiona."

As the two of them shook hands, there was a loud screech.

And that would be my sister, Natalie.

"Baby sis! You are *tres amazant*, or however they say it in French. Congratulations!" I was gripped in another hug. When Natalie released me, her eyes fell on Fiona. The two of them stared at each other, and there was a little ripple in the air, like an electrical field.

"Fiona, this is my sister, Natalie. Natalie, Fiona."

"It's such a pleasure to meet Mad's family," Fiona said in her best British way. "She's the bee's knees."

I was? Was that a compliment? I sometimes had difficulty keeping track of Fiona's British-isms.

I watched as Natalie and Fiona shook. Was it my imagination or did the two of them grip hands longer than necessary? Finally, Natalie dropped her arm and turned to the woman beside her. She was as tall as Natalie but with red hair, like red hair the color of a brilliant autumn leaf, not red hair that you got when you were born. "Let me introduce you to Francine."

"Pleased to meet you, Madeleine, and congratulations on this lovely place."

I shook hands with Francine and shot a glance at Natalie. Was this the woman with whom she was having an affair? I looked for signs of intimacy between them. And then Natalie pulled another person into the picture.

"And this is Francine's husband, Dr. Nash, my department head."

That would explain the lack of a frisson.

"Lovely to meet you," I said to him. And then the conversation faltered. Because, what do you say to the husband of the woman your sister was having an affair with? I plucked another glass of wine from the tray of a passing waiter.

But then there was the whine of a microphone and Fiona saying, "Can you hear me? Is this working?"

A chorus of "yeses" greeted Fiona, who stood on a raised platform near the macaron display case.

"We'd like to welcome you all to the grand opening of La Bonne Chance bakery!"

Her words were greeted with a round of cheers and a few shouts of "ole!" and "hooray!" It seemed the crowd was well lubricated. I swayed a little as I listened to Fiona, then slugged the rest of my wine down. Was it my third glass? I couldn't remember. But when I saw a waiter near me, I pushed my way past a couple of people and grabbed another one. Because, after all, it was my party, even if I was unhappy with the bakery and the macarons. More wine seemed like a good solution to things I had no control over.

And then I heard my name being called. I looked around and realized it was Fiona, calling me to the mic.

"And now I'd like to introduce you to the force behind this bakery, Madeleine Miller."

More cheers.

"Madeleine? Madeleine? Where are you, Mad? Come on up."

Well, okay. I felt ready for anything.

"Let her through, people," Fiona said through the microphone.

And, amazingly, the crowd parted for me. I held my wine glass up high so as not to bump anybody with it, but I might have sloshed someone anyway. I found myself next to Fiona. I squinted at her. She looked as perky and perfect as she had the second we'd walked out of the spa. I glanced down at myself. And I, well, I was covered with yellow ganache and a dribble of wine and Lord only knew what my hair and makeup looked like.

Also, as I stood there, I realized that I was sloshed.

"Everyone, welcome Madeleine Miller."

I raised my foot to step up onto the platform but somehow the heel of my shoe caught, and I ended up down on one knee. A man from the crowd helped me up and then boosted me onto the platform.

"Whoops," I said into the mic that I took from Fiona.

Laughter and applause.

I held up a hand to stop the clapping. Alcohol loosed my tongue. "Thank you sho much. While I'm the so-called genius behind the bakery, let's not forget the man who had the foresight to bring me down here to L.A., Richard Bishop!"

Loud cheers erupted and mad applause.

From my perch slightly above everyone, I scanned the crowd, looking for him. But there was no Richard. I swayed from foot to foot, wondering where he had gone. And then someone opened the front door, and through it I caught a glimpse of flashes of light—the paps' cameras and the sound of a door slamming. One of the Ryans stuck his head through the door and said, "He just left."

I put my hands on my hips in mock anger. "Well, isn't that shomething."

Laughter from the crowd.

"Oh well, I guess we don't need him anyway." I leaned closer into the microphone and mock whispered. "Don't tell anyone, but we do need his money."

More laughter.

Fiona was grabbing at my arm. "The script," she hissed. "Read from your script."

I looked at her. What was she talking about? Oh, right, the little speech they'd handed me at headquarters that morning. I hadn't the slightest clue where I'd put my copy.

"This iff Fiona, my keeper," I told the crowd. "Only thing is, she couldn't keep me from getting drunk." I slapped my knee as if I'd just said the funniest thing ever. And the crowd did laugh. Hard. Which kept me going. I'm not sure what got into me except for fatigue, and yeah, alcohol. But once I sensed I was entertaining the crowd, I couldn't help it. I was on a roll and I went with it.

"Anyhooo, I'm supposed to read to you from a script, but I haven't the faintest where it is."

Fiona thrust a sheaf of papers in my hands. I looked at her, then the papers, and then the crowd. "Well, wonders never cease; here we go." I squinted at the paper and began to read. "Welcome to the opening of the Los Angeles Bonne Chance bakery. We're so delighted you could come and share in our joy at this moment. Please be sure to—" I stopped reading and looked at Fiona. "Really? You expect me to read this crap? C'mon, these people are smarter than that! Eat, drink, and be merry, people! Life is short, so eat macarons!"

And then I fell off the stage.

CHAPTER 20

I finished the blog post and pushed *publish* just as the boarding call for my flight came. Shoving the computer into my messenger bag, I stood, rubbing the remnants of the bruise on my hip from where I'd fallen off the stage a few days earlier, and straggled onto the plane with the rest of the passengers. I plopped into my seat, buckled in, and closed my eyes. Oh God, I needed to be back home in Portland so bad.

After the debacle of the opening—yes, I really did fall off the dais, and no I wasn't hurt except for the bruise on my hip but I had a terrible hangover the next day—I didn't see Richard again for a while.

"He had to go to Montana and then London," Fiona told me, when she would deign to talk to me again. I couldn't figure out why she was so mad at me. Yeah, so I'd gotten drunk and flubbed the canned speech I was supposed to give. But the opening had continued for hours after my indelicate appearance and was talked about in the gossip columns as the party of the year. The *L.A. Examiner* had even mentioned my fall off the stage, calling it "a funny moment by an endearing new rising food star."

Never mind that the macarons still tasted terrible. And never mind that I'd probably blown my chance at a Cook & Eat Network show. "We haven't heard a word from Ted Palmer, or anyone else for that matter," Fiona had told me when I'd inquired. And then she'd fixed me with her look, wherein she jutted her chin out and opened her eyes wide.

"I wonder why not," I'd mused out loud, and I confess, I did it just to goad her.

"Oh, bloody hell, Madeleine, are you really so clueless? Might it not have something to do with the fact that you got bladdered at the opening?"

Fiona's zero to ninety responses were always so satisfying and besides, who knew that bladdered was British slang for getting smashed?

"Everyone else seemed to think that part was highly entertaining," I'd said.

"Just follow the script next time," Fiona said.

The plane taxied down the runway. I'd planned the trip to Portland because I knew Jack and Daisie were back from Dallas and because I'd suddenly felt overwhelmed with L.A. Fiona was mad at me, Richard was gone, and hanging out at the bakery was an exercise in frustration as we still couldn't quite get the macarons right. Cheap ingredients will kill a good macaron (or any pastry) all the time. But when I talked to the Ryans about it, they just shook their head and mumbled things like "net" and "overage" and "bottom line." I'd planned to talk to Richard about it if he ever reappeared.

And then he had, a few nights earlier, all smiles, bearing gifts—chocolates from his favorite London shop and a beautiful lavender cashmere shawl.

Fiona had just pulled into the driveway to drop me off after an interview with a local journalist. Once in a while she decided to drive instead of relying on the limo or town car and it was always an entertaining experience to listen to her curse in British as we tooled down the highway ("Blasted idiot," "Bollocks," and my own personal favorite, "Learn to drive, you rat arsed wank stain!"). As I opened the car door, a sleek black Porsche zoomed into the driveway beside me, nearly knocking me off my feet.

Richard grinned behind the wheel. He turned off the engine, grabbed the keys, and hopped out, then flung his arms out wide. "My sweet Madeleine, it is so wonderful to see you."

My first thought was that I was glad I'd dressed up for the interview at Fiona's insistence. I glanced down at the spiffy black suit and robin's egg blue blouse I had on, courtesy of another shopping trip with Fiona. My second thought was that I was annoyed with him for ditching the bakery opening without telling me—and then leaving town for a week, too. And my third thought was that he looked amazing, exactly like Ford Dooley in the opening scene of *The Light of Day*.

He took me into his arms, and I inhaled his musky leather and orange scent, rubbing my cheek against his wonderfully soft cotton shirt.

Behind us, I heard a car door shutting. Fiona. Richard broke the hug and stepped away from me.

"Hi." He grinned down at me, then looked over at Fiona and raised a hand in greeting.

"I'm mad at you," I said.

"I can tell that by the way you greeted me," Richard said with mock seriousness and then grinned. Since Fiona was there, the grin was a cross between the Public Option and the Private.

I felt my cheeks coloring. I was happy to see him, but I was also still pissed.

"You left the opening without telling me!"

Richard changed the expression on his face to very serious and concerned and nodded. "I had to leave to catch my plane, my sweet."

And it was only as I sat on my plane remembering the scene that I realized something: he flew on a private jet that could leave anytime he told it to. But in that moment, I didn't remember that. I didn't remember anything, even Fiona, until she spoke.

"And you missed Mad's grand gesture," Fiona said.

Richard grinned at me again. "I do so wish I could have seen you fall off the stage."

"Fiona still hasn't forgiven me," I said.

"Well, the Cook & Eat Network guys loved it. I spoke with Ted Palmer on the way over. The show is on."

I jumped up and down with excitement and grabbed Richard and kissed him.

Fiona shook her head and stared at me glumly. "You lead a charmed life, Madeleine, I swear to God, which this just proves He doesn't exist. I shall take my leave now."

Richard waved his hand in Fiona's direction and clutched me to him as his kiss deepened. Oh, his kisses. They were sunrise over the ocean, a field of untouched snow glittering in the sun, a foggy morning in the forest. He pulled away from me briefly enough to say, "I'm so proud of you, baby," and then Richard and I were inside, and I was pulling off his clothes, and he was doing the same to me.

Later, after we'd made love and I'd risen from the bed and thrown together a quick omelet and brought it back to bed, I asked him if he'd gone to see Grady.

Richard gulped egg and nodded. "I stopped in Montana briefly. Grady's looking at colleges."

I clutched this tiny morsel of information to my heart and exulted. Surely it meant that Richard was now going to start opening up to me.

"I'm looking forward to meeting him," I said. And then, emboldened by Richard's admission about Grady, I went further. "And does his mother live in Montana?"

Richard nodded again as he chewed, then swallowed. "Hey, you know what would taste good right now after this meal? A macaron. Do you have any?" Then he leaned over and kissed me on the nose.

"I'll get some in a second. Does Grady's mother live in Montana?"

"Oh darling, why talk about her when you are right in front of me?"

I shrugged. "Because I want to know more about your life."

"Fair enough," Richard said. "I'll tell you over dessert."

But by the time I'd arranged macarons on the plate he'd come into the kitchen.

"I've had another lovely idea, my sweet. I'm going to make you my special Manhattan. I'm famous for it in many circles." He fluttered his eyelashes as if to indicate he didn't take that fame seriously, and then set about making it as he told a story about visiting Antarctica.

He handed me a glass.

"What makes it special?"

"Sip it and tell me."

I sipped it. The drink was delicious but since I rarely drank hard liquor I hadn't a clue. "Um, it's because it's so cold?"

Richard laughed, and ruffled my hair. "No, silly, it's because I use orange bitters. I buy only the ones made with oranges from Seville."

"Oh, of course," I said, with mock seriousness and Richard laughed again.

It was only as the plane banked over Los Angeles that I remembered how he'd managed to dissemble again, telling me about his orange bitters instead of anything more personal. And I'd fallen for it yet again. A relationship with Richard Bishop took a lot of work, most of it on my part, ignoring all his little idiosyncrasies. *They're not idiosyncrasies; they're manipulations,* an insistent voice in my head told me. Was that true? I didn't know. Probably. But what in the hell could I do about it? I was totally powerless in this relationship. I needed Richard a whole hell of a lot more then he needed me. Oh, I just couldn't sort it all out at the moment. I opened my iPad to read the book I'd downloaded in the airport—a novel about a woman who goes to Paris to live and learns how to bake.

JACK PICKED me up at the curb outside baggage claim and it felt a little bit like déjà vu for the last time we'd done this, back in the fall, when I'd learned about the problems with the bakery financing. Then it had been raining and cold. Now it was raining and almost warm—April in Oregon was as changeable as my moods. Inside Jack's oversized SUV he had the defrost on full blast to counter the rain, which seemed to be increasing.

I plopped onto the front seat. "Phew! It's good to be home." And it was, sort of. It was good to breathe the glorious fresh Portland air and it had been good to walk through our quirky airport—small, with a brightly patterned rug, and full of bookstores, coffee shops, and brewpubs—just like the city, minus the rug. But it was wrenching, too. I felt like I was watching a tennis match. One minute the ball was in the court of L.A. and the next I needed to whip my head around because the ball was in the court of Portland.

I looked over at Jack. He looked even more handsome than he had at the opening. How was that even possible? I sat in my seat and stared at him.

"Hello to you, too, Lenie." Jack grinned. He grinned! I was going to have to get used to this new, happy Jack. It was weird.

I peered into the back seat to cover my discomfort. "Daisie's not here?"

"She agreed to stay home and babysit the Italian Delight while I came to get you."

"Oh God, you made Italian Delight?"

Jack nodded. He steered the car onto the airport access road.

"And Caesar salad?"

Another nod.

"And your divine garlic bread?"

Nothing.

"You didn't make the garlic bread?"

He broke into a smile. "Of course I did, I was teasing you."

"I cannot wait."

"Um, Lenie?" Jack's face turned serious as he reached to switch off the defrost. "I've got to warn you. It's been intense here. There's some stuff going on."

"Oh, God," I said. "Good stuff or bad stuff?"

"It's good." The muscles around Jack's mouth relaxed. Lord, he was good-looking. Why had I never noticed? I'd always thought of him as striking at most. But looking at him now, I realized he was plain old-fashioned handsome. And his presence filled the car and wrapped around me like a soft down quilt.

"Tell me over a glass of wine then," I said.

But even so, when we pulled up in front of his house, the *For sale* sign came as a shock. I stifled a scream.

Jack stopped the car and looked at me.

"Um, I should say you've got some stuff going on. Jesus, Jack, you're selling the house?"

He nodded. "Daisie and I are moving to L.A. to be with Carla."

All I could think of was the time I'd seen Carla outside the coffee shop, wrapped in the arms of another man. "But you can't!"

Jack pulled the car to the curb and turned the engine off. "It's already decided, Lenie. Anyway, I thought you'd be happy. We'll be in L.A., and we can see each other more."

"But…" But what? I should be happy. But it felt all wrong. I shook my head. "I don't live there, really. This is my home. And you and Daisie being here is part of it. I don't want you to leave that."

Jack pulled the keys from the ignition and turned to me, the keys jingling in his hand. "So, what's the deal? We can't leave you, but you can leave us?" He shook his head. "Doesn't work that way, Len. You don't get to waltz around doing whatever you damn well please while everyone else waits for you."

A burst of wind rattled the car and a spray of pink blossoms from a nearby cherry tree fanned across the windshield. "But I haven't been waltzing around! I've been saving the bakery!"

"Right." Jack threw the car keys in the air and caught them in his hand, clasping his fingers tight over them. "Because abandoning us to hit all the L.A. hot spots on the arm of Richard Bishop is certainly working hard to save the bakery."

I opened my mouth to protest but clamped it shut when I saw the look on his face. It was Jack's Thor, God of War look, the angry thunder god expression. He fixed me with it then turned and opened the car door. I exhaled a long stream of air and my shoulders sagged. I heard him at the back of the car, opening the hatchback and removing my luggage. But I sat slumped in the front seat, thinking. *Had* I abandoned Jack and Daisie?

Jack came around the side of the car and opened the door for me. I'd forgotten what a gentleman he was about things like that. Even Richard didn't bother with opening car doors for me. Of course, he was usually too busy waving at the paparazzi whenever we arrived anywhere to worry about such things. This time Jack didn't wait for me. He grabbed the handles of my suitcases and dragged them toward the stairs to his house, groaning as he did so. I'd be staying here for the time I was in Portland since I'd found a short-term renter for my house for a few months. It was nice to have it occupied, even though Richard was paying the mortgage.

Jack paused in the middle of the stairs and looked back at me. "You coming, Len?"

"Yes." I jumped out and followed him.

Daisie waited at the front door to greet us. "Mad!" She threw her arms around me and hugged me tight. Such displays of emotion were rare for Daisie. I looked at Jack above her head as if to say, what's up with this, but he ignored me in favor of fussing with the handle of one of the suitcases.

Now Daisie clutched my waist and looked up at me. "Save me! You're the only one who can save me!"

"What am I saving you from?" I expected her to say she wanted to spend the day with me the next day and not have to go to school. Or to have me help her get out of her home-work—which Daisie generally thought of as useless and far beneath her—that night.

"Moving to la-la land."

Oh, Daisie. I looked down at her. "I thought you loved L.A."

"From afar, Mad, from afar." She wrinkled her nose. "I don't actually want to live there. It would mean I'd need to learn to drive, and I've been planning to hold out on that in favor of waiting for self-driving cars to become feasible."

I stroked her hair. I didn't want her to go either, obviously, but it was not for me to get between her and her father.. "We'll be close by." And even as I said the words I wondered if Jack would allow that—or if he'd want me totally out of his life so he could focus on Carla.

"I could come live with you instead," Daisie said. "And Richard Bishop could hire me as an intern."

Oh, God, I was so out of my depth here. I looked at Jack for help, but once again he ignored me. This time he busied himself hanging up jackets in the front hall closet.

"I could be your social media consultant, " Daisie said. "Cuz you need one. I have, like, seven thousand followers on Twitter. And you only have a few hundred. I'm going to master TikTok next."

"Dais—" I said. "I would so love to have you come live with me in L.A., but you need to be with your father. He makes the decisions about your life."

"But I have skills that could help Richard. I've already come up with a plan for how he could improve the performance of his shoe stores. And it just so happens that I've written a business plan for him to invest in my own product, the ScarfPad."

Jack turned from the hall closet. "Daisie, you are not going to live with Mad. You are going to live with me and your mother."

Daisie's nose wrinkled. "She's not my mother. I had a virgin birth."

"To your room." Jack pointed. "I won't have you bad-mouthing Carla that way."

Daisie stood her ground. "She's stupid and lazy, Dad, and she's using you because A, she's run out of money and B, she wants to get to Richard Bishop so he can give her acting jobs. It's ridiculous that you can't see it."

"To your room, now."

She looked at me. "Tell him he's crazy, Mad."

I chewed the inside of my lip as I pondered Daisie's words. It did seem synchronistic that Carla reappeared in Jack's life at the same time we met Richard Bishop. And I couldn't get the image of her with another man out of my mind—even if I wasn't one hundred percent sure it was her. I remembered Carla at the grand opening, telling me I needed a psychic reading from her. And now I wondered—was that an attempt to get closer to Richard Bishop?

I chose my words carefully. "Maybe you can come stay with me once in a while. And I'll see if I can't get Richard to spend the day with us—" I glanced at Jack, whose eyebrows were furrowed so furiously they were halfway down his face. Clearly, he didn't approve, but I plunged on. "—or you could shadow him at the office."

"We have to go back to Texas for a while first," Daisie said. "So she can finish her movie there."

"Well, Texas wasn't so bad when you were there before, right? I hear Austin is a lot like Portland."

"We're not going to Austin anymore. It's going to be Dallas," Daisie said. "Which is better for Carla, actually. Because there are more stupid people there."

"That's it, that's enough, you are in your room right now young lady."

Daisie stalked off to the stairs, waggling her head and muttering. When she got to the bottom of them, she called out, "I guess you don't care that my life is ruined. Now I'll never get to marry Benjamin."

"Go," Jack said.

"Who is Benjamin?" I asked as Jack ushered me into the kitchen.

"He's her boyfriend." Jack used air quotes. "At least Daisie thinks so, though I'm not so sure Benjamin does. I keep expecting his parents to take out a restraining order against her. You know how she gets when she's obsessed about something."

"I'm not obsessed! We're in love!" A voice hollered down from upstairs.

"Get in your room and quit eavesdropping," Jack called. "The sooner you comply, the sooner you can come down." He waited for the sound of her door closing to continue. "He's actually not what you would expect at all. He's handsome, popular, and a big jock."

"Really? That doesn't sound like her."

Jack pulled a corkscrew from a drawer and spiraled it into the top of the bottle. "Yeah, well, he's president of the Entrepreneur's Club."

"Oh, that makes sense, then." I took the glass of wine Jack handed me and plopped myself down in a chair at the kitchen table. Jack's house was old, like all the rest in the neighborhood. Correction—like *most* in the neighborhood. Recently, an alarming trend of developers buying up old houses, razing them, and building a bigger house had started. City lots were valuable because of land-use laws which prohibited urban sprawl. But Jack's house had been built in the early part of the twentieth century and its old charm lingered. The kitchen had been carefully updated and now was an open, inviting space. The table I sat at was surrounded by windows that overlooked the backyard on two sides.

"I don't want you to leave," I blurted.

"I thought we'd gone over this," Jack said, taking a seat across from me at the table.

"I was just thinking how great this house is and how you won't have any trouble selling it. And that made me sad all over again."

Jack reached out and patted my hand, then left his hand on top of mine. The gesture made my whole body tingle. He squeezed my hand and then withdrew his, and my hand felt suddenly cold at its absence.

"Things change, Len."

I nodded.

"And change is not all for the worst."

I nodded again. To my surprise, the discussion had made me feel teary and I didn't quite trust myself with words. I blinked my eyes a few times and swallowed. "It's just that there's been a lot of it lately."

He patted my hand again. "Everything is going to be fine, Lenie," Jack said. He looked at me seriously for a moment, then his eyes brightened and a smile lit his face. "I almost forgot. I have something for you."

"A surprise?" I said, happy to be able to clear the air.

He nodded as he rose from his chair, then held up a finger and disappeared into the hall. When he returned, he held a large box, which he plopped on the table.

"Open it." He handed me a knife.

I raised my eyebrows at him.

"Just open it."

I took the knife and slit the top of the box carefully, then grasped the flaps of the box to yank the clear packing tape away from the cardboard. A plastic bag full of something white filled the box. I peered inside, then untapped the top of the bag. Inside was a neat stack of folded white…. I looked farther…aprons.

"Oh my God!" I knew immediately what they were as I pulled one from the box and held it up.

"Oh, Jack, I can't believe you did this!"

I clutched the apron in both hands and stared at it. The exact replica of my most precious possession, my mother's apron, only hers was hand-stitched and these were printed.

But they were the same design as the original. When we'd first opened the bakery, I'd gone on a site that made custom aprons and created the design. Somehow Jack had found it and ordered these.

"I know you've wanted them forever. And now that we're running in the black, it seemed a good time to do it."

"They are perfect. Thank you, thank you, thank you!" I ignored the little niggling voice in my head that whispered, *too bad you rarely bake anymore.*

I ran to him for a hug, burrowing my face against his denim shirt, and then raised my head from his chest to look up at him. He stared down at me, our eyes locking. And then he leaned toward me. I caught my breath, because for all the world it seemed like he was going to kiss me. At the last minute his face veered away and he stepped back.

"I better check the Italian Delight."

I stepped away from him then sat back down in my chair, gulping a large drink of my wine. Jack fussed with the salad bowl, and I willed my breathing to return to normal.

THREE DAYS LATER, I sat back in my chair at the airport boarding gate with a contented sigh. The little emotional moment between Jack and me had cleared the air of all the weirdness between us and we'd ended up having a great time —walking to the food carts near the bakery for lunch and cooking dinner together. I even got to pick Daisie up at school one day and lay eyes on the vaunted Benjamin. He was short and slight—what did I expect for a twelve-year-old? —and had been surrounded by other boys his age. They punched and shoved each other, of course. But as I watched, Daisie walked up to him and he immediately snapped to attention.

"What did you say to him?" I asked her when she'd gotten in the car.

"I told him the stock market was way up," she said matter-of-factly.

"It is?"

"Oh, Mad," Daisie said. "Don't you pay attention to anything?"

And now, sitting in the airport, I laughed, remembering. I felt good about the time I'd spent with both Jack and Daisie, thank God. But the best thing was the time I'd spent at the bakery—my bakery, the original Bonne Chance. Oh, it was wonderful to get up early and arrive at the shop before dawn. The new crew we'd hired before I left for L.A. seemed to be settling in nicely and the macarons were delicious. I spent every second I could there and left satisfied that all was well.

Jack had dropped me at the airport early because he had an appointment—something about a preliminary phone interview for an environmental consulting gig in Texas. But I didn't mind. I never minded time in airports for some odd reason. I loved watching people and the vast anonymity of it soothed me.

I whipped out my iPad, wanting to go over some notes about the book I was writing. It cracked me up every time I repeated that to myself—*the book I'm writing*. Richard's people had been responsible for putting together the book proposal and finding my editor, Amelia, but now I was responsible to write. I found I was enjoying the process, and Jack and I had had some good chats about it.

Once that was done, I still had a lot of time until the plane boarded. I scrolled over to some local L.A. news sites, thinking I'd catch up on news from the Southland, as the TV commentators called southern California. I scrolled through stories on the L.A. *Times* website. Nothing much of interest.

Until the word *macaron* caught my eye. Oh nice, it was a review of the bakery.

But my original opinion that it was "nice" faded fast as I scrolled through the article. I read it all the way through once, my jaw dropping. This was not good, not good at all. The review mentioned the "geegaw-laden" décor of the bakery. But worst of all, they panned the macarons, calling them "tasteless" and "dry as the Sahara Desert."

I reached for my phone and punched the Fiona button.

"I was about to call you," she said when she picked up. "I'm just leaving an emergency meeting."

"I told you and Ryan we couldn't use those cheap-ass ingredients."

"We think we've got a solution, Mad. I'm sending a car to pick you up at the airport and we'll go straight to the bakery. I'll see you in a couple of hours."

Suddenly, it wasn't so much fun to be hanging out in the airport. The time until we boarded passed slowly as I fussed and fidgeted and worried about the L.A. bakery. And being on the jet for two hours was like an enforced prison sentence. But finally—finally!—we landed at LAX, and sure enough, there was Fiona in the town car waiting for me.

"We are confident we've got a great solution for this problem," Fiona said. "We're working it from the bakery end, of course, but the P.R. people are on it big-time also."

"I sure hope the solution doesn't have to do with more cost cutting when it comes to supplies," I said.

Fiona waved her hand. "You'll see."

We pulled up at the bakery, which looked like an Easter egg dyed by a crazed Easter bunny in the glittering L.A. sunlight, and Fiona led me through the showroom—which was as empty as an ice cream store on a snowy night, I might add—to the back. I was surprised to see the big work area deserted also—no Jacques-Pierre, or Ellie, or Thomas. There was however, one jacketed and toqued man standing in the corner with his back to us.

Fiona smiled at me. "Mad, meet our secret weapon, the big gun who can get this bakery back on track." Then she spread her arms out in a ta-da motion. The man turned around.

It was Will.

CHAPTER 21

Will.

Will, alive and well—or apparently so, since he had a huge grin plastered across his face.

Will, intensely handsome, with his glossy black hair, eyes the blue-gray of the Pacific Ocean, and the cool swagger of a man who knows the effect he's having on his audience.

And his audience? Me.

I'm afraid I exhibited my trademark openmouthed, eyes glazed expression. Because—Will? In the L.A. Bonne Chance? This was Fiona's secret weapon, the big gun, her answer to all the problems that plagued us? All I could do was stare and try to ignore the way every molecule in my body tingled at the sight of him, and how what I really wanted to do was fling myself at him and feel myself enclosed in his arms.

The very arms that Will now spread wide, in an invitation for me to hug him.

I stared at him. Oh Lord, he looked good—tanned and muscular and vital. I stood close enough to gaze into his eyes, and in them I saw the sun and the moon and the stars and all the planets, along with galaxies unknown. The answers to all life's questions swirled in those eyes. All I had to do was take two steps toward him, place my head against his chest, and all my problems would be solved.

But I didn't do that. I couldn't get my feet to move.

"God, it's good to see you, Mad," he said, awkwardly dropping his arms when I didn't immediately fall into them. "I've missed you so."

My heart tugged toward him. But then I came to my senses. This was Will, the asshat, as Daisie would say, of the century.

"Um, right," I said. "You missed me so that you ran off with another woman when I was pregnant and started a bakery in Santa Fe, leaving Jack and me with a massive debt to Mafia thugs. Uh-huh, I can tell you missed me a lot."

The expression on his face never wavered, the smile never faltered, and I wondered if he'd somehow taken lessons from Richard on how to present oneself in public.

I glared at Fiona, who stood in the doorway to the baking area, watching our little drama. "What in the hell were you thinking, bringing Will here?"

"I'm the only one who can bake macarons like you, Mad. I'm the only one who can save the bakery," Will said.

"It was Richard's idea to hire him, actually," Fiona said. "He agreed that Will, with his flair for the dramatic, could save the bakery better than anyone."

"Yeah, right, except me."

I stood there, feeling the heat rise inside me like water about to boil over. I'd been kept from doing my best talent—baking macarons—in favor of becoming the public face of the bakery, and now somebody else had been hired to save the Bonne Chance, when by rights that's what I should be doing. And to top it all off that somebody was Will. And Richard had hired him?

"Well, I certainly hope you stick with this one longer than you did in Portland," I said, then pivoted on my heel and fled. I couldn't trust that roiling water within me not to overflow and scatter over everything in its wake. And I would not be responsible for any more damage to the bakery.

And so, I ran. I flew out the front door and turned right on Hollywood Boulevard. What I needed, I decided, was alcohol. Wine would calm me and help me to think straighter and if it didn't, well, too damn bad. I needed it anyway.

The problem with relying on town cars and limos for transportation was that it made fleeing an emotional scene problematic, because I had no car to hop into and speed away in. So, I hoofed it. A few blocks down was a wine bar with a vampire theme that I'd seen as I drove past a few times and as luck would have it, the place was just opening as I arrived. No doubt in an hour or so it would be packed with gorgeous Southlanders, but since it was just four, empty tables beckoned. I scooted inside and found a table in the back, beneath an ornate chandelier.

A waiter recommended a glass of the bar's branded red and I agreed, and only after he left did I realize the menu listed an outrageous price for it. Oh well, I thought, pulling out the credit card Richard had given me to use for business expenses. I used the card very sparingly, feeling odd about it, but if this wasn't a business expense, I didn't know what was. It was a business emergency of the highest order.

I had just slugged down half the glass when I heard the front door open. I looked up from staring into the burgundy of the wine and there stood Will.

"Go away," I said.

But he didn't. He pulled out the chair across from me, then signaled the waiter and ordered the same thing I had. "I'll have another, too," I told the waiter and then I downed the rest of my first glass. The wine tingled and sparkled all the way down my gullet and the alcohol cleared my brain enough to face Will.

"Madeleine," Will said. He reached his hand across the table and covered mine. I snatched mine away.

"I hate you," I said.

"No, you don't, Maddie. You're angry with me now but you don't hate me. I know you—and you don't hate people. You love them, sometimes too much, maybe, but love is the only thing you know."

"For God's sakes, stop with the Hallmark tripe."

Will studied me and then sipped his wine. "It's not tripe, it's truth, Mad. And that's why I left you. You were way too good for me and I couldn't handle that. I've got a bruised heart that sometimes seeks darkness and I'm afraid that's what happened with Hilary."

I rolled my eyes. "When did you turn into a poet? Oh, maybe when you first decided it would be cool to shag Hilary? Or how about when you thought it would be fun to open a bakery in Santa Fe? Oh no, wait, I've got it—no doubt when you sold my bakery's soul to the Mafia? Jesus, Will, I can't believe you have the nerve to waltz back into my life."

And I also couldn't believe how dramatically he was affecting me. I pressed a hand to my chest to still my heart from pounding so hard, but that just made my stomach churn again. I glanced away from Will, toward the bar, where the sommelier was wiping the countertops and trying hard not to look at us while he listened to every word. I downed another slug of wine.

Will reached for my hand across the table. I pulled mine away from him.

"I know it's strange, me showing up here, Mad. But I'm through with Hilary, I promise. It's you I want. It's the Bonne

Chance that I want to help bring back to profitability. I'm ready and willing. I know I can make it happen."

I shook my head. The hell part of it was that half of me believed him—or wanted to believe him. I gazed into his eyes, wondering where the truth lay.

"When Richard first flew me here—"

"Richard flew you here to interview? When?" I demanded.

"Last week."

Jesus, when I was innocently having a wonderful time in Portland, Richard had brought Will in to talk about the bakery. Likely as soon as I'd boarded the damn plane.

"Yeah, it was great. I stayed at the Peninsula Hotel, and Bishop and I had a couple long dinners to discuss business. Hey, have you ever tried his special Manhattan?"

"You and Richard had dinners and drank his stupid Manhattans together? Did it not occur to either of you that you taking a job at the L.A. Bonne Chance might upset me just the tiniest bit?"

I could tell by the look on his face that it hadn't. But what about Richard? How could he be so ridiculously clueless to think I'd be happy about having Will onboard?

He couldn't, the voice inside my head intoned. And if it were true, it changed everything. I put my head in my hands. I heard the front door open, and the *clip clip* of high heels on the polished floor. I tore my eyes away from Will's and looked up to see Fiona approaching our table.

"Mad, we've got to get you home now because I've got another meeting. Will, I'll meet you here in the morning to introduce you to the rest of the crew."

When I did nothing but sit and stare at her, Fiona yanked at my sleeve impatiently. "Come *on*, Mad."

And then I got up and followed her because it seemed like the simplest thing to do.

. . .

IN THE LIMO, I thanked Fiona.

"For what?"

"Rescuing me from Will."

She looked at me like she hadn't the least idea what I was saying, then shook her head slightly and went back to the message she was pecking out on her phone. Her fingernails were so long I never could figure out how she managed that. Nevertheless, she obviously had no idea what a catastrophe hiring Will was for me.

"Whose idea was it to hire Will, really?" I asked her, hoping she would say it was the Ryans.

She quit tapping and looked up. "Richard's." Then she looked back down again.

"Jesus," I said.

"What's the big deal? He comes highly recommended."

"Right, by whom? The Mafia?"

"Mad, I don't understand why you are so upset."

"Because he's my ex. The one who ran away with another woman and dumped me and the Portland bakery like we were useless garbage."

"Oh," Fiona said, and then waved her hand, as she was so fond of doing. "Well, in this case, can't you just let bygones be bygones? The future of the bakery is at stake here."

"But I'm the one who should be tasked with saving it."

I flopped back against the seat. Fiona didn't get it and clearly wasn't ever going to. I closed my eyes, thinking that I'd take a little nap and forget that Will even existed and make my head quit buzzing. I shouldn't have drunk that wine so fast. And then my eyes popped open again. No way in hell was I going to take a little nap. I fished for my cell in my purse and pulled it out, then dialed Richard's number. He didn't answer, of course. He never answered. It was such a common practice of his, not answering the phone, that I rarely bothered to call him, figuring he'd find me or call me or text me when the time was right.

And now, sitting in the back of the car I realized what a passive fool I'd been. I'd let Richard have his way with everything, including me. While in the meantime, he didn't give a shit about anything except my business. I was as easy as adding one plus one. Well, no more. I punched his number again. No answer. Tried it again. Nothing.

Fiona looked up from her phone. "What are you doing?"

"Calling Richard."

"He won't answer," she said.

"He will if I keep calling him."

"Hand me your phone."

I thought she wanted me to quit calling him, so I hid the phone at my side, like a little kid would. "No."

"Give me your phone, Mad, I know a number where you might be able to reach him."

That got my attention. I handed it to her. She punched a sequence of numbers onto the screen and then handed it back to me. Two rings later, Richard's voice came through the phone. "Fiona?"

"No, it's Madeleine," I said.

"Well, what a lovely surprise," Richard said. "How are you, my goddess?"

"Lousy," I said. "I just found out who you hired to resuscitate the bakery. Which should be my job in the first place, by the way."

"Oh Maddie, I'm so sorry I wasn't able to warn you. But we had to move fast on this decision. Can we discuss this in person, darling? Where are you? I'm about to board the plane for L.A., so how about I pick you up tomorrow?" There was a pause, as if he were checking his watch, or a schedule. "Is ten too early?"

He sounded genuinely concerned about my anger, like the contrite Richard I'd learned to love.

"Um, ten would be good."

Fiona screamed.

"Wait a second, Richard." I covered the phone and looked at Fiona. "What?"

"You can't meet Richard at ten because you have the freaking audition tomorrow morning."

"Audition?"

"For Cook & Eat!"

Oh, God. I'd totally forgotten about that in the rush of seeing Will.

I uncovered the phone. "Fiona says—"

"I know, I heard her. What about we meet for lunch after? I can come pick you up and take you to Kitt's. You've not experienced a meal there yet."

I'd heard amazing things about Kitt's, how their burgers were topped with unusual items like beets and cauliflower and the fries were made from apples and peppers. People stood in line for hours to get in at lunch. Of course, that wouldn't happen with Richard. He'd be ushered right in to the best table.

I started to agree. But then I stopped. Because, it dawned on me again that this was the man who had hired my ex-husband and was now trying to sweet-talk his way around it. Who thought he could manipulate me any way he wanted—and so far, had been right. But no longer, I vowed.

"No."

"No?" Richard asked.

"That's right, no. You're not going to come sweep me off my feet once again, Richard. We are going to meet some-where of my choosing and talk. And I will drive myself there."

I needed this to be on my own terms. My words were met

with silence and finally, "Okay. And where, pray tell, would you like to meet?"

Oh God, I hadn't thought that far. But then I had an idea. I quickly scrolled through my phone for the address and gave it to him.

"Sounds good. Can't wait to see you, babe," he said. And then the phone disconnected.

"You're meeting Richard Bishop at McDonald's?"

"How'd you figure that out?"

She held up her phone.

I shrugged. "It's where I take Tansy. And I figured it wouldn't hurt for him to see how the other half lives."

Fiona rolled her eyes and went back to her phone.

"Hey, what number was that you called?" I asked her.

"Oh, it's just his secret line that he can always be reached at. I'll probably get in trouble for dialing it for you, it's meant to be for business only."

I remembered to thank her for the chance she took before I huddled and glowered about the fact that she had access to his secret line, but I didn't. I also berated myself something fierce—what was I thinking, asking him to meet me at McDonald's? Oh well, it had seemed like a good idea at the time. When we got to the house, the driver carried my bags in and I waved goodbye to Fiona and then flopped on the couch in the living room. What a day. What a freaking day.

CHAPTER 22

$\mathcal{Y}$ou've probably heard how hot it is under the lights of a television set but hearing about it and experiencing it are two different things. When they say it's hot under the lights, it is hot.

As Fiona would say, *freaking* hot.

Sweat rolled down my back and sides and I blessed the little black dress I'd bought on a shopping trip with Fiona a couple weeks back, because it wouldn't show the perspiration.

They'd told me that the set we were using had been designed for a cupcake baking show, but it fit right in with the aesthetic of the Bonne Chance. It featured blue striped wallpaper and pink window shades, a sink, and accessories, and I swear all the baking utensils were the same salmony pink, which amazed me. Maybe it was the similarity to the color scheme at the Portland bakery, or perhaps it was because I was still stewing about Will—but for some reason I wasn't nervous. I smiled and nodded and mixed macarons— this time the prep person had arranged everything just right —and chatted about my favorite places to visit in Paris, the little café called LouLou on the Left Bank, the store on the Boulevard Haussmann that sold wonderful journals and stationery, and the flagship Ladurée store on the Champs Elysees—the mother ship of all macaron stores, in my humble opinion.

Suddenly, I realized I was in that lovely place that seems so difficult to get to and is so wonderful when you do—the place where you've let go of all attachment to what happens. It was the state of being Natalie had been talking about, the one my father always went on about. It was the best place to be ever. Because, I realized as I chattered and piped, that I just didn't care. If I got the show, it would be wonderful. And if I didn't, I'd do something else. Like bake. I'd go back to Portland and return to the original Bonne Chance and bake my macarons and I'd be happy. I nodded my head to myself. Yep, that's what I'd do—it's what I should have done long ago. I'd let Richard lead me away from all that I loved most with the promise of a glittery, luxurious life, a life that I never felt comfortable in.

"That's a wrap!" the producer called.

And that's when I heard it—applause. People on the set were clapping for me. I couldn't believe it, but apparently, I had nailed the audition. I said "thank you" to the dark space beyond the lit-up set, took a deep breath, grabbed a pink dish towel, and mopped sweat off my forehead.

"Great job, Madeleine," the producer called. "We'll be in touch shortly."

Fiona appeared out of nowhere. "Hard as it is for me to believe, you actually did an amazing job, Mad. Richard will be very pleased."

I cast a stink eye at her. "I don't give a rip what Richard thinks."

"C'mon." She pulled at my sleeve. "Let's go get a cup of

tea." She looked at her watch. "You still have time before you have to meet Richard at…McDonald's."

"Can we make it coffee?"

Fiona laughed. "Of course."

We found a cute coffee shop near the studio. And for once we didn't talk about the bakery or her next plans for me or what was up on the schedule. Instead, we talked about ourselves. I told her about growing up in Portland—how difficult it had been when my mother died, but how great Earl had been as a father. I talked about how close Natalie and I had always been, but how much I missed having the chance to know Cecily. And how odd it had been when Earl suddenly became very famous very fast. For once I didn't talk about Will, because right then, everything that had come before him seemed to be more interesting.

And she talked, too, amazingly enough. She told me about growing up in a dirt-poor part of London and seeing Richard Bishop on TV one night—the TV that her invalid mother always had blaring—and realizing that she could make something of herself, too. How from that point on, she quit rousting about with druggie friends and began to focus, getting her grades high enough that she passed the A levels and went on to university instead of straight into the workforce. From then on, her singular goal was to work for Richard Bishop, no matter what it took. She'd ignored family, friends, a social life, everything, to get to where she was. Which explained her ability to be so single-minded.

"And is working for Richard everything you thought it would be?" I asked her. I took a sip of my latte and looked at Fiona over the rim.

"Oh, it is!" Fiona smiled, but her enthusiasm seemed forced, and as I watched, her smile faded, and she took a large drink of tea. "At least it was."

"What do you mean?"

She set her teacup on the table and gazed across the room. "I'm not really sure. It's just a feeling I've had lately." She turned her head to gaze at me, brushing her bangs from her face as if to see me more clearly. "Sometimes it rankles me the way he treats people. I don't know." She sipped her tea. "It never used to bother me, but…"

I leaned toward her, eyebrows up, trying to be encouraging without interrupting.

"It's just…Okay, I'll just say it. I've grown fond of you and your lot, you see, and it's hard to watch him do his usual thing with you. That's all."

I set my glass down. "His usual thing?"

But, once again, my window of opportunity into Fiona's true thoughts seemed to shut down as quickly as it had opened. Her eyes, bright and lively moments before, glazed over, and she tipped her cup up to drink what little remained in the bottom, then set it harshly on the table.

"Let's go. You've got to get to your date." She used air quotes as she said the last word. I marveled at the sudden change in her as I followed her out the door.

I SAID goodbye to Fiona and found my own way back to my car, checking my phone as I walked. Which is why I nearly bumped into someone as I neared the parking lot. I looked up. Oh God, it was that odd journalist.

He stood before me with the same black messenger bag over his shoulder, the same notepad and pen in his hand. All he needed was a raincoat and fedora to look like an old-fashioned reporter from a detective novel. He stuck out his hand. "Winston Herman from the L.A. *Times*."

I kept walking, ignoring his extended hand. "I remember."

"I heard you just had an audition here at the Cook & Eat Network," he said.

I scowled at him. How did he know that? But probably the best tactic was to remain silent.

"Did Richard Bishop arrange that for you?"

The parking lot was in sight. My car was located on the edge of it. Just a few more steps.

"And how are you feeling about your relationship with Richard now that the bakery is struggling?"

I shot Winston what I hoped was a scathing look. "I am not going to talk to you, so you might as well just give up." And there, thank God, was my car. I opened the door and got in. Just as I shut the door Winston yelled, "You have my card if you change your mind." I slammed the door, and then watched out the window as he walked away. But then I rolled the window down and called after him.

"Winston!"

He paused midstep and looked over his shoulder. I motioned to him with my finger and he scurried back to the car.

"Remind me what your Richard Bishop story was about?"

His face lit up like a shooting star streaking across the sky. "How he romances female entrepreneurs like you."

I tapped a finger on the steering wheel. "And what is so bad about that?"

"I have evidence that he establishes relationships with women to take over their businesses."

"But that doesn't make any sense. If it were true, he'd have a whole stable of such businesses in his portfolio." Richard might be focused on business to the point at which he lost sight of the impact his actions had on people, but I couldn't see him actually destroying them. It was hard for me to imagine him being quite so conniving.

Winston leaned one hand against the car. "What I've discovered is a pattern of these businesses failing. It may not be intentional on his part, but it happens all the same. Once the business falters even a little, Bishop gets bored and moves on."

A worrisome niggle gnawed at the pit of my stomach. The Bonne Chance was faltering…a little, anyway. But I shook my head, refusing to believe it. "You're wrong."

"But your own bakery is proof, isn't it?"

No, I wouldn't listen to him any longer. I started to roll the window up. He put a hand out to stop it.

"All I need is one more interview to complete the story. Yours. His current girlfriend. And then we're going to print with it in a few days."

I shook my head harder. "No, I won't talk to you."

I started to raise the window, and he chucked a business card through it before it was fully closed. The card landed on the passenger seat. I stuffed it in my bag as I watched Winston trudge off. The niggle in my stomach had turned into a noisy rumble. I slapped my tum and put my car into gear.

But then I decided I was through with allowing men to ruin my life. No need to change plans. I would damn well sit in my car and check my messages, as I'd been meaning to do before Winston interrupted me. I put the car back in park and looked at my phone. A call from Natalie, no message; a call from Dad, glory be; and five hundred texts from Will. Well, maybe more like five. But still. I kept scrolling through the notifications and found one from a number I didn't recognize. Whoever it was left a message, so I clicked over to my voice mail.

A sweet, high voice sounded through the phone. "Oh hi, um, Madeleine? It's Tansy here." There was a long pause and the sound of people talking in the background. I narrowed my eyes, listening. She must have been calling from the souvenir shop. "There's nothing wrong or anything, I promise. I just wanted to call to make sure I had your phone number right. See ya!"

I looked at the phone. The message had come in two days ago. Damn it, I had to get better about checking with my phone. Hot friend I was—I'd given Tansy my number in case anything went wrong in her life and then I never bothered to answer calls. Just to check, I dialed the number back. But the person who answered said that Tansy was busy helping customers and couldn't come to the phone. I left a message for her, just in case.

And then I went on my merry way. Actually, the only merry thing about it was that there were french fries at my destination.

CHAPTER 23

I sat inside the McDonald's I'd visited so often with Tansy, drumming my fingers on the table with one hand and sipping a Diet Coke from the other. I'd ordered two supersized Big Mac meals and, thoughtfully, even made sure we had ketchup to go with them. In truth, I myself did not usually visit McDonald's all that often—though I'd eaten here a lot more since the advent of Tansy in my life. I frowned, thinking of the number of fries I'd eaten over the last months. I pinched the skin at my waist. Probably time to lay off them.

But first I needed to make my point with Richard.

If he ever arrived.

And if I ever figured out exactly what my point was. Something to do with bringing him down to the planet where real people lived and ate at fast food restaurants. And, oh yeah, meeting him on my own terms.

To talk about what a rat he was for hiring Will.

But maybe he wasn't going to show. I patted one of the Big Mac boxes. The food was getting cold. I checked my watch. He was five minutes late. If there was one thing Richard Bishop insisted on, it was timeliness. "I learned long ago, Maddie, that one should not only be on time, but strive to arrive early. It indicates such seriousness of intent."

At the time he'd uttered those lines to me I'd been scrambling to write them down for Daisie, so I hadn't noticed how ridiculously pompous they sounded. Now, I shook my head. Sometimes—often—the things Richard said sounded like a screenwriter who'd stayed up too late had written them. Why was I only just now realizing that?

I drummed my fingers harder and looked out the window. And there, sure enough, was a long black limo pulling into the parking lot. Leave it to Richard to choose a limo over a town car or driving himself. The better to emphasize his exalted status over the mere mortals who frequented Mickey D's?

The chatter of people around me fell to a hush as he walked in, grinning the Public Option, as he looked all about him, like a king blessing the serfs with his presence.

"It's Richard Bishop!" someone said.

Richard waved in his direction, then pivoted his head and waved in the other direction for good measure. I remembered when I'd first seen him alight in the Bonne Chance all those months ago. What had thrilled me then had grown tarnished. I shook my head. No, I still loved him. Didn't I?

"Rich jerk," I heard a woman near me say.

"Thinks his shit don't stink," a man answered her.

I winced, hoping Richard didn't hear and that they wouldn't keep up with their cranky comments when he sat down.

And then he stopped at the table and grinned down at me. I stood and allowed myself to be enfolded in a hug. He smelled, as usual, like orange and leather, which I knew came from a special kind of aftershave he bought in London. His shirt—one of his signature black tees—felt as soft as a worn apron against my cheek.

Richard stepped back first, then displayed the Public Option in blinding force. "Oh Maddie, you always like to surprise me, don't you? Coming here is genius. I do so like to keep in touch with the ways of real people. And you've given me an opportunity to do that."

I sat back down, hoping the so-called real people around him didn't hear his tripe about keeping in touch with them.

"So, refresh my memory as it's been a while. How does one order in a place like this?"

I waved my hand at the food on the red tray. "I took care of it. All you have to do is eat."

He stared at the molded plastic of the booth for a second, then grabbed a napkin from the wad on the tray and used it to wipe the seat before sliding in. I handed him a Coke. It was gargantuan. He held the cup at arm's length and inspected it, then took a careful sip through the straw I'd stuck in and managed a smile.

"And what have we here?" He pointed to the array of cardboard boxes and paper bags of fries.

"I got us both Big Mac meals. Supersized. Because the fries are so good, you're going to want a ton of them." Ostentatiously, I popped one in my mouth, and followed it with another one. "Mmm. So delicious. Try one."

For one fleeting moment, a look of distaste crossed his face, quickly followed by his usual composed mien. He reached for a fry.

"They're good with ketchup, too."

He set the fry down and picked up the ketchup packet instead, then fumbled as he tried to tear the plastic.

"How do you do this?" And just as he said it, the packet

opened, and red squirted all over his hands and the paper on the tray.

I heard someone nearby snickering. I figured it was the couple who'd made snide comments about him as he walked in.

"Those little guys can be a pain." I handed him a napkin.

Richard wiped his hands and then heaved a sigh, squared his shoulders, and looked at me. "So, Maddie."

"I want to eat before I talk, Richard."

Actually, I didn't care much about the food at the moment. But I was enjoying Richard's discomfort, because it was the first time I'd actually seen him wear it. Richard out of his element was as rare as snow in L.A. I took a bite of my Big Mac and allowed a look of rapture, or so I hoped, to cross my face.

"Try it," I commanded.

Richard opened the box and pulled the burger out, spilling the layers all over the tray.

More snickers from around us.

He took one bite of bun, then set it back down.

"Num."

It was the most half-hearted "num" I'd ever heard.

I was leaning toward putting him out of his misery, but he managed to speak first, probably because I had a mouthful of burger. Which was, I have to say, truly delicious.

"Thank you for agreeing to come here with me," Richard said, raising his paper cup full of Coke in a salute. Wait a minute. He'd agreed to come here with me, not vice versa. I started to protest but his next words stopped me.

"And now, shall we have that conversation about your ex-husband?"

"Yes, we shall." I set my food down and nodded. "I just can't understand why in the hell you thought hiring him was a good idea."

He stared into his drink then raised his gaze to mine. "Bakery sales have gone down, and we don't seem to be able to get the macarons to taste right. And, darling, I know that's your area of expertise." He sipped his drink. "It's your recipe, after all. But with you as the face and brand of the bakery, we simply can't have you spending all your time behind the scenes. I felt strongly that we needed to hire someone to take your place."

"But it's the baking that I love. I don't want to be the face and brand of the bakery. I want to bake."

And then his phone rang. He glanced at it and for one swift moment looked askance. He composed himself quickly and said, "I must take this, Mad. It will only be a minute." He stood, turned his back to me, and dipped his head as if he was trying to speak so nobody could hear.

At least we'd gotten the conversation about Will started. While he took the call, I picked up my phone to pass the time and realized I'd missed a text from Daisie. *Help! I can't stand living here in the land of big hair and bigger boobs!*

I smiled and shook my head. How I wished I could do something about her having to live with Carla. *Let's plan for you to visit L.A. soon.*

I got a smiley face emoticon and a whole row of hearts in return. I set my phone down and my ears picked up on Richard's conversation. He stepped a little farther away and perched at an empty table. Even so, I could hear bits and pieces, which seemed mostly to be about convincing somebody not to do something. I heard the word *no* a few times and, "this is not a good time."

Richard returned to the table, stashing his phone in the pocket of his jeans, and sliding back into the booth. He popped a fry in his mouth and then took a drink of Coke.

"I just had an idea," he said.

I cocked my head as if to ask what.

"I've just booked a room for you at your favorite hotel."

I must have looked at him blankly.

"The Peninsula. Where you stayed in October."

"But why would I want to do that?"

Richard took my hand across the table. I dropped the fry I'd been about to stuff in my mouth.

"I know things have been stressful for you lately, darling, and this would be a chance for you to recuperate. Hang out at the hotel pool, get room service, laze about." He grinned at me, a small boy pleased beyond measure with himself.

I remembered the downy white beds at the hotel, how soft the sheets had felt against my skin and the mattress that was the perfect hardness. And the shower! The nozzle had a spray I could adjust to prickle my skin or soothe it, and endless hot water. It sounded wonderful.

"You can get a massage and a facial at the spa."

I smiled dreamily, relaxing just at the thought. "I'll need to run by the house and get clothes. And toiletries. And other things I need."

"Oh no, darling. We'll have someone run by and pick some up for you. And you can just leave your car here and one of my people will deal with it."

"What about the bakery? I need to be able to get to the bakery."

Richard waved his hand. "We've got people who will drive you. I'll put one of my men at your beck and call. You can go bake to your heart's content." Then he leaned forward and clutched both my hands in his. "Although it seems to me you might want to take a well-earned break."

"Yeah, and thanks to you, my rat of an ex will be at the bakery." I shook my head. "I just don't think hiring Will was a good idea. Beyond the fact that he's my ex, he can be flaky."

"We'll see about that. Maddie, I have a suggestion. Stay at the hotel and relax for a few days. Think about things. Think about all the good you can do for us in the public realm, and what a relief it will be for you to have someone shepherding your macarons. And then, if you're still upset about it when I return from Zurich, we'll take action, I promise. But please do promise you will ponder how you can best represent us."

Us. Who did he mean by *us*? Did he mean him and me, or did he mean the Bonne Chance? The way he said it—the subtle intonation of his words—made it sound like he meant them, as in his company, as if I were an employee of his, not the founder and owner of the Bonne Chance bakery. I stared out the window for a minute to gather my thoughts.

"So, it's settled then? You'll stay at the hotel a few days?"

I started to say yes, pulled by the thought of diving into that cushy pile of bedding. But then I came to my senses. He was just manipulating me again.

"It is a generous offer, Richard. But I think I'll just go on back home."

A fleeting expression crossed his face. But it was gone so fast I could barely register it—panic? Alarm? But neither of those were words that I would equate with Richard Bishop, ever.

"Oh darling, the car can take you wherever you want to go, even to the bakery. And give the driver a list of what you need from the house, he'll pick things up for you."

Why was he so insistent about me staying at the hotel, especially since he wouldn't even be in town? But then, I let all my doubts and concerns float away, out over the streets of L.A., and my brain slid back into its old neural pathways. I started thinking about maybes. As in, *maybe* he was breaking down emotional walls and was ready to let me in. *Maybe* he was ready for a deeper relationship. *Maybe* I was over Will. *Maybe* Richard was really, truly, one hundred percent ready to commit. And *maybe* I was, too.

But then I got hold of myself once again.

"No thank you."

A stricken look crossed his face this time. But that was his issue, not mine. I stood to go, suddenly unsure of where we stood as a couple. Because suddenly all my *maybes* were starting to look more and more ridiculous.

"Wait, Maddie." He reached across the table to me. "Sit, darling. I've another idea."

What was going on? I plopped back down.

"How would you like to see my other residence? The one at the beach?"

The big one. The fancy one. The one he actually lived at when he was in town. The one he'd never taken me to, despite several discrete inquiries on my part.

"You can walk on the beach, or laze about all day. My housekeeper Flora will take care of your every desire. You can't imagine how good her cheesecake is!"

Was it my imagination, or did his words sound forced?

He clutched my fingers. "Please, Maddie? I'll be calmer while I'm gone if I know you are getting some much-deserved rest and being taken care of."

I caved. The thought of finally seeing his house was just too much for me. I nodded my acquiescence.

"I'll send a car to your house and have them pick up your things. And we can go right there now."

"Remember, I drove, Richard. I don't feel comfortable leaving my car here."

He pressed his lips together.

"I'll go to the house, pack my stuff, and you can have the car pick me up there."

"No!"

I don't think I'd ever heard him so vehement. Richard was nothing if not a well-modulated human.

"Oh darling, I have only a few hours before I need to leave

for Zurich and I'd so love to spend every minute left with you."

Oh what the hell. "Give me the address and I'll drive there now."

He clapped his hands. "Oh wonderful, darling. It will be amazing to finally get to show you the house."

CHAPTER 24

I waved goodbye to Richard's limo, then got in my car and plugged the address into the GPS, following the directions onto the freeway heading west. I tooled along, pleased with myself for luring Richard to McDonald's—though come to think of it he never ate more than a lame bite of bun and a couple of fries—and eager to see his house. His real house. My thoughts rolled along on a pleasant course. Would the décor be Zen and relaxing? Mid-century modern? Or full of art and color? I was thinking sharp angles, tall ceilings, and massive windows, furniture dwarfed by the magnitude of the house.

A car cut into my lane, causing me to swerve. It also caused my brain to swerve.

As in, what the hell was I thinking?

I'd let him do it to me again. I'd let him manipulate me into doing exactly what he wanted, what worked for him.

No. No more.

I couldn't believe it. And why had he suddenly been so insistent on me staying either at the hotel or his house? Somehow, his explanation that he'd worry about me while he was gone didn't hold up. He'd never worried about me before.

Nope, this time I wasn't going to do it.

I was going to return home and relax there. Maybe I'd bake there, since I couldn't do it at the bakery with Will there. I nodded my head. Yes, that was the perfect plan. I'd call Richard as soon as I got home to tell him I'd changed my mind. He'd be off on a plane to Zurich in a few hours anyway.

Just in time, I took the exit to the house and exhaled with relief. This was a much better plan.

I TURNED into the area where Richard's house was located, down past the neighbors who had horses in their front yard and pulled into the driveway behind a large silver SUV.

I sat up. Now who would that belong to? Had Richard changed his mind about going to Zurich and somehow ended up here instead? Or had he somehow gotten wind of my plan and come here to talk me out of it? But then I remembered he didn't have an SUV, as far as I knew.

Well, I'd just have to go figure it out.

I always used the side door, which was a slider that opened right into the dining room. As I came around that side of the house, I noticed someone sitting at the table as I fumbled with the key.

A teenage someone, with a lock of dark hair that fell just so over his forehead, a detail I noticed as he turned to look at me entering the house.

Richard had a piece of hair that fell that way also.

"Who are you?" the boy said.

"Um, I'm Madeleine. Who are you?"

"I'm Grady." He stood and extended his hand.

Grady. Richard's son. But what was he doing here, at the house?

Just then a woman appeared from down the hall. She had thick wavy red hair that cascaded around her shoulders and a face free of makeup. She was tall and stockier than most of the women I was used to seeing in L.A.

"Hello?" she said. Then she looked me up and down and an expression of recognition shadowed her eyes. "I wondered whose stuff was in the bedroom."

"Um, do I know you?"

She reached out her hand. "Sarah. Richard's wife." She turned to Grady and said, "Hey, go hang in your room for a bit, okay?"

"Okay," Grady said, heading off toward the hall. "But call Dad, Mom. He's been calling you all afternoon. God. You could at least talk to him."

My mouth fell open. Richard's wife? I must have turned the pale color of the sand on the Malibu beach. I couldn't get my brain to connect. Richard had a wife? I'd assumed that Grady's mother was still in his life, but I'd also assumed that they were divorced.

"Oh dear," she said. "You're another of his conquests, aren't you? He didn't bother to say anything."

"Richard is married?"

Sarah nodded. "To me. For twenty years."

No wonder he'd suddenly decided it would be great for me to stay at his other house. It must have been Sarah on the phone when we were at McDonald's, telling him she was coming to town. What was it I'd heard him say? *This isn't a good time.*

I stared at Sarah. She had wrinkles on her cheeks and a neck that looked like crepe paper. No wonder she preferred to stay in Montana. And then I thought about the absolute arrogance of Richard thinking he could keep his wife and his lover separate. All he had to do was tempt me with hot tubs and massages and facials, and the thought of seeing the house he'd so carefully kept me away from.

"You must be his latest project."

"Project?" I asked.

"Oh, he's always trying to save some woman or another. Or so he thinks." She shook her head. "All he's really doing is trying to save his first wife, over and over. What did you say your name was?"

"I'm Madeleine," I said absently. And then, "God. I'm so sorry. I had no idea. I never would have—"

Sarah shrugged her shoulders. "Don't be sorry. It's the way our marriage works. You're not the first and you won't be the last. I'm here to catch him when he falls. Which is always." She peered at me. "What is it you do?"

"I bake macarons."

"Ah yes, the baker he was so enamored with."

"You knew about me?"

"Not really. Not in the sense that he and I discussed you. But I do follow his press."

"Oh, God." I felt my shoulders slump and my head drop forward. "I can't believe Richard would do this to me."

The frown that had dominated her face softened. "Don't hate him. He's not a bad man. Just a deeply wounded one. But let me guess. When he learned I was coming to town, he convinced you to stay with him someplace else, somewhere luxurious and wonderful, where all your needs would be seen to."

"Yes." Oh Richard, so transparent to all but himself. "But then I decided I was done with him manipulating me." I spread my hands. "He thought I was going to the other house after we left McDonald's, but I decided to come here."

"Wait." A smile played at the corner of Sarah's lips. "You got Richard to McDonald's?"

For a moment I forgot who I was talking to, and the situation, and I laughed. "Yeah, it was pretty great. Sadly, he did not appreciate the french fries."

"I would have paid money to see that," Sarah said.

I nodded, and then remembered again what was happening. "Okay then. I guess I'll just get my stuff and go."

She looked around. "So you have been staying here?"

I nodded.

"I thought so. I knew someone had been. I packed at least some of your stuff—the obvious things—into the suitcase in the closet." She pointed to my little pink suitcase, the one I'd so recently emptied from my trip to Portland. "I figured you'd be along sooner or later."

I nodded again, unable to trust myself to speak, then darted across the room to grab my luggage and the keys to the car from the kitchen counter. I paused and looked at Sarah. What does one say to the wife—the actual *wife*—of the man you've been doing the hanky-panky with?

"I'm sorry. I really am. I had no idea." And then, inanely, I added, "It was nice to meet you," and hightailed it out the door.

"You've got a lot more oomph than most of his women," she called after me.

CHAPTER 25

I flung open the door of my car and then sat behind the wheel for a second, trying to think where to head.

As I steered away from the house, I realized I didn't have a clue where I was going. Heading to Richard's Malibu house was out of the question—anything to do with him was out of the question now—and I couldn't hang out at the place where I'd been living for the past few months. I couldn't go to the bakery because Will would likely be there.

I beat my hand against the steering wheel. God, I was an idiot. Worse, I was an idiot with nowhere to go.

I drove out onto the main road between the canyon house and Malibu and turned right, heading back toward L.A. Maybe I could rent a hotel room somewhere? Yeah, except for the anemic amount of credit I had on my credit cards. I'd been trying my best to wrestle my totals down, but half the time I forgot to pay them on time, which resulted in fines and more debt. That was the sort of thing that Jack had done for me. I missed him. I missed Daisie, too. I missed the life I'd forsaken for the idiot whose wife and son I had just met. For one brief moment, I considered using the company credit card Richard had given me to book a hotel room, but I quickly dismissed the thought. I shook my head. No way was I going to be any more beholden to that asshole than I already was. Nope, no way.

But then, right before I was about to hit the freeway entrance, I thought of one place I *could* go. I steered the car to the side of the road and then pulled a U-turn when traffic permitted and headed back toward the Pacific Coast Highway. Natalie lived down past Santa Monica, in the hip, arty town of Venice, and she'd offer me a port in the storm at her little house on the canal.

I punched the button for the phone to call her as I drove and then put it on speaker, so I wouldn't get busted for talking and driving. The phone rang repeatedly. Please pick up, please, please, please, I prayed as I drove. But she didn't. Her message clicked on. I pushed the button to end the call and then pushed it again immediately to call her again. Same thing happened. I called her again. This time she answered.

"Jesus Christ, you're persistent," she said.

"And you never answer your phone."

"Oh, baby sis, if that isn't the pot calling the kettle black, I don't know what is. I was on the other line until your constant calling made me decide I better switch over. What the hell is up? This better be a good emergency. Did the Illustrious One dump you?"

I steered the car through a curvy canyon road that would ultimately connect me to the PCH. "Actually, I dumped him. Turns out he's married."

"Richard Bishop is married? Baby, I'm sorry."

"I didn't find out until I ran into his wife and son at the house where I was staying."

Natalie whistled.

"He's a manipulative bastard," I said.

"There's a news flash," Natalie said.

Was I the last to realize the truth about Richard? "Anyway, that's why I'm calling. I need a place to stay."

"Come on over, baby sis. The fridge is stocked, and I've got a couple of good reds in the wine rack. I'm heading to San Diego with Francine for the weekend, so you can have the place to yourself. But I'll be here for a few hours yet."

I hung up the phone and stopped for a red light on the busy highway through Malibu. Richard's house was somewhere around here, or so I thought. But how would I know for sure? God. Richard was married, and he hadn't told me. I thought back to meeting Sarah, and her final words. Like hearing I had more oomph than most of his women meant anything to me. Because—*most of his women?* How many did Richard go through? And what was that she'd said about Richard trying to save his wife? Thoughts jumbled through my brain, but I couldn't make sense of them. That reporter—I couldn't remember his name now—asking me questions about Richard taking over women's businesses. Tansy, telling me how businesses had come and gone at the Noho location. I couldn't arrange them into any coherent picture.

I thought of someone I could call who could tell me more. Fiona. I punched her number.

"Hi, Mad," she said cheerfully after a few rings.

How to bring up this delicate topic?

"Mad, are you there? Oh Jesus, this is one of those stupid butt dials isn't it? Bollocks."

"No, wait Fiona, I'm here!"

"Well talk then," she snapped.

"I just, er, um, wanted to let you know I won't be available for publicity anymore."

"Oh, Beef Curtains. Of course, you will be. Come on, Madeleine, don't be ridiculous."

"No, it's true," I said. "And Richard and I are through, too."

"You're through?" She sounded incredulous.

"Yeah, because it turns out he's married."

"You didn't know he was married?"

"Did you?"

"Of course I did, you bloody fool."

Now it was my turn to be silent. Fiona knew all this time? And that meant Ryan—all the Ryans—and Jacques-Pierre and Thomas and Ellie and everyone else who had ever had anything to do with Richard knew? The paparazzi knew? "Everyone knows?"

"Everyone in his inner circle. He keeps Sarah and Grady's existence as quiet as possible to the outside world so they won't be bothered."

I thought back to the time Fiona had asked me about being with Richard, the naked desire for him on her face. "But…but…I thought…I mean…."

"This is the way the world works when you get to the elite levels, and if you can't handle it, I advise you to jump off the boat."

Well that wasn't helpful, in fact, the opposite. Now I felt like even more of an idiot. Everyone in his inner circle knew Richard was married, even as he paraded me around town? My humiliation was complete. I couldn't wait to collapse in a heap at Natalie's and hide from the world forever.

I hightailed it on down the highway until I reached her place. Well, it wasn't quite that easy. Natalie lived on the Venice canals, one of the most charming places to reside in the whole history of the world, except for one tiny little problem—parking. The residential streets between her canal and the busy neighboring boulevard were clogged with autos parked next to each other like clown cars. I blessed the size of my little car as I maneuvered my way into a spot with space for a motorcycle after nearly half an hour looking for a place. Both the front and back fenders kissed the cars on either side of me, but such was the case with every other parking job along the street, so I locked the car up and set off on foot, never mind that I had nearly half a mile to walk.

The voices in my head kept me company as I strode along the narrow streets. *Idiot. Dumbshit. Richard is married. Idiot. Dumbshit. How could you not have known? Idiot. Dumbshit.* On and on I lambasted myself as I walked. The wine Natalie said was stored in her cupboard was going to be a welcome relief. I looked at my watch. Holy crap, it was only four in the afternoon. I felt like I'd lived a lifetime since I'd done the audition that morning. And now that was likely worth nothing, though I'd totally nailed it.

Natalie rented a small, older home, which sat in the shadow of a huge modern redo. She leased the place from its plastic surgeon owner whose latest trophy wife didn't want any part of living in Venice—only a mansion in Beverly Hills would do for her. My sister lived in fear that the plastic surgeon would dump this wife and take up with one who did want to live on the canals, thus depriving her of her beloved abode. But in the meantime, she got to enjoy where she was. Birds sang, and a breeze rustled the magnolia blossoms. The branches of a lemon tree laden with fruit hung over the sidewalk. In the distance, I heard traffic along the boulevard, but if not for that, one truly could imagine themselves in a distant European town.

Nat's house was tiny, painted blue with white trim and a bright red door. "Buddhists consider a red door good luck," she'd explained the first time I visited her on the canal. I hoped the door's bright hue would perhaps turn my luck around. I walked up the front steps to the small porch and knocked on the door.

No answer.

I knocked again, then looked for a doorbell. Nothing. I knocked again, then looked around as I waited. Her canoe bobbed gently in the canal a short walk across the sidewalk, so she wasn't out on it. Had I misunderstood our conversation? No, she'd said she would still be there for a while.

I reached for my phone to text her just as she flung open the door. Her hair was awry, her cheeks flushed, and the hem of her white blouse was untucked from the white peasant skirt she wore with it. I checked to see if she wore white shoes to match, but she was barefoot. It was only when I saw another woman looming in the background that I realized. Duh, they'd been in bed together.

"Oh," I said. "Um, sorry to interrupt."

Natalie laughed. "Not to worry, baby sis. We just got distracted."

Francine greeted me with a cool smile and I tried not to stare too hard at her. She just looked so different than she had when I'd met her at the grand opening. Her hair was no longer red, but a deep blue, so that was one reason. But she also seemed infinitely more relaxed, perhaps because her husband was obviously nowhere in sight.

Natalie stood back from the door and motioned me in.

"So, um, you guys are going to San Diego for the weekend?" I asked.

Nat nodded, dreamy eyed.

"We are indeed," Francine said, suddenly all business, as if somebody had to step up and take control of the conversation. She pulled a tan linen shirt over the black skirt and tank —both slightly askew—that she wore and fastened a huge pendant around her neck. "And I must dash and do a couple of errands before we can leave. It's lovely to see you again, Madeleine. Natalie, you'll pick me up in an hour or so?'

After she left, Natalie ensconced me on the couch, which took up most of the tiny living room. It was a gorgeous purple velvet, pillows laden with embroidery and mirrors thrown just so on it. I sank back into its depths.

"Wine or water?" Nat called from the kitchen.

Before I could call out my answer, Natalie came into the room carrying a tray that held a big glass of water, a shot full of an amber liquid, and a bottle of bourbon.

"I thought perhaps some whiskey might be in order here." She handed me the shot glass and I sipped at it, then gulped it all in one drink. Natalie refilled it. I made a conscious effort to leave the glass on the table, at least for a minute, even though the warmth from the last drink lingered in the most comforting way in my stomach.

"Now tell me everything that's happened since I saw you at the grand opening," she said, sitting on a white easy chair that fronted the sofa, the only other seat in the room.

And so, I did. I told her about the bakery and how the macarons were crap because of the shitty ingredients, about the trip to Portland and how Jack and Daisie were moving, how Richard had hired Will to save the bakery, and worst of all, how he turned out to be married.

Nat sat calm and still as I related my woes and when I was finally finished, she shook her head. "Well, baby sis, you sure have been up against it."

I nodded in agreement and reached for my whiskey.

Nat pointed at me. "I'll tell you one thing, though, I'm not surprised about Richard. I'd heard a rumor that he was married, but he sure hides it well. And he's always seemed a little too perfect to me, a bit too *too*, if you know what I mean."

"I do." I sipped at the bourbon, then set the glass down and fell back against the couch cushions. "And I guess I thought I would be the one to puncture that perfect façade." I sighed. "But apparently not."

Nat reached out and straightened a row of Buddha statues that lined her coffee table. Then she pulled a feather duster out of a low cupboard and walked around the room swatting it at the few pieces of furniture—the coffee table, a squat, low chest covered with statues of angels, and a side table crammed in the corner between the couch and the front wall. Nat was a neat freak to my casual messiness, a constant cleaner and polisher and straightener. She flicked the duster across the lamp on the side table.

"Pretty sure you got the one speck of dust on that lamp."

Nat shrugged. "Can I help it if I like things to be clean?" She ran the duster over the coffee table *again*, and then, apparently satisfied with her efforts, stuffed the duster back into the cabinet. "Okay, baby, I've got to get going. But before I leave there's one more thing we've got to talk about."

"I promise I'll keep the place clean, Nat, truly. And I'll figure something out as soon as I can, so I won't be here forever."

She waved her hand again, this time sideways in front of her face. "No, I'm not worried about that, even though you are a gigantic slob. What we need to talk about is Will."

"Will?"

"Yes, Will. As in ex-husband-who-has-returned-to-the-fold Will."

I slugged the rest of the bourbon in my glass down and shook my head. "I got enough to worry about without adding him to the mix."

She tapped a finger against the living room wall. "My point exactly. You've never dealt with your feelings for him, which I for one consider to be the reason why you fell so quickly for the wretched Richard."

"He's not wretched," I protested. "And I didn't fall for him."

She fixed me with the Natalie look, the one she'd been using on me since we were kids, the one she no doubt used lavishly on her students: chin down, eyebrows up, eyes ablaze.

"Okay, okay," I said, hands in front of my face. "So I did a little."

She tapped the wall again and then used the same finger to point at me "Exactly. You have a bad habit of not facing things, baby sis. And methinks the only way you are going to get through this crisis is to start. That's all I have to say. Just think about it, okay?"

I plopped my head against the couch. I didn't want to think about anything. I just wanted to sit there and get drunk.

Natalie walked across the room and kissed me on the forehead. "Have a good weekend, sweetie. Take the canoe out. The water's low but its high enough for a spin."

"Have fun with Francine," I called.

After Natalie left, I poured myself a glass of wine. But within a few minutes, sitting in the tiny house felt confining. I was too antsy, feeling like bugs were crawling around inside me. I moved to the front porch, but that didn't feel right, either. I needed to move. I set my wine down, closed the door to the cottage, and stepped off the porch.

Walking along the canals was soothing. A light breeze coming off the ocean a few blocks away rippled the water and the smell of the sea relaxed me. I walked past yards dotted with succulents and other tropical flowers I didn't know the names of. The canals were such an eclectic area, small, older cottages cheek by jowl with large modern homes.

As I walked, I thought about Natalie's words. Was it true that I had a habit of not facing things? I paused and gazed out at the canal, waving at a kayaker who paddled by. I had to admit, maybe my sister had a point. I'd stuffed the grief of my miscarriage and funneled all my feelings into work. And I'd clearly not dealt with my feelings for Will particularly well, either.

But there was more. A lot more, I admitted.

And that was my sister Cecily's death. I still blamed myself for it. And rightfully so. I closed my eyes as the memories overtook me. Weirdly, when I allowed myself to remember, which was as seldom as possible, I never saw pictures; I just heard sounds. I heard the sound of the car crashing into ours and the sickening screech of metal that followed. I heard one brief cry from Cecily, one tiny baby wail, and then silence.

And then I heard the sound of my mother screaming my sister's name.

My eyes popped open as I realized something, something that had niggled at me all these years, but I'd never brought up to the light to look at.

My mother had screamed my sister's name, but not mine.

She'd yelled, "Cecily, Cecily," over and over again, but never once, at least in my memory, had she yelled, "Madeleine."

There was only one conclusion to come out of this.

My mother never loved me as much as she'd loved my baby sister. I fingered the scar on my jaw. How sad that my mother had preferred my dead baby sister to me.

From my pocket, I heard a sound—my phone ringing. I ignored it.

Because it jarred me into a second thought.

The idea that my mother preferred my dead sister to me was bullshit. My mother loved me as much as she loved anybody. *But she always thought I could take care of myself, so she didn't worry about me.* She'd told me that, repeatedly. "You're a smart girl, Madeleine; you'll figure things out."

And I could take care of myself, just as my mother thought. And I would, damn it. I'd get through this latest debacle somehow. I opened my eyes, squared my shoulders, and headed back to the cottage.

. . .

I was so lost in thought that I didn't notice things weren't the same as I'd left them when I returned. The signs registered subconsciously and were only readable in retrospect. Like the fact that all the lights were on in the house. The fact that the door was slightly ajar. The fact that somebody lounged on the couch.

I screamed.

"Mad, Mad, it's just me." Will leapt from the couch. "I texted you a million times to tell you I'd be here. I called. Don't you ever answer your texts or your phone?"

I stopped dead still in the doorway, clutching my heart. Lord, he'd given me a scare. "What are you doing here?"

Will laughed. "Waiting for you, of course."

"But...how—"

"Your sister, bless her heart, let me know where you were hiding."

That damn Natalie, always thinking she knew my business better than I knew it myself. "She called you?"

Will leapt from the couch. "Yes, yes she did. Come in, come in, Mad. There's wine, and beer, and look." He did a Vanna White motion with his hand. "Cold cuts and salads."

There was indeed quite a spread laid out on the table. Plates of salami, turkey, and cheese, and two bowls of salad, beside a small dish of olives and what looked like a bowl of popcorn—my favorite. At the far end of the table sat a bottle of wine and two glasses.

"Did you do all this?" I asked, impressed despite myself. I mean, he remembered *popcorn*.

"I did." He grinned, then frowned. "Okay, true confession, it was all here already, Natalie just told me about it. But come in, come in, and sit down. I thought we could have a nosh and a drink and then go for a moonlight canoe ride."

Will grinned. "C'mon, Mad, sit down and have a glass of wine."

Yes, wine sounded good. A lot of wine. Vats of wine.

Will poured a glass and held it out to me. I looked from the deep red of the wine to the ruddy sheen of his face. Goddamn it all to hell anyway, he was as freaking handsome as ever. And looking into his eyes still made my heart flop, sort of like a fish on the shore of a lake, but never mind. I took another step into the room and reached for the glass of wine. Our fingers touched, and electricity shot through me.

Maybe Nat was right. Maybe I did still need to deal with my feelings for Will. I plopped down on the couch with my wine.

Will grinned. "I'm so glad to see you, babe."

My ears prickled. "What's this 'babe' stuff?"

He shrugged. "Just a term of endearment."

"To which you have absolutely no right." Even if I was cheap, I wasn't easy. I took a big gulp of wine.

"Maddie."

I looked up at him, scowling.

"Maddie, I've got to say it again—I've never been so wrong about anything in my life as I was to leave you. I don't know what got into me—call it a midlife crisis."

"Great theory, except you're not middle-aged yet."

He waved his hand. "Call it whatever you like—"

"Maybe blinded by lust?"

"That works. I don't care! But what I do care about is you. I can't believe I was so stupid to throw away what we had. It's you I love, Maddie. It's you I missed every night—"

"Lying in bed next to Hilary," I added helpfully.

He nodded. "I couldn't stand it. All I wanted was to be with you. I'd wake up in the night and reach out, expecting to find you, and instead, there she was."

I drank the rest of my wine in one big swallow, hoping to

calm myself. Because not only was every cell in my body dancing, every synapse in my brain was firing as well. Cells and synapses were dancing in rhythm, screaming, "It's you he loves, it's you, it's you!"

He was leaning toward me now. Oh God, the familiar Will smell. Lemon and sandalwood. I never had been able to figure out how he got that smell. When first we'd been together, I'd searched the medicine cabinet in his apartment, looking for an aftershave lotion, but found nothing. I finally decided it magically emanated from him. And now I inhaled it like an elixir, letting it waft around me. I closed my eyes.

And then I felt Will's lips on mine. How could they feel so good! Will's lips were as smooth as cashmere. I allowed his tongue to part my lips a little and then, suddenly, we were kissing deeply, passionately, thrillingly. I felt myself dissolving into him, just wanting to be closer to his body. Will responded with his hands, which he smoothed up and down my arms and shoulders.

My mind went on a wild tumble. Will could be part of my dream of returning to Portland. He could go back, too. We could get back to where it had all started, the two of us, beginning the bakery.

Will moved his lips from mine. "Oh, Maddie," he breathed. "I've missed you so."

Maybe we were destined to be together, never mind the tiny, small voice in my brain I suddenly became aware of that was shouting, "Stop, stop."

Mentally, I swatted at it. Didn't Dad always say the ego would trick you away from your true self? Surely that voice was my ego and my desire to be with Will was my true self. But then the voice shouted, "Hilary." I ignored it again and concentrated on the way Will was running his tongue around the inside of my mouth. Then the voice shouted, "loan sharks."

I sighed again, this time not with pleasure. The voice was getting louder and more insistent, and suddenly I realized I'd gotten things confused—this was the voice of my true self, trying to save me. Suddenly Will's hands on me felt like sandpaper and his mouth on mine made me want to gag.

I pushed Will away.

"What are you doing? Don't make me stop." I scooted backwards on the couch, away from him.

"C'mon, Mad, you're torturing me. Look." He nodded towards the huge bulge in his pants. Will was nothing if not proud of his package, and he had liked to remind me of that every chance he got.

"I can't do this," I said.

"Yes, you can." He lunged toward me again. I shoved him away.

"I. Can't. Do. This," I said, enunciating each word clearly.

"You could a minute ago," Will said. And then he smiled his goofy-hangdog-surfer smile, the dopey lopsided grin that had made me fall in love with him. Oh God, he was such a boy. Peter Pan, the eternal boy-child.

I shook my head. "It's not right, Will. Yes, I'm still attracted to you and part of me would like nothing more than to lead you into the bedroom and play with you all night."

He waggled his eyebrows.

"But I can't just continue to let men set my course and go any which way the man-wind blows me. I still love you—I always will—but it doesn't mean I'm *in* love with you and it doesn't mean I can *be* with you."

Will's entire body deflated.

"At least you've got a job at the Bonne Chance Hollywood," I said.

"Sort of," he said. "I'm not so sure about it, though.

They've got me making more public appearances than baking."

I should have listened to him more carefully, but I didn't, because I was too eager to get away from Will. I stood. My legs felt a little shaky, as if I'd just gotten off a long boat trip, but I touched my fingertips to the wall to steady myself. I looked at Will, still huddled on the couch, and realized with a gasp I kept to myself that he looked pathetic—pale, shrunken, desiccated. Why hadn't I seen that earlier?

"But I need you, Mad."

"No, you don't. You need the memory of me, Will, but that's all. What we had is over, destroyed by Hilary, and oh yeah, those stupid loan sharks of yours."

He hung his head. "That was a terrible mistake, I will admit. But everything turned out okay in the end."

I thought about what had happened over the last few months, me leaving Portland to lead the glitzy life in L.A. Well, many a woman—and man—would have sold their souls just like I did to experience that life, so I couldn't really complain. "Yes, yes, it did."

"And Hilary is a bitch extraordinaire," Will said.

I caught the subtle tense shift. "Is? I thought the two of you broke up."

"We did," Will said. "But there's no getting rid of her. I might as well just tell you now, Maddie. She's pregnant."

Once, when Nat and I were wild teenagers, we'd gone out drinking one night and the next day I'd never bothered to eat anything. The two of us were goofing around outside on the front lawn when suddenly black dots crowded in on my vision and then everything went black and I fainted. And that was how I felt at that moment. The black dots started to crowd in on me.

I plopped down into the nearest seat and held my head in my hands. Hilary. Pregnant.

"Is it yours?" I raised my head long enough to ask, already knowing the answer.

He nodded. "I'm afraid so."

The dots hovered in my vision again and I put my head down. Will was having a baby. With Hilary. Will, the one who had told me repeatedly that he didn't want a child of his own because he himself was still a child. It was difficult to take a breath and the dark spots were becoming overpowering. I forced my head down farther and did my best to take deep breaths. Will was going to be a father, the one thing I'd wanted from him more than anything, the one thing he refused to give me. My pregnancy was one of the reasons he'd cited for leaving me, and I knew he'd been relieved when I miscarried.

"Maddie? You okay?" he said. "I know it's a shock and all. And you know how I am about wanting children anyway. Hell, for all I know it's *not* mine. I told her to get rid of it, but she wouldn't listen."

I whipped my head up at him. He and Hilary had what I wanted more than anything in the whole freaking wide world, and he had told her to get rid of it? "It's time for you to go, Will."

He spread his hands. "Aw, c'mon, Mad, I don't want to leave now. I'll sleep on the couch. I won't bother you at all, I promise. Just don't make me leave."

I took another deep breath. The black dots seemed to dissipate with my resolve, and I stood. "No, go."

"Where am I supposed to go on a Friday night?"

"How about back to Hilary and your unborn baby?" I asked. And then I stood over him until he got up and headed for the door.

"I love you, Mad," he said as he left.

"I love you, too, Will," I said. "I always will. But I don't want to be with you." And I shut the door behind him.

CHAPTER 26

I sobbed on the bed all night long after Will left. I sobbed out my anger over the fact that Hilary was pregnant—freaking pregnant!—and the way I'd almost succumbed to Will's charms. I sobbed because this time I knew it was over—really, truly over. I was done with Will Wilson.

And then I sobbed for most of the weekend. I sobbed for Will and I sobbed for the fact that Richard was married. I sobbed for my lost baby. And I sobbed for more—my mother, and my dead sister Cecily. I sobbed for Natalie, just because she was Natalie, and my Dad and his financial problems. And I sobbed for Jack and Daisie, saddled with Carla for wife and mother.

When I was done sobbing for everyone, I started all over again.

By Sunday night, I was sobbed out and finally I slept.

Then my eyes popped open early the next morning. Very early. I was exhausted from my weekend of crying, but in that weird fugue state where I was too tired to sleep. Instead,

I felt antsy and anxious. And I knew there was only one thing I could do to calm myself—bake.

But Natalie's kitchen was hopeless, about the size of a desktop, and she had notoriously few kitchen supplies as well. I stood in the living room in the pre-dawn darkness and switched on a lamp, which illuminated the remains of Will's aborted feast. Empty glasses sat on the table, specks of red wine dried on them like blood. Bits of popcorn littered the floor. The cheese on the platters on the table had dried and hardened, and the edges of the meat slices curled like little toy boats. In all my sobbing, I'd ignored the mess, hadn't even noticed it. I retrieved a garbage bag from Nat's closet and swept all the food into it, then rinsed the dishes and stacked everything neatly in the sink. I'd run the dishwasher later.

And then I threw on jeans and a T-shirt, grabbed my purse and keys, and ran out the door.

I ALWAYS LOVED BEING out and about in L.A. in the early morning hours before the rest of the city woke. I loved it in Portland, too, but I loved it even more in L.A., probably because the city was so huge and usually so full of people that it was amazing to drive through relatively empty freeways and streets. Relatively being the operative word because there was still more traffic than one would think possible so early in the morning.

But no matter what you think about the fifty-gazillion people that live in town, and their cars of course, too, and no matter if the whole idea of the place turns you off completely, there's one thing about L.A. that people don't talk about. And that is the light. There's a special light in southern California, a soft golden light I've not seen anywhere else. And I will admit that half the time you can't see the light because it's obscured by smog. But that morning I drove toward Beverly Hills and watched the sun light the sky and admired the stark urban beauty of the city.

I'd pulled into a Starbucks drive-through and bought the biggest size latte they sold, and I balanced it and my bag and the keys too as I arrived at the back door of the bakery. Out of habit, I glanced around for Tansy, but there was no sign of her. Heaving a deep breath, I fit my key into the lock. I was taking a big chance that Will might be there baking, but I was betting he wasn't. I was betting Will had gone back to Hilary as fast as his little feet would carry him after I'd given him the heave-ho.

But something weird happened. The key didn't fit. Hoisting my bag over my shoulder, I held the key ring up and checked to make sure I had the right key, then tried again. And again, it didn't fit. It took a minute to register. But then I got it.

The locks had been changed.

Blood rushed to my head and pounded. It must have been a problem with vandalism. Or maybe a break-in. Or something. I tried one last time, then gave up and started pounding on the door.

Jacques-Pierre looked surprised when he opened it. "Oh, Madeleine, hello. I didn't expect to see you here."

"Why not?" I asked, somewhat crankily. "Technically, I own the place."

"Um, yeah," Jacques-Pierre said.

I pointed behind him, into the bakery. "I thought I'd help you guys with some baking. So, how are the macarons coming? Did you get the ingredient issue worked out with Ryan?"

But Jacques-Pierre didn't budge from the doorway.

"Can you move, please, so I can come in?"

The look on his face was a combination of terror and pity. His eyes widened and then narrowed. Jacques-Pierre always had a jaunty demeanor, with his handlebar moustache and dark, glittery eyes, but right then he just looked scared. He leaned toward me and dropped his voice to a whisper. "I'm not supposed to let you in, Madeleine."

I laughed. "Come on, it's me! Of course, you can let me in." I stepped toward him.

But Jacques-Pierre used his body, clad in his baking whites, to step sideways and fill the doorway. "I'm sorry, Mad. I like you and if it was up to me, I'd let you in." He lowered his voice another register. "But I can't afford to lose my job. I've got a little one at home and my wife is pregnant. I can't let you in."

I stared at him, trying to make sense of what he was saying. He wasn't supposed to let me in? He was worried about losing his job if he did? And as I stood there squinting at Jacques-Pierre, the sun rising behind me and just starting to wash the wall of the bakery in gold, I remembered something Will had said. *They've got me doing more public appearances than baking.* I pondered. Why would he be doing public appearances? Wasn't that my domain?

"Well, I'll just call Richard and see about that."

And then, before I could whip out my phone, Jacques-Pierre did a funny thing. He nodded his head behind him, toward the inside of the bakery. I scowled at him, not understanding. He pointed toward the phone and then nodded his head toward the bakery.

"Richard is here?"

Jacques-Pierre nodded. My heart did a gallop so huge I thought it was going to fly out of my body like a whirlybird. I pressed my hand to my chest. Why was Richard at the bakery? Especially so early in the morning?

"He appeared early this morning, without warning," Jacques-Pierre whispered. "He's in the other room, giving a pep talk." He looked over his shoulder, into the bakery. "He even called the sales staff in."

But not me. He'd convened everybody else, but not me.

I leaned around Jacques-Pierre and hollered. "Richard! Richard, its Mad, come let me in."

A great echoing silence filled the bakery beyond the door. I stood there, jingling my keys. I could leave. I could turn around and get back in my car and drive back to Natalie's cute little place on the canal and flop on the couch and forget about the bakery. Yes, indeedy, I could. But I was tired. I was tired from sobbing all weekend. I was tired of letting man-storms blow in and out of my life, and me bending like a tree in a squall—any which way the man-wind blew, there went Madeleine.

Uh-uh.

I was done.

I looked at Jacques-Pierre and said, "Step aside. You won't get in trouble for this because I'll take the blame. Hell hath no fury like a baker who can't bake." And I walked around him into the bakery, yelling, "Richard! Richard!"

There's an amazing thing that happens when you let go of everything that has been binding and confining you. It may happen that you don't even know what's been binding and confining you until the moment when you release those shackles. And in that moment, there is power—sheer, amaz-ing, intelligent power. I felt that power as I walked through the dark rooms of the bakery toward the front showroom. I was done. And right here, right now, I was going to find out what the hell was going on with my bakery—and my life.

I found Richard in the showroom, standing near the front door, surrounded by the other bakers—Thomas and Ellie and a couple of women who I didn't recognize. He was talking to them with an earnest expression on his face, and I noticed the rapt looks on the faces of his audience, especially the women.

"Richard."

He looked up and for one second it flashed—a momentary look of despair, replaced so quickly by the Public Option that I wondered if I'd really seen it. "Oh, Madeleine, dear, how lovely to see you."

"It is not freaking lovely to see me and you know it. You changed the locks and you told everyone not to let me in. That does not constitute *lovely to see me*, Richard."

"Oh now," he said.

"Oh now what?" I asked him. "Now fucking what?"

"I don't think the situation calls for profanity, do you?" Richard walked closer to me and he held his hands out in front of him in a beseeching manner.

"Yes, I do! Yes, I fucking goddamn do! You lock me out of my bakery and you pretend you're in love with me when the whole time you are not only married but you have a son! If that doesn't call for some goddamn profanity I don't know what does."

"Richard Bishop is married?" Ellie said to the woman beside her. "I didn't know that."

"Nobody knows." I turned to Ellie and the other woman— was she a baker or a clerk or what? "He keeps it a secret so he can have his way with as many women as he can. Like me."

Richard put his hands in front of him as if to push me down, and he had the nerve, the utter nerve, to continue to use the Public Option on me. Couldn't he at least have gone for the Private Option? Jesus! "Madeleine, this is not the time or place for you and me to discuss personal business." He turned to the assembled group. "We'll finish this business meeting later, okay? You may return to your posts now."

"It's not just about our personal business, is it?" I gestured around me. "It's about this business, too. It's about the bakery."

Richard looked at the employees, still standing around us, gaping, and made his little shooing motion, the one he used so many times on me. They obeyed, scattering throughout the bakery, and Richard pulled me into a corner by the front window. "Madeleine, we have a few things to talk about. The business is going through some, ah, changes."

"You bet your ass it is. Because now that I know you're married, you're not quite so interested in me anymore, are you? It's time for you to move on to another woman, another business, right?"

I watched as a variety of expressions flitted across Richard's face. Panic, and then a flash of anger, and I knew there was truth in what I'd said. And then, lo and behold, both those emotions were replaced with something else—the Public Option. Again.

"Oh, Maddie," Richard said.

"Don't freaking oh, Maddie me," I said.

The Public Option dimmed for one moment and then it grew even bigger. "Remember what Ford Dooley always says. 'Life is what happens when you're busy making other plans.' That's what happened when I met you, Mad. I just couldn't help myself."

"Really, Richard? You're invoking Ford Dooley at a time like this? That's not even a quote from him; it's John Lennon. I know Ford Dooley said it, but Lennon said it first. And you're not half the freaking man that Ford Dooley was. You said you played him because you wanted to be him. Well maybe you ought to start by copying some of his integrity."

The Public Option did not dim for even one second. "Listen, Mad, Fiona and Ryan have scheduled a meeting for tomorrow, at headquarters, and I think it would be best if we waited until then for our review."

"I want to know the truth now. I want to know why the locks were changed. I want to know what's going on."

"Mad, darling." Richard grasped my shoulder, and he looked all business. "It'll be best if we wait until tomorrow, when all parties will be present."

"All parties? What the fuck are you talking about?" My voice was getting shriller and shriller. And so much profanity coming out of my mouth was shocking, even to me. I swatted Richard's hand away. "Don't touch me."

"Oh, Mad," Richard said and he looked so sad for a moment that I almost reached out to touch him and comfort him. "Oh, my darling Mad."

"I can't believe you let me find out you were married by running into Sarah and Grady."

"Madeleine, this is not the time or place to talk about personal issues." Richard glanced around, and then he gazed deeply into my eyes, the way he had so many times onscreen, the way he did when he wanted to convince me of something. "But I've just had the best idea. I'm going to bundle you up and take you home where Flora can care for you and then tonight you and I will have a lovely dinner together."

I stared into his eyes. God, he was gorgeous, those eyes insanely appealing, as was the rest of his face. But as I gazed into those amazing eyes—the eyes that had mesmerized me so many times—I realized that my anger was gone. Because it was difficult to be angry at an empty shell. In its place was a new emotion. Sadness. Sadness for him, sadness for me, sadness for all we'd gone through together and that it had to end this way. I had loved him, well and truly, just as I'd loved Will.

And, I had wanted to save him. Like I wanted to save everybody. And even though what Winston Herman had said about him was true, he wasn't a bad person. I wasn't trying to save him from terrible bad deeds, just his deeply wounded self. But I knew now that was impossible—Richard was so used to public adulation and so adept at milking it that he'd never give himself a chance to recover. And it was not up to me to help him try.

"I'm not going to go have dinner with you, Richard."

An expression of surprise crossed his face, quickly replaced by the Public Option, as if he couldn't believe I'd refused him. "Oh come now, Mad, it will be lovely."

"There's not going to be a lovely dinner with you tonight." I held my hand out, and to my surprise he took it.

"Mad—"

I spoke before he could go farther. "Thank you for everything you've done for me—I never would have gotten to experience this lifestyle if I hadn't met you. But here's the thing you keep forgetting. At the end of the last Ford Dooley movie, he wakes up, and everything he experienced was all a dream. None of it was real, Richard." I shook my head. "And neither is this life. This lifestyle does not suit me at all, and I never would have realized that any other way. So, thank you, Richard. And goodbye."

I squared my shoulders and headed toward the door.

"Madeleine."

I turned back to him.

He paused for a moment, as if searching for the right words, then he took a deep breath. "I love you. I truly do. There's just so many other things to take into consideration. In another time, in another place, we could have been so good together."

I would have thought it all yet another one of his acts, but for the look I saw on his face. It was Richard, plain and simple, no Public Option, no Private Option, no calculated presence. It was the real Richard, the one I'd caught only fleeting glimpses of throughout our time together.

He shrugged both his hands out. "I don't know what gets

into me. I get carried away with everything and then…" Richard's shoulders slumped and he shrank in on himself. "I wish it could have ended differently for us."

I nodded, then headed to leave once again. But at the last minute I turned and ran back to him.

I threw myself into his arms and we stood there, hugging each other for a long, long time.

CHAPTER 27

As I left out the back door, it occurred to me to be worried about Tansy. I looked around her usual smoking area for her with no luck. I drove by the apartment where I'd picked her up one day but saw no sign of her. I pulled over into a truck-loading zone and idled for a minute, peering up at the apartment. I could hardly knock on the door and ask for her. That might set Brad off for another round of hitting. If only she had a phone number, I could call to check up on her.

I didn't want to leave town without connecting with her. I bit my lip as I steered the bug onto the freeway. Tansy was one reason—the only reason—that I hesitated to leave L.A. It felt like abandoning her to an uncertain fate. But what could I do? What choice did I have? I had no options left in L.A., other than staying at Natalie's and her place was way too small for the two of us. Besides, I apparently no longer had a job at the L.A. Bonne Chance. I'd find out tomorrow at the meeting they'd arranged.

A cool breeze off the ocean ruffled my hair, but the morning sun promised a warm day. Birds called to each other as I parked the car and ducked down a walkway to Natalie's canal. As I neared Nat's house, I heard a strange noise. At first, I thought it was a baby crying, and then I thought maybe it was a cat howling. As I climbed the stairs to the porch of the house, I realized the sound was coming from within and it was a human, weeping as if the depths of their pain had no bounds. There was a pause and then the sound began again. I scowled, listening. It sure sounded like Natalie.

I was about to open the door and go in when I noticed a very faint movement to my left. A person. A male person, sitting in the lotus position on the wood floor of the porch. A male person in the form of my father, eyes closed, hands in his lap, apparently in a deep meditative state. How could he sit out here meditating when all hell was breaking loose inside?

I nudged him with my toe.

No movement.

The wails from inside grew louder.

I nudged him again. Nothing.

I was about to leave my father to his meditating and go inside to check on Natalie when he opened his eyes.

"Your sister is having a crisis," Earl said. "I came to comfort her."

I looked at him, still as a rock on the front porch, and listened to the sobs within.

"Sure looks like you're doing a great job of it, Dad."

"I've done all I could. She refuses to listen to me." He unfolded his legs and stood up, far more gracefully than I could have managed from a sitting position. He wore white pants and a loose white shirt that flapped in the breeze.

"What happened?" I asked.

"They got caught."

"You mean Natalie and Francine? Who'd they get caught by?"

"Francine's husband." Earl dipped his chin and gave me a look.

"That would be the dean of the religious studies department and Natalie's boss?"

"That very person."

"Oh lord," I said. "Does she still have a job?"

"Debatable," Dad said. "Remains to be seen. If I were a betting man, I'd say no."

"Do I dare try to talk to her?"

Dad perched on the edge of Nat's wicker love seat and took a swig of a bottle of water he'd plucked from the floor. "You might have better luck than me."

I went inside and found Nat lying on the couch, pale as the yellow outfit she was wearing, a long billowy skirt which was fanned out around her ankles, and a lemony tank top. Her sobs seemed to have subsided but every few seconds she sniffed and warbled as she caught her breath.

I walked across the room and stood over her. "Are you okay?"

She took in another ragged breath and opened her eyes. "Oh, Maddie, I'm so happy to see you. It was awful, just awful."

I pulled up a chair. "Tell me."

And she did, all about how Francine's husband, Natalie's boss, got suspicious when he caught glimpse of a reservation email on his wife's computer, which he never, ever in a million years used except his was broken and he needed to send one email, just one tiny email. And how he'd taken note of the address of the inn in San Diego where the women were staying and waited until they were all settled in and then arrived there late Saturday morning at a most inopportune moment.

"Oh Madeleine, what am I going to do?"

Like I could give anybody relationship advice. I stared at

her. "Haven't a clue, sis. I really don't. I'm sorry. I just don't know."

I DON'T KNOW what I expected to happen at the meeting the next day, but at least I was rested, hydrated, and full as I went into it. Earl, Natalie, and I had enjoyed—or tried to enjoy, given the emotional states Nat and I were in—a simple dinner on her porch and then turned in early. And now I stood in front of Richard Bishop's gleaming L.A. headquarters building, the heat of the unseasonably hot spring day starting its slow rise from the sidewalk concrete. I looked up at the building. The smoked glass windows of the tower deflected the light all the way up, but somehow at that moment the sun illuminated the gold RB sign at the top so that it shone like a jeweled crown.

Nope, I wasn't going to miss L.A., with its glittery, empty promises. Yes, I was ready to return home. A sudden image of the Portland Bonne Chance rose in my mind—its sweet little front showroom, simple in its pastel décor. I smiled, thinking about it. How wonderful it would be to be home in Portland and back to my regular routine of rising early to bake macarons. All I had to do was get through this meeting, and formally say goodbye to the Ryans, and then I'd be free to go home. I started for the door.

"Wait up there, Lenie," a familiar voice called.

Could it be? It sounded like...but no. That would be impossible. I pivoted my head to see who was hailing me. And oh God, I was right, it was Jack. Jack! Right here on the sidewalk in downtown L.A. My mouth fell open as I stared. Because there he was in all his Jackness, not edited for L.A. at all, just firmly and totally himself. He wore wrinkled jeans that had seen better days and a plaid shirt beneath a tweedy sport coat. And his face! It was tanned, but he looked haggard and thinner than when I'd last seen him in Portland a couple of months ago. What stood out the most was the several weeks' growth of hair sprouting on his chin. His dark beard was flecked with gray. But I didn't care, because it was Jack, just when I needed him most, come to be with me in L.A.

"Is that all the greeting I get after all this time?" he said.

And then I squealed and ran toward him and threw myself into his arms. "God, I'm happy to see you." I stepped back from the hug and looked at him more closely. A shadow crossed his eyes as he gazed down at me and his sharp intake of breath told me he was in pain. "Why are you here?"

"To see you, of course." Jack grinned and then kissed me on the cheek. The contrast of his soft lips and scratchy beard set my stomach aquiver and a sweet shiver ran up my spine. "And because I was summoned to appear." He gestured to his body. "I literally just got off the plane from Dallas."

"Where's Daisie?"

Jack's shoulders slumped.

"Is she okay?"

He nodded. "She's fine, just a handful." He shook his head. "I thought she would get used to being with Carla, but you know how she is."

"Yeah, I can't quite picture the two of them getting along."

"They're hopeless together. They hate each other, and nothing I do seems to change that. I'm hoping the two days they have alone together right now will help."

I had visions of me swooping in and rescuing Daisie, bringing her back to Portland to live with me. Jack's eyes had that haunted look in them again. But then something cleared, and his face changed as he looked at me and smiled. I was happy just to be in his presence.

I lunged at him again and rested my head against his chest as his arms enfolded me. For a moment, all was right with the world. And then he patted me on the back and took a step backwards. "I think we'll be late if we don't get up there."

ALL THE USUAL suspects were arrayed around the conference room table—Fiona and all the Ryans. This time, there seemed to be a couple of near-Fiona clones as well, and I wondered if the cloning happened before or after they were hired. Then I realized that the one person I had half feared and half hoped would be there was absent—Richard Bishop was nowhere in sight. Fiona stood beside the window, staring out, something I had never been able to accomplish in that room with its floor to ceiling glass. It gave me the sensation I was going to pitch out over the city and fall twenty-seven floors to oblivion.

"Hello, Mad. Hello, Jack." Fiona greeted us with her most clipped British accent and no sign of the woman who had shared personal stories over a cup of tea in evidence. She wore all black, a snug black pencil skirt and tightly fitted buttoned-up jacket with white piping, along with black hose and black stiletto heels.

"Going to a funeral, Fiona?" I said brightly and then laughed at my own joke until I realized that nobody else was laughing.

She shot me her patented Fiona stink-eye look. "Richard wanted me to tell you that he will be unable to join us today."

Of course, he wouldn't. But I have to admit, I was relieved. I didn't feel the need to see him again at all, ever. We were ushered to seats facing the window and the expansive view of the city, which was a relief, because with the table between me and the glass I didn't have the constant fear of falling. A moment later a mini-Fiona fussed about, pouring us water and asking for our coffee order. It appeared soon thereafter, in white mugs emblazoned with the Richard

Bishop logo in gold. As I raised the mug to my lips, I realized it also had a thin gold strip of color along the rim, and at the same time, the chief Ryan stood and smoothed the cover of the giant pad of paper on a stand.

A trickle of coffee dribbled down my chin and I wiped it and looked around to make sure nobody had seen. All the Ryans and Fionas were staring at the chief Ryan but Jack was staring at me. And when he caught my eye he grinned and nodded his head ever so slightly toward my chin and I knew he'd seen. I grinned back and there was a moment when the rest of the world fell away. Gone were the crazy-big view, the gleaming coffee table that never seemed to get fingerprints on it no matter what, the coffee mugs with gold rims. Gone were the Ryans and Fiona and the mini-coffee-bringing-Fiona who had stationed herself against the wall, behind the table. There was only Jack. And me.

"Ahem. Let's get started then," the chief Ryan said.

I shook myself and turned my attention to him, as did Jack.

He flipped over the top page on the stand. "I'm happy to report that the outlook for the L.A. La Bonne Chance is improving." He pointed to a graph on the paper that showed a rising red line. "Sales have improved dramatically since we brought Will Wilson on to fix the problems with the macarons."

Well, la-di-dah, as Daffy Duck used to say. He flipped the paper and went on about consumer strategy and market opportunity analysis and other boring business calculations I didn't have the least bit of interest in. I glanced over at Jack, who appeared rapt. This was his area of expertise, I reminded myself, and he liked studying it. He'd always tried to school me on the bare bones basics of accounting, but I was tone deaf. It was the same way with math—Daisie had explained to me at least fifty times what a prime number was, and I didn't seem to be able to hold it in my head.

I never saw that lack as a detriment, or as evidence that I had an inferior brain. As far as I was concerned, I just had a *different* brain, one that solved creative problems with ease, math problems not so much. Just as there was emotional intelligence, I believed there was creative intelligence and that's what I'd been handed in the brains department. My mind dipped and rolled along this pleasant train of thought until Ryan flipped to a chart with the headline, *Portland La Bonne Chance.* I sat up and paid attention.

As far as I could tell, the lines on this chart looked similar to the ones on the graphs for the L.A. Bonne Chance—a rising red line. I expected more of the same kind of talk about profit and loss and market segmentation and add-on sales. But instead Ryan said, "So you can see why we've had to make the difficult decision to close the Portland bakery."

I sat up. "What?"

Ryan nodded his head toward me in a slow, gracious manner as if talking to a child. "We have decided to close the Portland La Bonne Chance."

I stood, my chair clattering backwards behind me. "But that line goes up! It looks just like the graph for the L.A. bakery that you said was doing great!"

"But this line is not the whole picture." Ryan flipped to another chart that showed a green line snaking across the page in a straight horizontal line. "This is the indicator of monthly growth." He flipped to another chart. "And here is the schematic for the Portland La Bonne Chance costs."

On that chart a blue line rose to the top of the page. I was having a hard time making sense of any of it. I looked toward Jack, whose eyebrows were knotted so fiercely they looked like nooses and when he spoke, his voice came out terse and clipped. "These charts don't jibe with what you're saying."

Ryan made some vague comments about profit and loss and Jack's eyebrows furrowed farther, which I wouldn't have thought possible.

And as I sat there, trying to take it all in, a bubble grew inside me. It was a bubble of knowledge, the certain knowledge of why all this was happening. The bubble grew bigger and bigger until I had no choice but to open my mouth and let it pop out of me.

"You're doing this because Richard and I broke up," I said. "You're doing it because we broke up and you wanted to steal my business and make it into something else. Which you seem to have succeeded in doing."

Jack's eyebrows unknotted a tiny bit as he looked at me. "You and Richard Bishop broke up?"

I nodded. "We certainly did. Because who in their right mind wants to be with a man who happens to have a wife and a son—a teenage son, I might add—that they never bother to tell you about?"

A strange expression crossed Jack's face, but I didn't have time to focus on it because things were happening fast.

"Now, Mad, calm down." Fiona piped up from the other end of the table. "You know Richard Bishop doesn't make business decisions on whims."

I glared at her down the table, hoping my glare was as effective as her stink-eye look. "No, I actually don't know that. Fiona. Because I really don't know anything about Richard Bishop. He doesn't let anybody know him."

"Ahem." The chief Ryan cleared his throat. "All of your speculation is neither here nor there, I'm afraid. We've decided to close the Portland bakery, and that is that. We'll be shuttering it at the end of the month."

"Let me get one thing straight," I said. "You're closing the Portland bakery."

"Yes, that's correct." Ryan raised his eyebrows and nodded at me as if I were a small child.

"But what's to prevent me from reopening it?"

"The terms of your agreement with Richard Bishop Enterprises. He owns the name, and all the equipment, of La Bonne Chance Bakery."

I slumped into myself then and the rest of the meeting passed in a fog. I saw people talking, Fiona speaking up, Ryan pointing to charts and flipping pages, but I couldn't comprehend anything anybody said. All I could think about was that my bakery was gone. My dream, my ideal, my love, my baby —gone. Along with everything else as well. I'd said goodbye to Will and to Richard Bishop and I apparently no longer had a job or a place to live, at least in L.A.

When the meeting broke up, Ryan ignored me, but Fiona came over to me. To my surprise, she wrapped me a hug. "I'm so sorry, Mad. I went to bat for you with Richard, but when that man makes up his mind, that's it. You know how he is."

I shook my head sadly. "No, I really don't know how he is, Fiona. I don't think anybody does."

And then Fiona surprised me even more. "Let's keep in touch, okay? I really want to stay connected with you."

Jack and I rode down the elevator together in silence. A floor or two down, he stepped closer to me, and put his arm around my shoulders. I rested my head on his chest and we rode that way the rest of the way down. Outside on the street, he spoke.

"I'm sorry about your breakup with Richard."

It had gotten warmer during the time we were in the meeting. Heat rose in little shimmers from the sidewalk and the smell of exhaust tickled the back of my throat. I waved my hand in response to Jack's comment and shrugged.

But Jack wasn't letting it go that easily. He peered at me more closely. "He's really married?"

"It's something he hides well," I said and then sighed. "I don't know how much longer the whole thing would have lasted anyway. This whole rich and famous lifestyle? It's not for me. I just want to wear yoga pants and a hoodie to work and not worry about the paparazzi catching me without makeup."

Jack laughed. "Oh, Lenie, I miss you."

"And I miss you." I stared at him for a long, long moment. "What happens now? Are you going back to Dallas?"

He stiffened and nodded.

I cocked my head. "Really, Jack? Because whenever I say the words Dallas or Carla your whole demeanor shifts. You slump. And your eyes get all hooded, like I can't see the real Jack anywhere."

His eyes looked that way at that very moment, come to think of it. But I couldn't get him out of whatever it was that told him he had to stay with Carla. "She needs me, Lenie."

"I'm quite sure she does. But the question I have is, do you need her?"

The startled expression on his face told me everything I needed to know.

"C'mon Jack," I said on a whim. "Get a later flight. We can go have lunch somewhere, drink a few beers. Mourn the loss of the Portland bakery."

But Jack shook his head. "Can't. I'm heading up to Olympia on the way home to talk to the real estate agent about my house up there. Maybe light a fire under her. I've got to get to the airport, Lenie."

I offered him a ride, but he said he'd take a Lyft, even after I promised I wouldn't say bad things about Carla. I watched him walk away from me, down the hot L.A. sidewalk and wondered what I was going to do without him in my life.

CHAPTER 28

I steered my car back toward Natalie's, stopping by a wine store to pick up a good bottle of red because I planned to sit on the front porch and get drunk. Good and drunk. And then I was going to wake up the next morning and bake something, because that's what I did when I got sad or depressed. I baked. Even though Nat's kitchen wasn't big enough, maybe I'd experiment with a new flavor of macaron. Berry, I decided, since all kinds of varieties were coming into season. Or maybe I'd branch out and bake a pie. And hopefully while I baked a vision of the future would unfurl itself to me. And then, as I thought about baking, it hit me.

The most horrible thought ever.

Oh God, how could I have been such an idiotic fool?

Because I had left my apron at Richard Bishop's house. The one where Sarah and Grady were staying. Fiona had arranged to have my things picked up and taken to Natalie's, but I'd forgotten to tell her about the apron. Oh my God, I'd left my apron there. My *apron.* My most precious possession.

The thing I carried with me wherever I roamed. The one thing that remained of my mother.

And I had left it at Richard's house.

This aggression will not stand, I thought. I would get that apron back if it killed me. And I knew just the person to help me do it. If only I could find her.

I turned the car around and headed to the bakery, then drove down the alley behind it, hoping against hope that I'd find Tansy in her usual smoking spot, even though I hadn't seen her there in days. I peered out the front windshield and side window, desperate to see a glint of her purple hair. I collapsed my shoulders when I didn't see her, then turned the car around in a parking lot and cruised back.

And then, a flash of reddish-purple.

Just as I drew even with the back door of the souvenir shop, Tansy walked out. She didn't see me and so I could get a good eyeful of her. She looked like a sullen hipster, wearing black tights with huge holes in them—even on this hot, hot day—and short jean cutoffs. She had an army jacket on over a red T, and in her hair she wore a matching red bandana tied as a headband. Her platinum blonde and magenta tresses stuck out in little tufts above the scarf, and she had a good-looking leather messenger bag slung over her shoulder. I peered at her through the window. If I was seeing things correctly, that was a very expensive bag she carried, and I wondered what boutique she'd lifted it from. Well, I could hardly call her out on it when I was going to ask her to utilize those very same skills.

I couldn't get over all the layers she was wearing on this sweltering day. And even with all of that, she was the most gorgeous thing I'd seen in ages. My heart pounded. God, it was good to see her.

"Tansy," I called out the window as I maneuvered the car to a stop next to the curb.

She turned and glanced toward the car with that slack look I'd come to expect, the one she used on the men (and women) who took her for an easy mark and tried to hit on her all day long. But then when she saw me, the blank eyes disappeared, and a huge smile lit her face.

"Hey, Mad, long time no see." She walked to the car and leaned her head in. "What's up?"

A sudden blast of sadness wrapped my heart as I stared at her open, sweet face. What would become of her when I wasn't around to watch over her? And how would I explain to her that I was moving back to Portland? I took the chicken's way out and decided not to explain any of that until later.

"Oh god, you don't even want to know. Hey, I need some help with a little project. Are you available?"

She shrugged. "I just got off work. Brad's expecting me at home, but…" Tansy glanced around as if Brad would jump from behind a garbage can and grab her.

"Can he wait? This will only take an hour or so. And there's a Deluxe Quarter Pounder with cheese and fries with ranch at the end of it."

I'd taken Tansy to McDonald's enough to know her order by heart. She stood staring at me through the open car window. "And a chocolate milkshake," I added when she didn't immediately respond.

"Okay." She shrugged again and opened the car door. "I guess Brad can hang out a few minutes without me."

"Did you guys have plans?" I asked as we buzzed off down the street.

She shook her head. "Nah. He just likes to know where I am."

"Seat belt," I reminded her.

She shrugged her green army jacket off and glared at me.

"Do I have to? I hate these things. Brad says they are just another way the man controls us."

"Yes, you have to. Seat belt laws may well be the man controlling us, but in this case it's a good idea. "

Tansy rolled her eyes and clicked herself into her seat belt, then reached into the messenger bag she'd placed on the floor and pulled out a package of gum, offering a piece to me and then popping one in her own mouth after I declined. Out of the corner of my eye, I watched her with fascination as she rustled about in her purse. Stolen or not, she had the kind of bag that was like a magical receptacle for all things exotic and wonderful, such as filmy scarves and emery boards and butterscotch candies and pieces of paper with notes scrawled on them. Fiona had a bag like that, too, though the items she pulled from hers tended to be sleek, leather, and expensive. My purse was a simple fabric square with a zipper on top and out of it came nothing more interesting than my phone, credit cards, and lipstick.

"So what's this little project you need me for?" She chomped on her gum, like a caricature of a hapless secretary, glanced up at me and then down at the bottle of bright blue nail polish she had pulled from the depths of her bag and was now opening.

"Don't smack your gum and don't spill that," I said.

"Your attempts to civilize me will get you nowhere."

"I like you without your button, but you'll be more comfortable with one, so I'll sew it on."

"Um, yeah," Tansy said. "Not following."

I laughed. "Oh, it's just a line I always remembered from a children's book called *A Pocket for Corduroy*. A little stuffed bear was missing a button and went on an adventure in a department store to find one. Then a little girl buys him and takes him home and sews a button on for him. But the ultimate message is that it's okay to be yourself. My Mom used to read it to me. I always loved that book."

Tansy painted a swath of blue on her nail and looked at me sideways. "Must have been nice to have a mom who read to you."

"It was," I said cheerfully, remembering how I'd loved to cuddle next to my mother on our blue couch. She smelled of vanilla and lemon because she baked so much and, in my memory, at least, she always wore white and had lipstick perfectly applied on her mouth.

Tansy grunted, and I realized that such a simple pleasure I'd taken for granted had not been part of her growing up. "Since we don't have all night, or at least I don't, could you fill me in on this project?"

"Oh right," I said as I steered onto the 10 freeway. "It's to recover my apron."

The disgusted noise that came from Tansy's mouth could have stripped the set-in grease stain on my white T-shirt that I never seemed to be able to eradicate right off the fabric.

"You dragged me along with you to find an apron?"

I nodded. "It's not just any apron. It's my special apron. I can't bake without it. I inherited it from my mother."

"The mom that read to you?"

"Of course, I only had one."

She made the disgusted noise again. "I had about ten different mothers growing up."

"Oh baby, I'm sorry."

Tansy shrugged and held the brush of the nail polish in the air as I sailed over a bump. "It's just the way it was, that's all. So where is this super special apron of yours?"

And so, I explained. She interrupted me once to ask, "And what makes you think I'm the one who can rescue your precious apron?"

"Well, um, er, because…."

She waved the hand that held the nail polish brush and I grimaced at the idea of the blue liquid spattering inside the car, never mind that I was not going to be able to get the smell out for weeks anyway. "I know, it's because I'm such a good thief." She hunched up her shoulders and then collapsed them and heaved a huge sigh. "What can I say? It's my superpower."

I continued with the explanation of the house and who was staying there and how I thought we would get into the kitchen (by the side sliding door, which I hoped would have a lock that was pickable).

By the time I was finished, Tansy had put away her nail polish and was rubbing her hands together. "I get to break into Richard Bishop's house. Woo-ee. Talk about sticking it to the man. But I don't get it. Why don't you just tell him you want it and let him get it for you?"

"It's been an eventful time since I last saw you. Richard and I are finito. I broke it off with him."

I expected her to be happy, seeing as how she'd called him a jerk. But Tansy was always full of surprises.

"God, are you freaking nuts? Why would you break up with Richard Bishop? Even if you hated him, it would be worth it to stay together. Jesus, the man gave you everything you wanted and more."

"Except his real self," I said.

"Huh?"

"Never mind." I waved my hand. "It just wasn't working out, Tansy. He's got a wife and a child. A teenage child. Neither of which he found important enough to tell me about."

"Dude, Richard Bishop is married? You could have fooled me, the way he looks at every woman around him."

"Like how?" I put my turn signal on and tooled the car off

the freeway exit to join the winding road that led to Richard's canyon house.

"He's a leerer," Tansy said. "He's got those amazing eyes and he uses them on you."

"Boy, does he ever. Anyway, you told me you thought he was a womanizing jerk. I thought you'd be happy we'd broken up."

She cast a stink eye at me. "But dude's a gazillionaire. I could put up with a lot of jerkiness for that."

For a minute, I felt a pang. Maybe I had done the wrong thing, breaking up with him. I mean, he did have all the money in the world. And I'd blown it for the bakery, too. What would have happened if I'd called Richard up, batted my eyes—and asked him for the money to keep the Portland Bonne Chance open? Then I shook my head. Nope, that wasn't me anymore. It never had been, only I just had to walk through Richard's glitzy life to find that out. I looked over at Tansy. It made me sad that her definition of a satisfying relationship was based on what it could give her.

"So, what are you going to do now?" Tansy said.

I took a deep breath. This was the part I dreaded, telling Tansy that I needed to move back to Portland. But the intersection for the road that led to Richard's house appeared, and we were just minutes away. I moved into the left turn lane. "I'll tell you that when we're done, but we're almost there so let's review our plan."

Taking the left turn, I edged into a small pullout by the side of the road. In another fifty feet came the turn for entry to Richard's little enclave. "Okay, so I'm going to drive through the neighborhood and point out the house to you, then I'm going to park a house away, by the horse. You'll get out and walk as if you belong here and head right up to the door. Look around, pick the lock, get the apron—it should be hanging on a hook near the kitchen door—and walk back to the car. Okay?"

"What if someone asks me what I'm doing?" Tansy said.

I pointed a finger at her. "My hope is that won't happen." I glanced at the clock on the dash. "It's two p.m. I'm thinking most people will be at work. This isn't the wealthiest neighborhood in Malibu by a long shot. It's probably about the least expensive. But least expensive still means a crapload of money." Crapload? Every time I hung out with Tansy I found myself talking like her. "And for most residents, that means they need to leave the house and go to work."

"As far as I'm concerned, you can take your hope and shove it. Hope never got me anywhere. I deal in reality, Mad. What do I say if someone asks me what I'm doing?"

"Nobody will," I said firmly, hoping I was right. "But if they do, say you're here to visit a friend. Grady is Richard's son's name. You could always use his name."

Tansy nodded, seemingly satisfied. On the drive through the neighborhood, she peered out the window, as if taking every detail in, as I pointed out Richard's house.

My tour elicited a squawk. "That's his house? It's tiny. And really plain. I thought he'd live in a mansion."

"Oh, this is just the starter house. His real place is a mansion. Looks like something in a movie." I spoke authoritatively, even though I'd given up my chance to see it. But I had done an internet search and found one photo of it, such as it was. Someone had taken a telephoto shot from the beach, and all I could really see was a ton of windows. But it did look big.

I pulled over to the side of the street. The problem with committing a crime in this neighborhood was the lack of privacy. The streets were not normal streets like in my northeast Portland neighborhood, with curbs and parking strips and sidewalks and backyards to hide in. No, these were more like lanes, and curvy ones at that. There was no clear demarcation between the street and the residents' yards, leaving me uncertain if I was parked on somebody's grass, or a right of way. At least we were under the shade of a large tree, which would offer some protection.

And then I had a thought. "Remember, the apron is mine anyway. So, we're not technically stealing."

"Even though we are breaking in."

"Well, there is that. Are you ready?"

"Sure." Tansy climbed out of the car, not the least bit ruffled or rushed. I shook my head, watching her. The girl was clearly a born thief. Too bad there wasn't a career based on stealing things. She'd excel at it. And here I was, encouraging her. Ah well. The desperate do desperate things. I *needed* that apron back.

She closed the car door behind her and I watched her walk off down the lane. Tansy did confident well. She walked slowly, but not too slowly, and she really did look like a young woman about to visit a friend. I shook my head, watching her. She *faked* confident so well, and I knew that it truly was all a fake, that beneath it all she was a mass of insecurities, anxieties, and fear. Well, who wasn't?

I didn't dare put my head back and close my eyes, though that's what I most felt like doing. I knew, though, that I would fall asleep. And that would not work. Because I couldn't run the risk that someone would walk by, see me with my eyes closed, think I was a vagrant, and call the police.

I looked at my watch. Tansy had been gone two minutes. I continued my line of thought. I was a vagrant of sorts these days. Ah, that was something I could do while I waited—check my email. Which I did. Then I looked at my watch. Oh crap, ten minutes had gone by.

I peered out the front windshield. No sign of Tansy. I

leaned my head out the window and listened for the sound of sirens. As in, Sarah was home, had caught Tansy, and had called the police. Nothing. Shit. What to do? I was just getting out of the car when Tansy appeared around the hedge that separated the side yard of Richard's house from the neighbor's yard. When she saw me, she grinned, and held up the apron.

"Oh God, thank you," I cried and ran to her, hugging her and jumping up and down. I snatched the apron from her hand and hugged it to my chest, then held it in front of my face and stared at it. The apron was no worse for wear. Its embroidered images were still visible, and it felt as soft as ever.

Then I remembered where we were. "We have to get out of here."

Tansy shrugged. "It's all cool. Grady was there. I talked to him."

"Jesus, are you kidding?" I made hand motions toward the car and followed her back to it, carefully folding my apron and placing it on the backseat, where it would be safe. Then I buckled myself in, glared at Tansy until she pulled her seat belt across herself, and roared out of Richard's neighborhood, saying goodbye under my breath. Once we were on the road I breathed easier. "Now tell me everything. And thank you again."

"You really didn't have to rush out of there. Grady's totally cool." And she explained how she had snuck into the side yard of the house, hugging her body close to the hedge, and then stopped in a place where she had a good view of the dining room. And there noticed Grady at the table. She was so surprised to see somebody there that she crunched on some dead leaves and he must have heard her, because he came to the door and looked out.

Tansy shrugged. "And that was that. I was caught. I

explained what I was doing, and he was awesome."

"How awesome?" I inquired.

"He just told me that his mom had noticed the apron and wondered about it and because of that he knew right where it was. He grabbed it for me. He told me that you were cool."

"He did?" Was it my imagination or was it the wee-est bit odd that Richard Bishop's son was calling his father's lover cool?

Tansy nodded. "I don't think he quite got that you and Richard were doing the hanky-panky, you know? Although maybe he did, he seemed pretty with-it." She stared out the window as I entered the freeway, heading north this time, toward Agoura Hills. "So anyway, it was a lot easier than I thought. And now I'm starving."

"There's a McDonald's right down here."

I suddenly realized I was starving, too, and so I pulled into a parking spot instead of heading for the drive-through. Inside, we ordered Tansy's meal and a Filet-O-Fish and fries for me.

Tansy wrinkled her nose after we'd carried our trays to a table and unwrapped our food. "You actually like the Filet-O-Fish?"

I finished chewing a huge bite of fried fish, tartar sauce, and bread and smiled dreamily. "I love me a Filet-O-Fish." I popped a fry into my mouth. "The only thing better is the fries. Best fries on the planet."

"I'm pretty sure this is the only place I've ever had fries," Tansy said. "Unless you count Burger King or Wendy's."

I thought about the pile of frites I'd had at the little café in Paris on the Left Bank, how they'd almost melted in my mouth. That was a terrible cliché, but in this case, it had been true. I ate another fry. Yes, delicious, but did they surpass the ones I'd had in New York City at that small restaurant in the Village that Will and I had frequented when we'd spent a week in town? And then I was sad that Tansy had only eaten fast food french fries, even if McDonald's fries were the best on earth.

"What?" Tansy said, bringing me back to the present. "Why are you shaking your head?"

"Just thinking about something." I waved my hand. "It's nothing."

"When are you going to tell me the rest of the story?" She spoke around a mouthful of fries. "Like, the whole Richard thing."

"Ah yes, the whole Richard story." I sat back against the bright orange molded booth. "Well, after I broke up with him the fallout was fast and furious. First they told me that I am no longer associated with the L.A. bakery—"

"You mean I won't see you there anymore?"

I shook my head. "Nope. And they also announced that they were closing the Portland location."

"Damn, that's cold."

"I thought so."

"I know it's disappointing and all that, but it, like, doesn't matter all that much since you live down here and all, right?"

"That's what I need to talk to you about, Tansy. I'm moving back to Portland."

Tansy set her burger on the paper she'd opened atop the tray to create a place for her burgers, fries, and ranch sauce. The look on her face stabbed my heart. "No. No, you can't. You can't move to Portland because you live here."

It broke my heart, but I had to tell her the truth. "There's nothing for me here anymore." I lifted my shoulders and dropped them again. "I don't even have a place to live. For now, I'm couch-surfing at my sister's."

Tansy slurped at her Coke and scowled. "You could move in with her."

"She doesn't have room. And, L.A. is not my scene, Tansy.

It's big and there are too damn many people and cars."

Tansy shook her head. "Why did you have to break up with Richard? Why couldn't you just put up with how he acted so you could stay here?" I could see that she was almost in tears.

I reached across the table to touch her hand, but she pulled it away from me.

Tansy slammed her cup down on the table and shook her head. "I can't believe you'd do this to me. I just can't believe it."

"Tansy, I'm not doing it to you. I'm doing it because I have no choice."

"I'll never see you again," she said.

"Of course you will!"

She shook her head. "You'll lose track of me. Then you'll forget about me. Like everyone else."

"I can guarantee you one thing, Tansy, and that is that I will never forget about you. Ever." I shook my head. "And I'm not going to lose track of you."

"But what if we move or something? How will you know where to find me?"

"There's such a thing as email," I said.

She looked at me like I was insane. "Like I have access to a computer."

"You could go to the library?" I suggested weakly. And then I realized something. Tansy didn't have a phone.

"How about this? How about we buy you a phone? Then you could email me. Or text me. Or even call."

Her face brightened. "You'd do that for me?"

I nodded.

And then her face fell. "But I can't afford the monthly payments."

"I'll cover them, too. I want to be able to stay in touch with you."

She got up from the booth and came around and hugged me. "You're the best, Mad."

"Well, I think you're pretty awesome, too," I said.

And later that day, after we'd gotten her a phone and she'd promised that she wouldn't let Brad get his hands on it, and we'd sent each other texts to confirm phone numbers, and she had oohed and aahed over all the things she could do with the phone, we said goodbye.

I pulled the car into a visitor's spot at her crappy apartment building. When she wasn't looking earlier, when she'd been obsessing joyfully over her phone, I had slipped three twenty-dollar bills into her purse. I wished it was more, but it was all the cash I had on hand.

"I guess this is it," Tansy said.

"I'll be back down in October," I said, though I had no idea if that were true or not. I nodded toward her phone. "We'll coordinate via text, okay? And maybe you can still get up to Portland."

"That's not going to happen." Tansy hugged me across the seat. "Thank you for everything."

I hugged her and kissed her cheek and then I watched her get out of the car and walk away from me one last time. I hoped to God she would be okay. And silently I cursed Richard for lifting me up and then dropping me again. But as I sat watching Tansy climb the stairs to her second-floor apartment, I made a vow to myself. I wasn't going to rely on anyone else—most particularly, a man—to lift me up. I'd lift my own self up in the future. I wasn't quite sure how that would happen, and I had to admit my options looked grim. But by God, I would figure it out. If I hadn't been in the middle of L.A. I would have gotten out of the car and shaken my fist at the sky in a Scarlett O'Hara moment. Instead, I looked up at the sky, said, "Watch me," and tooled off toward Natalie's.

CHAPTER 29

$\mathcal{I}$t wasn't that bad.

Yeah, right. Truthfully? It was awful. My worst nightmare come to pass. Me back to a rootless, purposeless life. I got a job at the coffee shop next door to the bakery, and spent my mornings pouring coffee, steaming milk, and doling out doughnuts and scones. Let me tell you, going from working for myself and setting my own hours to working for someone else was tough. Not I-have-no-money-and-my-lover-beats-me tough, like Tansy's life, but tough in a different way. And worse was feeling that I was marking time until something happened, even though without goals or forward motion I had no idea what that something might be.

In some ways, it was as if I'd never left, even though Jack and Daisie were gone and the bakery was shuttered. I resumed my old routine, rising early to walk from my house to work, even though work was now very, very different. Walking by the shuttered bakery every day was discouraging, especially since all the equipment was still inside. I couldn't figure it out—the Ryans had said that the bakery needed to be closed because it wasn't making any money, but once it had been closed nobody made the least bit of effort to move things out. Some mornings on my walks to work, I wondered if my time with Richard had all been a dream.

At least I was back in my little house, which now, after all my time in Malibu among ranch homes and mansions, looked to me like a little fairy tale cottage. Although I'd previously never been the slightest bit interested in gardening, since I'd been back in Portland, I'd planted a riot of blooming annuals. Geraniums, cosmos, zinnias, lobelia, and petunia spilled out of the pots in front of my house.

Daisie told me it was because I now hankered to stay put. That girl. We still Skyped every Thursday night like clockwork and when I told her about my garden, she insisted on a Skype tour.

"It is because you've had so many upheavals in your life lately, you're now desiring to put down roots." Daisie wore a red crocheted hat, the chullo kind that looked like a helmet, with flaps covering her ears, even though the weather in Dallas was hot and humid.

"Aren't you warm in that hat, Dais?" I'd asked her.

She clutched her ears for a moment and shook her head. "It's my flak helmet. I need it to protect me from the stupidness of that woman."

That woman was, of course, Carla, and despite my repeated protests that Daisie should try to establish a relationship with her, she refused. Daisie saw no good in her mother and needled her father to return to Portland constantly.

"Oh baby, I'm sorry. Hang in there, okay?"

"She's getting worse," Daisie said mournfully. "I think it's because she realizes she no longer has access to Richard Bishop."

I was not going down that road with her. Daisie had been

horrified and refused to Skype or text with me for a week when she learned I'd broken up with Richard. "Hey, sweetie pie, where's your dad? I wanted to ask him something."

I didn't have anything to ask him; I just wanted to see him. I missed him something terrible.

"He's lying down," Daisie said.

"What?" Jack was not the sort to lie down. Like, ever. No matter how much pain he was in.

"He said his back hurt really bad."

"Is he okay, Dais? I don't like the sound of that."

She sighed, and her entire skinny chest folded in on itself. "I think so. I don't know. I hope so. I keep telling him to go to the doctor, but you know Dad."

"Can you carry the computer into his room so I can talk to him?"

But just then, Carla yelled that she needed her help and Daisie scrambled to sign off. Oh *lord.* I just could not understand what Jack was thinking, staying in Dallas with Carla when clearly Daisie hated her.

Later that morning I walked past the shuttered Bonne Chance, eyeing all the equipment still inside. The outside looked pristine, the windows clean, the awnings that Richard's infusion of cash had bought still in great condition. The sidewalk was even swept. Somebody was keeping it clean. I got an idea. I'd call my landlord and ask what was up. Checking my watch, I realized I still had five minutes before my shift started, so I turned my phone on and searched for the number. Yes, despite my best efforts to be more connected, I had left my phone off again. I decided to ignore the messages and texts that had come through and go ahead and call the landlord. Standing outside the bakery, I punched his number. He was evasive, but what I got was that the same people who had been writing the checks recently were still sending them. That would be Richard's people.

Well, that was interesting. I pressed my nose against the glass and peered inside. Bad mistake, because it brought a lump to my throat. Everything was just how I had seen it just a few months ago—the blue and pink striped wallpaper, the lacy doilies at the edge of the display case, the sparkly Eiffel Tower statue I'd bought in Paris by the cash register. The only thing that was missing was the macarons—and people to eat them. I blinked back sudden tears. All I'd ever wanted was to make my little bakery into a success. Well, I had tried my best. It just hadn't worked out very well.

I turned away as my phone dinged its annoying alert that I'd gotten a text. This was why I ignored it as often as possible, I realized, because the constant dinging and buzzing enervated me and ratcheted up my anxiety. I was the kind of person who felt a stupid and immediate responsibility to others, and once somebody texted or called, I felt beholden to respond to them *right away.* Which was why leaving the phone off worked best.

But this time I was glad I had the phone on because it was a text from Natalie.

Baby sis call me when you get the chance.

And so, I did. Turned out Natalie had nothing new to say, just the usual obsessing about her girlfriend, or sudden lack thereof, seeing as how Francine had apparently decided to go back to her husband.

"Oh, and hey, did you see the latest on Richard Bishop?"

"Nope," I said. I'd been determinedly not reading entertainment or celebrity websites. I'd had enough of that world, thank you very much.

"Well, apparently he's now dating Jolie March."

"Am I supposed to know who that is?"

"She's famous for her perfume," Nat said. "She owns a small chain of perfume boutiques."

Well, wasn't that interesting. No, I told myself. No, it wasn't.

Almost as an afterthought, Natalie told me about her lack of a job and complete lack of prospects. "Turns out there's not a huge job market for over-educated religion profs."

I had nothing to offer her, of course, except my love and support, because, well, look where I was. Things hadn't exactly worked out for me, either. I sighed as I hung up. Earl would tell me to put it all in perspective, and I tried to. I did have a job, I did have a house, and so far, said job with tips seemed to be stretching to pay my monthly mortgage, even though it was tight. Okay, so I had to dip into my savings last month. Alright, and yes, dipping into it pretty much cleaned it out. If things didn't change soon, I'd be pounding the pavement looking for a job writing ad copy again. If I could get one, seeing as how I'd been out of the job market for years and the economy was stuttering. But still, in theory, I could go back to sitting in a cubicle writing blog posts for sucky businesses whose mission statements went against every fiber of my being.

There were worse fates, right?

Yes, yes there were. Like digging ditches. Or sitting on the street begging. Or being completely flat out broke. People all over the world were suffering way more than I and I needed to remember that and be grateful for what I had.

My phone rang just as I was about to silence it again and I answered it absently, thinking it was likely Earl, since I'd been thinking about him and he often called when that happened, as if he'd picked up my brainwaves. But it was the unfamiliar voice of a woman.

"Hello, Madeleine, this is Amelia."

I was silent for a long moment, trying to recollect the name. Amelia, Amelia. It had a familiar ring to it, but lord, I'd met a lot of people over the last few months, in L.A. and here in Portland as well, what with working at the coffee shop.

"Amelia, from Timmons & Thatcher."

I barely heard the last part as a surge of traffic passed by on busy Sandy Boulevard. Then it hit me—Timmons & Thatcher. The publishing house! Oh God, she was the editor who had accepted the book proposal—the book about macarons and Paris. I said hello and uttered all the niceties of social chitchat, all the while wondering why she'd called me. Finally, she got to the point.

"How's the book coming? You know you can send me pages as you write, in case you need an objective eye to look at them. Well, I'm hardly objective, seeing as how I'm your editor, but still."

I was stunned into silence. Because I'd thought that the book had been taken from me, too, like the bakery, and the Cook & Eat show and everything else, and thus, I hadn't been working on it. Out of the corner of my eye I noticed Lola, my shift manager, open the coffee shop door and beckon to me. I glanced at my watch. I was five minutes late for work. I waved at Lola and held up one finger to indicate I'd be there in a second.

"We're very excited about this title, and eager to get it released," Amelia said, apparently mistaking my silence for something other than shock.

"Um..." I managed to say. "Um...I've been working on some short pieces." She didn't have to know they were blog posts, now, did she? I had been blogging like a madwoman, and I wondered if that counted. Something about that medium suited my style and I found it easy to pound out blog posts with surprising regularity, though I'd long since abandoned the blog Richard's people had designed for me and started my own.

"Short pieces are good," Amelia said. "A lot of short pieces add up to a long book. Why don't you put some of them together in a Word file and send them to me and we'll go from there?"

I nodded my head, even though she couldn't see me. "I can do that," I said, clutching my hand to my heart. The book! They still wanted me to write the book! This was the most exciting thing that had happened to me since I'd left L.A.

"Great, pop me an email then and let me know when you think you can send them."

"Will do," I said. I saw Lola waving madly and turned my back to her. "Can I ask you something, though?" My heart pounded as I inquired, because I didn't want to know the answer. But I *needed* to know it.

"Ask away," Amelia said.

"Has anyone from the L.A. Bonne Chance contacted you about the book?" Pound, pound, pound. I pressed my hand to my chest and took a deep breath. Because now, suddenly, I'd been given back something good. Something really freaking good, as Fiona would say. And I didn't want it taken away from me again.

"No," Amelia said, and I let all the air out of my chest. I hadn't even realized I'd been holding my breath.

"Why would they?" Amelia continued. "It's your name on the contract. You're the author we want, not some bean counter from the bakery."

"Okay, good, just checking." I said it as cheerily as I could. "And so, um, I guess I'll get those pages to you pronto, then."

"Sounds good," Amelia said. "Talk soon. Oh wait, don't hang up. One more thing. When do you think you'll be going to Paris? Because we were thinking that if you could blog while you're there, we could start to tie those posts into promoting the book. We're thinking about building a whole social media campaign around it. How do you feel about that?"

My mouth fell open. "Um, Paris?" I managed to stammer out.

"You know, like it said in the proposal. Part of the advance money we allocated you is for the trip to Paris to visit the macaron bakeries there."

Oh, God. Really? Was she kidding me? Was this a joke someone had decided to play on me? Was I on a candid camera even as we spoke? If not, I'd died and gone to heaven. Because, *Paris.* My life might have totally and completely fallen apart but if I got to go to Paris, everything would be okay.

"Advance?"

"I looked into it just before I called, and the check is on its way to you, enough to cover expenses for you and a companion. Sorry it's taken so long. Sometimes accounting is very slow. When do you think you'll go?"

"As soon as possible," I blurted. To hell with the coffee shop, to hell with Lola, to hell with the bakery equipment sitting unused in a dusty storefront. I was going to Paris.

"Fabulous," Amelia said. "Let me know as soon as your arrangements are made, and we'll start to coordinate social media. And send me those pieces."

"I will," I said weakly as I pressed *End.*

Paris! I was going to Paris! And I got to take someone with me. But who? My first thought was Jack, but he was cranky these days and no doubt would not leave the beloved Carla. Earl was too busy with his dying retreat center and his writing career, and besides, we'd not be able to walk two feet down the street without fawning fans stopping us. Natalie? No offense to my beloved sister, but even in the best of times she tended to take all the air out of a room, and now, in her current misery, she wouldn't be the best of travel companions.

Well, I could always go alone. I trudged toward the coffee

shop, now a good ten minutes late and sure to invoke the wrath of Lola. Yes, I could do Paris alone. Couldn't I? Just then my phone buzzed with a text. I glanced down. It was from Tansy.

Hey lady, how are things? I miss you. What's up in the land of rain and clouds?

An idea formed. I grinned at the thought of it.

I texted her back.

What's up is that I'm going to Paris. Want to come? All expenses paid.

The answer came immediately.

Jesus H. Christ, are you fucking kidding me? Of course, I want to come. But you're not serious, are you?

And I wrote her back.

I am indeed serious. But you'll have to leave Brad.

Nothing came back. I stared at my phone, willing a text to come in, hoping that leaving Brad was not the sticking point. Because suddenly all I could think about was how much fun it would be to show Tansy Paris. I shook the phone in my hand, as if that might make something happen. And then, finally, a ding.

Brad can stuff it.

And that was that. I strode into the coffee shop to tell Lola I needed a couple of weeks off. That would go over big. But who cared? I was going to Paris.

As THINGS DO when the stars align and everything is right as rain, the arrangements for Paris came together quickly and smoothly. I enlisted Natalie, figuring she had plenty of time at the moment, to help Tansy get a rush passport. Tansy herself was like a kid in a candy shop, more so after I sent her money from the advance check and told her to buy some clothes. I probably should have been more careful with the money, but the check was generous, and hey, when the book got published, I'd get more. Never mind that I had a minimum wage job and a mortgage to pay. Everything would be alright once I got to Paris.

We were set to leave on a Tuesday, and I booked myself through L.A. so that I could hook up with Tansy at the airport and head overseas. I was excited about the trip, but even more excited to see Tansy again. I had missed that girl something fierce. I knew that she had some hurdles to leap to take the trip, like convincing jerk-ass boyfriend it was okay for her to leave and praying that she'd have a job upon her return.

"It's okay, Mad," she'd say every time I'd anxiously question her. "I can handle Brad. And if I lose my job, I'll find another one. It's not like selling souvenirs to tourists is a specialized skill."

Still, I held my breath. Bringing Tansy to Paris seemed like the most important thing in the world to me, because I felt it would be a life-changing trip for her. And God knew, her life could use changing. I held my breath and visualized that all would be well just the way Dad taught me.

We made it to Monday, the day prior, before things fell apart.

The call came from an unfamiliar number as I sat at my kitchen table sipping coffee. My two-week vacation started that day, and I was reveling in a morning where I didn't need to rush out the door when the cell rang. Even though I didn't recognize the number, I pushed the accept button anyway. This was part of my new regime of being responsible, keeping my phone on, and responding to calls and texts. I mean, look at some of the things I could have missed. The Paris trip being Exhibit A.

"Madeleine, this is Carla."

"Oh hi, Carla," I said cheerily. I was cheerful about everything. Because, Paris. But then I realized that it was weird for her to phone me.

"Jack asked me to call you."

"Oh God, is he okay?" Something in her tone of voice worried me.

"Um, he's in the hospital."

I leapt from my chair, knocking my coffee mug over, screeching. "Is he okay?"

"Oh, he's fine. He got an infection at the scar site. He was in a lot of pain, but it took a while for them to figure it out."

Oh, he's fine? When he had an infection and was in a lot of pain? For God's sake. My heart thudded a steady beat: *Jack in the hospital. Jack in pain.* I missed him so much and now he was lying in a hospital bed far away from me. Coffee from the spill splattered onto the floor and I rose to grab a wad of paper towels.

"But he…he's going to be okay? Should I come see him?" And then I had another thought. "Is Daisie okay?"

"Well, that's why I'm calling."

I didn't think it was possible, but my heart thudded faster. "Is she okay?"

"She is fine."

Carla had a hesitancy in her speaking that, in person, was mitigated by her beauty, but drove me crazy over the phone.

"But I need to go to Croatia," she said.

I sat in silence for a minute, not sure I'd heard her correctly. "Wait. Your husband is in the hospital with an infection, you have a daughter to care for, and you're telling me you need to go to Croatia?"

"I know it is terrible timing, but it's for my career. You know how psychic I am. And I'm hearing from my guides that this next movie is the one. It's the one that will be my breakthrough. But I have to leave in two days."

There was a pause, as if she was listening to someone else

and then she spoke again. "And now, with Jack in the hospital, there's nobody to watch Daisie."

Oh, my freaking God. She was even worse than I thought. Because, she had the best man in the whole world and the most amazing daughter ever, and she was going to waltz off to Croatia in their hour of need. I shook my head. "I'll figure out how to get there, Carla." And then I pressed *End*, longing for the days when one could slam down a phone to make a point.

I wondered why I hadn't gotten a call from Daisie, informing me about the situation. And Jack in the hospital. The thought made my heart pound with anxiety. Oh God, I hoped he was okay. I knew he dealt with the aftereffects of his wound on a regular basis, but I thought they manifested in pain, which was bad enough certainly, and not infection. I tried his cell, but he didn't answer, so I settled for a text saying, *You okay, Jack? I'm worried.*

What to do, what to do? It was clear that I was going to need to get myself to Dallas on the way to Paris. I stood, refilling my coffee and then paced the kitchen while I punched the button for Daisie's phone.

"Hello?"

Daisie's voice came through the phone weak and uncertain, not at all like the Dais I knew and loved.

"Daisie, it's Mad."

"I know." Her voice was weak and quivery.

"What's going on? Why do you sound so funny?"

"Dad's in the hospital. And I'm hiding from Carla. She hates me, Mad. And with Dad sick, I'm stuck with her. She's so nicey-nice around him, but when it's just the two of us she's mean to me."

Lord, Daisie sounded like a weak schoolgirl, not the strong quirky kid who would someday run the world.

This was a situation I could not allow. I bit my lip, thinking, and then heaved a heavy sigh. It was no doubt going to take vast amounts of energy and even more money, but it was the only plan that presented itself to me. And besides, the longer I didn't hear back from Jack the more anxious I became. I needed to get to him, no matter what.

"You should have called me, Dais."

"It happened fast. And I didn't want to bug you. Things haven't exactly been going well for you lately, either."

"Oh Daisie, my love, please don't ever hesitate to call me. Okay, listen, can you hang tight until tomorrow?"

"I think." Her voice sounded like a five-year-old's.

"Do whatever you have to do, and I'll be there, okay?"

"Are you going to take me home to Portland?" Daisie asked.

"No," I said. "You're coming with me to Paris, Dais."

I'M NOT QUITE sure how I did it, but I managed to get everything arranged and rearranged by the next morning, the day when I was originally slated to leave. I informed Tansy that she'd have to meet me in Paris and gave her step-by-step directions for getting on the plane and through customs once she landed. This would be her first plane trip anywhere. I shook my head, laughing. And here it was to an international destination. Paris, no less.

But I didn't laugh for long because I was worried about Jack. I rerouted my plane to Paris through Dallas and gave Daisie a good idea about what she should pack. Thank goodness, she had a valid passport—she and Jack had gone to Mexico a few years back.

Okay. I took a deep breath as I left my house, messenger bag over my shoulder, and dragging my rolly bag behind me as I headed toward the Uber that idled in front of my house at four o'clock the next morning. I ran through the list in my head, hoping I'd gotten everything figured out. I'd finally gotten through to Jack the night before and he'd assured me he was fine, and the infection was abating. I wouldn't believe him until I saw him, though. But I was proceeding on the idea that he was okay, because I didn't know what else to do. The way I had things worked out, there'd be time to see Jack in the hospital, grab Daisie, and get the flight to Paris that left in the evening. With luck, Daisie and I would land an hour later than Tansy the next morning, and with even more luck, she'd be waiting for us at the apartment I'd found on Airbnb, a charming (or so it looked in the online photos) little spot in Montparnasse, a neighborhood I thought the girls would enjoy.

It would all work out. One more deep breath and I checked what I had in my hand: messenger bag filled with book, iPad, passport, and wallet. I checked my other hand—it was on my suitcase. I nodded my head decisively. Yes. It would all work out. Jack would be okay, and Tansy and Daisie and I would make it to Paris. I sure hoped that was true.

CHAPTER 30

Oh, Paris. There really was no place like it on the planet. I lifted my head to inhale the aroma of coffee from the boulangerie that Tansy, Daisie, and I sat outside of. I watched the two of them plow through their breakfasts—chocolate croissants, of course. I say *of course* because as soon as the girls discovered their prevalence here, it was all they wanted to eat every morning. Daisie wore a patterned chiffon scarf around her neck that she had bought in honor of her new hero—Marianne Majors, the CEO of Hooray.com, who had grown up in Paris and was famous for her signature scarves. Daisie's adoration of Richard Bishop had faded as soon as she realized she no longer had a direct pipeline to him through me. Now she was scheming on how to reach Majors.

"Six degrees of separation," she was saying to Tansy.

"Huh?"

I was learning that Tansy had a, shall we say, *interesting* grasp of popular concepts and current events. Growing up in a succession of foster homes, she'd had spotty access to a computer, and thus had missed some things here and there. I watched as Daisie explained the concept of six degrees of separation; Dais delighted in her role as Know-It-All. I worried about what Tansy was teaching Daisie in return—last night I'd heard Dais ask Tansy to explain, once again, how her boyfriend sold pot at a profit, despite the prevalence of legal marijuana dispensaries, though Daisie referred to it as "the economics of drugs." But Dais seemed to be a good influence on Tansy—Tansy more and more often asking to use my iPad to read a book she'd discovered on my Kindle app.

And Tansy may have had a spotty grasp of things, but she'd managed the trip alone from L.A. to Paris on her first airplane flight ever with aplomb, navigating the airport and finding her way to the apartment with no problem. And, she had never looked better, I thought as I gazed at her. The purple streaks had grown out and she'd told me she couldn't afford the hair dye, which made me suspect she'd snitched it from the drugstore before, but what was left behind was a lovely shade of dark ash blonde that highlighted her Mediterranean toned skin and dark eyes. She'd filled out in our time here, too, likely due to the chocolate croissants and huge meals of luscious French food we ate every night. Tansy had also discovered a love for the Croque Monsieur, that tasty grilled French sandwich of cheese and ham, and she ate one nearly every day. Watching how her cheeks and body plumped, I realized she'd probably never had as consistent a run of daily nutrition. At dinner the other evening, when I'd asked her what she usually had to eat at night her reply had been, "Cereal."

A gaggle of French teens walked past us, book bags slung over their shoulders, laughing and looking very Parisian. I couldn't help but notice how the two male teens at the back of the group glanced back at Tansy. She was a knockout these days.

Well, I was happy to see both girls looking so hale and hearty, although the one problem I had was that every time I mentioned Daisie going home to Dallas she put her hand out in front of her face and refused to let me go farther. She was laboring under the delusion that she'd get to go back to Portland after Paris.

And I got it, I did. Because of what had happened in Dallas right before we left. And: Jack. Yes, *Jack.*

When I'd walked into the hospital room and saw him lying there, all the cells in my stomach turned over and my heart flipped. I swear to God, *it flipped.* I pressed a hand to my chest, thinking it was something to do with having just gotten off the airplane. Jack looked drawn and pale and like a thinner version of the Jack I knew and loved but it didn't matter. Because there he was. *Jack.* He smiled at me. And then my heart leapt again. I mean, it literally felt like it somersaulted in my chest and I had to clutch a hand to it to make it stop. Was I having a heart attack? I looked around the room, wondering if I should call a nurse. Well, if I was having a heart attack, at least I was in the right place for it. But then my gaze landed on Jack and my heart did its funny little dance again.

Jack. My *Jack.* The man who had stood by me through thick and thin, the man who had held my hand when the bakery was in dire straits, the man who had figured out ways to keep us open during the first lean days when nobody knew we existed. The man who had cooked dinners for me every Thursday night for years, the man who made the best Italian cheesy casserole—not to mention garlic bread—in the world, bar none.

He looked up from his bed and smiled. Every feature in his face lit up—his brown eyes lively and alert, the crow's feet at their sides crinkled, his cheeks suddenly rosy.

"Hey, Lenie."

My knees felt weak. It was if the angels had suddenly poured golden light on him. Was it just me feeling this? Suddenly I remembered Richard saying something about the way Jack looked at me. And Natalie telling me that Jack was in love with me. Could it be possible that I was the only one that hadn't figured it out? The thought overwhelmed me.

"Hi, Jack," I said weakly.

"Thank you for taking my girl with you to Paris."

I nodded. I couldn't seem to find words to say anything.

He reached his hand out to me and I took it. He wrapped his palm around my hand. I suddenly felt warm and secure. "I know she's having a hard time here. She and Carla just can't seem to find a way to get along."

Suddenly Carla was more than just the ditzy wife of my dear friend, she was my rival for Jack's affections. His *wife*, I reminded myself. I couldn't help myself. "And you and Carla are getting along?"

Jack shrugged, and I swear to God his eyes dimmed. "We have our moments. You know how it is."

"I do." His hand tightened around mine. I waved my other one. "But I don't want to talk about me. How are you?"

"Better. Getting better." He shifted in the bed. "It was a nasty infection, Len. A little scary. And who knew how painful an infection could be?" His expression changed, and he smiled at me again. "But the doctor says I can go home in the next few days."

"That's great, Jack." All I could seem to do was smile at him dopily.

"You okay?" he said.

"I am. I'm just happy to see you."

He tightened his hand around mine again and pulled me closer, until I was right next to the bed and my face inches away from him. "I'm happy to see you, too," he said.

I leaned a little closer. Our eyes locked. Every molecule in my being sang halleluiah. Rainbows danced around us. I saw it in his eyes. It wasn't just me. I knew it. I *knew* it.

I could practically feel his lips on mine as I leaned toward him. I wanted to feel him closer to me. I wanted to feel him kiss me. I wanted Jack.

"Time for your meds!" A nurse bustled in.

I leapt back from the bed and felt for the chair beside it with my hand, then sank down into it. Jack focused all his attention on the nurse.

The nurse and Jack chattered while I sat and stared out the window. God Almighty Jesus, it was a good thing that I was going to Paris in—I looked at my watch—four hours. And that as soon as Daisie arrived, we'd have to jet off to the airport to make our flight and thank heavens for that. Because that was the strongest hit of emotion I had felt in quite some time. I glanced covertly at Jack. It wasn't so covert, he looked at me and grinned. I remembered how many times we'd both reacted to something in a crowded room and met each other's knowing gaze.

And then I heard a scream, and something flew toward me. It was Daisie, and all I saw at first was the chullo hat she said protected her from Carla's idiocy. "Mad! Je suis si heureuse de vous voir."

I laughed. "Vous avez appris le francais."

Daisie stepped back from me. "I think you should have used the familiar in that sentence."

I pointed at her. "You are correct, my love. Tu as appris le francais."

She ripped off her hat. "Two weeks without the idiot—"

"Daisie," Jack warned.

She shot him a look and continued. "So I don't need this hat. And Dad, you know it's true—she's dumber than a block of ice."

"That may well be so, but I haven't raised you to be rude."

My heart leapt again. If it kept doing this, I really would be in the ICU with a heart attack. Because Jack had all but agreed with Daisie that Carla was dumb. And how could he be in love with someone who was stupid? Oh, how I wanted to say something, but Daisie spoke instead.

"She was just using you to get closer to Richard Bishop, Dad. Now that Mad's given him the heave-ho, I bet she's not so interested in hanging out with us anymore."

Daisie leveled the accusation blithely and I held my breath and looked to Jack to see his reaction. But instead of the hurt I expected to witness, his face was as devoid of expression as his white bedsheet.

"Do you like my outfit? I chose it just for France." Daisie stepped back for me to view her. She wore leggings, and a pink and black polka dot dress with a large black flower on its bodice.

I was so entranced I leapt up and hugged her again. "We are going to have so much fun in Paris!"

And now, a few days later, I was sipping my café au lait in that very city and I smiled. Because we *were* having fun. And I didn't have to worry about Jack's health because he'd been texting me every day, several times a day actually, with updates. He'd gotten home from the hospital, he was up and about, he'd gone out and walked a mile—all his texts were upbeat, and none of them mentioned Carla.

I read each one eagerly and tried to parse out any hidden meanings. He'd never been much of a texter before. Of course, I did have sole custody of his only child for the moment. Once in a while I asked myself if he was yet one more person that I was trying to save. The answer always came swift and sure: feck no, he was saving me.

And, life was good. If only I could stay here forever and forestall going back home. Well, at least I had the book. I'd worked on my writing every morning while the girls went in search of chocolate croissants, and I'd written blog posts, too, dutifully sending links to Amelia, and Daisie was tweeting up a storm. I'd risen early that very morning and gotten more pages done, as a matter of fact. It was a fantastic schedule—write, drink coffee and eat luscious pastries, and then wander the city with the girls and ponder writing love notes disguised as texts to Jack.

"So, what's on the agenda for today?" I asked the girls, trying to get my mind off my lovesick Jack quandary.

"No more macaron stores," Tansy said. "I never thought I'd say this, but I'm sick of macarons."

"Quel blasphemy!" I cried. "How can one get sick of macarons?"

"When you've eaten them every day at every place in Paris, you can, trust me," Daisie said. "But we do want to go back to Angelina's. And the Eiffel Tower. You promised. And we only have a few days left. It's time."

"Can't we just go to Angelina's and skip the Eiffel Tower? We saw it from the bus tour last week," I said.

"That's not enough, I want to go up in it," Daisie pouted.

"I can't go back to L.A. and tell people I was in Paris and didn't go to the top of the Eiffel Tower," Tansy said.

I don't know why I was so averse to going up the tower, maybe because it felt so touristy and kitschy. Of course, I had the advantage of having been here before numerous times, and I'd been up the tower on several of those occasions. Then I remembered something and brightened. "Don't you have to get tickets way ahead of time? They are probably sold out."

Daisie waved her iPad in the air. "Done. We've got tickets for three p.m."

"Well, if you guys get your wish, I get mine, too—"

Daisie put her hand together in a prayer position. "Please, no macarons."

"I want to go to the Shakespeare and Company bookstore," I said.

"What's that?" Tansy asked.

"It's an English language bookstore on the Left Bank," Daisie said. "First opened by Sylvia Beach in 1919, it was a gathering place to a large expat community during the 1920s."

"What's an expat?" Tansy said.

"Expatriate," Daisie explained. "An American who lives in another country. Anyway, she catered to them and also published *Ulysses* when nobody else would."

I could tell by the look on Tansy's face that she wasn't familiar with *Ulysses*. So, apparently, could Daisie. "*Ulysses* is James Joyce's most famous book. It was considered controversial because it features his wife doing the nasty at the end."

Oh lord, there was nothing I could do but grin.

Daisie stood up. "The bookstore closed during the war but was reopened in a new location by George Whitman in 1951. His daughter runs it now. And I would like to go, too." She glanced at her watch and looked at Tansy.

"Let's go," Tansy said. "Sounds cool."

And so we did. And it was as we strolled there, as we walked along the banks of the river Seine, which was lined with stalls selling books and art, that I had the epiphany.

Daisie had stopped to look at a book and was holding it up, sounding out the French words, doing it, of course, far, far better than I would have. Tansy was looking through a stack of cute bookmarks featuring cats. I was gazing at the two of them, thinking how cool the stalls were and why didn't we have anything similar in the States, when it hit me.

We did.

And I could sell macarons there.

Okay, so we didn't have stalls, per se, but we did have food carts. Portlanders were rabid for food carts, with nearly every vacant lot given over to a collection of them. We called them food cart pods, and there was one right down the street from the bakery. I could start small, very small, even, as I didn't need a whole truck in which to bake them. I'd get a domestic food license, bake at home, and then sell them out of a cart, which would cut costs enormously.

"Oh, my God," I said. I wasn't sure how much it would cost, or how I would get the money, but suddenly getting back in the macaron business seemed doable. And the first thought I had was to text Jack. I checked my watch. It was a little past two p.m., Paris time, which made it eight a.m. in Dallas. Jack was an early riser, so he'd be awake.

I just had the best idea ever, I texted. *We could sell macarons at a food cart. Maybe even the one down the street from the bakery.*

And then I stood staring at my phone and waited for a reply. Which was stupid, I know, but Jack usually texted back right away. He wasn't doing much, except taking it easy and resting up. A minute ticked by, then another.

"What are you doing, Mad?" Daisie asked. "And can I buy this book?" She held up a tome in French.

"I'm waiting for your father to answer my text." I dug in my purse for some cash and handed it to her. A funny look crossed her face, but then she grabbed the euros and pranced off to make her purchase.

Tansy appeared at my side. "We've got to get going to the Eiffel Tower," she said.

"Oh lord, you two are incorrigible." I couldn't believe that even Tansy was pestering me about timing, she who had the loosest concept of time of all. But as soon as Daisie reappeared we set off.

"Where are you going?" Daisie asked as I set off.

I spread my hands in front of me. "To the Eiffel Tower." And then I added, "duh" for good effect.

But Daisie shook her head. "No time to walk."

"For the love of all things sugary; of course there is time."

"No." And Daisie strode to a taxi stand and stuck out her arm. Clearly this day was spinning out of my control. I couldn't figure out what had happened to the girls, as usually they were content to let me set the pace of our days—and they had loved our walks all over town. But before I could protest, a cab had pulled up and Daisie was ushering us in. I grumbled about paying the money and Paris traffic, but really, I was complaining about being herded around. If there was anything I hated, it was being told what to do.

Daisie's phone kept dinging, her own peculiar tone that signaled she had gotten a text. No matter how many times I asked her to put it on silent, she refused. "What would be the point of that?" she would say, looking over her glasses at me. "I wouldn't know I had a text then, would I? I mean, duh."

So that day in the back of the cab, I asked her who was texting her. She shot me a look that said I was overstepping bounds—or something—and growled. "A girl my age needs to have some secrets from parental authority," she said.

"Good thing I'm not your parent," I mumbled, though secretly I was pleased.

"You sure act like you are," Daisie said.

We inched along through Paris traffic, but it didn't take us all that long to get there, a fact I could see caused Daisie much relief. She checked her watch as we approached the broad grassy park beneath the tower and the cab pulled over and let us off. Geez, I had no idea that going up in the Eiffel Tower was so important to the girls. If I had, I wouldn't have kept blowing it off. Except, I realized as I stepped out of the cab, that it was only suddenly today that they'd started bugging me about it. Oh well. Who knew how teenage minds worked? Though, in truth, Daisie wasn't quite yet a teenager. And Tansy was beyond her teenage years. Well, that made them even more mysterious.

"C'mon, Mad, quit dawdling," Daisie said. She pulled on my arm. I scowled at Tansy, as if to say, "What's up with Daisie acting so weird?" but she just smiled and shrugged.

"This way," Daisie said, even though she was leading us away from the place where the ticket pickup lines formed and toward a side of the park that was less crowded.

"But it's the wrong direction," I said. "If you want to get in line for the ride up, we've got to go this way." I pointed toward the tower.

"This is a better way. A shortcut," she said. Tansy seemed to be following her without complaint, so I went along. The least I could do was humor the girls. We reached a corner of a broad grassy area and knots of people formed and reformed around me. My phone dinged to tell me a text had come in. I hoped it was Jack, responding to my text about the food cart idea, so I paused to look at it. And it was.

But his text didn't say anything about a food cart. Or macarons.

It said, *Look up.*

Huh? Look up? Why was Jack telling me to look up? I was so confused. But I did anyway.

And saw Jack.

Standing in front of me.

In Paris.

At the Eiffel Tower.

I looked at him. And then I looked at Daisie. She was grinning and jumping up and down. I looked at Tansy. She was smiling broadly. I looked back at Jack. He looked much heartier and healthier than he had in the hospital. He'd bulked up and gotten some color from all those walks he'd said via text he'd been taking. And he looked even more appealing to me. My heart pounded wildly. Jack. Here, in Paris.

"But...what...why..."

Jack held his arms out to me and I did the only thing I could do. I ran into them. His hug was as substantial and secure as ever and this time he smelled different, like my favorite orange macaron, though God only knew where he'd picked up that scent. I burrowed my head into his chest and just breathed, feeling his arms tighten around me. But then I had to know. I stepped back.

"But what are you doing here?"

Jack grinned and shrugged his hands out wide in front of him. "I couldn't let you girls have all the fun now, could I?"

I smiled up at him. "I'm so happy."

And then I had a terrible thought. "Is Carla here, too?" I glanced around me, half expecting to see her pop out of the crowd wearing a miniskirt and stiletto heels.

But Jack shook his head. "She's not here now, and she's not going to be with me ever again."

"But...you mean..."

"We're done, Len. Over, finito, finished. I tried my best, and I just can't make it work. Because here's the thing."

Oh, God. I held my breath.

"It was really hard to concentrate on building a relationship with Carla when I couldn't stop thinking about you."

And then he leaned down and kissed me.

We spent two wonderful days shepherding the girls around Paris, but on Jack's last night, he and I went to a favorite café on the Boulevard Montparnasse where we ate steak and fries and drank wine. Jack needed to leave Paris two days before the rest of us because he had meetings about one of his consulting projects that couldn't be missed. But, luckily for me, those meetings were in L.A.—so he would be able to pick us up upon our arrival there. Though I was due to change planes to Portland from LAX, he'd convinced me to stay over a couple of nights.

"It won't be the same as the places you stayed with Richard, but the company I'm working for puts me up at a pretty decent place in Beverly Hills," he said.

I reached across the table and grabbed his hand. "I'd stay with you in the worst hovel in the world, " I said, and I meant it. "Those places I stayed with Richard were too ritzy for my blood anyway."

"Speaking of Richard." Jack took a sip of wine and peered at me over its rim.

"Do we have to?"

"That L.A. *Times* article is getting a lot of play."

"And Richard's PR people are doing their best to counter Winston Herman's allegations." I took a bite of the *amuse-bouche* we'd been served, which was a tiny bit of lobster toast served on a white ceramic spoon. Heaven. In very un-French fashion, I could have eaten a pound of them. "And Richard is all over the news with his rot about creating and funding a foundation so that he can do even more for women." I rolled my eyes. "What a load of crap."

"He talks a great game, though."

I'd just noticed that Jack hadn't touched his *amuse-bouche*. "You going to eat—"

He pushed the spoon across the table before I could finish. I gobbled the toast in one bite, closing my eyes in rapture for a moment.

"You did good talking to that reporter, Len."

I winced. "I still feel a little funny about it. I mean, Richard did save the bakery." My lips twisted. "At least for a few months."

Jack had a momentary funny look on his face but it passed when he spoke. "He also deceived and demeaned you, Mad, as it suited his purposes."

"True dat." Sipping my wine, I nodded. And thought how madly, desperately, crazily lucky I was to be in love with Jack *and* have him in love with me. No more prostrating myself to a man's interests.

"Have you heard from him?"

I scoffed. "Are you kidding me? I'm now persona non grata as far as Richard is concerned. And that is okay with me. I don't even want to *think* about Richard anymore. I wish him well and I'm grateful for what he did for us. And how he showed me what I *don't* want. But." I waved my hand as if swatting a bug. "Let's talk about something else."

"Okay then," Jack said. He poured me wine from a carafe.

One of the best things about cafes in Paris was the wine they served. "How about that Tansy? You think she's going to do okay in Portland?"

I grinned. "You know she is." The thought of having Tansy with me in Portland made me want to about burst.

The day after Jack arrived in Paris, after conferring with him, I'd asked Tansy if I could change her ticket from L.A. to Portland. We were sitting outside at a café, the girls' favorite, where they'd insisted we come one last time. I was goofy with love for Jack, especially after I'd spent the previous night in his arms—and more—in bed, and goofily happy for everything else in the whole world. Daisie had pulled Jack off down the street to look at a shop she'd seen something in.

Tansy looked at me, her brows curled above her eyes. "And what would I do in Portland?"

"Live with us. Help me get the food cart started. Learn how to bake macarons. Go back to school. Study fashion design. Whatever you want. But after this time here, we're a family. And I can't let you go back to L.A. to live with Brad."

She sat silently and stared at me.

Maybe I had misread the situation. Maybe she had no interest in changing her life. Maybe she missed Brad. "Unless you want to go back to L.A., that is."

More long silence. Parisians walked by us on the sidewalk. A woman wearing all black with an elegant leopard print scarf held a poodle in her arms and accidentally jostled our table. A young man walked by and tried to catch Tansy's eye. But she was still staring at me.

"You'd do that for me? You'd let me come to Portland and live with you?"

I nodded. "I want you to, Tansy. I would miss you something fierce if you went back to L.A."

And suddenly, her chair scraped, and she leapt at me, her arms around my neck. I felt dampness on my face and realized she was crying. I held onto her with both arms as tightly as I could and let her cry. Finally, she exhausted herself and returned to her chair.

"I've been worrying all week about going back to L.A. I've never wanted anything more than to be with all you guys."

Just then Daisie and Jack walked up, Daisie clutching a bag from the store. "Look, I got that briefcase," she said. Then she noticed the tears on Tansy's face. "What's wrong?"

"What happened?" Jack asked.

I smiled. "Tansy's coming to live with us in Portland."

Daisie was even faster than Tansy had been. She thrust her bag at Jack and fell onto Tansy, hugging her in a rare display of emotion. All Jack and I could do was just smile.

It seemed like that's all we'd been doing since Jack arrived. Smile. But that was okay by me. And that's what we did on our last night together in Paris, as we sat at the café drinking and eating.

AFTER THE INTERMINABLE FLIGHT, I stood with Daisie and Tansy on the sidewalk outside the Delta baggage claim, waiting for Jack to pick us up. He'd texted a couple of times that he was stuck in traffic, which wasn't unusual in L.A., but we'd been cooling our heels for half an hour and the girls were getting cranky.

My phone buzzed, the signal I had a text. It was from Jack.

Here.

Oh good. I looked up. But where was he? All I saw in front of me was a truck, and a big bulky one at that. I peered around it, wondering if Jack had gotten stuck behind it. The truck's horn honked. I looked closer. And realized that the truck was painted all over in broad pastel pink and blue stripes, just like my color scheme for the original bakery.

"Mad, Mad, look!" Daisie yelled.

Tansy looked up from her phone—I hoped to God she wasn't tweeting with the cute young French boy she'd met at the Orsay—and started laughing.

And then I saw it, stenciled on the side of the truck in ornate letters: The Bonne Chance Bakery.

He didn't.

He couldn't have.

The door to the truck opened and there he was. Jack. My Jack. Grinning from ear to ear. I looked from the truck to him, and back again.

"But…how…what?"

Jack made a Vanna White gesture with his hand and said, "Your chariot awaits, madam."

"You got us a food truck!" I ran to him and threw my arms around his neck and my legs around his waist. "Oh my God, you are the best ever!" I kissed him all over his face and then hard on his mouth before breaking away. "But you only left Paris three days ago. How did you manage all this?"

Jack grinned down at me. "I had a little help."

He walked to the back of the truck, which featured another door, and knocked. And who should step down from it but Fiona.

"No," I said.

"Yes," she said.

I gaped. There was no other word for it—I gaped. Because, Fiona. She looked like a different person. Her hair was pulled off her face with a headband, and while her makeup was still as impeccable as ever, it had been applied with a much lighter hand. She wore jeans and a black cotton sweater with the sleeves pushed up to the elbows. And red sneakers. Fiona was wearing *sneakers,* and red ones at that. The coolest thing was that she looked fantastic, fresh and energetic, with glowing skin.

"Are you Fiona's twin sister that I didn't know about?"

She shook her head and laughed. "I'm Fiona, the one and the same."

"But...but..." I quit trying to formulate words and just pointed up and down at her.

"I know. This is what ditching Richard Bishop will do for a woman."

"You quit working for Richard?"

"Of course she did—he's a tool, Mom," Daisie said, before skipping off to climb into the back of the truck.

Jack and I met each other's eyes. Daisie had just called me Mom. I took a deep breath and smiled, worrying that my heart might shatter from happiness right there on the spot.

"Love that girl," Fiona said. "She's really something."

I forced my attention back to her.

"But I thought you loved working for Richard," I said.

"Yeah, but it was getting more and more difficult to watch the way he operated. All that rot about his first wife." Fiona shook her head. "And I liked you, Mad. You drove me crazy, but I liked you anyway. You weren't like his other ones. Having you around made me look at things differently. Oh, and your sister isn't so bad, either."

And then Natalie appeared from behind the truck.

I gaped. Natalie looked fantastic—as vital and glowing as she had in the early days of her affair with Francine. My sister enfolded me in a hug. "Isn't this just so much fun?"

But then Fiona clapped her hands together. "Now, chop chop, Jack. Didn't you tell me we had somewhere to be this afternoon?"

At least some things never changed.

Just then a young man wearing khakis and a neatly pressed blue and white pin-striped shirt walked up to us. "Excuse me, but I'd like to buy some macarons?"

"Oh, I'm sorry, sir, but this is just the truck, we don't actually have the macarons yet," I said

Fiona inserted herself between the man and me. "Don't mind her—she just got off a transatlantic flight and you know how dingy that can make you. Step right this way and we will fix you up. I'm afraid we don't yet have a full complement of flavors, but will raspberry, vanilla, coconut, and chocolate do?"

I turned, openmouthed, to Jack, as Fiona led the man toward the truck. "How on earth...?"

"That Fiona," Jack said. "She's a dynamo. She got Jacques-Pierre and Ellie working on macarons at a commercial kitchen before my plane had even landed. Your recipe, of course. With the quality ingredients you used, not the crap Richard's people foisted on you."

"You planned all this from Paris?"

Jack nodded.

"But how did you pay for it all?"

"You can thank my real estate agent for that. I finally sold the house in Olympia."

"Hey, Mad." Tansy stuck her head out the back of the truck. "You've got to come see this—it's amazing."

"I will—just a second, hon," I called. I turned back to Jack. "*You're* amazing."

He shrugged an elaborate shrug. "I try."

I cocked my head and eyed him. "There was no business meeting here, was there?"

He shook his head.

"I can't believe all this. But how are we going to get back to Portland?"

"I figure we'll rent an SUV and caravan home. And, I thought we could make a couple stops along the way; see if we can't drum up some interest in the macaron truck. I'm hoping we can lease a spot in the food cart pod down the street from the bakery when we get back to town. That's the one thing I didn't get tied down. But I can work on it from the road."

I pursed my lips while I gazed up at Jack. He was the same Jack I'd worked alongside for years, the same Jack I'd seen lying in a hospital bed and laughing up at me from a tangle of sheets in Paris. But there was something different about him, too. Because this Jack was confident, purposeful. This Jack shot off sparks as he ordered people around. This Jack was the man I wanted. This one, and no other. This one was the man I loved. Truly, deeply, fully.

I started laughing.

"What?" he said.

It didn't seem the exact right time to tell him that I loved him. And I'd already said it to him just shy of a million times already. So I said the next best thing. "Let's go drum up some interest in macarons."

WHICH IS WHY, an hour later, I found myself standing on Hollywood Boulevard, just down the street from the L.A. Bonne Chance. To my surprise, Jack found a prime parking spot immediately, pulling the truck—Daisie and Tansy together had started calling her Mabel—to the curb.

Daisie saw my perplexed look. "Tansy phoned her old co-worker at the souvenir store to mark the place off with cones."

"Oh," I said. "Of course." Why not? I seemed to be in one of those magical places where everything happened easily and gracefully and all there was left to do was go with it.

But that still didn't explain the crowd on the sidewalk.

"Is it some kind of tourist show?" I asked, staring out the window as Jack maneuvered the truck into its parking spot.

"Nope, they're waiting for macarons," Jack said.

"But...?"

"Mad." Daisie called me from the back of the truck, where she and Tansy and Fiona had strapped themselves into a bench seat. Daisie held up her iPad. "I've been tweeting. Duh."

"And I've been doing Instagram Stories," Tansy said.

"You guys are amazing," I said. But then I had a thought and grimaced. "Don't we need a permit or something, though?"

"Handled," Fiona said, waving a piece of paper. "Now get your ass out there and sell macarons to the people."

I had the time of my life that afternoon, even though I was exhausted from the long flight from Paris. I didn't care. I wouldn't have missed it for the world. I handed out paper bags stamped with images of our macarons and took money and happily listened to people exclaiming over how good they tasted. At one point a coiffed and bejeweled middle-aged woman, clearly a denizen of the wealthy enclaves in the hills beyond, stopped me.

"I'm so happy to see you! I've just got to have my macaron fix," she said. "We so miss the macaron bakery that used to be right down the street."

"Excuse me?" I asked. "The macaron bakery is gone?"

"Yeah, I don't know what happened to it." She had a thick manner of speech that betrayed Jersey origins, and she waved a hand covered in diamond rings. "One day I went by there to buy macarons and it was just empty."

My heart hammered in my chest. The L.A. Bonne Chance, gone? After everything we'd been through, the last vestige of my dream was gone? I reminded myself it had long since been co-opted so that it didn't resemble my dream, but still. When the crowds thinned enough for me to get away, I walked the half-block up the street to see for myself.

And sure enough, the storefront was empty. No garish pile of Easter-egg-colored macarons in the window, no twinkling lights fastened on every window, no mock-ups of the Eiffel Tower everywhere you looked. Even the name of the business painted on the window and door was gone. Someone had scraped it off. Instead, there was a sign hung on the door that read, *Coming Soon, The Precious Parfumerie.*

It was disconcerting to stare at the empty space that had contained so many of my dreams, but at the same time I felt a sense of relief. I narrowed my eyes at the sign advertising the perfume store, remembering how Natalie had told me Richard's new squeeze was the owner of a small chain of perfume shops.

But as I stood there, a lanky woman brushed past me and went into the shop. Was she the perfume lady? Damn, I hadn't gotten a good glimpse of her. And I wanted to—oh, how I wanted to. I wanted to meet the woman who had taken my place on Richard's arm. On a whim I knocked on the door of the store.

"Yes?" The woman stood beside the open door, holding a screwdriver. I peered behind her into the space, which was completely empty, save for a plastic tarp and some dust on the floor, and then looked at her. Her dark hair was swept up into a messy ponytail, and her brown eyes were friendly and warm. Was she the woman who had replaced me in Richard's affections?

"Are you the one opening the perfume store here?"

"What? Perfume? No. Oh, you mean because of the sign." She took a step behind the door and ripped the sign down. "No, I sell jewelry. My own designs."

"But...but..."

"Yeah, I was damned lucky to get the lease for this space. The last folks who were going to rent it fell through at the last minute. I'm not sure why, but I'm glad for me."

I couldn't stop the smile that spread over my face. "That's great, just great. I wish you all the luck in the world."

* * *

FOUR DAYS LATER, I drove Mabel the last stretch up I-5. Another hour, and I'd be home in Portland. We'd stopped in San Francisco, Sacramento, Ashland, and Eugene along the way, and been met by crowds at every stop, thanks to the social media efforts of Daisie and Tansy. We'd gotten a ton of press, too, especially once the media figured out my connection to Richard Bishop, and I'd given TV interviews while standing in front of the truck, and radio and press interviews on my phone from the passenger seat. I usually spent half my airtime steering the conversation away from Richard, but if I could mention where the macaron truck would be, I didn't mind.

Everyone else had gone on ahead of me in the rented SUV from Eugene, as I'd promised to stay and finish selling the macarons. The college crowd was ravenous for them, and we sold out of the entire supply that Jacques-Pierre and Ellie had made. But I'd seen the look of exhaustion that made Jack's face sag and noted Tansy and Daisie snapping at each other. Even Fiona's brisk demeanor had gone slack. They'd all done so much for me already, I'd agreed when Fiona suggested they get a head start, promising I could handle the rest of the sales and telling them I'd meet them at Jack's house in Portland.

I didn't mind. I liked driving Mabel. And I liked having time to process everything that had happened so quickly over the past few weeks. All in all, it had been a remarkable run. The only thing that made me sad was the loss of the bakery. Selling macarons from the food truck had made me realize how much I missed it. I missed early mornings there, shuffling batches of pastel-colored macarons in and out of the ovens, and then grabbing a latte from the coffee shop next door, my former employer, once they opened. I missed

Jack and Daisie working across the hall in the bakery office, and the camaraderie that meant I could pop in to take a break, chatting with them any time I wanted. The bakery had been everything I'd wanted and more, and somehow, I'd let it slip through my hands. On the bright side, I told myself, looking around the body of the truck, at least I had a place to bake macarons, and if Jack's negotiations worked out, we'd have a spot in the food cart pod.

I yawned. I was getting tired myself. Ahead off a freeway exit I saw an ad for a drive-through espresso shop and pulled off to grab a latte. As I idled in line, my phone dinged. It was a text from Daisie.

Dad says to bring the truck to the bakery building.

That didn't make sense. *Why? There won't be any place to park along Sandy.*

The car in front of me finished its order and I pulled through and talked to the barista. Another text dinged.

Dad says it's illegal to park a big truck like Mabel in our neighborhood.

I picked up the phone and shook my head. Really? Since when had that law been enacted? But I knew that Daisie, once she got an idea in her head, wouldn't let go of it, so I just texted back, *Well, try to save me a spot then.*

An hour later, as I pulled into Portland, I wondered if it really was illegal to park the truck in front of Jack's, and if so, what would we do with it then? Well, I guess we'd find a parking lot or rent a space somewhere to stow it. I turned onto Sandy Boulevard and headed down the hill that the old Bonne Chance sat on.

And saw a huge crowd amassed on the sidewalk. Oh crap, I'd never find a place to park now. The bento café on the corner was probably having a lunch special or something. I knew I should have taken the truck to Jack's, illegal or not. Damn it. I was too tired for this. I pounded the steering wheel as I cruised down the street, craning my neck to see what was going on.

But...why was the crowd standing outside the Bonne Chance? And why were there pink and blue balloons tied to the building? And...was that Jack standing in front of it, waving madly? And Daisie and Tansy jumping up and down beside him? Um, it was. And Fiona, too. She raised her arm and beckoned me to the curb, where, lo and behold, a parking space awaited. I pulled the truck over and squinted at the building and the crowd. It looked like the bakery doors were open. But that was impossible, because Richard Bishop's people owned it now and they'd abandoned it.

And then Jack was at Mabel's door, pulling me out and escorting me to the sidewalk, where probably fifty people milled about, including, I was surprised to see, a TV reporter.

"What's going on?" I asked.

"What's going on is that the bakery has reopened," Jack said, pointing to the door.

"But it can't. We don't own it anymore."

I was so confused. A bright light switched on, illuminating the grey day, and I realized it was a TV camera. Oh man, whatever was going on, I was not ready for it.

"Oh, but we do," Jack said.

"Um...I think I'm missing something here, unless there was a time warp while we drove home."

Jack grinned. "It took me awhile, but I remembered something that had been bugging me. Richard's people referred to the bakery as *La* Bonne Chance, not *The* Bonne Chance. Remember how you were always correcting them? So, I started thinking about it. Sure enough, all the paperwork is under that name. Which is a business entity that doesn't exist. So, everything is null and void. We still own the Bonne Chance."

A spatter of rain hit my shoulders and head, but I didn't

care. Because I felt like all the flowers everywhere in the world had bloomed at once, that every bird alive on the planet was singing. The Bonne Chance was mine again? I ran to the door and peeked in. Everything inside it was just how I'd left it on that January day nine months ago. Caroline stood behind the counter.

"Hi, Mad," she said.

I waved a weak hand. There were stacks of macarons in their slots behind the Plexiglass shield, their hues of rose and green and blue and yellow and white like the most gorgeous display of jewelry I'd ever seen. I turned back toward Jack, tears stinging my eyes.

"I don't know how you did this, but I've never been so happy in my life."

"Fiona did it," Daisie piped up. "But I helped her some."

I pressed Daisie to me in a fierce hug. "You're amazing." Tansy smiled behind her, and I reached over to pat her shoulder.

Daisie pushed me away and looked at Jack. "Do the rest, Dad."

And that's when it happened.

Jack fell to one knee on the sidewalk outside the Bonne Chance bakery, despite the grimace of pain that crossed his face, despite the rain that had begun to fall, despite the crowd that looked on, despite the TV cameras. He held out a box.

I pressed my hand to my heart and gasped.

Jack opened the top of the box and displayed a sparkling diamond ring. I covered my mouth in amazement, staring from him to the ring.

"Lenie," he said, "will you marry me?"

I couldn't, wouldn't ever feel this full of love again. Or maybe I could. Maybe that's what this whole journey had been about, learning that things could work out for me, that good was all around me if I would only open my eyes. That I didn't have to save everyone, only myself. I stared down at Jack.

"I've been in love with you from the first time I met you," Jack said. "But I was with Carla. And after Will left, you didn't seem the slightest bit interested in me and I felt it was too soon anyway. And then Richard came along." He shook his head and his body wavered for a minute. I realized that crouching in that position must be very uncomfortable for him, what with his injury and all. But he kept going.

"And I felt I owed it to Carla to try to make it work with her. For Daisie's sake."

Dimly, I heard Daisie make a noise, but I didn't tear my gaze away from Jack. Couldn't, even though I was vaguely aware of the people who formed a ring around us, watching. It might as well have been just Jack and me, alone somewhere in a moonlit garden.

Tears splashed my cheeks as I stared at Jack and I whispered a silent thank you to the universe for bringing him to me. "I've never wanted anything more in my life."

The crowd cheered and clapped.

But then I had an awful thought.

"Wait," I said.

Jack wobbled on his knee and wrinkled his brow.

"Aren't you technically still married to Carla?"

He waved his hand, and then used it to hoist himself up to a standing position. "Not anymore. Or at least I won't be soon. She's already been served with divorce papers. And it won't take her long to sign them, because from what I hear, she's already got a new man in Croatia."

Jack put the ring on my finger. I held my hand up to the crowd to show it off. More clapping and more cheers. And then someone yelled, "Now can we please buy some macarons?"

I looked at Jack.

"We made them wait for you," he said. "We wanted you to be here for the first sale."

And so, I led the crowd into the bakery. My bakery. The Bonne Chance Bakery of Portland, Oregon, specializing in macarons.

EPILOGUE

Bakery reopens to long lines, adds food cart, Oregon Live article, November 20

Fans of the Parisian delicacy known as the macaron, rejoice! Madeleine Miller's deeply lamented Bonne Chance bakery has reopened in its original location on Sandy Boulevard. Miller has also added a second location in the form of a food truck currently parked at the Division Street Food Cart pod. She's selling the same pillowy pastel French sandwiches that we all came to love. "We're excited to be back in business, allowing Portlanders their macaron fix!" Miller said. According to Jack Rogers, her business partner and fiancé, the former bakery got into financial trouble due to bad loans of one of the original owners, Miller's former husband, now in jail for tax fraud. A rescue effort by famed entrepreneur and actor Richard Bishop "was disastrous as it took us in the wrong direction," according to Rogers. "We're happy to be back doing what we do best—baking macarons."

. . .

I POURED eggs into the frying pan and stirred, then waited until they were a little set and sprinkled grated cheese on top. I pushed down the toaster lever for the first batch of English muffins.

"This glue is not working," Daisie said.

"You're using too much of it," Tansy said. She held up a piece of pale blue paper. "Look, you have to squirt out just a tiny bit, enough so the glitter sticks but not so much that it gets all glumpy."

"Your breakfast is almost done anyway, girls, so clear a spot for it," I said.

Jack entered the kitchen then and came up behind me to nuzzle my ear. "Is there enough for me?"

"Always," I said. "You get everything I got," and I turned to give him a kiss.

"Ee-uw," Daisie said. "I never would have helped you two get together if I'd known how gooey you were always going to be."

Tansy stood and started gathering up craft supplies. "We'll put this away for now, but we've got to finish after breakfast. They have to go out today. Or tomorrow at the latest. The party is only a few weeks away."

I slid place mats, napkins, and silverware onto the table and Tansy arranged it, and then Jack pulled plates out of the cupboard and served eggs while I buttered the English muffins. Fortunately for us, his house hadn't sold and as soon as we'd arrived back from Paris, he'd taken it off the market. It was much bigger than my little cottage and had four bedrooms, which was perfect for all of us, including Tansy.

I watched as the girls gobbled eggs and bit into English muffins. I couldn't imagine how we'd ever lived without Tansy among us. She was turning out to have quite the knack for organizing things and events. The project the girls were working on was invitations for an engagement party slated for New Year's Eve. We planned a very small event with only close friends and family here at the house, seeing as how Jack was still not technically divorced and it seemed better to be at least a little bit circumspect. By small, I meant small, with Earl, Natalie, Fiona, and Caroline, our one employee from the food cart, in attendance, though Amelia, my editor, was also coming and several of my local blog readers had threatened to crash the party.

Though there was the small matter of the film crew that planned to be there. Yes, a film crew. The Cook & Eat Network had declined my show, after the debacle with the L.A. bakery—Richard's influence, of course. But once they noticed the press our food truck journey created, they were interested all over again. We were still in negotiation, but the film crew planned an initial foray to town to see the bakery and the food truck in operation.

The front door banged, and a voice called out, "hoo-hoo." Then Natalie appeared in the kitchen. Even though it was ten o'clock on Sunday morning, she was fully dressed in shades of blue—a long tunic over leggings, complete with blue shoes and turquoise jewelry. "Ooh, smells good, I'm starving."

Jack put another English muffin in the toaster and I scrambled more eggs.

"What's with the makeup?" Natalie asked Daisie.

Daisie wore thick black eyeliner on her lids, and she'd painted black tails off the corners of her eyes. She had a thick bronze collar around her neck.

"Cleopatra," Tansy said, as Daisie chewed. "She's discovered Egypt."

"Mad says we can go next year," Daisie said.

"I said nothing of the sort."

Daisie shrugged. "It was worth a try. Can we?"

"I'll come," Natalie said. "I've always wanted to see Egypt."

"I want to go, too," Tansy said. She and Natalie had started to develop a special bond, with Tansy often wandering down the street to visit her at my little house where Natalie had taken up residence. Tansy seemed to have an unlimited appetite for spiritual information, and between Natalie and Earl, she was soaking up data like a sea anemone drinking ocean water. She'd be starting classes at the community college in January, and I couldn't wait to see what she decided to study. Something to do with fashion design, likely, but she wasn't sure yet.

I would not be going to Egypt or anywhere else next year, but I hoped that Natalie would stick around. While she figured out her next move she had started writing a book proposal that Amelia said she'd be happy to look at.

"Where's Earl?" I asked.

"On his way," Natalie said around a mouthful of egg.

"On whose way?" A voice boomed and there he was in the kitchen, my dad, looking as hale and hearty as ever, even as his seventy-first birthday approached. Daisie jumped up and hugged him and Earl hugged her back and kissed her on the cheek before taking a seat at the table. Every time I looked at my father, my heart swelled even further. I loved him so much and I was so happy that he spent much of his time back in Portland these days. I also loved what he had decided to do—ditch the retreat center in Santa Fe and open a scaled-back version here in town, in the same building as the Bonne Chance, which had several vacancies.

"Where's Fiona?"

"She'll be along. She had a call with someone in England," Natalie said.

The world works in mysterious and wonderful ways. Natalie and Fiona were seeing each other. Ever since Fiona had met Nat at the bakery's grand opening, she'd had her eye out for a chance with her. And now Fiona was starting her own P.R. firm here in town. Which was one reason the Bonne Chance bakery was getting a ton of press.

"Oh, bloody hell, who thought breakfast at this ungodly hour on Sunday morning was a good idea?"

That would be Fiona, entering the kitchen, looking adorable and very English in jeans and a sweater. She touched Natalie on the shoulder and pulled in a chair beside Tansy. Jack set a mug of coffee in front of her.

He and I looked at each other and I nodded. I walked across the room and took his hand. He cleared his throat. "Okay, now that you're all here…"

"There was a reason we wanted you here together…"

Jack and I looked at each other and laughed. I could tell by the look on his face that he was feeling the same thing as me, that this was surprisingly hard to say. I don't know why, because it was happy news. *Momentous* happy news.

"Because we have an announcement…" Jack said.

Daisie looked at me and then Jack. Earl narrowed his eyes and swept them up and down my body. Tansy cocked her head to one side, and Natalie and Fiona joined hands.

I took a deep breath. "I'm pregnant."

The happy clamor that ensued lasted for a long time, and when it finally died down, we opened champagne and sparkling cider for Daisie and me, though she managed to snitch some champagne, I noticed. After everyone had a glass, Jack raised a toast.

"To new life," he said.

I held my glass of cider up. "To family," I said. I looked around the kitchen at everyone assembled there. They were my family. Some by blood, some by choice. I couldn't be happier that we'd all ended up together.

I took a sip of cider and glanced over at Jack. He set his glass on the counter and held his arms out to me. I stepped into them. I was home at last.

ACKNOWLEDGMENTS

This book had a long and torturous journey to publication with many fits and starts along the way. I'm grateful to all who helped it along its path.

When the Bonne Chance was barely a glimmer in my eye, I got helpful first chapter reads from Kate Kaufmann, Jenny Bates, and Rachel Saffel, and also from a Spalding MFA alumni workshop with members Rae Cobb, Leah Henderson, and Harriet Leach.

Once upon a time, agent Erin Niumata plucked the Bonne Chance manuscript from the query slush pile and took a chance on me. It didn't quite work out the way we expected, but she had a huge influence on this book's development along the way. I'm grateful for all that she did for me.

To the team who always has my back—Debbie Guyol and Jenni Gainsborough. You guys did a thorough beta read on the Bonne Chance and offered insightful comments. I'm also grateful for our little team's trips to McMinnville and Manzanita (not to mention England and France) and all the Otto's pizza and red wine we've consumed along the way.

To all my students and clients, including the Wednesday Writers—I learn as much from you as you do from me! To my Zoomers, thanks for forming such a great community so quickly. And to the early reading team, thank you, thank you, thank you for your support!

To Camille Pagán and Heather Demetrios for incredibly helpful coaching. (Writers, if you want to move ahead in the world, hire a coach.)

To my family: sisters, children, grandchildren, nieces and nephews, cats, grand-dog, fish (just kidding about the fish), I'm lucky to be a part of such a nutty, exuberant bunch. I'd have a lot more time to write without you all around, but I'd have a lot less to write about, too.

And finally, to Steve, mostly known as Poppi these days. Thank you, honey for putting up with me for all these years and for finally having learned not to groan when I say, "I've had an idea!" Love you.

ABOUT THE AUTHOR

Sign up for Charlotte's newsletter to be the first to find out about her new books, giveaways, and updates. Charlotterainsd.substack.com

The great-granddaughter of pioneers who walked across the Oregon Trail, Charlotte Rains Dixon considers herself a westerner through and through. Many of her stories are set in her home state of Oregon, where her characters reside in fictional versions of her favorite wine area (Calderwood Grove) and coast towns (Star Haven Beach and Wayfarer Cove), as well as Portland, where she resides. She is the author of the novel Emma Jean's Bad Behavior, as well as the forthcoming titles The Matchmaker's Temptation and The Journalist's Passion, both part of the Calderwood Grove series.

When not writing fiction, Charlotte teaches writing in Portland, England, the south of France, and on the Oregon Coast. She also coaches writers privately. She is Director Emeritus and a current mentor at the Writer's Loft, a certificate-in-writing program at Middle Tennessee State University. She earned her MFA in creative writing from Spalding University and is the author of a dozen non-fiction books. Her fiction and articles have appeared in numerous publications.

Charlotte lives with her husband in Portland, Oregon, in a multi-generational home that is by turns boisterous and exuberant but seldom quiet. She believes no breakfast is complete without a crossword puzzle to work and no Happy Hour can actually be happy without popcorn. (Wine goes without saying.) Despite frequent stays in France, she regularly fractures the language. She is, however, fluent in Carney. Charlotte writes stories about places you long to live filled with people you'd love to know.

twitter.com/wordstrumpet

instagram.com/wordstrumpet

amazon.com/Charlotte-Rains-Dixon

pinterest.com/charlotterdixon